Praise from readers for *Take*

*Loved this dark and often humorous portrayal of death and its aftermath. Laughed, cried and felt every emotional tug.*
**Sandra, Freuchie**

*So good to read a book about East Lothian. Couldn't put in down.*
**Helen, Port Seton**

*A blooming brilliant read. Five stars from me.*
**Diane, Fife**

*Held my breath several times. Lots of twists and turns that I didn't see coming. Couldn't stop crying at the end.*
**Maureen, Brentwood**

*Honestly? I didn't expect this book to be so good. I totally forgot that I was reading a debut novel. Loved it.*
**Val, Pitlessie**

*What a predicament for Ruby! Fantastic plot.*
**Yasmin, Enniskillen**

# TAKE ME INSTEAD

*Faye Stevenson*

First published in 2023 by Faye Stevenson

Publishing services provided by Lumphanan Press
www.lumphananpress.co.uk

Front cover photography by Mark Stevenson
www.markstevensonphotography.com

*To my family. Love you.*

*O wad some Pow'r the giftie gie us*
*To see oursels as others see us!*

ROBERT BURNS (1786)

# PROLOGUE

*Wednesday 24th April 2019*

*My darling mum,*

*If you are reading this then it means I am no longer here and somehow you have returned.*

# ONE

## *Sunday 5th of January 2020*

Rachel tried to make sense of her surroundings. She was definitely lying down – on her back. The surface was soft, she thought, but couldn't be sure. Her eyes were refusing to open and it was an effort to move her arms or legs. They felt as heavy as her head: which throbbed. Bloody agony. She could hear noises but they were being swallowed by the silence. Voices perhaps? Or the wind? Concentrating on nothing was exhausting. After what seemed like an age, a door opened and muffled footsteps came closer. Someone was fumbling near her feet.

'Good morning, Rachel. Agata here. How are you today? Now, I'm just going to take your temperature and blood pressure.' She sounded young and there was a definite Eastern European lilt there; a rhythm that seemed familiar.

Rachel surmised she might be in a hospital but had no idea why. Icy fingers brushed her skin and she must have flinched because the kind voice apologised for her cold hands. The hands were rubbed vigorously together. Rachel forced her eyes to open and a reassuring smile leaned in.

'Hello Rachel. My name is Agata. How are you feeling? You've given yourself a nasty bang to the head.' Agata's elfin face was as reassuring as her voice. When no response was elicited, the young nurse continued. 'You're in hospital, Rachel – the Royal Infirmary in Edinburgh.' Agata held her hand and gave it a gentle squeeze. 'Doctor will be here shortly and he will answer all your questions.'

Rachel closed her eyes to think. Flashes of white, blinding light speared the blackness, quickly replaced with big, red, watery bubbles that would burst when the jagged light stabbed at them. When the maelstrom in her head abated and some sort of calm crept in, she thought back to her last memory.

It was a Thursday morning. She was meeting with Ruby but she was agitated. Her husband sat at the kitchen table nursing a mug of coffee. He didn't want her to go.

'What time d'ye intend to be back from your jolly?' asked Colin.

'It's hardly a jolly. I won't be eating much and I'll be back long before tea-time. I'm sorry Colin but I can't wriggle out of this one.'

'She uses you. They all do. I dinnae understand why ye cannae see it... but nah. You always make excuses for them.' His moan was full of spite.

Rachel refused to be drawn into a spat. For once, could he not be happy for her? She put his favourite dish on a chopping board to cool for later. Fish pie infused the air. She kissed him on the cheek but he shrugged off her attempt to hug him.

She could remember parking near St Margaret's Loch at the entrance of Holyrood Park in Edinburgh. She squeezed in between two black cars; the driver of one of them was reading a newspaper while stuffing his face with a huge doughnut. She pulled off her grey jumper; beneath it was a cheery pink floral blouse. The jumper was placed carefully on the back seat and she hid her sensible black loafers under her old black jacket. Ruby, her daughter, had bought her a pale pink trench coat for her last birthday and she put it on the front seat for later. She zipped up her cream ankle boots and pulled her jeans down over them. The contents of her black shoulder bag were emptied into a woven straw bag – one of Ruby's castoffs. She slipped into the driver's seat and headed towards the Grange. Everything after that flashed past. It was as if someone had activated the fast forward button in her brain, flicking through memory frames, desperate to find where they had left off. Arthur's Seat. Holyrood Palace. Radical Road. Salisbury Crags. The Commonwealth Pool. The beginning of the Meadows. The Sick Kids, the Grange then Ruby's.

Parked outside the drive of the elegant Victorian house in Dick Place, Rachel dusted her pale cheeks with blusher and smoothed pink lip balm over her lips. Blusher on her cheeks. Pink swipes of balm on her lips. *Bronze blusher. Pink balm.* Repeat. Repeat.

The pace decelerated abruptly. In sluggish motion, Rachel crrrr... unched the grey pebbles leading to Ruby's front door. Her daughter stood in the porch and gracefully opened her arms wide. It reminded Rachel of her dad's Livingstone daisies when they opened their petals to welcome the morning sun. Funny how random thoughts spring to mind. Ruby, tall and slim in a cream jumpsuit. Her long blond hair swished back and forth. Sw... ish, Sw... ish. Somewhere far off, Ruby laughed but it was all so hollow and distant. She picked up her grey, Stella McCartney satchel and looped it ever so slowly over her head. A long, cream cardigan fell softly from the crease of her arm.

Lying on her hospital bed, tears trickled down Rachel's cheeks. Wet pools settled in her ears. She had so much love for this daughter of hers. Suddenly, she was wrenched back to that moment. The Thursday in March before Mothering Sunday.

Ruby smiled. 'You look great, mum,' and tucked several

strands of her mother's grey hair behind her ears. She scrunched her nose and nodded approvingly. 'Let's have a lovely day.'

Mother and daughter were having a rare girlie day out. Ruby had bunked off early. Most unusual; it was kind of frowned upon at the radio station. They sauntered arm in arm through Marchmont's wide streets – an area of smart, four and five storey Victorian tenement blocks, popular with students and young professionals – as they headed towards the Meadows. Chatting and giggling all the way, they crossed over to the vast expanse of green and up the Middle Walkway that passed what used to be Edinburgh's old Royal Infirmary; now converted into overly priced (in Rachel's opinion) up-market apartments. Twice on the way there, someone asked for a selfie with Ruby. Her beautiful daughter graciously obliged. Rachel was bursting with pride. She felt safe with Ruby. For a few hours, the tension she held in her neck and shoulders would melt away.

They stood at the busy junction on Lauriston Place and waited, hand in hand, for the green man. Half a dozen folk lined up and leaned in behind them. At five feet nine Ruby seemed much taller than her mother; her slender frame and high heel boots probably helped. They took one step. Only one. There was a loud screeching of brakes. Someone behind them screamed: a piercing shrill that seemed to last an eternity. The hard surface of the road walloped the side of Rachel's face. Through the slits in her eyes, she could see her Ruby lying like a mannequin doll that had been tossed aside on a shop floor – the legs at a funny angle. Her long blond hair covered her face. Before the darkness engulfed her, Rachel made a pact.

'Please God, don't take my precious girl. If you have to take anyone – take me instead.'

# TWO

A scream exploded from the pit of Rachel's stomach like something escaping from the depths of Hell.

'NURSE! ... NURSE!'

'I'm still here, Rachel,' Agata reassured her.

'How's my daughter? How's Ruby? Please tell me.' Her cry was now a throttled rasp.

'Ssshhhh. You've had a fall and bumped your head. Doctor'll be here soon with your results. Try and stay calm for me.' The petite slim nurse patted the back of Rachel's hand.

Rachel could feel another exasperated wail resonate within her. 'I didn't fall. We were hit by a van. A large white van... and Ruby, just lying there. Please. How is she?' Her nails dug deep into the young woman's skin.

'I'm not aware of a motor accident, Rachel. You were brought in to hospital alone as far as I know.'

'No. A van hit us. The green man came on and we stepped on to the road. Ruby held my hand.' Behind closed lids, Rachel's eyes scoured her brain for confirmation. Deep inside, her head pounded harder and faster.

The nurse fussed around the bed. Tugging at the sheets and fluffing the pillows. She was tiny. Her blue tunic top and navy trousers could have fitted a twelve-year-old.

'How long have I been here?' asked Rachel.

'You were brought in late yesterday morning to A&E and admitted to this ward in the evening,' answered Agata.

'Does my husband know I'm here?'

'A young woman sat with you last night.'

'Ruby?'

'I'm not sure, Rachel.' There was a note of hesitancy in her voice. 'Let's wait until the doctor comes.'

'I'd like to sit up. I'm thirsty.'

Agata raised the bed slightly as Rachel pushed down with her right heel and with a great deal of effort, heaved her body awkwardly into a sitting position. The stiff white sheet was folded over the blue cotton bedspread and tucked in around the patient. The nurse filled a plastic tumbler with water. She popped in a straw and handed it to Rachel who took a few tentative sips. It felt good, refreshing, but when she coughed, sharp spasms shot through her head. The pain was excruciating. Reluctantly, she drank some more.

A young man entered the room and greeted Agata briefly in another language. Rachel's next-door neighbour was from Tallinn in Estonia and sounded just like the two youngsters. The auxiliary nurse picked up the water jug and replaced it with a fresh one. Ice cubes clinked as the liquid settled.

'Where did this nightie come from? It isn't mine,' Rachel explained with a renewed strength to her voice.

She tugged the material closer to her face. It was a white, shirt-styled nightdress with penguins on it. Rachel would never have worn something so silky or frivolous. It couldn't possibly have been hers.

'Your young friend brought in your things last night.'

'It's not mine. What else did she bring? Can I see?' It was more of a demand than a request.

'There's a long leather coat hanging up here with a black scarf and a pair of black trainers on the shelf,' Agata informed her patient as she unhooked the hanger to allow Rachel to get a better look at the coat and scarf. 'A pair of red velvet jeggings and a white jumper's on the other one.'

'Not mine. I think the wrong clothes have been allocated to my room.'

The nurse pursed her lips but said nothing. She lifted a holdall from the locker and put it on the bed. Rachel recognised it. The beige Armani canvas bag belonged to Ruby.

Rachel turned the contents over slowly with her left hand as her right elbow had taken a battering from the accident; a pair of pyjamas, a lacy bra, some skimpy pants and a soap bag. Nothing in there was familiar to her. Nothing at all. They must belong to Ruby. A glimmer of hope was emerging. Rachel had no idea why she raised the next question but she asked to see the clothes she was wearing when she was brought in. Agata placed a plastic hospital laundry bag on Rachel's knee. The clothes had been rolled into a sausage ball. Rachel cautiously unfurled them. There was a pair of black jogging bottoms with a thin red and white stripe down the sides and a matching roll neck top plus some socks and underwear. Rachel checked the labels. They were from Zara; a shop she had only ever been in with Ruby. She checked the tag on the jogging top: size 10. Rachel hadn't been that thin in years.

'You have good taste in clothing for...'

'A woman of my age?' Rachel finished the sentence for her.

Agata apologised. She was not going to say that.

'They. Are. Not. MINE!' Rachel was confused. 'I was wearing my jeans and a pink blouse yesterday.'

She looked at her hands. Her nails were painted white. She

held her fingers closer. A little Christmas emoji was glued on to every nail – each one different from the next. Then she noticed how slim her arms were. She fumbled with her left arm and rolled up her nightdress. Her naked body was on display for all to see. How the hell had she lost so much weight?

Agata looked as startled as Rachel felt.

'A…A… Am no me.' Rachel's voice was tinny and panicky. 'I'm not me!'

She searched for the compact mirror she had seen earlier when she had unzipped the wash bag and held it to her face. Rachel stared at her reflection. Rachel Gordon glared back. She was relieved. She was definitely herself. Yet she looked different. Her face was thinner. She patted and rubbed her skin for some sort of reassurance. She angled the mirror and examined her eyes. The tip of her middle finger swept over her eyebrows. Fine thread-like lines had been etched to form an arc. She licked her finger and rubbed at the bone above her eye but the colour remained intact. As she stretched her arm further away, she could see that her hair was different. Gone was the salt and pepper mop of grey. Beneath the bandaging, several tones of blond strands were peeking out. Rachel slumped back into her pillow and dropped the round mirror on to her lap. She couldn't make sense of it all. When she pulled up the covers for comfort, the small mirror fell off the bed, rolled over the speckled grey flooring and stopped at a pair of brown shoes. The young recipient bent down to pick it up. A stethoscope swung jauntily from his neck.

Doctor Harry Garland introduced himself. He jiggled the clipboard free from the bottom of Rachel's bed to read her notes. Rachel sighed; they got younger every day. No one wore white coats anymore. They could have walked in off the street and no-one would bloody notice.

Harry Garland approached her bed. A pale blue, stripy shirt that had been poorly ironed was tucked into navy chinos. He looked like a rugby player with his broad shoulders and sticky-out ears.

'Obs are all good doctor,' said Agata, 'but Rachel seems a little confused today.'

The broad shoulders gave her an equally broad smile. 'The results from the CT scan are good. No lasting damage. Mild concussion. Only five stitches in the small head wound – caused by the impact as the back of your head met the ground, I'm assuming. The doctor shone a bright light into both her eyes and asked her to look right and left. 'Can you remember what happened before you fell, Rachel?'

'I didn't fall,' she insisted. 'I was in an accident. A white van ploughed into me and my daughter and I would like to know how she is?' Rachel's steely stare said it all.

Agata shrugged.

'Perhaps we can start with some basic questions, Rachel. What is your full name?' asked the young man. His tone was pleasant yet authoritative.

'Mrs Rachel MacDonald Gordon.'

The nurse and the doctor exchanged looks.

'And your date of birth, please,' he coaxed.

'June the thirtieth, nineteen sixty-two.'

'And that makes you?'

'Fifty-six but soon to be fifty-seven.'

Doctor Garland frowned. 'What day is this, Rachel?'

'If I've been in here overnight then this must be Friday. Mother's Day is on Sunday so... 31st, 30th... this is the 29th of March.' Rachel felt smug. Did they think she was incapable of working out a simple date?

The doctor pulled up a chair. It scraped across the floor then he sat down; it creaked beneath his beefy bulk. He would ask more questions later. Agata excused herself as she had other patients to see. Harry Garland cleared his throat several times.

'If you've got something to say, say it,' urged Rachel. She wanted an explanation.

'On Thursday 28th of March 2019, you were admitted to Accident and Emergency here at Edinburgh's Royal Infirmary after you were hit by a moving vehicle in the city centre. Apart from severe bruising to your body and the side of your face, you sustained two hairline cracks to your ribs. There were no other breakages. Although, there was no obvious signs of traumatic brain injury, you were displaying classic symptoms of post-traumatic amnesia. This was very distressing not only for you but all your family.'

Rachel interrupted him. 'Wait a minute. Are you saying all of this happened yesterday? The nurse told me my only visitor was a young woman.'

Harry took a deep breath. 'There's no easy way to say this Rachel but your first admission to A&E was nine months ago. Your second was yesterday. Today is Sunday the 4th of January 2020.'

Rachel took time to process what he was saying. 'No. Not possible. I can remember it all so clearly. Right up until I saw her on the road next to me. So, what have I been doing since then? What about Ruby?'

'I am so sorry Mrs Martin but...'

'Martin was my married name,' snarled Rachel. 'To my first husband.' She couldn't care less about being polite now. Her patience had been stretched too far. 'I'm Rachel Gordon now. I need to speak to my husband Colin please,' she demanded.

'Again Rachel, I can only follow procedure. We have a letter here from your lawyer, as instructed by you, that should you be readmitted to hospital at any time your only visitors must be Annabelle Jeffries, Lisa Hamilton or your son, Rory Martin. No one else. Under no circumstances should Colin Gordon be granted permission to see you. Nor his daughter, Claire Rennie. You have taken a restraining order out against both of them.'

'Is this a joke? Colin is my husband. He will be absolutely furious when he finds out. Does he know I'm here? I have to see him.' Rachel was physically choking as she spoke. Colin would blame her even though she had not orchestrated it. 'Annabelle is Ruby's best friend. Why on earth would I choose her over Colin?' Rachel barely whispered her next words. The truth frightened her.

'Is my Ruby dead? I need to know.'

# THREE

Doctor Garland didn't have to confirm Rachel's question. The regret in his eyes told her all she needed to know. Ruby was gone.

Rachel listened to her sobs. She'd barely stopped since she was left alone. It came from the soles of her feet, swam up through her legs and throbbed in her chest. The bed juddered. She'd never experienced such pain and there was no-one to share it with. Admittedly, she was distraught when her mother had died, her father less so (she had been prepared for his death), but this was different: they were older. Ruby was too young. No mother should outlive her child. It wasn't the order of things. The ceiling and the walls seemed to close in on her; threatening to suffocate her prostrate body.

They had been so happy walking through the Meadows. They kept looking at each other, leaning in and giggling like two naughty teenagers who had bunked off school for the day. Pink blossom from the flowering cherry sprinkled the branches of the trees like confetti as they strolled through the middle of the park. University students were sitting around on rugs reading books and chatting. A group of young men were kicking a ball not far from the path. When the ball landed in front of them, one of the teenagers scooped it up and whistled as Ruby and Rachel passed him.

'Looking good, Ruby Martin,' he shouted.

'You too,' laughed Ruby and she flicked her long hair away from her face. The wide legs of her cream jumpsuit flapped in the spring breeze.

Before running off, he hollered the obligatory 'Hey Ruby, haud yer wheesht!'

The two women sniggered and rolled their eyes.

'If I had a pound for every time that was said,' Ruby nudged her mother's head affectionately with hers.

*Haud Yer Wheesht* (hold your tongue) was a popular, evening TV show on Best Scotland. It was a Scottish version of the old *Give us a Clue*; a mixture of charades meets pictogram but with edgy adult humour. Ruby was one of the main panellists. She had taken over (temporarily) from her good friend Kit Hendry, another well-known presenter from one of the bigger, commercial radio stations. It was the break that Ruby had been longing for. It had catapulted her onto the path of celebrity recognition. New and exciting propositions had been pouring in from radio and TV ever since. With her film star good looks and her down to earth humour, she had been an instant hit with audiences and fellow panellists. Not forgetting the big-wigs in charge.

The clouds parted and the warm sun added to the glow that Rachel was basking in until a big, bloody white van destroyed it. Stole her Ruby.

Rachel longed to hold her grandchildren: to see them. Her wee cherubs. She planted an imaginary kiss on their innocent, happy foreheads. Alfie with his cheeky grin; nearly five – actually, he would *be* five now. Had she missed it? And little Nola; a clone of her mother. How were they coping?

People spoke about living nightmares. Rachel was surely

drowning in hers. Was her head thumping because of the blow she had sustained or were her tormented thoughts pummelling her skull in a bid to escape the madness? Because this was *NOT* normal.

According to Doctor Garland, after the collision with the van, Rachel had experienced extreme lapses of memory – huge chunks were missing. At first her behaviour had been erratic and aggressive; common symptoms with people suffering from post-traumatic amnesia. Her family and friends had been asked to be patient and not to question what she would be convinced was fact – when it clearly was not. With the absence of evidence of a specific brain injury (although it couldn't be ruled out), the medical powers that be began considering PTSD: post-traumatic stress disorder, resulting from the aftermath of the accident and/or the reluctance of Rachel willing to accept that Ruby had died. Words like hippocampus and prefrontal cortex were thrown into the mix but by that time Rachel had lost the will to live.

After she had been discharged from the Royal last April, she had continued to see a Professor James Warnock, an eminent consultant neurologist.

It was a lot to take in. What bothered Rachel most, apart from the loss of her beloved Ruby, was what had she been doing for the past nine months? When she was brought in yesterday, she had been found on Portobello promenade. Saturday morning strollers claimed she had dropped like a stone. One passerby told the paramedics that she thought Rachel had slipped. No-one else was with her. Why Portobello?

Every Saturday, Rachel drove to Aldi in Tranent with her carefully planned shopping list. She walked round the store whilst Colin waited in the car with a flask of coffee and a newspaper. It was her routine and she rarely deviated; not without sufficient justification.

When she had asked one of the hospital lunch ladies to hand her her phone, she didn't recognise it. Nor did she know the pass code. There were two bank cards tucked in the flap next to the IPhone. One was a Bank of Scotland debit card and the other a Nationwide credit card. Both newish with Mrs Rachel M Gordon etched on them. When had she acquired her own cards solely in her name? As a fifteen-year-old, she had opened a Bank of Scotland account when she started working in 'Irene's' on Saturdays, sweeping up hair and making copious amounts of tea. She'd been loyal to B of S ever since. When she remarried, she changed it to a joint account. She'd never ever been with Nationwide. My God, did Colin know? What would he think?

She took a sneaky peek at her body again. Although she was thin, she seemed to be fairly toned. Her skin wasn't at all mottled or wobbly. She lifted her right leg high into the air to examine it more carefully. The little bit of lunch and tea she had nibbled on had refuelled her energy levels. With little effort, she was able to hold it close to her face; no big rolls of fat around her belly forming a barrier. And even more surprisingly, when she wrapped her hands around the top of her thigh, her thumbs and middle fingers could almost touch. Gone was the unsightly cellulite that forced her to wrap a sarong around her hips when she holidayed abroad; not that that had happened for a long time.

She studied her hands again. They seemed smoother; less wrinkly and her nails were beautifully manicured. Only twice in her lifetime had she succumbed to having her nails done – the first was the wedding of her son, Rory, and the second was Ruby's wedding. She would never ever have considered having little emojis painted on them. She cringed as she felt her husband's disapproval. And what about Colin? Why on earth would she have prevented him from visiting her?

A quiet knock on the open door jolted her from her reverie. It happened again, with a little more force.

'Only me.' Annabelle Jeffries paused in the doorway as if seeking permission to enter. 'Hiya bbz, how ye doin?' Not really waiting for a reply, she continued, 'You're looking better. Are ye feeling better?' She sounded nervous.

She was wearing a bright red puffer jacket and wide black culottes. Black high-heeled boots gave Annabelle much needed height. She had always been envious of Ruby's long legs. She tucked her white woollen hat and gloves into her handbag and ruffled her thick, shoulder length, dark brown hair. Ever since Annabelle was a wee girl, she had worn glasses. They were now part of her DNA. Her latest pair were large, round and black.

'Babes? I've been waiting for you.' There was a hint of menace in Rachel's tone.

Annabelle giggled. It was a giggle that dried in her throat. She walked to the window and loosened a blue plastic chair at the top of a pile. She paused momentarily and stared into the darkness outside, exhaled loudly then turned to face Rachel. She carried the seat over to the head of Rachel's bed and draped her jacket around the back. The bright red was in stark contrast to the grey, drab interior of the small room. She acknowledged the older woman with a thin smile and sighed again.

'How are you?' enquired Ruby's childhood friend as she polished her steamed-up glasses with the corner of Rachel's bed sheet.

'Confused,' admitted Rachel, 'and I was hoping you could set the record straight.'

Annabelle squirmed in her seat then took Rachel's hand.

'Do you know who you are?'

'Oh, not you too!' Rachel yanked her hand from Annabelle's grip. 'I've had enough of the interrogations thank you very much. For God's sake, just tell me what's going on.'

Annabelle stuttered, 'I am so so sorry but I really need to ask you this. Do you really know who you are?'

'Well, the last time I looked in the mirror TODAY, I was definitely Rachel Gordon,' she snapped sarcastically. 'And if I am not mistaken you are Annabelle Jeffries my Ruby's best...' she faltered.

The two women stared at each other, their eyes desperately searching for answers. The younger one bit hard into her lower lip and was visibly shaking. She was the first to swipe some tears from her face then the water works began – both lost in their grief. Annabelle stood up and wrapped her arms around the woman she often referred to as her second mum. Their tears soaked each other's shoulders.

It took several minutes before either of them were composed enough to engage in a conversation. As soon as one of them attempted to speak, their trembling lips rendered them incapable again. Rachel was shocked at Annabelle's distress.

'I'm so sorry Mrs. M but it's a lot for me to take in.'

Rachel gave her time to cry although she did think she was a tad melodramatic. Ruby's pal had had nine months to grieve; Rachel had had less than nine hours.

Eventually, Annabelle picked up the box of tissues she had brought in the night before. She grabbed a handful for herself and passed the box to Rachel. She dried off her glasses again, blew her nose and laughed nervously.

It was Rachel that took control next. 'I can't remember

anything after the accident. I saw Ruby on the road…' She puffed her cheeks. 'And the next thing I know is that I am in here. They tell me it's the beginning of January 2020. So, what the hell have I been doing for nine months and why are you here and not Colin? It makes no sense.'

'I honestly don't know where to begin.' Annabelle covered her face with the palms of her hands then she lowered them on to the bed. 'I have something for ye, Rachel, and I have to warn you that it will seem utterly, utterly unbelievable but I'll answer any of your questions as honestly as I can.'

Annabelle rummaged in her bag and brought out a clear, plastic wallet with a red zip. Inside was a navy hardback book (a little smaller than A4 in size) with a beach scene on the front: a yellow and red deck chair sat under a palm tree. The background was as blue as a cloudless sky. A thick red elastic band held the bulging pages together.

'Ruby asked me to give you this should anything happen to her.' Annabelle's voice was so full of emotion that Rachel was afraid to take it.

'Is it something she bought for me?' asked Rachel.

'It's a journal. It will tell you everything you need to know about the last nine months,' explained Annabelle.

Rachel furrowed her forehead. Her eyebrows seemed to rest on her eyelashes. 'And Ruby organised this before she died?'

'Please read it Mrs M. I'm the only one that knows of its existence and that's how it has to remain.'

Rachel hoisted herself into a more comfortable position. She pulled her knees up and rested the thick book on her lap. She traced the palm tree with her finger and smiled. Ruby loved her summer holidays. She prised off the tight binding.

'I'm frightened to open it.'

Annabelle pressed the back of Rachel's hand into her lips. 'You'll be fine. I'm right here.'

Rachel opened the hard back cover and gently ran her finger down the join. There was a piece of lined paper folded in half with *READ FIRST* on it. She flicked it open. The handwriting was instantly recognisable. At least, it looked like her own. Small and neat.

*My darling mum,*

*If you are reading this then it means I am no longer here and somehow you have returned.*

# FOUR

Rachel lowered the letter, her mouth tightened. Her piercing glare demanded a plausible explanation.

'This is definitely my handwriting... so who the hell am I writing to? My mum's been dead for years.'

Annabelle's anguished brown eyes darted everywhere except at Rachel. She clasped her fingers together and tapped her thumbs against her chin. As Ruby's friend twisted a strand of her dark hair around her finger, Rachel sensed she was struggling to divulge what she had to say.

'The diary was started a few weeks after the road accident. It explains why Ruby decided to write it all down. God, Rachel, I know this must seem mad. It was all mad to me at first and I refused to believe it. You can believe what you want but at least you'll know what you've been doing for the past nine months. I've only had time to glance at the first few paragraphs this morning. As soon as I realised that you might be you... ye kept calling for Ruby last night, I nipped into your flat to fetch it.'

'My flat?'

'You live in Portobello now. I'll explain later.'

Rachel squeezed her eyes tight and tilted her head to the right and left whilst massaging her neck and shoulders with her good arm. She inhaled deeply and continued to read.

*I don't know where to start or what to say or who I'm actually writing to. You or me? Will there ever be a proper you or me ever again? The whole thing is totally bizarre. Weird. Crazy. But sure, I have to do this. I owe it to you to write down everything that has happened to me so far. It's only fair. And to be perfectly honest, I'm terrified that I might wake up tomorrow and I've forgotten the past four weeks and I have to start from scratch. This way, I know exactly what I've done and said!!!!*

*So, I'm going to give you all the details once I can sort them in my head.*

*I woke up in hospital in YOUR body. I know!!! Absolutely fucking unbelievable.*

*A few weeks after the accident, I realised I had to record everything that had happened. I had been jotting down bits and pieces every day (just in case!!!) but it wasn't an accurate account and nowhere detailed enough. I have no idea how or why this has happened to me, to us. It's a nightmare. We were good people, I think. I have no idea how long I'll be here. Will it be forever or am I living on borrowed time? I miss you so much, Mum and I have only Annabelle to confide in. Every time I look in the mirror and see your beautiful face, I crumple. BUT I have to be strong for both of our sakes and for my beautiful babies or Ben won't let me see them or be close to them. I've got to prove to him that I'm over believing I'm me, Ruby. That has been the hardest part of this nightmare, not being honest with Alfie and Nola but I can't. Too too difficult. Too complicated.*

*Part of me hopes that you will never read this as it means that I will be somewhere else. Totally selfish, I know. Please please let it be Heaven as this is a living Hell. That's not aimed at you by the way. I hope I don't spoil anything for you, Mum. I'll try to be true to you but you know what I'm like. Big mouth, short fuse.*

*I am so sorry that we didn't spend enough time together when we had the chance. My fault probably. And I'm so sorry that I didn't see what you were going through. Please Mum, read this before you ever think about contacting Colin especially after what I now know.*

*HE IS A DANGEROUS MAN.*

*Perhaps you are reading this decades later and Colin will be long gone. Hope so. I love you so so much and I miss you even more. You were such a good mum to me and Rory. I should have told you that more often. I'm going to fill you in on everything that has happened so far in this new notebook then I'll write to you every day. Just in case.*

    *Love you so much*
    *Your Precious Ruby xxxxxx*

Rachel repeated the words out loud to allow Annabelle to hear them and to confirm that she had interpreted correctly what had been written. Her thoughts were all over the place yet Annabelle's face was devoid of shock. She obviously accepted that Ruby had written it. Rachel laughed; an odd agitated laugh. She could hardly begin to rationalise what she was about to say.

'Did I believe that I was Ruby? Is this what this is all about? What did everyone else think?'

Annabelle coughed nervously. 'Nobody believed her, well you. Not even me at first. But she told me things that only Ruby and me knew.'

'This is bloody nonsense,' announced Rachel. 'Farfetched and farcical. I want you to leave and I want to talk to Colin. I mean it. I want Colin here NOW!'

'That's not going to happen.' Annabelle seemed full of remorse. 'Rory is down as your next of kin. You'll have to go through him.'

Rachel threw the diary on to the grey, non-slip flooring. Her face dared Annabelle to challenge her.

'Oh...oh...,' squeaked Annabelle and as if her life depended on it, she jumped up to gather in the bits and pieces that had fallen out and scattered; tickets, scraps of paper, cards and photographs. All of them dated.

'Please Rachel, don't do that,' begged Ruby's friend. 'Remember what Ruby wrote? Colin is dangerous. He'll have you put away. He tried it before. You must know what he was like. Please... read some more on your own. Take your time.' Collapsing into her chair, Annabelle sucked in some air and threw her head back. Eyes clamped, she expelled the air from her lungs, flapping her dark brown fringe in the process. She looked totally washed out. As she opened her eyes, she squeezed Rachel's hand tightly. 'I promised Ruby that I would look after you no matter how hard you pleaded with me to let you see Colin. Ruby had that injunction taken out to protect her and you. She never gave up on you. Don't give up on her. Don't give up on me.'

Annabelle's face seemed to slurp into her very bones. Her forehead dropped onto Rachel's blue bedspread and she began to cry. She buried her face deeper into the covers as if to smother the unnatural groaning that was escaping from her throat. She sounded done.

Rachel picked up two of the photographs from the pile that had been rescued from the floor. She recognised the first one. It was a snap of Ruby, Ben, Alfie and Nola taken while holidaying in the Florida Keys a couple of years ago. They were on the beach in their bare feet. The sun was setting behind them; it was just about to sink into the sea. Little blond Nola, a toddler, was perched on Ruby's hip, her bare chubby legs dangling, and Alfie was standing in front of Ben with their matching tropical shirts. Ruby, in a smart pink playsuit, was staring lovingly into her handsome husband's equally smiley face. They all looked a picture of happiness; dressed up and ready for dinner. Rachel had the very same photo. It sat framed on her bedside table or at least it used to. Now it was in her drawer. She would look at it most nights before she climbed into bed. Colin claimed they were showing off and rubbing their noses in it. A holiday that neither he nor Rachel could ever afford. It was easier to hide the reminder. Less hassle.

The second was another holiday shot of the family – except Rachel was in it. No Ruby. On the back was the destination and date; Playa de Las Americas October 2019. Rachel's stomach lurched. She had no recollection of it and yet she too was gazing into the face of her son-in-law with the same adulation that Ruby had shown in the first photo. She studied the two prints as her eyes ping-ponged between the two scenes. There was no doubting the look of love on both women's faces. Rachel would never have stared at her son-in-law like that.

Rachel looked down at Ruby's lifelong pal. As a regular visitor to the Martin household, Annabelle always lit up their house when she bounced in. She was the happy go lucky Yang to Ruby's often pragmatic Yin. Secretly, Rachel had always thought that Annabelle would end up marrying Rory. They rubbed along so easily compared to the two squabbling siblings yet as adults, Ruby and Rory had mutual respect and admiration for each other. Most of the time.

'Please don't. I'm sorry.' And she stroked the young woman's dark head.

Rachel lifted Annabelle's chin with her fingers and promised to read more of the diary with an open mind. Ruby's best friend blew her nose again – loud honking filled the room. There were only a few tissues left in the box.

'Would you like me to stay a little longer?' she asked sniffing.

Rachel shook her head. She needed some time on her own to digest what was unfolding. She watched as Annabelle fastened up her red jacket and pulled her hat down over her ears and flattened her waves. It was cold outside. Her young friend pecked her on the cheek and promised to return tomorrow night. As she disappeared into the corridor, Rachel had meant to ask her if she knew the pin code to her mobile but she was too late. It would have to wait until the following evening.

Rachel kissed the Florida Keys photo and placed it carefully on her bedside trolley. The other one was placed in the front page and the rest were tucked into the back along with the other scraps for the time being. The book had been well used. It looked as if it could fall apart any minute. She plumped up her pillows and made sure she was comfortable before tackling the journal again. She looked at the Christmas emojis on her fingernails – a bemused smile pushed her cheeks apart. She swallowed what little saliva remained in her mouth. Her middle finger hovered above the palm tree. Apprehensively, she opened the thick navy cover and turned to the first dated entry.

# FIVE

## *Ruby's Journal*

**Wednesday 24th April 2019.**

It's almost four weeks since the accident and I have a key to Annabelle's flat in Pitt Street. I can't tell you what this means to me. FAB-U-LOUS!! A safe haven away from Colin. I now have a phone, your old one but not for long – had no time yet to buy a decent one but will do asap. God Mum, how did you manage with that relic? I've been borrowing a look at other folks every chance I get. And I have use of a computer. At Auntie Vera's of all places. Plus, here obviously. Was able to sort out new passwords that Colin doesn't know about. He is pissed off about that. Tough. I've also set up a Blog called 'Ray of Hope' which I hope will help other women like you. More of that later. Annabelle has said that I can move in with her anytime but I have a few things to sort out in Alderburn first. I'll tell you soon how I managed to convince Annabelle that I was me. Meanwhile, I'll try to explain what has happened so far in some sort of chronological order. I had been scribbling things down since the accident anyway, in case I lost all that memory too. Colin reads it but pays scant regard to it. Obviously, I never write anything derogatory about him or Claire. Just the basic outline of my day. Nothing that he could use against me. I will be moving out as soon as, before I bloody murder him or more than likely he will have murdered me. And I'm not joking. It is way too menacing for me to stay there for much longer. He is a fucking nightmare by the way. I sorted out all your banking and salary but will fill you in later. You MUST read everything about Colin. PLEASE. And don't attempt to contact him.

Sorry, I digress and must keep to the point.

*

Back to the beginning. **Thursday March 28th.**

You looked great Mum. Best I had seen you look in ages. Gone were the frumpy jumpers and old woman jacket. I was so pleased to see you looking like your old self again. Thank you for wearing the pink trench, you really suited it. I'd managed to get away sharp. Lucky me. Had to beg the programme controller for it but he owed me one. Long story. Got him out of a jam recently. Silly eejit is cheating on his wife and I foolishly gave him an alibi. Not proud of myself but don't really rate his wife. Not that I know her well. She snubbed me once at a big bash in the Dome. Remember we went there last year for brunch? Smart place on George Street. Anyway, I pinned you down and you agreed. Thankfully. Why had we let things slip? We were always so close. Was it Colin or me to blame or both of us? I am truly sorry mum. I was too absorbed in my own career and wee world to notice what was happening to you. Totally selfish. You should've said something. Instead of you rushing out our door on Thursday evenings after looking after the kids, I should have insisted you stay for a chat or overnight. You always seemed so keen to get back to Colin.

All I can remember was us waiting at the traffic lights. I held your hand and when the green man popped up, I pulled you on to the road. That's when the van ploughed into us. WHAM!

Three of us as it turned out. An old man was next to you. He suffered a broken leg and collar bone. I need to track him down and find out what is happening with his claim as regards compensation. It might help me (as in you). Ben will be fine. I was well insured. But I need to make sure that I take care of me now and you, if there is a you, in the future. Sorry, that sounds crass but we need to look after our finances. Ben is useless at that sort of thing. Always left it to me. Somehow, I need to steer him in the right direction. Not sure how as I'm most definitely persona non grata at the moment. When I say me, I mean me as you. He's not forgiven me yet. Still too wary. God, I miss Alfie and Nola so so much. I'm finally getting somewhere with your bank accounts. Why on earth did you stop having a card of your own? It's called being independent.

Waking up in the hospital was the scariest thing ever. Actually, so many things in the past four weeks have scared me shitless that it would be hard to rate them in order.

The first thing I remember was the pain. My whole body throbbed. The right side was worse. It was hard to work out what ached most. The pain in my chest was excruciating – I could hardly breathe. It felt as if I was being flattened by an elephant. I shouted out for you and felt someone take my hand then there was that smell. Yeuch! When I opened my eyes, Colin's ugly mug was millimetres from my face. His breath seriously stinks. First degree halitosis. Pawing my face. FUCK! WHAT WAS HE DOING? Then he kissed me!!!!! On the lips. Can you imagine?

'Ssshhhhhhh,' he whispered. 'You're safe. Safe and reasonably well, considering.'

Considering?? We were rammed by a white van. I shouted for you again. He kissed my hand. Practically snogged it. Not nice.

First reaction (apart from what the fuck?) was – why was your Colin slobbering over my hand? Second one – I screamed and I mean screamed. Colin looked terrified. The nurse ran into the small ward and Colin backed away. He got tangled in the yellow privacy curtain that had been pulled around my bed and kicked out with his legs to free himself from the material. I shouted out for you and then Ben then the kids. I wanted to know what had happened to you. Wanted to see the kids. Desperately. I wanted to see dad too. Every time Colin edged towards me, I became hysterical. I couldn't work out why he was there. Other than needing to find out what had happened to us. I demanded to see you or Ben or Dad. I heard Colin mumble that 'her mother died years ago.' The nurse had to usher him out of the room. He was not for budging.

'She needs me.'

She had to practically shove him out.

The poor nurse. No matter how hard she tried, I was not for calming down. They must have given me an injection, or maybe it was just the morphine, because I conked out. When I came to, I felt groggy. Colin was back fussing over me but he had a look in his eye. Cold. Like he could see right into my soul. I had no idea why I was pissing him off. Why wasn't he with you? Thank goodness the nurse was there. Then the doctor came in. I could hear myself trying to shout but I was tongue-tied. Every time Colin approached me, I must have raised my arms as I could feel myself wrestling with him but I was aching. The pain in my side was unbearable and yet I was determined to lash out.

'STOP IT!' he yelled. 'It's me, Colin. Your husband.'

'You are NOT. HE IS NOT!' I could hear my muffled shout. I held on to that doc's hand as hard as I could. 'He is not. Please help me.'

The doctor and nurse were so kind. They listened patiently while I slurred who I was and what had happened to us. I think I drifted off to sleep. Can't be sure but the next thing I could recall was that I was calling for Ben again, over and over. Begging the nurse to let me see him. You would've thought that I would've recognised your voice (it's your voice that comes from my throat). I can only assume that the drowsiness had duped me. When Ben appeared at the door, I dissolved. I stretched my hand out for him to take it. I can't tell you how reassuring it felt to have my hand in his even though I thought my elbow was snapping with the effort. He was so gentle. My Ben. He looked dreadful. Dark shadows under his eyes. His beautiful blue eyes were so grey, so was his skin. His lips were trembling and he was choking on his words. He kept saying sorry over and over.

'I'm so sorry, Rachel.'

He was confused. Obviously. Or so I thought. He should've said that he was sorry about Rachel. About you. But he said it again. Through his snot and tears. Then-

'She's gone.'

He held my hand tightly to his mouth. I could feel the warmth of his breath on my knuckles. His tears trickled down my wrist and I cried too. For you, Mum.

'It's 'e,' I smiled. 'Ru'y.' To be fair, my bottom lip was twice the size and I was speaking with a strange numb-like lisp.

He dropped my hand and turned to Colin. 'What's she saying that for?'

As if I wasn't in the room, the nurse explained to Ben that I was in shock. It can happen after an accident. The trauma. Confusion. Survivor's guilt. Wishing that Ruby (me) was still here. I would soon settle down and I would begin to remember things properly again. She left to find the doctor. Ben looked broken.

I assured him I would be okay and that I loved him. I knew the right-hand side of my face must have been swollen after the accident because I could only touch the dressing ever so lightly with the tips of my fingers and that was why he wasn't recognising me. I reached for his warm hand and squeezed it. He crouched by the bed and looked straight at me.

'Ruby's gone, Rachel. She didn't make it. Doctors say she wouldn't have suffered.' He blubbed more. He was so upset.

'I did survive, 'abe. Look at my eyes. It's me.' I was worried that he wouldn't be able to recognise me and I kept blinking. 'It's me, Mr 'ean.' (Bean was my nickname for him) 'Your Scoody Doo.'

All my gang used to call me Ruby Roo but Ben changed it to Scooby Doo (I'm hopeless in quizzes). I used to call him Mr Bean because of the funny faces he could pull. Ben shook his head. Got up and walked away. I can't begin to tell you how useless it all felt. I screamed 'fuck' a lot. Too much for them.

Colin was pretending to be distraught. I know now he would have been pretending because I understand him better now. I had to learn quickly or he would have had me committed. I've Auntie Lisa to thank for that not happening.

Colin had his hands on Ben's shoulders. Their foreheads were touching. I could remember thinking that they were similarly dressed. Jeans and grey jumpers. Only Colin's was V neck and he had a checked shirt underneath. Ben seemed to tower above him even though I knew they were roughly the same height and build. An inch taller than me. Five ten. That's why I always wore flats when I was out with Ben. My handsome Ben with his dark blond wavy hair swept back from his face and his neatly trimmed stubble. Colin could do worse than take some hair taming hints from Ben. It's that strange side parting that Colin's got. His hair's too thick and wavy for it. It looks like a pile of Brillo pads lined up on the top of his head (de-pinked). Maybe if he kind of ruffled it a bit, it would look more natural. And his ridiculous white trainers. Brand new and cheap. The kind certain Brits buy for their summer holidays. Not for an unfashionable sixty-year-old. Sorry Mum. What did you ever see in him?

Anyway, they kept glancing in my direction and muttering quietly. Not hiding the fact that they were discussing me. I was surprised when Ben approached the bed first. He sat down on a chair.

'Rachel,' he said almost in a whisper. 'Do you remember what happened?'

I told him that we were holding hands and the green man came on and we stepped out. I think I heard brakes screeching then I woke up here with bad breath seeping into my nostrils. I'm sure he smiled at that.

'What happened to 'um?' I asked.

'Ruby didn't... I'm sorry.'

He scrunched his eyes and sighed then looked towards Colin seeking support. Colin shuffled in beside him. Up until then, I still kinda liked Colin. Trusted him, I suppose. Just didn't want his close contact. Him touching me.

Colin leaned in. 'Rachel, there's no Ruby here. Only you my darling. Only you. The doctor believes you have suffered short term memory loss. It can happen after a severe blow to the head. You're only trying to hold on to Ruby in your own mind, my love (something like that but you get the gist). Ruby's no longer with us. You have to be strong for Ben and for Alfie and Nola. Please don't upset them anymore.'

I couldn't believe it. Don't upset them! How fucking dare he say that to me. Sorry Mum but I can't help swearing. So much anger inside me. A bad habit and one that you don't like. (I think it's my generation or maybe Ben and me have stressful lives. Had stressful lives. Definitely still do). I gripped Ben's hand with all my strength. I'm sure my nails dug into his skin.

'Lishen to nee,' I pleaded. 'LISHEN.'

I'm NOT going to write exactly how I was speaking (can't be arsed!!!) but try to picture what I must've sounded like. Any letter that needed me to work my lips was difficult.

'I bought you those jeans from Top Man, 32 inch waist 32 length. That sweatshirt is from Fat Face. You hate heavy jumpers. They make you claustrophobic. (shouldn't have used that word. Had to say it twice!!) It cost me £39.99 and you said that there was a similar one in Asda for ten pounds and that I was robbed.'

'Ruby probably told you that,' he said. 'Everyone knows I hate thick clothing.' His eyes were full of pity for me.

I was getting angrier. Typical me. You always said that I should count to ten and think. I'm just like my dad. I wish I had your temperament. Rory's got it. Everything and anything was pouring out my mouth. Holidays we had shared, parties, cinema visits with the kids, books we had read to them, when they were ill, places we had humped in. My mouth was twisting. Surely, he must have registered something. I begged him to think about what I was saying. It HAD to be me.

'You're always the same,' I screamed. 'When the obvious is staring you in the face, you have to question it. Question me. *For fuck's sake Ven, o'en your ears. It's neeeee.*'

Don't know where I got the strength but I reached for him and grabbed the cuff of his jumper. Tight. He staggered backwards but I held on. The look on his face! You'd have thought I had leprosy. Colin waded in and roughly prised my fingers from him. Fortunately, it was Ben who settled me and tucked me in. That's when I took my chance. I deliberately lowered my voice causing him to come closer. I wanted to kiss him there and then but realised that it wasn't the right moment. Plus, throbbing lip. I worked through the agony to emphasise the next bit.

'You have a Master Beano and I have a Miss Do-little,' I said, nodding to his man bit then lifting up the covers to allow him to squint at mine. That was definitely our little secret. Nobody else knew that.

It's absurdly funny, looking back. (I'm actually giggling now!!) The colour drained from his face and he was grey enough already.

'RIGHT,' he roared and he scooped me up.

I was in agony. Stupid bastard. But at least now he had understood. He was taking me home. He staggered towards the toilet (ward ensuite). The two patients in the other beds looked stunned. Ben's face was puce from carrying you (me). Sorry Mum but you're no light weight and although he is quite muscular for his size, he's a wee beanpole. He caught his breath then kicked open the door with one of his feet. My head snuggled into his shoulder. We stumbled in and stopped in front of the mirror. I was too busy studying his nose and stubble.

'LOOK!' he shouted. 'LOOK!'

I turned my head to the mirror. I couldn't take it in. I could feel my husband holding me up yet it was you staring back at me in HIS arms. I screamed. He screamed. I screamed louder. You were in a hospital gown yelling *MUM* out loud. The room stopped. It was as if someone had taken our picture when we weren't ready. We looked stunned. Then I felt as if I was being sucked backwards at breakneck speed and according to what I now know, I fainted.

# SIX

*Rachel's Ward. Sunday 5th January 2020.*

Rachel lay back on her pillows and stared at the white ceiling. This was madness. She was reading a diary supposedly written by her dead daughter and what's more, part of her was beginning to believe it might be true. She tried to remember. She willed herself to try harder but she had no recollection of waking up in hospital before today.

The door of her room opened and a woman not much younger than Rachel popped her grey head through the door.

'A tea or milky drink and a wee biscuit?' she asked.

'A tea would be grand. I'm feeling a bit parched,' replied Rachel as she tucked the photograph of her and Ruby's family into the pages to keep her place.

A male nurse bustled in and looked at Rachel's notes hooked over the end of her bed.

'Do you need any pain relief, Rachel?'

Rachel hadn't realised that her head was still thumping and agreed that she needed something. Two paracetamols were dropped into a tiny white paper cup. She swallowed them with her tea and demolished the two digestive biscuits on her tray. She was surprisingly hungry.

In the solitude of her room, she deliberated whether to continue with the journal or to leave it until the morning. It must have been a terrible shock for Ruby to see her mother's reflection in the bathroom mirror. Rachel remembered how relieved she was when she saw her own face staring back from the compact mirror several hours ago. How would she have reacted if Ruby's startled face had bounced back at her?

The lure of the diary proved too much and Rachel used the Tenerife photograph to find her place. The Rachel in the snap looked fantastic. Slim, tanned, happy and confident. Nothing like the overweight and worthless woman she actually was. She examined the handwriting for the umpteenth time. The scrawl was definitely hers. Yet the Ys were different – more creative like Ruby's. And Ruby drew little circles instead of dots above her I's. There were other tiny discrepancies that only Rachel would probably notice. When she took her time, Rachel could produce exceptionally neat handwriting but when she was in a hurry, it was spidery and untidy just as it was on the pages she had read.

# SEVEN

## *Ruby's Journal*

Every time I relive that mirror scene, it sends a shiver down my spine that's why I had to put down my pen and take a short walk around the block. Stood at the bridge at Bonnington that arches over the Water of Leith and stared at nothing for ages. Just thought about the water and the hum of the cars passing me by. Bliss. I'm sure I saw a wee flash of blue. A kingfisher maybe? I thought of Dad. Remember when we used to have our picnics at Gifford and we would paddle in the burn next to the park? Bloody freezing. Rory loved it. Not me. I always had to come out for a pee. Were there kingfishers there or am I making it up? Anyway, it was a wee ray of hope. Exactly like my blog.

It's strange to be writing this diary by hand but hopefully it means I can take it anywhere and write in it. I'll have to leave it here at Annabelle's for the moment. Can't risk the weasel seeing it. He would have me sectioned without a second thought.

To see you in Ben's arms instead of me was petrifying. So back to the morning after the shock.

*

**Friday 29th March.**

I cried all that night. Thinking of you. I was the only person alive (surely, I was alive) that was mourning you. My nightmare was on repeat. I kept running up to random people, shouting at them to listen but no one was interested. As the dream went on, I couldn't catch anyone I was chasing and my screaming was lost in the long empty road. So distressing. My pillow was drenched. Sweat and tears.

I woke up to find Colin and Claire rummaging through your bag. What the fuck? What is she like? Shifty shifty shifty!!!!! Totally untrustworthy. She's like a skinny, manky black cat. When I challenged her, Colin turned on me saying that Claire was only trying to help and that she had rushed to the hospital first thing to support him and me. Really? Probably rushed round to check out how much money you had in your purse. I had always thought that Colin was a decent guy and when he told us (me and Rory) that you were suffering from panic attacks and anxiety, I actually believed him. He was so plausible. I should have demanded more proof or at least helped more. Why did you allow him to say those things about you? I'm so ashamed that I went along with it all.

After my shenanigans the night before, one of the other patients was hysterical because of it. Her husband complained and demanded that I be moved. So I was, to a room on my own.

Claire sashayed up to me (I was still lying down as my ribcage ached) and asked who was I today? Honestly, I could have yanked her dyed, navy-black hair and punched her in the face but hadn't the strength. PLUS, alarm bells were ringing. If I picked a fight with Colin's only daughter it would not bode well for me, so I said nothing.

I know it's daft but I could feel you warning me. Like you were my sensible wee conscience, tapping the inside of my skull to rein me in.

'Cat got yer tongue?' she sneered.

Then she cackled like a witch. (She could easily play *Bellatrix Lestrange* from *Harry Potter* – same teeth) Worse still, Colin joined in. A coven in my room! Part of me was terrified and the other part had sprung into overdrive as I was trying to work out what to say next. Be tactful pummelled the conscience hammer.

Fortunately, a nurse and an auxiliary came in to get me up. Colin had brought in your nightie and dressing gown. With my fingers, I motioned to one of the helpers to come closer and asked if she would help me into my nightie as there was no way that Claire was putting her skanky mitts on me. The nurse suggested that Colin and Claire could go for a walk and reminded Claire that it should only be Colin in the room at this time. It gave me a chance to have a chat with them. I explained that I had lost huge chunks of my memory and I couldn't remember my life with Colin and that I was really frightened to be alone with him. Then I began to sob. Because I was terrified. Ben hadn't believed me nor had Colin. Annabelle was on holiday and I wasn't sure if any of the other girls would be allowed in. Truthfully, I wasn't sure if I believed it myself. The senior nurse was great. She explained to Colin when he returned, minus the witch, that I was confused and very agitated and perhaps he should wait in the relative's room until the doctor was doing his rounds. She promised to find him shortly.

'She's at it,' he snarled. 'It's what she does.' He shot me a warning as he left.

He is what you would call a wee nyaff. A nasty wee nyaff at that.

Eventually, Doctor Miah turned up. He was lovely, same one as the day before. Thank you, NHS. He listened to everything I was saying. Obviously didn't believe I was me but was sympathetic and didn't call me a liar either. He arranged for me to have another CT scan to ensure they hadn't missed anything. He asked Colin to be patient with me and insisted that my memory would return in time. Familiar surroundings and my normal routine should help to jog things.

Being left alone with Colin was awful. My heart was racing. Colin deliberately said nothing. It's strange how silence can be as intimidating as the spoken word. He stuffed your handbag into his black holdall. I could hear him opening and closing cupboard doors on my blind side. (His whiter than white trainers squeaked on the floor. Each squeak shredded my nerves further.) He took your mobile from the pink trench coat. The phone went in his pocket and the coat was roughly rolled up before being wedged in beside your bag. Your cream boots were waggled in front of my face. He muttered something about the length of the heels and made a big gesture of putting them in the bag. He zipped it up and dropped it on to the floor. I watched him pull up a chair. My heartbeat filled the space between my ears to bursting point.

'All being well, ye'll get hame the morn.' There was no emotion in his tone yet it was laced with menace. 'If ye behave, Ben will drop in to discuss the funeral arrangements.' Then he made an odd grunt in his throat. 'I wonder if she made a will.'

That's when I knew that Colin had never liked me. In seven little snidey words.

'Lisa!' Colin rose to greet Auntie Lisa who broke down in his arms.

'Hey,' he said (he is so slippery) 'she's okay. Doctors say she'll make a full recovery.'

She had obviously been told about the memory problem. Colin was convinced that I would be back to normal in a day or two. I knew a threat when I heard one. Auntie Lisa stood over me and stroked my hair and frowned at my dressing. Kissed my forehead. Her familiar perfume (Molecule 01, Harvey Nics, where else?) was as comforting as her kiss.

'It's me Auntie Lisa. Ruby.' I couldn't help myself.

'What's she saying?' snapped Colin.

Lisa said that I had asked about 'Ruby'. Then she declared that she could murder a coffee and would Colin be a darling and get a skinny latte from the cafe for her. He did remonstrate but she ignored his excuses. No sooner had he disappeared through the door when she turned on me. And she didn't hold back.

'Right, lady. You listen and you listen good. Whatever is going on in that head of yours has to stop. GET A GRIP! I'm sorry, Rachel,' she said, 'I promised you a long time ago that I wouldn't interfere after the last time but if you don't put a stop to this then Colin will. Please. We've been friends for a long time and I know what he is capable of. You do too, even though you always denied it.'

I had no idea what she meant but I knew that she was confirming what I was already coming to realise – Colin was not to be crossed. I didn't get a chance to interrogate her further as Colin burst into the room claiming that he had left his wallet in his jacket pocket. It was porkies of course. He was making sure that we couldn't chat in private.

'So, Rach, what do you remember?' asked Auntie Lisa.

Colin hovered at her shoulder.

'About what?'

'About everything,' she urged.

I played the 'woe is Rachel' card. Had to. I informed them both that I could only recall snippets. I recognised them. Knew them. Despite Lisa trying to coach me, I couldn't remember anything about your school life (only what you and Lisa had already told me about you being pals since you met at a drama club when you were nine then being in the same class at High School, all the way through). All of my memories are my own or what you and Auntie Lisa have shared with us. Didn't convey that to them, naturally. I told Colin that my time with him was a blur. Although I was able to talk a wee bit about your wedding day, I had nothing to say about the honeymoon (thank God) or about anything else. That's when I realised that we (me, Ben and the kids) hadn't spent any significant amount of time with Colin at all. Why was that?

Colin raised his voice. Accused me of making it all up. Lisa put her hand on his forearm to calm him down but he flicked it off. Awkward. If I couldn't remember much about my oldest friend, she emphasised, the same could be said of him.

'I am the most important person in Rachel's life,' he yelled. 'She loves ME.' And then as if it was an afterthought, 'and I love her.'

Auntie Lisa and I exchanged glances. No more needed to be said. No, he did not. Sorry Mum but it's the truth. He only loves himself and that mad cow of a daughter and her equally sneaky squirt of a girl. Bellatrix Junior. Ten going on twenty. Actually, I'm being unfair. The wee one does seem to be very fond of you and she has been a bit of an ally to me.

Auntie Lisa kissed me again and rubbed my cheek with the back of her cold hand. She's always had cold hands. Warm heart, you said. And that she was too thin. I think she looks great. Lisa straightened up all official-like with her immaculately groomed long bob and fastened her Karen Millen, dusty blue jacket over a smart woollen navy dress. Smart dresses, thick tights, brogue shoes. Her signature look. What's she like? Once she finds a brand or shop she likes, she sticks to it like glue. Works for her and she rocks it. You definitely used to be like that. Maybe not sticking to a particular style but you used to dress smartly. Lisa fired a smile at Colin.

'While Rachel is under such duress, understandably, given the death of her daughter, I hope that you will be kind enough to allow me to visit more often. I'll pass on your regards to Rory. He's driving up from Brentwood tonight and staying with me. He'll be in tomorrow morning.' And she blew us a kiss. She's not a senior civil servant for nothing.

Colin was a little taken aback and muttered 'of course.'

Her scent lingered long enough to remind us both that she may have left but she was not forgotten.

# EIGHT

## *Ruby's Journal*

**Saturday morning.**

I got another scan at 7 o'clock on Friday night. CT again. Odd time but I suppose they work twenty-four seven. At least it would prove that I had a brain. The drink that they give you beforehand was diabolical. Yuck!!!

The weasel was still scuttling around. My new name for Colin. He tried to give me some tablets that he had taken from his jacket pocket and he wasn't happy when I intimated we should ask the nurse first.

'It's the medication you take at home,' he goaded.

'Then discuss it with the nurse.'

I asked him for your phone but he refused to hand it over. In the huff over the pills. (Sad to admit this considering everything else that was going on but I was having serious Twitter and Instagram withdrawals.) Didn't need it, he said. Same with your purse.

'What's the code?' he demanded.

Obviously, I didn't know.

'There ye are then and nothin here ye need to buy.'

'But I might want to phone someone and it would be good to have a card. Plus, I might fancy a stroll to the shop in the foyer or watch T.V.'

'Oh, ye can remember the foyer then?' he snapped.

For the hundredth time, I apologised for not knowing everything.

'If I could, I would,' I said on loop.

I instinctively knew that things would be no better back in Alderburn. I would have to be one step ahead of him. If only Annabelle hadn't been on holiday, I'd have called her to come ASAP. Australia's not the easiest of places to fly back from in an emergency.

I can't tell you how excited I was about seeing Rory. Doom and gloom Weasel threw plenty derogatory comments around the room before he turned up. Although, he was slightly more complimentary about Rory than me. When Rory entered and we locked eyes our sadness was tangible. He climbed on to the bed to cradle me (you). A big baby on my little brother's knee. Unbearable emotion swirling around us. My heart seemed too big for my chest and I could hear Rory's heart thudding on the side of my face. Rory was crying for me and I was sobbing for you. We rocked together for ages. Colin was all agitated as if we had committed incest.

'Ye'll be asked to leave,' he yelled at us.

Rory kept telling him to relax.

Once we had both recovered, I asked Colin to leave the room to give me a chance to be alone with my *son*. He refused, reiterating that it was imperative that I remained calm. I pleaded with him. Rory intervened (he should have jumped in sooner).

'I understand that you're only looking out for Mum, Colin, but it would be appreciated if we could have some time on our own. For a little while? (He flashed his famous charming smile) I'm really grateful for everything you have done for her this past year. It hasn't been easy.'

'Likesy what?' I piped up.

'You've had a lot of problems this year, Mum, and Colin has taken good care of you.'

'What kind of problems?'

'Mental health,' Colin butted in. 'Depression. Anxiety. Nasty moods.' He spat that last bit!

'And the whole family appreciates what you have endured but I would like some privacy with my mother, mate. Not a lot to ask.'

Colin mumbled that he was the one that would be left to clean up the mess. (The nerve of the wee shite!) Rory assured him that he wouldn't allow that to happen. I could sense Rory itching to say more but he didn't. Colin skulked out. Drama queen.

I was right in there. 'What was that all about? Endured? Ruby never said.'

'Sorry, mum, Ruby was too busy to listen.'

'Not true,' I screamed. 'I would have done anything to help mum. You know that.'

Rory did that funny thing with his jaw and nose when he gets riled. Squinty fierce face.

'MUM! You are NOT Ruby.' He took my hand and addressed me more kindly. 'I spoke with your doctor yesterday and he thinks that you have survivor's guilt. Rather than accept Ruby's death, you find it easier to pretend to be her.'

'I'm not pretending,' I whimpered.

'Maybe not pretending, more that you want to be her.'

I started to cry. To be fair, Colin did tell me you were depressed, Mum, and that you had anxiety attacks but he made light of it. Told me he was coping. It was his job to look after you and I shouldn't worry. So I didn't. Sorry. Plus, I've hardly seen you this year. Properly, I mean. Every second Thursday like ships in the night doesn't count. When I did try to pin you down, there was always an excuse. Too busy with your school work. You had a headache. Colin wasn't well. You were resting.

'I can't help it. I feel she's still with me,' I whimpered. (What else could I say?) 'I even think like her.'

'Then control her mouth, Mum. Colin's at breaking point. He's a good bloke. Been good for you. He's had a lot to put up with. Don't push him over the edge. Remember what happened last time?'

'What?' I had no idea what he was referring to.

'Last summer, you had to go in for respite care. At Abbotsford Priory. For four weeks. To give Colin a break. I paid for it.'

'You? Why?'

I knew nothing about it. Mum, I thought you were all on holiday. Why didn't you say where you really were? The kids and I had gone to the south of France for two weeks and Ben joined us for six of the days. How could I have known? When we came back, Colin made out that he had treated you to a Wellness Centre. A fortnight of mindfulness and meditation. I believed him. And Auntie Lisa never hinted. Colin, apparently, was about to have you sectioned because he'd had enough but Rory talked him out of it and arranged with Lisa to drive you down to the Borders. You should have come to stay with me, Mum. I would have looked after you.

'I thought they had all gone to Spain and that the Wellness Centre was a tag on,' I explained.

Rory coughed nervously. Turns out he had paid for Colin and the Bellatrixes to holiday in Benidorm for two weeks. Two effing whole weeks and I had been kept out of the loop!! A HUGE kick in the teeth. Rory must have clocked that I was struggling to comprehend it so he changed the subject and poured me some diluting orange. A young nurse came in and was all giggly and flustered around Rory. He has that effect on woman. Has that effect on JJ. He takes his height and dark hair off Dad whereas I'm more like you. Not the height but your colouring. Did you ever notice that Rory never wears jeans. Ben lives in them. Needs a wrench to lever them off. Our Rory looks like he's stepped out of the front page of a glossy mag. Wouldn't swap my Ben though. Can't now even if I wanted to.

(Had to splash my face with cold water just now. So hard.)

'I saw Ben and the kids last night,' Rory said.

'How were they? Do you think he'll allow the kids to see me?' I asked.

He explained that Ben was in bits. Alex (Ben's sous chef and manager of Suthiez) was in charge of the restaurant for a few days to give Ben a chance to sort out the funeral arrangements. Karl and Louisa were more than capable of running Rubiez. Kids were unusually quiet. I could've cried. Alfie was refusing to discuss me with anyone. Kept disappearing to his room. Nola was convinced I'd be back *tomorrow*. Bless her. Libby and Ros had been to visit. Two of my besties. As if you didn't know. Libby had baked a big batch of scones and Ros had taken the kids to give Ben time to organise things. JJ (my co-host) and Arjun had popped in. The kids went to nursery on the Monday to keep things normal for them. Normal? Without me? I ached for them, Mum. Still do. How could my babies be coping without me? No mummy cuddles. My wee munchkins didn't deserve this. Ben was adamant that I wouldn't be allowed to see the kids until I had sorted myself out. Until no delusions of being me (Ruby).

Sorry for the splodges. I had to wash my face again.

Tributes had been pouring into the station since the accident.

A bystander had posted it on Facebook (along with a picture!!!) before Ben had even been informed. The gall of some folk. Unbelievably callous. One of his staff had to pull him aside. How can people be so cruel? I hadn't even thought about my work. Can you believe that? Ruby Martin hadn't missed the job she lived and breathed. JJ had to take the Friday and the Monday off. Totally bereft. Wee soul. He couldn't face going in without me. Every time he spoke about me on air, he broke down. Also, can you believe it's six years since I started presenting with JJ. 2013!!! Bloody hell. I insisted on doing the Friday with him as my original start date was Monday 1st April and I was terrified the listeners would think it was an April Fool. Six years!!

Simon Ward had to take over our show the day after the accident. Remember him? Si Fi? (Science geek). Sly Si more like. He would think he had died and gone to heaven. The breakfast slot had been his dream number for years. Thank God Jacob, aka JJ, pulled himself together. He is so chicken hearted. His husband Arjun is the total opposite. Held Jacob together. I tuned in the following morning. Had to. Curiosity got the better of me. I'm not kidding, Mum, I had no idea one person (me) could cry so many tears. People were saying such lovely things about me.

Ben wanted to talk things over with you/me – the funeral mainly. It's a Northern Ireland thing. Discussing the funeral asap AND burying them within three or four days. Didn't happen with me. He doesn't believe in cremation so I assumed correctly that he would plump for a burial. Before then, I couldn't have cared less but now I do. No way would I have condoned a burning. What if in some perverse way, I needed my body back. Daft I know but I couldn't risk it. Not that my body could be rescued from six feet under either. Oooooooh!!

Someone or something has just walked over my grave. A cold, ghostly finger thrummed every bone on my spine.

I asked Rory if he planned to say a few words on behalf of the family and he agreed but only if Dad could contribute too. At the end of the day, it was up to Ben. I suggested your favourite sad song – Eva Cassidy's *Songbird*. If Rory thought it was an odd choice, he didn't comment. It was your funeral as well as mine so you needed to be represented in some way. You must be thinking that I'm talking about our final goodbyes so matter of factly but trust me it was the total opposite. I was a wreck on the day. But I could hardly announce that it was your final farewell and not mine. Colin had successfully planted the seed that you were a fruitcake. Constantly shouting from the roof tops would've made things a lot worse.

My funeral had tentatively been arranged for Tuesday 16th April. On condition there was nothing untoward with the post mortem. I didn't want us to be interfered with in that way but what could I say? Felt surreal. School holidays and I was supposed to be going to Centre Parcs with Ros and her two on the 12th and 13th. I planned to travel back on the Sunday for work and Ros would stay until the Monday. The kids were so looking forward to it.

I meant to say that Rory bumped into Kenneth at Edinburgh airport. He'd travelled from Enniskillen in the afternoon. Thank God for that. Ben's always been close to his dad and Kenneth kept him grounded. No mother though.

Margaret was waiting for the actual funeral. She should've been there but no no, her daughter's needs were greater than her son's. Carrie needed a babysitter. For f's sake – she has a nanny!! In order for her to attend my funeral, she had to finalise some deal or other for the company. And no surprises but when

Carrie did turn up in Edinburgh, she was darker than whatsisname from that antique TV programme, David somebody. For someone with her brains and business acumen you think she would see that the blonde bimbo, crispy-tanned look is not the best. Yet, they go nuts for her in Sharm El Sheikh. Drooling apparently. She gets the best service. Must work as Sutherland's do a hell of a lot of refurbishing there. Egypt and Dubai make up more than half of their turnover.

Rory FaceTimed Alana and Jack. Wee Jack is a lovely boy. He was so concerned about you. His posh Essex voice, 'gran-nee!' He was so relieved to see your face. A lot of questions though!! And he asked to see under the dressing. What's he like? Alana told him off. Quickly redeemed himself. He'd made a beautiful card for Alfie and Nola. A detailed drawing of the big cousin in the middle with his protective arms around the shoulders of my two. Beautiful. More tears. Poor Alana, she was sobbing as hard as me. And her face was as bad as mine. Her eczema had flared up with all the stress. She kept saying that she would miss me. I had been her friend and confidante as well as a fantastic sister-in-law. Someone else I should have given more time to.

I had to tell Rory about my fears regarding Colin. Left out all my mounting doubts about Colin's integrity. Kept that for much later. But I had to explain that because of the memory loss I was terrified to go to your house with him. I hardly knew Colin. Totally true. Had no love for him. Very true. Even truer now. Rory promised to chat with him when he came back. In front of me.

Then the bomb was dropped. Hadn't expected it. BOOM! The pit of my stomach exploded. Ricocheted off every fibre of my being.

'Would you like to go with me to see Ruby?'

# NINE

Rachel checked the time on the big grey clock on the opposite wall. She had to squint in the dimmed light. It was nearly half past two in the morning. The hospital was eerily quiet. She listened for a few moments. Not a sound was to be heard. She had drifted off to sleep thinking about Ruby and Rory and Colin but now she was wide awake.

She couldn't face reading any more, especially about the funeral. Ruby had been dead for nine months and she hadn't mourned her properly – actually not at all. Nine whole months had passed without her precious daughter in this world and she would never see her again. Never hold her hand or hold her close. The opportunity to reassure her and tell her funny Ruby how much she loved her was gone; snatched by a nasty, white van driver. She had an overwhelming urge to phone Rory but she had no idea how to unlock Ruby's phone and regardless of what mind games her memory had been playing, remembering a mobile number had never been within her skill remit. How was Ben coping without Ruby? She did everything for him: all the admin and practicalities for the house and the family were organised by her. Rachel used to be the same when she was married to Rob, the father of her children. Like Ben, Rob concentrated all his energy on his business and left Rachel to deal with the home side of things. She was good at it too. Ran like clockwork so why had she fallen apart when she married Colin?

When Rob and her parted (his secretary – typical cliché), she hadn't disintegrated. Quite the opposite. She'd thrived. She bought a small semi-detached bungalow in Alderburn where she had grown up. Mortgage free. At least Rob had had the decency not to hassle with what was due to her. With a renewed energy, she had taken up new challenges (some weight loss helped) and it was at an evening class (five years later) where she met Colin. Geology was not a subject she would normally have gone for but she had read an article in a Sunday magazine about James Hutton, a famous geologist, and how his theories about the age of the earth had been shunned by the Christian zealots of his time (Georgian era – you didn't challenge the bible). Plus, the naughty James had been a bit of a lad in his day. It had tickled her interest.

Along with the rest of the budding geologists, Rachel had gone on a weekend expedition (piss up more like) to Siccar Point near Cockburnspath. She seemed to always be in the same walking group as Colin and they ended up sliding down an extremely steep slope on their arses all the way from the cliff top towards the dangerous rocky edge of the sea, solely to get a better vantage point of the two layers of rock at the famous Point. They had to use ropes to pull themselves back to the top. Several times Colin apologised for having to put his hands on her dirty bum to give her a much-needed push up. It was exhilarating and exciting. They ended up sitting together at dinner and breakfast where he was funny and attentive. She felt very relaxed in his company. About three weeks after the trip, it was Rachel who asked him out for a drink and why not? He could only have said no. To her surprise, the fifty-eight-year-old widower agreed. He had introduced himself as a widower to the evening group at the first meeting and technically it was true. Only, he had omitted to inform Rachel until much further into their relationship that he was in fact separated from his first wife when she died. Had been for five years. Rachel had decided it was irrelevant. She loved him and that was good enough for her.

Rachel thought about Colin and what Ruby would probably have faced when she returned to Alderburn with him. Perhaps Ruby had refused to go. Her stomach constricted. She was about to say *please God look out for her* but the last time she had made a pact with God, it had gone horribly wrong.

Next thing Rachel knew was the gentle hand of Agata jiggling her shoulder.

'Good morning, Rachel. How are you today? Do you feel well enough to sit in your chair this morning and have a cup of tea?'

Rachel was happy to comply.

'Did you sleep well?'

Rachel had not. Harrowing nightmares had peppered her sleep. As she sat on the chair, she admired her penguin nightie and smiled. She had so many questions for Annabelle, not least about where she was going to stay when she was allowed out. Annabelle had given her little information about her current situation and how she fended for herself. This was exactly how Ruby must have felt – alone and totally bewildered. Reliant on others to function properly.

After some tea and toast, she asked if she could have a shower. It wasn't a problem as long as she didn't get hair wet, for the time being at least. The bandaging was there to prevent Rachel from touching her head wound. A small area around the stitching had been cut away. The same Eastern European auxiliary who seemed to be friendly with nurse Agata, found her a shower cap and added that she would have to be quick as they were moving her bed onto the ward shortly.

Rachel stood in front of the mirror to admire her hair and her naked toned body, turning one way then another, checking every angle, as if she were in the changing rooms. In spite of her hair needing a good wash – it was clapped to her head – she could see that it had had a decent cut and knowing Ruby, it wouldn't be cheap. Not too short and the dreary former salt and pepper look had been banished. Light and dark blond highlights added warmth to her face. She reckoned she had lost about three stone maybe more. It was actually four. She had never really lost her baby weight gain. In truth, she had never really tried or cared. What daft diet had Ruby used to transform all her flab and wobbly bits? Vegan probably. She knew Ruby was a vegan dabbler. She only dabbled as Ben liked his meat and Ruby couldn't resist his cooking.

She patted and smoothed the skin around her upper arms with the palm of her hands. She had muscles. The last time her arms were like that was when she was at Moray House teaching college – a long time ago now. She had helped out a male friend of hers who had a weekend job loading up vans with daily news-papers at Waverley Railway Station. It was back breaking work with a wearily early start, usually around 2.00am, but very well paid. Much more than she could make working in a bar or any of the shops on Princes Street or George Street. Her boyfriend at the time hated the idea that she had bigger biceps than him so she packed it in. Looking back, he was a lazy wee bastard. She considered that she had always been too eager to please the men in her life.

After a refreshing shower, Rachel's bed was wheeled through

to a ward holding three other beds. She trotted behind it as the nursing staff slotted it in and organised her lockers. A loud-mouthed patient in the bed opposite (there's always one) introduced everyone. Rachel wasn't really interested but she did note that motor mouth, in her big, furry pink housecoat, was called Evelyn and the poor wee soul in the corner bed was Alma. Alma was facing the window and had her back to the ward. She lay curled in the foetal position. Her body barely twitched as Evelyn called her name.

'New arrival, Alma! What did you say your name wis hen?'

'Rachel.'

'An what are ye in fir?

None of your bloody business. 'Em... concussion,' replied Rachel in a creaky bird-like warble.

With little concern for any of the other women and with no subtlety, a ruddy faced Evelyn reeled off their ailments starting with tiny Alma. *Benign tumour* she mouthed but it was still loud enough for Alma to have heard. She pointed to the side of her head and pulled a sorry long face then swiped her fingers across her throat as if to indicate there was little hope for poor Alma. *Jaw alignment* (who didn't look up from her magazine and ignored Evelyn as she sang it out) was singled out next and just as she was about to announce her own debility, one of the nurses interrupted her.

'The shower room is free, Evelyn.' And she rolled her eyes in mock indignation at Rachel.

A stocky built Evelyn struggled out of her chair and shuffled to the toilet. As one burly patient left, a burly doctor sauntered in. Doctor Harry Garland. Same navy chinos, different badly ironed cream shirt. Reminded Rachel of Princess Diana's wedding dress. Obviously doesn't live with his mother, she thought. Although, none of the youngsters seemed to bother with ironing these days. Ruby had the most luxurious bedding yet it was given a quick shake after it had been dried and roughly folded up ready for the next use. They weren't brought up like that.

'You look so much better today, Rachel. How are you feeling this morning?' Without waiting for a reply, his eyes tracked her chart. 'Hmmm. With some luck, it looks like you will be allowed home today.'

'I can't,' she protested, 'I don't know where I live. I'll have to wait on my young friend to tell me and she won't be back until this evening.'

Harry Garland stared at his patient. 'Ah, your memory problem. No better then?'

Rachel considered how she should play this. Deduction; remain calm.

'I'm truly sorry, doctor. I'm perfectly aware of who I am and my young visitor has filled me in with some of the details about my first admission and what happened afterwards but I have no recollection of the time from my first accident to this one. I wish I did but I don't. I've been told that my behaviour was bizarre. Frightening at times yet I can't remember anything. The last nine months are a blank.'

'Your notes from Professor Warnock make interesting reading. You must have friends in high places. Not many get the chance to work with him directly. I looked over his findings again last night. Fascinating. You could only remember fragments of your life after the last accident. Huge gaps were missing. Is that still the case?' he asked.

'Oddly enough, no. Now, I can remember everything about my life before Ruby and I were knocked down BUT from that moment until I regained consciousness yesterday, I have no memory of the past nine months.'

Dr Garland smiled. This juicy turn of events would be right up the Professor's street. There was so much about the brain and its reaction to and recovery from trauma that was impossible to diagnose or treat. A vast grey wilderness of supposition. He would write to him, of course, yet there was no medical reason as to why Rachel couldn't be discharged today. However, given the circumstances of her predicament and with his patient's permission, he instructed a nurse to contact Annabelle Jeffries to notify her of Ms Martin's imminent discharge. Hopefully, Miss Jeffries would organise transport for her friend.

There was little else that Rachel could do other than wait. The plastic wallet with the diary inside lay on her trolley. She unzipped it, carefully retrieved the navy book, and settled into the comfy hospital chair.

# TEN

## *Ruby's Journal*

**Friday 26th April. Annabelle's flat.**

Had to leave my diary at 'did I want to see me?' No, not really but I was supposed to be a grieving mother so what option did I have?

I'm trying hard not to arouse Colin's suspicions about me being friendly with Annabelle and I don't want him to find out where she lives so I get off the bus in Princes Street. I'm still not confident enough to take the car too far. Driving forward isn't a problem but twisting to reverse is awkward. Not just the ribs but I must have a trapped nerve in my neck. Plus, I think I've lost my confidence. Once I'm off the bus I cut through Markie's into Rose Street and down to York Place for the bus to Pitt Street. It's a big faff but I'm convinced he follows me when I leave the house. This way, I can lose him easily. I refuse to discuss where I'm going only that I need space to think and breathe.

Back to where I left off on Tuesday.

\*

**Saturday 30th March.**

So much happened after Rory went away that day. The police came to see me. I had to make a statement about the accident.

It didn't take long. The driver of the van admitted liability unequivocally. A young lad. Rhys Jones. Didn't know Edinburgh that well and was fiddling with his phone for the satnav. Took his eyes off the road for a second. One bloody second to wipe us out. Fuck! Fuck! Fuck! If it was any consolation, said the policeman, he was inconsolable. So he should have been. I hate him. Hate him.

Ben and Rory went to see where it all happened and managed to track down one of paramedics that brought us back. I died at the scene. Suspected broken neck. A freak accident. Shouldn't have happened as the twenty-year-old Rhys wasn't driving that fast. It seems that I rolled backwards off the bonnet and landed awkwardly on my head. Just my fucking luck!!!!

Someone, (who knows?) phoned the radio station and told them I had been screaming that I was too young to die. Total bollocks. The paramedic swore that that didn't happen. I was pronounced dead at the side of the road. Surreal, isn't it? Somebody wanted their two minutes of fame. Thank God Adrian boycotted that wee snippet of untruths but it did reach the Evening Gazette. I am NEVER buying that paper again.

GOT DISCHARGED!!! Out of hospital. Into the hands of eager beaver weasel. Hardly had time to prepare myself (mentally). Whisked 'home' to your wee semi in Carberry Crescent, in your wee Corsa, through all the wee back roads. Felt like someone who had just got out of prison.

A sense of foreboding engulfed me as I walked up your path. Nightmare. He just wouldn't listen. Colin that is. The doctors told him, Rory told him, Lisa told him and I made it perfectly clear that I WOULDN'T BE SHARING A ROOM WITH HIM (never mind a BED). He threw open your bedroom door and dropped his holdall on the carpet. Tah dah!! (Didn't actually sing that part but he might well as had). Furious was an understatement. For him and me. I thought his bulging eyes were going to pop onto his cheeks. As far as he was concerned, I was his wife and that was the end of it. If I explained once, I explained a hundred times that I hardly knew him. 'Why would I sleep with a stranger?' I kept shouting. Your small hallway only served to amplify our voices. We hurtled some nasty insults back and forth. Him to me – cold, frigid, uncaring, hopeless, weak etc. Me to him – controlling, uncaring, self-centred, something not quite right and of course toe curdling halitosis. He was truly convinced that I was putting it on. (Did notice that for the rest of the evening he kept breathing into his palms and having a good sniff. Serves him right.)

Then the caution hammer thumped its warning. I stopped. Started crying. Out of frustration. Plus, I was knackered. I asked him to call Rory to come and collect me. Not sure if that spooked him but he agreed to let me sleep in Jade's room for a few nights. Only to get a good night's sleep. So, the PINK girly room it was, in all its glorious shades, textures and soft toys. He chucked your nightwear from the hospital onto the floor and slammed the door. With my left hand, I teased your jumper over my head and shimmied your trousers and pants to my ankles. Tugging them off with my toes. Thank God I wasn't wearing a bra. (That was another mountain.)

Nola would love that room. You know Mum, my two have never had a sleepover in your home since you got married. You always chose to babysit at my house. Actually, the room made me smile and I hadn't done that since my awakening. I went out like a light and slept through from 8pm until 9am the following morning.

Then and now, the second I'm awake, the overwhelming

sense of loss engulfs me. It fills my lungs and feels like I'm drowning. I just want my babies.

Colin took to sneaking in and out but I kept my eyes firmly shut. My body was aching and the pain eventually forced me to roll out of bed in search of ibuprofen. We skirted around each other mumbling under our breaths, deliberately, just to antagonise each other. He did find ibuprofen and made me a cup of tea but demanded I take those tablets again. For your depression!! When I refused, he sulked for another half hour. Does he do it for attention? Or manipulation? Definitely both.

Showering was an effort and agony but there was no way I was not locking the bathroom door. He kept bleating that I would fall and he needed to check on me. I'm convinced he parked outside listening, ear to the door. I peed ever so slowly – teaspoon size dribbles so that he wouldn't hear me. Painful to do while still trying to breathe so I stuffed toilet roll down the loo to absorb the sound. When I unsnibbed the door he was nowhere to be seen. Then I heard the voices. Bellatrix and her sidekick. The glass living room doors give a clear view of the hallway so there was no way I could have sneaked across from the bathroom to Jade's pink den. To be fair, Jade ran out and greeted me like a long-lost friend. 'Gently...' I puffed. There was an odd smell about her.

Claire growled and reined her in. 'Morning... sorry who are you this morning?' she taunted, encouraging her audience, well Colin, to snigger with her. Not the slightest bit empathetic given that I must have looked like shit.

'Give it a rest,' I spat. Should've spat at her but was in no fit state to take her on. (Give me time!!) Plus, I felt vulnerable – bare feet, burgundy dressing gown, aching all over and wet trickles meandering down my back.

She jumped out the chair, ran into the hallway and bared her teeth millimetres from my face. 'You're an ungrateful bitch after everything my dad's done for you.'

Her nasty wheeze condensed on my face. I wrapped your housecoat (that's what you call it) tighter around me 'Remind me.' I could be just as sarcastic as her.

'He runs after you hand and foot. And he's put up with all your crap for years,' she screamed.

'What crap would that be, Claire?' I asked. I was ultra calm. You would've been proud of me.

'Your madness, you daft cow. What are you sniffing at?'

I had no idea I was. I'd poked my crinkled nose into her shoulder and sniffed. OOPS!! That smell again! Overbearing. Then it dawned on me. Sour clothing. Claire obviously didn't dry or air her wet washing properly. Ben used to stink like that when he shared a flat with Pascal. I forced them to buy a tumble dryer.

I excused myself most politely and fumbled my way back to my pink sanctuary. I would pick my battles later when I had more information about you and your situation and more strength to retaliate.

As I sat on the bed, I realised I would have to go into Colin's room for your clothes. Bless her, Jade knocked quietly on the door and asked if she could come in. I needed help to dry my hair and she was unexpectedly gentle. You have lovely soft bouncy hair. With each brush, Jade questioned what I could remember about her and would she still be your favourite grandchild. That did make me bristle. I'm pretty sure you would never have said that. She does seem to be very fond of you but I can't fully trust her even though she's only a child. I brushed your hair, oops my hair, back off my face and tucked it behind my ears. What a difference it made, if you forgot about the nasty abrasions and bruising on my face. I'd taken off the dressing. You always used to say to let the air into it. God Mum, am I never to hear those words of wisdom ever again? I suggested that Jade and I rummage through your wardrobe so I could choose something suitable to wear. Rory was picking me up at 11.30.

I don't think I have been in your bedroom since Colin moved in. Hadn't changed much. Same oak furniture that you had in the guest room in our family house. The pretty lemon curtains that you bought in Morningside not long after I had moved to the Grange. New grey carpet but it lacked something. It was very tidy, just like you, but all your little bits and pieces had gone. The lovely porcelain white figurine of two cuddling friends that Auntie Lisa gave you for your fortieth wasn't there. It was always on your bedside table. That's when I noticed there were no photographs of any of us yet there were of Claire and Jade. Claire and Jade on their own. Claire and Jade with Colin and one of the four of you but none of us. Not Alfie nor Nola or Rory's Jack. Why not?

It was hard to pick an outfit. You hadn't much to choose from that actually fitted you. All your lovely 'thin' stuff was hanging at the back of your wardrobe with old sheets draped over them, like you were hiding them. Colin had to put his tuppence worth in, shuffling in the doorway, complaining that it was only a mortuary visit and why couldn't I put on a pair of slacks (who calls them that?) and a jumper. Jade enquired what a mortuary was. It wasn't a fashion parade, he sneered, and Miss Fancy Pants (must have meant me) wouldn't know what you had on. What a bastard! A wee insignificant tactless gobshite.

I settled for your cream dress. The one you wore at Nola's naming day. Jade helped me with your bra. I had no other option.

I asked Colin for your cream ankle boots. At first, he pretended that he didn't know you had cream boots but Jade exclaimed they were in the bottom of the hall cupboard along with the pink trench coat. She ran to fetch the white bin bag. Colin looked like he could have gladly strangled her. Unfortunately, the trench had been ruined in the accident. The back seam had burst open and dirty grey streaks scratched the pink material. Sorry, Mum. I'll buy another one. I found the brown suede jacket that dad bought you years ago. It couldn't meet at the front but it was the only thing that complimented your dress. Colin said that I looked ridiculous and that everyone would be staring at me. Mutton dressed as lamb. Quite honestly, your face was such a mess, I doubted anyone would look beyond that. Fortunately, your big brown bag was ideal but that's when the fun started. There was only twelve pounds and a few coins in your purse. It looked like a purse that someone no longer wanted and would give a child to play with. It was empty. No cards. No receipts. I wiggled my fingers inside the tight side pockets. Nothing there to indicate it was yours. Yet it was. A gift last Christmas from Alfie and Nola. No phone either. When I asked Colin what had happened to your cards and phone, he mumbled and muttered something about you preferring to handle cash.

'Every adult has a bank card. At least two. A debit and a credit.'

'You don't. No for a long time,' he insisted.

'Why?' I demanded

That's when motor mouth jumped in. 'You can't be trusted. You squander your money. Waste it. Dad has to monitor what you spend.'

I could hear the incredulity in my laugh. 'On what?'

It certainly wasn't on your family. No harm, Mum. You

bought the kids and us well chosen gifts but the monetary value had decreased over the years. Not that we minded. We had no need for expensive presents and I wasn't aware that you lavished treats on anyone else, including yourself. I thought, well we thought, that with Colin having to retire because of his back problem that you were being more cautious with your spending.

Colin coughed and spluttered, 'You..ye were careless with the cards. Ye were constantly losing them.'

'That's not the same as squandering money. So, which is it? Losing or wasting?' It needed to be asked.

The doorbell rang and the unsaid words that we all had lined up to counter attack hung in the air. Stored away for later, for round two, three, four and countless more.

Rory strode in and said I looked lovely then suggested a little make-up would help. Claire and Colin exchange raised eyebrows. My skin was too sore to cover in make-up but I hadn't been able to find any anyway. As we were leaving, I eyeballed Colin and asked for my cards or if that wasn't possible could I have a hundred pounds to keep in my purse. I swear he was foaming at the mouth. Of course, with a flick of his wrist, Rory dismissed my request and assured Colin that I wouldn't need any money while I was with him. Then it was Rory's turn not to listen as we drove away. Every single time I presented something that didn't seem right, he had a plausible explanation to refute my claims. Honestly, I was shaking. What woman walks around with an empty purse, I argued? No bank cards, no loyalty cards, no bits and pieces. It's not natural. I begged him to discuss it with Alana and seek her opinion.

His grip tightened on the steering wheel, his eyes were steadfast on the road. 'Mum, you're reading into things for the sake of it.' He sighed. 'Colin is a decent, kind guy and has always spoken fondly of you – even when you made his life a misery. Please, give him a chance.' He gave me a quick glance; a mixture of disgust and pity then resumed his concentration. Matter closed.

Also, I needed your glasses. I kept rubbing my eyes as I thought they had misted over. I couldn't see a thing. Not at a distance.

The moment I was alone with Rory, I realised I missed the kids again. There was a tonne weight of emptiness teetering on my shoulders and it took every drop of willpower to stop me from caving in. I told him I needed to see them.

Rory seemed perplexed. 'I think you should see Ruby first.'

# ELEVEN

## *Ruby's Journal*

After my big moan about the purse and its significant lack of contents, we drove to the mortuary at the Royal Infirmary in silence. Both lost in our thoughts. The autopsy had been held back until Monday. Too busy, apparently. I was bricking it. What if when I walked in you wanted your soul back and I didn't want to give it? What would happen? An invisible fight? Could you imagine? Poor Rory would be wondering what the fuck!!!!! Then I felt terrible. Of course, I would exchange places. Instantly, the thought of not seeing Alfie and Nola overwhelmed me so I ran through the negotiations. Yes, I would change places but surely you would allow me to go and say goodbye to my kids. That was only fair. BUT what if I saw them and didn't want to swap? I could feel that fucker of a van all over again. WHAM!

We drove around for ages looking for a parking space. Rory didn't want to scratch the rented white BMW. Not cheap to park. Hospitals must make a fortune out of other folk's misery.

I was like a cartoon character getting out of the car. The bones supporting my legs had disappeared and they were literally wobbling like two shaky elastic bands. If it hadn't been for Rory wrapping his big strong reassuring arms around me, I would never have made it.

Rory looked lovely, Mum. He had chosen to wear a grey tweed jacket that you had given him several Christmases ago, with a white, brushed cotton shirt and black jeans (with a fine cord). He was so handsome and reminded me so much of dad. I was desperate to see dad but that was another game I would have to play with a great deal of fine-line walking.

The walk to the mortuary took an eternity on my jelly legs dragging lead boots. Every corridor took longer than the last one.

The young guy who looked after us was called Daniel (his last name ended in Insky so I'm assuming that his parents or grandparents were Polish but he was as broad as Gran and Grandad when he spoke). I think he introduced himself as an assistant to the pathologist but again not sure. Everything was a blur. I remember he was kind. We stopped at a huge black window and a light flicked on and there I was under a sheet.

Someone carefully rolled back the cloth. When my pale white face was finally revealed, I could feel Rory's bony arms digging into the flesh around my armpits, holding me up. My eyes were closed. I looked like an exhibit from Madam Tussauds; closely resembling the real person but something was missing. Life. My head seemed too big for my body like one of my old Barbie dolls. Maybe it was the way my hair was arranged. All plastic. I wanted to brush it.

There was no mad fanfare. Nothing was said between us (you and me). Only silence filled the void. I whispered to Rory to leave us for a minute. To give us a chance to communicate. Inwardly, I screamed that I was here and if you had something to say then now was your chance. I half expected Daniel to mouth something on your behalf. Obviously, nothing happened. It was horrible. Too final. Then I began to sob. I wanted to live. To hold the kids again. Have sex with Ben. And if that meant existing in your body, it was a price I was prepared to pay.

I vaguely remember shuffling out into the fresh air. We stood outside, just breathing. People filtered in and out of the main entrance of the building ignoring that we existed. All ages, all shapes, colours and sizes. Ignoring our plight and why not? They had their own problems to mull over and I couldn't have given a monkey's about any of them.

That's when the next drama unfolded.

'DAD!' yelled Rory then he was off. Darted over the pedestrian crossing and man-hugged dad.

Naturally, I followed and muscled in and blubbed into Dad's chest. I could feel him tense and wife number two did nothing to disguise her sharp intake of breath. Her eyes were like saucers and her eyeballs didn't know where to go. As far as I was concerned, I was cuddling my dad. I needed his protection. To make it all go away. You and dad hadn't embraced in years and probably only exchanged polite hellos at Nola's naming ceremony. Dad stood ram-rod still. That annoyed me. As the mother of his daughter, he should have hugged you properly. Rory felt the need to apologise for my behaviour. Dad grumbled that it wasn't important but he did eventually comfort me back, sort of. Once it twigged, I stepped back and mouthed sorry to Patricia then Dad. It took me a long time to be you or at least act like you. I'm still making mistakes especially when I bump into someone I haven't seen in months. Years even.

I kind of stood aside while Rory put Dad in the picture about the memory loss. It was so obvious that they were referring to me as both were trying to smile at me nonchalantly while engrossed in listening to or divulging the gory details. Dad cleared his throat.

'You've been through the mill, Rachel.' He was scrutinising my bruises. 'If there's anything we can do?'

'You could lend me your apartment in Spain for a while. That might help.' I was totally jesting. Actually, I knew I was being spiteful but couldn't help it.

Patricia's eyes began to expand again. 'Er, um, we would have to check the calendar,' she choked, searching Dad's face for back up.

'Not a problem,' I said sincerely. 'So, it's not a no then? Rob?' I looked directly at him.

'I'm sure we can sort something out. After the funeral.'

I shook Dad's hand firmly and smiled. 'Thank you.'

I kid you not, something changed. He patted my hand and returned my smile. It was warm and wholeheartedly meant. I couldn't resist a sly peek at Patricia. Wife number two was not amused. Brownie points to me.

Dad and Rory chatted for a few minutes. Patricia bounced on her red Jimmy Choo heels and smiled awkwardly. She dresses well but just can't carry it off. I honestly mean this, Mum. You are so much better looking than Pat (she doesn't like us calling her that). She was wearing a smart red and black dress yet it did nothing for her. She buys stuff a size smaller than she is. I'm convinced she's a fourteen. The black pony-tail doesn't work either. Too severe. Her head is too small for it. Ooooh it's good to bitch. Dad was same old, same old. Navy chinos and a pastel V-Neck and check shirt poking out the top. Older middle-aged men. Clones in cashmere. Kenneth Sutherland dresses in exactly the same way. Dad's greying a lot at the temples though. Can't be accused (falsely) of using Grecian anymore. He was never that vain.

They walked off and left Rory and me to watch them make their way into the hospital. Dad's shoulders sagged. He looked as if he had shrunk drastically in seconds. I wanted to rush up and tell my daddy that his wee princess was still here. Alive and well. But how could I?

My wee brother and I grabbed some lunch at the Polish Deli on Melville Terrace overlooking the Meadows. I could see our path (where we walked) and pictured you and me there a few days ago. I took the opportunity to prise Rory's phone from him and check out what was happening on my Facebook page. So much junk to wade through that needed deleted. I checked out the twitter accounts of my pals at Fourth Waves. JJ's following had almost doubled and everyone was discussing me. The Likes on my Instagram had quadrupled. If Rory was intrigued that you had suddenly acquired social media acumen, he didn't voice it.

I must have gasped really loudly. 'What's wrong?' he asked.

Amongst all the lovely comments there were two particularly nasty ones. One female offered to keep Ben cosy and busy in bed. He only had to ask!!!! The other one read,

'R.I.P. ... NOT!!! Welcome to the lives of the have nots bitch.'

'Ignore them, Mum. You'll always get negative comments. It's what Trolls do. They have nothing else interesting in their miserable lives so they target other folk. You can't court publicity like Ruby and Ben and not expect the nasty stuff as well.'

'That's not fair,' I screamed.

Rory agreed that it wasn't but it was the way things were. The chances of them being caught or confronted were slim and anonymity made them bolder.

I knew it was true. I also knew that I could receive hundreds of likes and positive feedback everyday yet I automatically homed in on the nasty ones. *What possessed you to wear that dress? Your hair was a mess. Should have gone to Specsavers.* I could reel them off.

However, I did persuade Rory to buy me a new phone. (Didn't happen straight away). I could tell that he was getting grumpy with me. Not that he said anything. The puffing and sighing were enough. It's what he didn't say when I asked, 'WHAT?' each time.

When he finally managed to wrestle his phone back, he texted Ben. I think I had been deliberately distracting myself.

Ben replied. Those two bleeps kicked me hard in the stomach. It was time to face Ben and see the kids at Deacon House.

\*

I'm going to have to go, Mum. I've been away from Alderburn for ages. Love you xxxxx

# TWELVE

*Rachel's Ward. 6th January 2020.*

Rachel pushed her food around her plate with her fork. She ate the peas and mixed the mashed potatoes in with what little insipid gravy was left. She finished the mash and decided to forgo the remainder of the unappetising pieces of chicken. The coconut sponge and custard reminded her of something that was served up in her old primary school in Alderburn although her school meals would have tasted so much better. Her granny was one of the dinner ladies.

Mouthy Evelyn had scoffed her lunch in record time. One of her pals, who was an auxiliary in another ward, had signalled to Evelyn that she was nipping outside for a quick puff. It never failed to amuse Rachel that seriously sick folk could still crave a cigarette and be willing to walk hundreds of yards through the hospital to get to the front door for 'fresh' air. She had never smoked. Never wanted to yet Lisa had smoked since she was thirteen. With three older sisters, all smokers, it was inevitable she would follow suit. All of Rachel's family would whinge when she had been at Lisa's – her clothes stank of smoke. If you walked into their tiny lobby blindfolded you would always be able to sniff out Rachel's coat. She must have absorbed it like a piece of lint. The funny thing was, they never complained about Lisa. She never seemed to smell of fag reek. Same applies today but the menthols probably help. And Rachel reckoned it helped Lisa stay slim. Gave her something to do with her hands.

Rachel missed Lisa and longed to talk to her again. Her practical, straight-talking friend, whom she had shut out this past year; actually, past year and nine months if you counted what she couldn't remember, would make sense of all of this. Not that Rachel had really wanted to lose the friendship. It just happened and it was her fault entirely. Yet Lisa had never stopped trying.

When Colin had first moved in, the honeymoon period, they were loved up – long walks, long lunches out and about, very cosy nights in, meeting up with friends (mostly hers, in fact only hers) and socialising with their families. After they got married, Colin changed. Black moods. He would pick fault with everything and anything. At first, Rachel presumed that it was his sore back wearing him down. He used to work as a fork lift driver at a food processing plant out near Broxburn in West Lothian but an injury had forced him to pack in his work before he moved in with Rachel. When she pressed him about compensation, he claimed that his colleagues had closed ranks and sided with the bosses. It was his word against several others.

He would moan that Rachel's friends and family would regard him as a leach; living off his wife. Rachel assured him that was not the case. She never discussed her financial affairs or his with anyone nor was it anybody else's business. Not wholly true as she used to disclose everything to Lisa and vice versa. They had no secrets until Lisa began to nitpick at things pertaining to Colin which Rachel found annoying. She was rarely derogatory about Lisa's Brian so what gave Lisa the right to challenge what Colin was doing or saying.

'Cos he's shifty and tells lies,' she would say. 'You have to have a good memory if you want to be a good liar, Rachel. That's what your mother always used to say. And just let's say that there are plenty of holes in Colin's stories.'

Rachel refused to listen. She made excuses for him. Supported his white lies and in time began to believe them as much as Colin did. She distanced herself from Lisa, from her family and even from the other teachers she worked with. The less they had to do with Colin, concluded Rachel, the more she could shield him from their scrutiny. Yet, for reasons unfathomable to her, that seemed to backfire. Suddenly, it was Colin who was protecting her from other folk's disparaging remarks. All Colin's insecurities had latched on to Rachel. She was now the anxious one, mistrusting others and herself. Reliant on Colin and benzodiazepines to keep her sane and normal. How had that happened?

Lisa had dared to challenge her. During that long drive down to Abbotsford in the Borders, Lisa kept banging on and on.

'You're as sane as I am, Rachel. It's that devious wee bastard. He's filled your head with all this nonsense and you fucking believe it.'

'NOT TRUE!'

'Look at you. You're a shadow of your former self. Where's my happy, gutsy wee pal gone? Where are all your nice clothes? And don't you dare make putting on weight the excuse. Doesn't stop you wearing nice things. Colin's no shy when it comes to the best walking gear. You never have any money. Where's your bank cards? And don't say you've lost them again. You never phone me or answer your house phone. It's always Colin who speaks to me. If it wasn't for Rory, you would be in a fucking nut joint. Wake up and smell the coffee, honey. He wants your money and if he gets his way, he will have your house too while you are rocking merrily in a bloody straight jacket far, far away. Why can't you see it?' she ranted. Ranted and ranted.

It was okay for Lisa, grumbled Rachel, with her big fancy car and big fancy house and important fancy well paid job. She had zero understanding of the money struggles of ordinary folk. At that insult, Lisa had to pull over and have a ciggie to calm down. In fact, she had two. One after the other. Rachel could see her friend was crying yet she stayed in the car. Devoid of sympathy. Colin was her rock and there was no way she would agree with her friend's perceptions. Lisa prowled back and forth like a trapped wild animal but all Rachel could think about was her washing. It was a beautiful summer's day. Not a cloud in the sky and there was a slight breeze. A perfect drying day. Her washing was still in the machine when it should have been out on the rope.

Rachel shuddered. What gave her the right to have demeaned her loyal pal like that? At the first opportunity, she would apologise to Lisa for her flippancy. She hadn't seen Colin in ages and there was something reassuring in knowing that she wouldn't have to, just yet. Plus, she was less nervy, les jittery. Sure, she was anxious about what was going to happen once Annabelle came for her but she was more fixated on Ruby's problems and how she was going to solve them.

Rachel couldn't be certain but perhaps she no longer took pills to manage her anxiety.

# THIRTEEN

*Ruby's Journal*

**Sunday 31st March cont'd.**

'Where are you going?' Rory questioned why I was heading round the side of the house.

I always go round the back in daylight. Habit, I suppose.

'We should knock at the door.' It was a polite, if terse, reprimand.

'It's my bloody house!' I wanted to shout but I complied instead.

Kenneth answered the door. 'Rachel pet, don't you look a sight. C'mere.' And Ben's daddy suffocated me in his embrace. He's always been like that. Another round of sobbing entailed.

Then I felt the tug; from my jacket to my heart. I guessed it would be Nola.

'Don't cry, granny. I'm here.'

Oh, my days. I was beyond consoling. I breathed her in. Devouring every morsel that I could smell and taste. Her hair. Her skin, Her clothes. It was as if God had gifted me Heaven. I had no idea I had fallen to my knees until Rory hoisted me to my feet. Nola's little confused face stared into mine. She squeezed my hand and the little 'Elsa' – she was wearing the blue outfit from 'Frozen' (hair in a side ponytail, daddy useless at plaits) led me through the family room and into the kitchen.

I half expected to see Ben sweating over the Aga but he was

bent over our large coffee table in the conservatory which was sprawled with letters and papers, as was the floor. The big grey briefcase that held all our birth certificates and other personal information lay empty on its side. He had emptied the whole lot out and messed up my filing system. I stomped through the dining area and stopped at the French doors, hands on hips.

'What the fuck, Ben? That took me ages to organise. Look at the labels on the folders.' I screamed at the top of my voice.

As soon as I had shot my mouth off, I felt gruff hands on my shoulders and I was pushed out into the kitchen and steered back to the family lounge. Rory had that nasty squinty face again.

'MUM! What's got into you? How dare you upset Ben. Get back in there and apologise. No. Forget it. Stay here instead and don't come through until I send for you.' Then he disappeared.

I was mortified. I kept forgetting that I wasn't me and worst of all I kept forgetting that I'm supposed to be dead (still do) and that people are grieving for me. I could hear Rory. Tones of remorsefulness. (I had perfected that same tone over the following weeks.) Not so my not so understanding husband. He was raging. Couldn't quite make out everything but heard enough. He was demanding that I should leave. That it wasn't fair on the kids. I was a nut job. Etcetera, etcetera. Rory trying to placate him.

The door squeaked open. Slowly. A tussled blond head peeked round. Alfie grinned.

'You're in trouble, granny.'

'What's new?' I half smiled.

He edged in and sat next to me. 'Did that happen in the crash?' His tender finger traced a circle around the scabbing near my right eye and whole cheek.

'It did wee mannie,' I uttered feebly.

'Mummy calls me wee mannie.'

'Is it okay if I do too?'

Yeh, he said and crawled onto my knee in his camouflage joggers and top. We snuggled in and sat like that for a long time. No need for words just cuddles. I played with his hair as I always did. Rubbing it gently between my thumb and middle finger. It puts him into a wee trance-like state. The mantelpiece was covered in sympathy cards. Two handmade Mother Day cards, dripping in glue and glitter were propped against the coal scuttle in the hearth. Beautiful. My heart sank to my ankles. Heartbreaking. I desperately wanted to read them but Alfie was so settled.

When Ben burst through the door, he was ready for an argument but seeing us together must have thrown him.

'He hasn't hugged anyone since... the accident.'

I gazed into my husband's eyes. Alfie buried his face deeper into me. 'Can we stay here a little longer, please?' he pleaded looking up at me. I wasn't hopeful.

Ben nodded and left. Kenneth brought me a cup of tea. I would have preferred a coffee but graciously accepted it. He's cooling down, he mouthed quietly, hoping that Alfie wouldn't hear. Alfie smiled. He had heard. Grandpa went to fetch Alfie some apple juice. Rory slithered back in.

'Sorry, mum. I was a bit...'

'Rough?' I interjected. Well, it served him right. Manhandling me as if he was a bouncer and I was some obnoxious drunk at a nightclub door.

I was instructed to go through to the conservatory. Ben apologised for losing it and accepted that he should be more tolerant of my "condition". He was about to do that air quotes thing with his fingers and stopped. I hate that. Jemma Courtney on the station does it all the time. I've actually thought about how I could break her fingers and make it look like an accident. Seems pretty pathetic now. Rory coughed and agreed that he would try harder too. Hmmmm. I didn't know whether to laugh or cry. They pair of them were so contrite.

I was ushered to the big comfy recliner. Ben stood beside me in his bare feet, jeans and white tee-shirt and demonstrated how the controls worked. I had to bite my tongue. It was odd being so close to my husband and him not sensing it was me. I tried hard not to stare. It was disconcerting to be sitting in my house, in my conservatory, on my favourite chair but as a stranger. I looked out on to my huge sheltered garden with fresh eyes. The summer house was too close to the patio and should have been erected further back, away from the barbecue area. Our big paving stones were covered in algae from last winter never mind this one. We're always too busy. I don't know why Ben convinced me to have the clothes poles removed. The whirly gig was ugly by comparison.

Ben went over the funeral arrangements. Rory was level headed as always and pointed out that everything might need to be put on hold until the coroner's report was complete. We should be prepared for a delay. I pointed out that we have procurators fiscal in Scotland. Coroners are for the rest of the U.K. (I had Grant Hamilton on breakfast time after I heard him at a Burns Supper. He's hilarious. A retired P.F. Learned a lot.) Dirty look from Rory. Men don't like it when their little errors are highlighted. Frightened to open my mouth again.

Alfie and Nola were in the playroom – in my direct line of vision. Nola was bathing her dolls. Alfie had lined up all his dinosaurs for a showdown. I couldn't concentrate on anything but them. My wee Irish twins like me and Rory. (Not technically as they are 16 months apart but close enough). Every so often, Alfie would look up and smile. I'm sure he knew.

Although Ben is half-heartedly religious and his family are church goers he confirmed that I (Ruby) had always spoken about preferring a humanist service should the need arise. I (as you) agreed and nodded approvingly. So, it would be in a church but Olive Watson who was another regular on my show would give the eulogy. Agreed again. Ben read aloud what he had written about my childhood and teenage years. I had to correct him on a few things but backed off when some things were too trivial for rectification. I went to both Brownies and Guides not just the Guides. And I learned to swim under water before I could swim on the top. Annabelle and I met at playgroup not in Primary one. I never wanted to be a teacher like you but had contemplated drama for a while. Once we got to the part where Annabelle introduced us, he was fairly accurate from there and that's when my input was no longer required as he would consult my friends and work colleges for their happy memories. God, what would some of them have to say? That I was a cow? Hope not. Not blowing my own trumpet but I think I was fairly popular at the station.

Ben dithered about 'Songbird'. If it had to be played it would be the Fleetwood Mac version. The jury was still out on that one when we left.

My hubby insisted my karaoke song be inserted somewhere in the service. 'My Life would Suck Without You' by Kelly Clarkson. I suggested it might be a bit loud so perhaps best left until the end. Alfie and Nola wanted 'Let it Go' from Frozen. I glimpsed Nola in her dressing up frock and could have crumpled. Not for the first time. Or last. Thank goodness for

Kenneth. As Ben's song choices became increasingly off radar, it was Kenneth who reeled him in, reminding him that funerals, for some, were a solemn occasion and perhaps the music should reflect that too.

'It should also be a celebration of Ruby's life,' he groaned. 'She was vibrant and feisty. I want her personality to shine through.' He decided he would seek advice from JJ. That's why I love my Ben. He so gets me.

Rubiez would host the funeral tea. It was usually closed on a Tuesday so would be the ideal venue. Rubiez for Ruby. I was touched. As a mark of respect, Ben wanted to close Suthiez that day too to allow the staff to attend. I was glad about that. I had done maître d' in both restaurants and knew all the staff. Ben's school pals had called him Suthie since first year, hence the name Suthies for his first solo venture. The Z was added for a wee bit razzmatazz. Naturally (to him), his second venue was named after me. Remember we laughed when Alfie asked if the third one would be Rachiez? You insisted it would be Alfiez. He was so chuffed at that.

The events side of me was itching to jump in with ideas. Only I couldn't, YET. Ben wanted to liaise with Karl (Rubiez head chef) about the nibbles. It would be a gourmet feast. I did pop in the following Thursday after the lunchtime shift (I knew Ben wouldn't be there) and cornered Karl and Louisa. I casually dropped in some ideas. Louisa snapped them up. Being you had its advantages. You were beneath suspicion.

After forty-five minutes of funeral chat, I felt as if I was disappearing into the recliner. I must have looked as bad as I felt because Rory asked if I wanted to go home. Too late. I had vomited all over our cream tiles and started to shake. Quite violently. My first thought was that I was going to die again and you would reclaim me. That was part of my negotiation strategy in the mortuary. Let me see the kids and then we could swap. FUCK!!! I passed out. Only for a few seconds. Rory grappled with my upper body and Ben struggled with my legs. They carried me up the stairs like a sack of potatoes – a very big sack – I thought my ribs were bound to crack further. I was unceremoniously tossed (felt like a toss) on to Alfie's bed. That's when I had my Dorothy Gale moment. Well, the bed did – birling around in the eye of the twister. Rory had had the sense to bring a basin. More spewing!!!!

Kenneth claimed that I had overdone things and wasn't surprised. I hadn't the energy to argue and let sleep take me.

Dung breath assaulted my senses like smelling salts. Colin hovered like a vulture. Rory had phoned Colin to explain what had happened and he had driven through to Edinburgh in record time. He was insisting that he would take me home but Rory was having none of it.

'Let her rest. She's in no fit state to be moved.' (Very true. I had to keep swallowing my puke. Aggghhh!!!) 'I'll stay with her and if she feels well enough later, I'll bring her home. If not, then first thing tomorrow morning.'

'It's what happens in a crisis,' he was yelling. 'She can't cope. She needs her medication. Refused to take it this morning. I'm the only one who can handle her.'

Rory assured him that if I became problematic, he would send for him but as I seemed calm enough for the moment it would be better to let me sleep. No point in him losing another night as well. Honestly? I couldn't have cared less. I was away with the fairies. I thought they had all gone as I heard the door close behind them but that's when I felt it. Warm nasty breath spitting on my face.

'You think you've pulled a fast one? NOT ON ME! This will be sorted when you get home.'

The bedroom door opened again. Not sure who it was but I was so grateful.

'Just giving my darling a kiss,' he said.

He pressed his clenched teeth into my cheek. I could feel the outline of each rectangle digging in.

*

I'm going to leave it there as I promised Annabelle I would clean her place. It's the least I can do. Did I say already she has given me a key? I can come and go as I please. She has no man on the horizon so she doesn't mind. A quick breath of fresh air, a coffee and cake (carry out) from the wee cafe on Ferry Road then I'll bash on in here.

# FOURTEEN

## *Ruby's Journal*

I'm back. God, how Annabelle lives in all this clutter? It would do my head in. I'm itching to totally sort it all out for her. Too soon me thinks. It's a hell of a lot tidier (and cleaner) than it was. The table is set. Candles are in place. All ready for her returning home from work. I'll write for another hour max.

*

**Monday morning 1st April.**

Colin opened the front door when Rory's car pulled up outside your house. He waved to us and had a welcoming smile on his face (APRIL FOOL!). His eyes connected with mine. They were menacing. God Mum, were you terrified of him cos a huge part of me definitely was?

Colin rushed up the path. He had a thick, ribbed knitted grey cardigan on, zipped up to the neck. Conclusion – a bit heavy for a warm spring morning but he'd only just finished a five mile hike up and around Traprain Law. Pity one of the wild ponies hadn't kicked him in the goolies. He wrapped his arm around my waist and made a big show of supporting my limp body.

A car tooted. Saved by the horn. Doctor Eleanor Riddle, your new GP, followed us up the path and into the house. I counted the paving slabs. Fourteen. Why? Unless it reminded me of our old path in Haddington. I used to do that then.

'Good morning, Mr Gordon and you must be Rachel?' she sang. There was something about her that I instinctively liked.

Colin was obviously not expecting her so soon. Nor was she the doctor he had requested for an urgent home visit.

A. She was female.

B. She was youngish and

C. Trendy for a GP. Her hair was blood red (short, pixie crop) and her lipstick was competing to outdo her hair. Everything else, contrasting black. Black polo neck, black trousers, her black medical bag and backpack. And black trainers. Birkenstock. Not cheap.

He was all flustered and couldn't get his words out properly. He said to Rory that he would 'take things from here' and was not happy when I urged Rory to stay and explain my memory loss to the doctor.

'I'm Eleanor Riddle. New to the practice and so pleased to be able to assess you at home, Rachel. You've had a rough time.'

She followed me through to Jade's room. I was still experiencing dizziness and nausea. Colin squeezed in behind us and sat on the wicker chair as I collapsed onto the bed, apologising for my lack of energy. She allowed Colin and Rory to stay to confirm some things about you. Colin was keen to share how difficult life had been with you for the past two years and that you often refused to take your prescription which led to extreme violent behaviour from you. Really?

But somehow, she had the measure of him.

'You've been married for two years, Rachel, according to your notes and I'm not aware of previous episodes of anxiety or depression.' She looked directly at Colin. 'And would you say that Rachel displayed any insecurities before you were married, Mr Gordon?'

Colin didn't get a chance to answer because Rory spouted that you had coped extraordinary well after Dad left you and that when you and Colin started dating, you were positively glowing with health and happiness. However, he did reiterate what a stalwart Colin had been since your diagnosis and that the family were indebted to his dedication to you.

Doctor Riddle ushered both of them out of the room as she wished to examine me and question me in private. Again, Colin was not for leaving but Eleanor was not for budging. She spoke quietly, almost in a whisper. We both knew he would be straining to listen in from behind the door. There was substantial bruising to your body. It was all coming out now. I winced several times as she tapped her fingers over me. She had a good look inside the mouth and was surprised that your teeth were intact. Strong teeth and gums, Mum. She urged me to keep an eye on the abrasions on your face as it looked inflamed. Once the physical examination was over, we talked about the memory loss. She was as fascinated as she was sympathetic.

'Nothing? Nothing at all?' she kept asking.

She explained that I could be referred to a neurologist if there were no signs of improvement but she doubted it would come to that. These things usually sort themselves out after a few days. She did say that her godfather was a consultant neurologist at the Inglis Trust, Kelvingrove in Glasgow. (Meant nothing to me at that point but did later after I googled it.) Then asked if I had any questions. I did. Lots.

Was I (you) in good general health apart from the anxiety problems? You were. But overweight – not obese (think you were) but too heavy for your age. Postmenopausal (no periods. Weird. Bonus for me).

HRT? No but you did get sterilised when you were forty. (Thought that was a bit young? Your choice. Your body.)

Heart problems? None. But keeping an eye on your cholesterol. Over five but below six. Serious diet plans put into action.

High blood pressure? No. (Surprising given that you live with the weasel.)

Varicose veins/haemorrhoids? (Happens with old folk) but no. (I'm sure you had piles after Rory – big boy. Big bloody head. Same as Alfie. Ouch! Even now as I think about it.)

Broken bones/ unexplained injuries? None. Relieved.

That question intrigued her.

I emphasised that under the circumstances, Colin was a stranger to me. He appeared hostile most of the time but conceded that it could be frustration with my memory loss. I was being gracious as I was fully aware that in spite of her warm personality, I was being assessed. Had to guard what I said about Colin but I needed to be sure that I wasn't in a physically abusive relationship. She drew back her head as if to take me in but agreed that if she had to suddenly share a house with a partner she barely knew, she would be more than anxious. It was the way she said partner. The intonation. Don't think she is into men.

Did I have anywhere else to go, she asked? That was the problem. How the hell would I know? And let's face it, who would want me? I don't mean the normal you but the unhinged me in my mother's body. I pleaded with her to talk to Colin on my behalf and intimated that I would be extremely grateful if she would make another appointment for me soon, as I was sure to have more questions once I had had a chance to consider them properly.

Anxiety and Depression? On that note, I tucked my paranoia way below my gut instinct, for the time being. You had been taking medication on and off for two years. Gradually increasing the strength e.g. sertraline, duloxetine then diazepam (got her to scribble them down and just found the piece of paper in my file today hence the reason I could spell the bloody stuff). Yes, I have a file on you. And on my memory stick. A must. To keep abreast of everything that was new to me. It has been a bombardment of information on a daily/hourly basis.

Dr Riddle hazarded a guess but my symptoms indicated sudden withdrawal from the antidepressants and given that Colin had already dobbed on me, it was probably the case. It could have been at least a week since you had last swallowed them. I asked if there was any chance that I could be weaned off them as I had felt okay since the accident. She looked at me and a huge mocking smile lit up her face. (She was really quite pretty.)

'I have to assume that your memory loss has actually increased your anxiety levels. Perhaps now is not the time for drastic action. Let's review your prescription at a later date. Make an appointment to see me in a week's time.'

I had no idea where the surgery was or the telephone number. I agreed to continue with the meds but had every intention of cutting back with or without her knowledge. BLESS HER, she left Colin in no doubt that until my memory returned or that I felt comfortable in sharing my personal space with him that he would have to be inordinately patient with me. Then there was the little beacon of light or was it a warning?

'I'll try to pop in the next time I'm passing your way to ensure that both you and Rachel are coping.'

She didn't but the cautionary smirk indicated that she might.

Before Rory left, he reluctantly promised to give Auntie Lisa £500 for me. He wasn't happy doing business behind Colin's back. Doing business? I only wanted to buy a phone (albeit a cheap one) and survive. However, he did and I can't tell you how much of a life saver it was. Your bestest buddy slipped in another £150. Woo hoo!!

Couldn't believe that Ruby Martin had been reduced to begging from family and friends.

# FIFTEEN

*Ruby's Journal*

It took me until the Thursday (4th April) before I felt strong enough to leave the house. The sympathy cards were comforting: the words, not the depressing designs. Samey greys, creams and silvers. Dozens of them. Thank God for Ros's bee and a poppy. The only splash of colour on your sideboard. The first card I opened was from Auntie Vera. She remembered the beautiful, happy girl who would sit and draw for ages. Aww!! Nearly all your neighbours had handed one in and all my pals had sent one too. Tanya next door had written something in Estonian. Sean translated it. You must have been very kind to them, Mum. Made me cry. What's new? Uncle Iain said that Auntie Lillian wouldn't be able to fly from Canada for the funeral (not enough money) but if you fancied a holiday in Toronto then you were to jump on the first available plane to join your sister. He and Auntie Bertha would drive down from Fraserburgh but not stay the night. Gran and Grandad sent one. Gran's wee shaky handwriting – so cute. They couldn't face the funeral but were comforted that dad would be representing them.

Colin was keen to engage with Rhys Jones's insurance company. Turns out he has something to do with a university near Aberystwyth, Wales. Colin spent the whole day Tuesday chasing up anybody and everybody. He could smell the compensation. Salivating on the phone to them. I hadn't the energy to contribute properly. (I did later).

The antidepressants appeared to have been working. I was much calmer but still determined to cut back when I had more control. Felt I needed my wits about me to manage Colin and Claire. Doctor Riddle called in on the Wednesday night with a course of antibiotics. The big scab under my eye fell off in the shower. It was oozing with puss. Yuck!!

Everything Colin did for me was begrudged. He kept moaning that we were running out of homemade meals (previously frozen) and he was NOT prepared to eat the crap that was poured into supermarket ready meals. As the wife of a Michelin star chef, I couldn't agree more but I had been in no fit state to chop anything (even whilst sitting – I tried and failed miserably) never mind stand at a hot cooker. Thank you, Mum, for all the carefully labelled Tupperware in the freezer. A God send!! You'd have thought that he could have prepared something or coaxed his thick wit of a daughter to help out but no. You must have done everything for him and her.

And my biggest sin to date? I forgot his bloody birthday. 1st April. How would I have known? And after everything that had happened, was it really that important? A very apt day for such a twisted git. I missed the birthday celebrations. (Gutted-not!). He was glad I was in bed, out of the way, as I would have stolen the limelight. If it hadn't been for the Bellatrixes, his special day would have been ruined. They made a point of balling out 'Happy Birthday'. Tuneless.

Auntie Lisa remembered. Brought him a beautiful home-made cheesecake on the Wednesday and a box of real ales. I didn't get the opportunity to taste it as Claire had it on the backseat of the car before Lisa had driven out of Alderburn. I wasn't bothered as I was £650 better off. Huge thanks to Lisa. Half of it was stuffed into one of the cream boots and the rest under the mattress. Not much imagination but I couldn't think of anywhere else to hide it. There was no way that Colin would have changed my bedding so it was as safe there as anywhere.

I found a pair of black trousers to wear and an emerald green blouse. Not exactly modern but not unstylish either. Had to use a wooden spoon to help me ease up my knickers and trousers. No bra – too complicated. Plumped for Sellotape to bind the front of your boobs and a vest top lurking at the back of your sock drawer. Decided to leave the cream boots (minus the dosh as it was now in my pocket) and settled for your black loafers. The brown jacket had its second airing. Demanding your bank card was futile, as the worm was not for turning on that one, so I headed out with what he assumed was twelve pounds in my purse. Face tripping him when I insisted I was happy to be on my own.

'Where the hell are ye going?' I could see his tonsils vibrate. He was that close.

In fact, he was always close. A real space invader. I could barely turn around but he was there. Leaning in. Backing me into a corner or forcing me to squeeze past him when I went through a doorway. Or as he walked behind me, he would push me with his body to intimate that I was too slow. Holding him up.

'Just out. Some fresh air. Won't be long.' I tried to sound nonchalant but the earlier encounter had frightened me.

Let me explain.

I had so missed my phone and my laptop and tablet. Colin had refused me access to your one. Why? Because I wasn't well enough yet. I was too exasperated to argue. Plus, your passwords were unknown to me. However, two days after I got out of hospital, I actually found him thumbing through your mobile. He denied it, of course. Accused me of being paranoid. All along he had been pretending that he had no knowledge of your pass code when he obviously did. What a knob! Your school I.D was in your school bag along with your planning folder. There were some passwords written at the back of your folder so I was hoping that they would unlock something once I got my hands on a computer. (He also claimed your computer was being repaired. Another question mark.) BUT I needed paper documents that had your name and address on them in order to purchase a decent phone. Your school pass didn't hack it. Where the hell did you keep personal stuff? I never found them in the house until much later.

That same morning, when he'd gone out for his walk, I hunted for them. I found three grey filing boxes in your big dresser next to your dining table. Everything inside, bills and receipts, all neat and tidy, had Colin's name on them or both your names. Not one thing addressed only to you. When I challenged him, he claimed that he dealt with everything because you were no longer capable. Then I asked, 'how the hell were you able to hold down a teaching position? A job that requires you to have your wits about you.' God! He went off on one. Mum, I was petrified.

He emptied out everything that was in one of the boxes. It was like a ticker tape parade. Bits of paper fluttering and covering the carpet.

I screamed, 'No! don't!' when he lifted another box high into the air.

He dropped to his knees, picked up handfuls and started throwing individual letters at me.

'Look. Nothin in your name cos I have tae do it all. YOU

ARE BLOODY USELESS!' With one big sweep of his arm, he knocked all my sympathy cards on to the floor as well.

I had been sitting on the armchair but when I got up, he grabbed my wrist. It shot out like a frog's tongue catching a fly.

'D'ye think I'm picking this up all by mysel?'

He held on tight and forced me into a kneeling position in front of him. Your housecoat opened revealing my naked body. Hadn't dressed after my shower. I felt so exposed.

I considered my options. I wasn't physically strong enough to defend myself if things escalated so I appeased him and began gathering up the paper work. The sheets were shaking in my hands. Tear drops were spattering the letters as I slipped them in one behind the other.

'Hey,' he said, 'What's all this?' And ever so calmly he swiped his thumb over my wet cheek but with just enough pressure to ensure that I felt it.

Together and in silence, we placed all the accounts into the box.

'I'm not expecting you to file them properly today. I'm not that unreasonable. So how about a nice cup of tea?'

I made it but I didn't have one. That's when I got dressed and left.

I hadn't a clue where I was going only that I had to get away. I deliberately avoided walking through the village. I took the short cut through Grey's farm, out onto the main road and walked (I would have run if I'd had the energy) about quarter of a mile outside Alderburn to the next bus stop. I kept looking round – half expecting Colin to be stalking me. Fortunately, there was no one else at the bus shelter. I leant my forehead against the cold glass to ease my breathing. A white cloud formed on the pane. With my finger, I drew a circle and a squeaky, sad mouth.

Up until then, I felt that I had been a match for Colin. An equal adversary. But his behaviour with the filing case spooked me big time.

The number 113 pulled up. A single decker. I sat right at the back. Craned my neck to check for his car. The bus ride gave me time to calm down and most of all to think. For the time being, I would have to let Colin believe that I was toeing the line for some things. I would never give in to sharing his bed. NEVER. But there were other things like cooking, cleaning, being more welcoming to Claire and Jade. Engaging in polite conversation. Reining in the sarcasm. I was fully aware of the necessity to be on guard. I didn't want to find myself being sucked in by Colin. Relying on him. When the funeral was over, I would plan my escape.

I needed money. Couldn't expect Rory or Lisa to bail me out indefinitely. If I had a computer, I could access my own bank accounts but how could that be explained away other than putting Ben at risk of fraudulent activity? I had to fathom out how to get my hands on your salary. A visit to your school was inevitable.

I got off in Princes Street and flagged down a taxi for Bruntsfield. Rubiez was still open. Didn't know where else to go. That's when I cornered Louisa and made my suggestions for the funeral. Looking around, I concluded quickly that Rubiez wouldn't be large enough to hold everyone. Not that I was being all luvvie or anything but I was pretty sure there would be a big turnout. Perhaps she and Karl could suggest an alternative venue to Ben. Tread carefully!

I could see Karl surveying the tables that were still occupied from the serving/preparation area at the back of the restaurant. Diners can view the cooking area from most of the tables.

Rubiez is so different from Suthiez. Different dining scene and experience. Posher probably. The interior and furnishings are more formal. Dark wood and parquet flooring. Don't think you've eaten in Rubiez. Food is equally as good. That's what we wanted. You would have enjoyed it. Karl summoned Louisa over and she told him who I was. Big cuddles ensued and did I want something to eat? Guess what? He rustled up a beef stir fry for me to take home before dropping me off in Princes Street. Typical Karl. Lunches had finished – at least for him.

We even did a wee detour to the house. Only a minute or two. Enough to cuddle the kids. Kenneth was in. No Ben. I made out I had popped in to apologise for Sunday. Asked Kenneth when would be the best time to phone the kids, if possible. He knew what I meant. Saturday morning, any time after 8.00 am. Ben was jogging with one of his running buddies to Arthur's Seat and back. I phoned at nine then liaised with Kenneth for future calls.

Stir fry big hit with Colin. Passed it off as my own. Pity he hadn't choked on it. Not sure he believed I had gone back to the Meadows to reflect on that day. It was the first thing I blurted when he had asked where I had been and it was plausible. He did show a smidgen of sympathy. If he'd known how desperate I was to go there then he would have driven me. Maybe not genuine but then neither was I.

*

That's Annabelle home. On that note. I'm logging off. Well closing the page! Ha ha.

Our first girly meal. So excited. I've prepared her favourite dish (if I'm cooking that is) chicken and asparagus risotto.

Easy peasy. I have a big day tomorrow so I hope I don't over indulge. Did I just say that? Of course, we shall have too much wine. We always do BUT I do need a clear head for tomorrow. SHOWDOWN!!!!!!!!

# SIXTEEN

*Rachel's Ward. Monday 6th January 2020*

Rachel felt extremely conspicuous sitting in clothes she hadn't chosen nor would she have, given her prior body shape. The velvet leggings and soft white polo neck were surprisingly comfortable. Even the trainers; like feathers cushioning her feet.

She had emptied the lockers earlier and placed everything carefully into Ruby's Armani holdall – particularly the diary. She mustn't lose that. Not now.

Annabelle breezed through the door. Dressed almost identically as she had the night before. Big puffy red jacket, big hair and big black glasses.

'Ready?' Her sunny face asked.

Rachel was not ready. She dreaded having to leave the security of the hospital and yet she felt remorseful. The uncertainty of what lay ahead unnerved her, at least she was in her own body, but for Ruby it must have been utterly terrifying.

The cold winter air nipped the back of her throat. She pulled the zip of her leather coat up to the bottom of her chin and tightened the thick black scarf wrapped around her neck and ears.

'Not far to the car and your flat should be nice and cosy. I left the heating on at low for you,' said Annabelle.

It didn't take long to drive from Little France to Portobello.

About fifteen minutes. Annabelle parked her blue Micra behind a block of new flats right on the promenade.

'I'll come in to make sure you are settled. There's plenty in the fridge. Ruby's always ultra organised.'

There was a sudden chill in the car despite the heat that was blasting out. Annabelle switched off the engine and didn't say anything else. Rachel could sense that her young driver was struggling to hold it together.

'By the way, the mini next to mine is yours,' she mumbled. Tears not far away. 'You bought it not long after you left Colin.' A cream, 5-door hatchback.

They could hear the waves breaking quietly as they turned the corner: their white tips, just visible, lolloped on to the sand in the darkness. Annabelle retrieved a set of keys from Rachel's bag and opened the glass door to the wide and bright entrance. Rachel's flat was on the first floor, second left.

Annabelle flicked on the light. The large square hallway was modern and fresh. The delicate light display above her head looked like the heads of dandelions that had turned wispy white. Rachel was sure if she blew hard enough, they would disperse and float to the ground. A grey and black rug sat in the middle of the floor surrounded by white ceramic tiles. Annabelle pointed out all the doors starting at her right, anticlockwise.

'Lounge, airing cupboard, second bedroom, bathroom'.

'Where's the first bedroom?'

Annabelle grinned and held the lounge door open for her friend. A glass dining table faced Rachel as she entered the room. Rachel felt as though she had stepped into a glossy magazine.

To her right, a slim, dark grey sideboard nestled against the white wall. Two white leather sofas, with chrome legs, formed an L shape in front of a large patio window and separated the open-plan, slate grey kitchen from the rest of the surprisingly spacious area. A shaggy rug, similar to the one in the hall (but black and white), supported a low glass coffee table. Rich, dark wooden flooring finished the look.

'Through here.' Annabelle ushered her through the door adjacent to the patio window.

She dropped Rachel's bag beside the king size bed bedecked in luxurious, white Egyptian cotton and festooned with an array of opulent, silver cushions. Typical Rubyesque styling. The room was a mirror image of Ruby and Ben's bedroom at the Grange, right down to the white leather headboard dominating the wall – only their room was much, much larger and instead of mirrored floor to ceiling wardrobes, they had a roll top bath in the bedroom, a huge ensuite and two walk-in dressing rooms. Rachel's ensuite was behind the wall with the headboard on it.

Another patio window. The white, vertical blinds had yet to be closed. Rachel saw the twinkling lights of Fife on the opposite side of the black stretch of water (the Firth of Forth) that separates the coastlines of Fife and East Lothian.

'You should see it in daylight,' said Annabelle referring to the view. 'Stunning.'

'Is that a balcony out there?'

'It's the same private balcony all the way along,' explained Annabelle.

Rachel wandered back into the lounge and asked if there were any slippers. The wooden flooring looked too clean to spoil with outdoor shoes.

'In the airing cupboard, I think.'

Ruby didn't do clutter. She was very minimalistic. Everything had its place. Abandoned footwear would not have been tolerated. Rachel liked to think that she was as tidy but Ruby's benchmark was extreme.

'Did Ruby buy this?' asked Rachel worriedly, waving her hand as if showcasing the room. Ruby had a tendency to splash the cash. Her organisational skills often seemed at odds with her spending frivolity.

'Rented. She... she was... She never knew how long she had here. She was frightened to take the risk.'

The flood gates opened. Annabelle slumped onto a sofa and let it all out: head bent with her dark curls licking the toes of her boots. These past couple of days, she had focussed all her energy on Rachel and now that they were both there, in Ruby's flat, the reality that she had lost her friend all over again was too much to bear.

Rachel collapsed onto her knees beside her and held her tight, desperately trying to absorb the grief escaping from Annabelle's lungs and body. Every time Ruby's pal attempted to rationalise her feelings, the sobbing drowned them out. In the end, she was too exhausted to continue. Her head and shoulders flopped into the cushions. Rachel lifted the young woman's feet onto the sofa, slipped off her boots and placed the white throw over her upper body. Annabelle lay there: half asleep, with intermittent strange humming sounds vibrating in her nose.

Rachel made a cup of coffee and wandered through the beautifully presented apartment, cup in hand. The second bedroom had been decorated and furnished for Alfie and Nola. The bunk bed was the same as Alfie had at home. The bottom bunk was a double bed and a single on top. The bottom duvet was pink with unicorns and the top, cream with dinosaurs. Rachel smiled. If there was one, there must have been twenty soft toys and dolls lined up along the pillows on Nola's bed. She loved her teddies and dollies. Rachel and Nola would line them up ranking them in order. The current favourite was close to the top, the least at the bottom. That could change daily. Before the road accident, Rachel used to babysit every second Thursday. It used to be every Thursday but Colin objected to her slaving for them. Funnily enough, he was quite happy for his wife to run after *HIS* daughter and granddaughter. The soft carpet reminded Rachel to look in the cupboard for slippers. She found a pair of Ugg slides on top of a basket of trainers.

She practically tiptoed over the floor and into Ruby's bedroom. Annabelle was snoring softly. She was curious to see what kind of clothing Ruby had bought for her. The wardrobe was full to bursting. Surely Ruby hadn't bought so many clothes in nine months? Rachel was relieved to see there were skirts and dresses that she would actually wear and more importantly, suitable for a woman of her age. Familiar bits and pieces that had belonged to Ruby previously and some things from Alderburn that Rachel had purchased years ago hung alongside new and well-chosen outfits. If life wasn't so absurd, Rachel would have thought that Christmas had come early. While fingering all the jumpers and tops, she heard Annabelle stirring. She slipped on the glasses she had found on the bedside table. Ruby had started using contacts. Not Rachel's thing.

'Coffee or something stronger?' asked Rachel.

'Coffee please. I can't risk a wine right now.' Annabelle smirked.

Rachel handed a Christmas mug to Ruby's best friend and topped up her own. She sat on the other sofa.

'I can't thank you enough for your bravery and loyalty. Supporting us both through this. It's mad. Unbelievably mad. I can't believe that I am buying into it. But when I see this flat and read the diary, I'm sucked in.'

'Same here. When Ruby, you, first suggested that your souls had switched, I thought you had lost it. Sorry, but there was something in the back of my mind that things weren't quite right with you, mentally, and that you gave Colin a hard time in the past. Not that I ever saw it. To me you were exactly the same anytime we met. Perfectly normal. But Ruby had always been so grateful to Colin for looking out for you. So, I assumed you had flipped.'

'How did he take to Ruby?' Rachel shook her head. 'I can only imagine.'

'Not great. Spiteful. Nasty. But God, when Ruby got stronger, she sorted him out. And Bellatrix.' Annabelle chortled. 'That's what she called Claire.'

Rachel grinned. 'She wrote that in her diary.'

Annabelle urged Rachel to read the diary to the end and if there was anything that needed further explanation, she should phone her. Annabelle rummaged through her bag and ended up emptying it onto the coffee table. How the hell did all that fit into her bag? She was never as organised as Ruby. Opposites attract; probably why they got on so well, concluded Rachel. She plucked a postcard from the enormous pile. Ruby's passwords were written on the card for all her software and banking requirements. She had given a copy to Annabelle for safe keeping. Annabelle scribbled her own mobile phone at the bottom.

'You've nothing else on this week. I've cancelled your Podcast. Elaine will cope without you.'

'What the hell is a Podcast and who is Elaine?' squeaked Rachel. Another big hurdle for her. What else had her daughter been up to in her body?

'You know what, Mrs M? Everyone knows you are resting. Ben, the kids, Rory and Lisa. Take your time. Finish the diary in comfort and we can discuss anything you want when you are ready. My number is on the card and on your phone. Give me your phone for a second.'

Deftly, Annabelle's two thumbs worked their magic. Rachel watched in awe.

'Right. I've fired off a message to all your key contacts explaining that you've had a fall but are okay and are under strict instructions to rest. You'll let them know when you are ready to text or chat. Rory will be here at the weekend. There's a curry in the fridge. You've plenty money for supplies. There's an Aldi's at the top of the road if you need anything. That's me.' She zipped up her boots. 'I'll see you again on Thursday.'

Annabelle ruffled her hair, straightened her coat and hugged Rachel then pulled a very serious face.

'Nobody knows about the journal. Please, don't discuss it with anyone else. They wouldn't believe you anyway,' she scoffed.

Once her visitor had gone, Rachel sat in the silence and surveyed the room. She was sure she would waken tomorrow and all of this would be gone. She would say to Colin that she had had the strangest of dreams but the details would be washed away as she showered; lost down the drain and forgotten. She would dress in her frumpy jumper and slacks and head for school. She job-shared with Marian Welsh. Rachel did Monday, Tuesdays and Wednesdays and Marian finished the week. When she needed extra money – more to the truth, when Colin demanded extra cash, she would pick up supply work on her days off.

Rachel pulled open the patio door. It slid with the slightest touch. The salty, icy air blasted in. She scooped up the white boucle throw and wrapped it around her shoulders. The promenade was quiet. Further along, towards the sports centre, a young couple were walking a dog. Apart from the lamp lights, it was black dark, especially out at sea. But it was beautiful.

Rachel sauntered back and forth. If she had the choice, would she choose her old life or this one? Obviously, any life without Ruby was out of the question but a future without Colin would be joyous. If she had to choose it would be 2016 before she met Colin. She was divorced but surviving. Independent. Had a wonderful relationship with Ruby and her beautiful family. She could help them. Give them her time. Her friendship with Lisa was as strong as ever. She loved her work. Switching to job-share had given her a great work/life balance. Yet, just like that fucking white van, Colin had destroyed what she had had. Maybe not a full-on collision but a slow corrosive erosion of her happiness. Worst of all, she had allowed it to happen. So, no. She may be in a living nightmare without her Ruby but to go back to Colin now, would be a travesty.

It was nine thirty. She cooried into the sofa with the delicious vegetable korma Ruby had prepared and opened the journal. She was on a mission. To finish it before Rory flew up from Stansted on Friday night.

# SEVENTEEN

*Ruby's Journal*

**Monday 29th April: Annabelle's Flat.**

Too much has happened this weekend. Honestly, Mum, so much drama has been packed into five weeks of my life as you than into my thirty-four years and ten months as Ruby Martin. Absolutely fucking crazy!!!!

A HUGE confrontation with Colin on Saturday, followed by a stomach-churning clash with Ben yesterday. I don't know where to turn. Surely, I deserve some good fortune. Actually, someone did bail me out last night. Don't know why I contacted him.

I've come to Pitt Street early (thanks to my lift) to gather my thoughts and think about where I go from here. Maybe I'll just run away. Is there a female version of the Foreign Legion? Actually, what is that? Gran used to say that Grandad had joined them when he had gone to the pub for the night.

I've listened to the radio for donkeys. Had far too much strong coffee. I'm buzzing. On a positive note, my Ray of Hope blog has exploded, as in fully taken off. I can't believe how many people have contacted the site. So many heartbreaking stories (men and women). I am NOT alone.

*

Right – back to where I left off. One week later. **Wednesday 10th April.**

Colin had not been pleased that I had gone off to Edinburgh last week without him. Made that perfectly clear. He was still oppressive. Not physically violent but it was like the threat of violence was never far away. It was the way he would look at me. Boring those nyaffy eyes right into my very being yet smirking at the same time. Seriously creepy and unnerving. Decided to stay close to Alderburn. Appeasement. I called in to see your Auntie Vera a couple of times (a bit boring but passed the time) plus I was able to have a good mooch around your house when Colin went for his morning walk. Taking in what went where.

I filed all those papers that he had emptied over the floor. Very interesting. Not much for you, Mum, apart from receipts in a brown envelope. All in the name of Rachel Martin. There were invoices for gardening equipment bought for Colin before you were married. I took a mental note of the account the money came out of. Same each time. You were funding Colin before he had moved in. Even coughing up payment for Claire and Jade's mobile phones last year. Strange. The other box had all your utility bills and car documents. The gas and electricity were in Colin's name (but you pay it!!!) and a lot of stuff in both your names. From what I could make out the car insurance was in your name and Colin and Claire were named drivers (that info would be very handy and advantageous for later). Fortunately, the purchase documents for your car are in your name. Rachel MacDonald Martin. The other box was locked. Why? (Did break into it much later but I'll not spoil that juicy piece for you just yet).

I tried hard, very hard, to give Colin little reason to doubt that my new behaviour was for real but I think he suspected that I was up to something. Hoped not. Playing housemaid to such an ungrateful git had not been easy. Thankfully, I was getting a little stronger. Walking helped (usually a loop around the village with Colin) not fast. It gave me a chance to spear him about your life together. If I got too close to rattling him, I changed the subject. Was getting good at avoidance tactics.

As soon as Colin had left the house that Wednesday, I showered, dressed and raced to the bus-stop. Only kidding – walked. Have to say that at long last I'd got my hands on a Bic razor and tackled the jungles under your arms. Seriously? When was the last time you de-fuzzed? And how come you have so much hair in your armpits but hardly any down below? I did your legs a full week later. Was frightened that the blade had been blunted (is that a word?). Until I could get a tach wax, I made do with plucking.

Anyway, Colin was heading for a coastal walk at Longniddry and I wasn't expecting him back until around ten. I suspect his walks used to be much longer but he wasn't prepared to give me a lot of leeway. Is he really a serious hiker? Yeh, he likes the gear but he doesn't exactly tackle difficult terrain. Also, I think he has taken up another hobby. Been very secretive about parcels that have been delivered. As usual, he took the car. Not bothered. I had little faith in my ability to drive safely. My ribs still restricted my movement.

I needed to go into your school. I was convinced that there might be something in your desk with all your personal data.

At least four people approached me at or on the way to the bus stop in Alderburn to enquire how you were. It was easier to tell them the truth.

'Sorry I don't know you. Memory loss after my accident but thanks for asking'.

Same reaction from each one. Could I remember this, that and the next thing? That would be a firm (hopefully apologetic) NO. (Absolutely FUCKING not. Didn't say that.) Why did they feel the need to test me when I knew nothing? Forget the Spanish inquisition, the Alderburn was worse. One of them asked if I knew who was in government. Another if I could remember her sister. I didn't know HER so how the hell would I remember her sister??!!! Glad the bus came. One old biddy wrote the bus times down. Knew you from the church. When did you and Colin start Sunday worshipping? Kind of her, even though the timetable was on full view at the shelter. Maybe thought I'd forgotten how to read!

I couldn't remember the last time I visited Musselburgh High Street. I was pleased to see that all the retail units were occupied. The walk to the school was arduous. Forgot how far it was from the bus stop. When I approached your primary school, the playground was a sea of bright red sweatshirts screaming and squealing at the top of their voices. All school playgrounds sound the same. Happy. I skulked in the doorway of the carpet shop near the school. Didn't open til ten so fat chance of anyone hijacking me, particularly any passing parent. I held back until the bell rang and they were all indoors. I gave it fifteen minutes.

I pushed the intercom button on the wall under the notice that read 'main entrance'. A sharp buzzing meant that the door was opening. Once inside, I was questioned through the intercom. When I announced who I was, a flustered OH, OH, OH followed. A tall, chubby lady with curly auburn hair greeted me in the corridor. More squealing – more like a shrill – ensued. Two more bodies appeared. I recognised none of them. A couple of bemused pupils shouted your name. I was led/pushed/coerced into the staff room and bombarded with questions. I had to raise my hand to silence them. Again, repeated my mantra. 'Huge apologies. Don't recognise you'. Stifled gasps. It's like being in the middle of a badly written sitcom and somehow you/me/we are the main character.

A cup of milky coffee, one sugar, was placed on the coffee table in front of me. Yuck. I prefer Americana, milk on the side or a little froth but kept shtum. The cellophane of a mixed box of biscuits was peeled back. Three faces introduced themselves: Tilly from the office, Anna the head teacher and Muriel the jannie then they waited for further explanations. I did my best. I was sorely tempted to carry photocopies of a well prepared and detailed account of RACHEL'S MEMORY LOSS. What to ask and what (quite effing frankly) not to bother asking? I handed in my sick note. Courtesy of Eleanor Riddle.

'Did I want to see the children?'

'Absolutely not!!!!'

'So why are you here,' Tilly asked (auburn hair).

I wanted to know more about you. Personal information that I would need. How were you paid and into what account? Your employment number, insurance number and general teaching council number were duly given. Tilly was great. Despite being constantly interrupted by children who had either forgotten their packed lunch box or P.E. kit that required a phone call home, Tilly dutifully found and wrote down everything I needed. One piece of really good news, you/me would be on full pay for the next six months unless you were able to return to class. Fat chance. I didn't have the patience to teach. Ever!! Not that I would have had a Ruby Roo (scooby to you).

Anna offered to take me to see your class. I insisted that I would prefer not to. Fell on deaf ears.

'A quick in and out. It will reassure the children that you are well. They have been most upset. I won't allow questions.'

Fucking hell. It was a hundred times harsher than the Alderburn inquisition. P2 launched their attack. Would I be back? What team did I support? Did I know what day it was? Could I remember them? (I felt awful when I had to shake my head). Did I have supernatural powers? A little too close that one. AND did I know when I needed the toilet? I pretended to check my pants and answered 'yes thankfully'. That got a few laughs. Not from your pal, your job-share, Ms Marian Welsh. One was not amused. Looked like she was chewing something that had gone off. She was now doing five days a week. She had always wanted to do more days but you hadn't been keen. Felt there was a dig there. Or maybe a kick in the teeth? BUT she had a question,

'Does Colin know you are here?'

'Of course,' said I.

She knew I was lying and I knew that she knew. Grateful when Anna terminated the interrogations.

Out in the corridor, we bumped into a lovely young woman, Sarah Goulding. A blond, well-presented Goth (had toned down the make-up and piercings slightly). You mentored her a few years ago and she proclaimed that you were instrumental in keeping her on and was thrilled to be working with you. You were the best teacher ever. Very inspiring and supportive. I was choked at that. The staff had been forewarned by Colin last week of the amnesia and she was dreadfully sorry. Tears hovered. Her and me.

Fortunately, she was out of her room for the rest of the morning, NCCT, (non class contact time that had been owed to her) and would I wait in the staff room as she had something for me. The rest of the staff regretted that they had work to do and deserted the small room. I sat on one of the low chairs (doctor's waiting room scenario) and waited for Sarah. I checked that the sheet of paper Tilly had typed for me was in my bag.

Sarah returned with a huge white plastic storage box. Your name was on one label and PERSONAL on the other label below it. She apologised for being late. She'd had to deal with a tricky challenging child. (I knew that meant a naughty wee shite.) She asked me to follow her to the learning support room at the end of another corridor. Three tables had been pushed together and eight chairs were arranged around them – like a mini boardroom. The tables rattled as the heavy box was dropped on to them.

Sarah had retrieved the box from your cupboard and thought I might want to rummage through it. You bet I did. She asked how I was coping being at home with no memory of my time there. Colin had been in earlier in the week to update the staff on my condition. He was finding it all very stressful. Turns out he has been a regular visitor to the school behind your back. Ensuring that everyone knew about your anxiety attacks and how difficult it had been for him. He pleaded with them to say nothing as it would only stress you more and that was the last thing he wanted. Sympathy was overflowing.

'And you?' I asked. 'What did you think?'

'Truthfully Rachel? ... I'm sorry if I'm speaking out of turn but I didn't like the idea of Colin coming in without your knowledge. I got the impression that all was not well with the two of you. You'd changed since he moved in with you. You were on your guard all the time. Not with me... but with the rest of the staff. You didn't come to anything anymore. When you mentored me four years ago, you were happy, energetic. Then...'

'I distanced myself from everybody?'

She nodded and blushed. Her eyes were very blue.

I explained that although I had no proof, I was sure that Colin had some kind of control over me (you). Perhaps not violent but I had the impression that I had been submissive. Not now though. I was trying to break free but it would only be when I had gathered enough information to leave.

She hoped the box would help. Maybe trigger some memories. She was as desperate for a coffee as I was. She left to make me one and I fingered all your folders. Most of them were to do with work – courses you had been on and personal development files. There was one though, a bright flowery yellow one, that had PRIVATE/PERSONAL on it.

Mum, you little minx. There was everything I needed. All your passwords. Copies of your birth certificate and of mine and Rory's. Copies of your marriage certificates and your divorce papers from Dad. A copy of your driving licence and passport. No originals. AND copies of your recent bank statements. I wanted to kiss you. Thank you. Thank you.

Sarah returned with our coffees and I slipped the papers back into the flowery envelope. Before we had finished, Tilly popped her head through the door, slightly flustered.

'Colin's in the office!' she gasped. 'Looking for you. And he seems a little perturbed.'

'How?' then it twigged. Snake in the grass Welsh. 'Tell him I'm just coming. Thank you.'

Sussing my predicament, Sarah led me to the fire door immediately next to the wee boardroom. She would put your box back in the classroom.

'Cut across the infant playground and out that gate. It leads to the park. I'll stall him.'

I blew her a kiss and legged it. Yellow folder in hand.

# EIGHTEEN

## Ruby's Journal

I scarpered across that playground half convinced that Colin would rugby tackle me to the ground. I had an inkling that he would drive around the school then down to the High Street seeking me out so had no alternative but to keep away from the main bus route. I didn't know Musselburgh backstreets that well but I had parked near your school once when Alfie was a baby. For a school fete. I hadn't long started working for Fourth Waves when I found out I was pregnant and you said that when I was famous folk would be clamouring to have me open Gala Days and the like. I laughed but you were right. Maybe not hugely famous but well enough known thanks to *Haud Yer Wheesht*. At least, it feels that way to me. And I've opened plenty of everything since then. Not that it matters now and if I'm honest it doesn't matter at all. The fame thing.

Anyway, I guessed if I carried on in the same direction I was scurrying, it would bring me out near the High School and another bus route. It did. I jumped on the first bus that came and climbed the stairs. Less chance of being spotted. I scoured the streets for Colin but saw no sign of him or your wee grey Corsa. Decided I might as well be hanged for a sheep than a lamb (think that's what you say) so ended up standing outside Lisa's place of work in Edinburgh on Regent Road. St Andrews House. Very grand building. A hop, skip and a jump from

Waterloo Place. A very well, presented guy at the reception eyed me up and down but did buzz Lisa for me. I think she was stunned to see you in her foyer and was worried that something serious had happened.

She couldn't stay for long as she had an important meeting that she couldn't wriggle out of. I quickly explained that I couldn't take the file home and would she keep it safe for me. She was more than happy to oblige then suddenly she gave me a piece of advice.

'For Christ's sake, Rachel. Get your hair cut before the funeral and buy yourself a decent outfit. You deserve it and so does Ruby.'

She hugged me and pushed the button for the lift. Before the doors closed, she smiled and winked mischievously. In that moment, I wanted you to look like her. Immaculately groomed. Smart dress. Expensive tailored jacket. Salon perfect hair.

I was off. Straight to George Street. Straight to Amber Rose.

As I opened the door, that familiar gorgeous fragrance bombarded the senses. Sensual Heaven. Roses and linen. It was like passing *Lush* only less intense. Toned down. Yummy, scrummy. Nobody gave me a second glance when I walked in. Usually there would be a flurry of excitement. A little WHOOP. Someone rushing to take my coat. Greeting me with a couple of air kisses. I knew everyone by name and they knew me. Pale Sally was first to acknowledge me. She gave my healing face the once over. It was still bright pink and flaky (scabby).

'Good afternoon. Can I help?' she asked but not really meaning it.

'I know it's short notice', I said, 'but I was wondering if someone is free to cut my hair?'

The look of astonishment on her face was laughable that I

would dare to assume that someone could possibly be free in Amber Rose.

'Hmmmmm,' she replied flicking over the screen.

'It's for my daughter's funeral,' I explained. 'Ruby. Ruby Martin.'

Her eyes widened and she squealed. 'OMG!'

Then did a funny running jig on the spot. Reminded me of Alfie when he was desperate for a pee. She danced out behind the pedestal (their desk) and threw her arms around me. There were real tears. The salon stopped. All eyes were on us. Pale Sally (her skin was never exposed to the sun) shouted over to Lloyd that I was Ruby's mum. The flurry started. A whirlpool of fashionable stylists swirled around me. All very sympathetic. Despite feeling a fraud, I was overwhelmed again. Then a vision in white appeared. White floaty blouse over white wide trousers. She liked to keep those big hips well hidden. Amber Rose herself. She and I got on so well.

'You must be Rachel. Ruby spoke so highly of you. Thank you so much for coming in,' she sang. She always sang. She was larger than life. Masses of white, blond hair (courtesy of fabulous extensions), elongated eyelashes and always one block of colour right down to the shoes: whites or pastels.

'You my darling are coming with me. Driving?'

When I shook my head a glass of bubbly appeared. I was seated in front of a mirror at the back of the salon. A little more private, I was assured. Or more probably, the salon was full and that was the only spare seat. Amber Rose pulled up a chair and gazed at your hair. I gave her free rein. A plate of teensy macaroons was placed in front of me. The foils were on and the fun started. And the craic (Ben's word for a fab blether). Reminiscing ensued.

Amber Rose was eternally grateful for all the free publicity I had given her on air on a regular basis. Quadrupled her business. I doubted that. Her reputation preceded her but it was kind of her to imply it. She did throw in a lot of freebies even for Ben and the kids. One of the many advantages of being a presenter on the morning show. Every stylist in the salon had a Ruby and/or JJ anecdote to share. Slip ups. Funny guests. Famous guests. Favourite games. It was uplifting.

Then it was Lloyd's turn. If you met Lloyd for the first time, you would immediately presume he was gay. Wrong. Totally camp – maybe it's his posh Glasgow twang – but one hundred percent a babe magnet. Drop dead gorgeous. Six foot four. Dark olive skin. Dark hair. Dreamy dark brown eyes.

He recalled the evening with Kevin King, an author from Dundee. That was the funniest thing ever. Self-published. Plenty of money. Probably sixty but pretended to be nearer fifty. Would have liked to have been a babe magnet. Not a hope in hell. Hence the book; A Cut Above the Rest. He'd hired out the salon at an eye watering price and invited his audience to have their hair styled as he did his X-rated readings. It was Fifty Shades of Edinburgh under the dryer. Gangbang shenanigans in an up-market hair salon. Cringe worthy.

Hair drying had to be done through the back. Didn't want his delivery drowned out. Amber Rose was mortified. I would have insisted on reading the book before agreeing to the event. Lesson learned. JJ and I had been invited to interview him before and after the readings. The champagne was on tap.

'Remember old Miss Smith?' Lloyd was creasing himself. Then he checked that you wouldn't be offended by what he was about to say. 'It's crude'.

The others nodded enthusiastically.

I knew exactly what was coming. 'I'm thick skinned and same sense of humour as Ruby plus I need cheering up,' I assured him.

Miss Smith was one of their regular clients. 86 years old and came every week for a shampoo and set. Lived in one of the apartments round the corner in Charlotte Square. Very desirable property. Well, Kevin King trotted out one of his toe-curling lines from one of the middle chapters and Lloyd's take on it was pitch perfect.

'Miss Smith, will you please shut your legs? I can smell you from here?'

I kid you not, you could have heard a hair grip drop. Mouth dropping silence. Then, bless her, old Miss Smith called out (head full of rollers), 'Young man are you addressing me?'

'Only if you are eighteen years old, my darling, and your pussy is on display.'

She replied as innocent as could be, 'Much, much older and my pussy is waiting patiently on my window sill for my return.'

The whole salon (then and now) erupted and wailed at her retort. You had to be there.

At the end of the launch, all of us, tumbled out half cut (not the hairstyles, I hope) on to George Street then some tagged on with me down to Suthiez to finish off the evening. Most of the customers who were left in the restaurant were polishing of sweets and coffees (Ben often slipped away after the last main meal had been dished up). Fortunately, he had not long clocked off and was cajoled into joining us for a few drinks. What a laugh! To be fair, they didn't stay long. A couple of rounds tops. That night, I'm fairly sure, little Nola was conceived. On a table in Suthiez. After everyone had gone. Obviously.

My ribs ached but from laughter. Once the highlights had been done, Amber Rose cut my/your hair. Mum, it was beautiful. Honestly. What a transformation!! Shortish, blonde and funky modern. I felt a little like me again.

The champagne had gone to my head. Woozy, woozy. AR refused payment. She couldn't possibly. We hugged and promised to chat at the funeral.

Amber Rose summoned her chauffeur. The appointed driver was actually her brother (older than Amber) and he took me home. Flashy black Mercedes-Benz.

Don't know why but poured my heart out about being frightened of Colin and the whole memory loss thing. Jasper walked me to the door. He warned Colin that if he called me tomorrow and I was upset, he would be there asap to find out what had been going on. He was a brute of a guy but interesting looking – in a good way. (They have a sister called Topaz Lily, not joking, their mother must have had a thing for precious stones and flowers as Jasper's full name was Jasper THISTLE Christie.)

I staggered in the door at Alderburn and put my middle finger up to Colin as I swanned in. OOPS!!!!

# NINETEEN

## Ruby's Journal

Next morning, Colin sulked and growled under his breath. He was in his usual walking garb and I was sitting at your kitchen table with your dressing gown on, sipping a vegetable smoothie. He commented on the muck I was drinking then declared that I was a slut and a harlot for having my hair dyed and that was another example of how I had lost my marbles. The evidence was mounting, he said. For what? I did inform him that he would be laughed out of court trying to prove that one. Four fifths of women and girls over sixteen have had their hair dyed. Even Claire. He tried to defend her by insisting it was for medical reasons. His daughter was NOT VAIN. Not like Ruby. Apparently, vanity ran through my veins. I did remind him that 'Ruby' was lying on a mortuary slab and had his boundaries of decency sunk to an all-time low.

He was at my throat in seconds. I was shocked. Totally. Nearly knocked me off my chair. He had gripped my throat with his right hand and his thumb and middle finger squeezed hard. His eyes were bulging.

'How dare you humiliate me in front of the staff at your school. What were they to think when you snuck off like that?'

The phone rang. That'll be Jasper I rasped. Hadn't a clue who it would be but his hand dropped to his side and he stormed off. As Colin answered 'good morning', I was hard on his heels and blurted out loudly that I would be there in a second. It was Jasper. Bless him. What could Colin do? He handed me the phone but pressed my body with his, hard into the wall as a threat.

'Morning, Rachel. You okay? You asked me to call at eight thirty.'

The wee bastard had the hard neck to poke my sore side with his finger. The look of hate on his face. I yelped and he put his hand over my mouth, for a second or two. Seemed longer. We could hear Jasper repeating your name. 'Rachel? Rachel are you okay?'

'No. No I'm not fine.' I could feel myself gasping for control. 'He's just had his hands around my throat.'

'LIAR. SHE'S A NASTY LIAR,' Colin spat down the phone as he tried to wrestle it from my grasp.

'Do you want me to drive over? I can come now,' asked Jasper, a mixture of seething and serious worry in his tone.

I lowered the phone and looked directly at Colin. 'That's Jasper enquiring if he should drive over, right now?'

'What? To beat me up?' Colin attempted a snigger.

'If that's what it fucking takes mate,' yelled my Guardian Angel.

'I'm calling the police,' Colin hollered. For once it was him that was shitting his pants.

'Fine by me,' I spoke very calmly. 'I'm sure your finger prints will be embedded on my throat.' Then in the same calm manner, I addressed Jasper. 'I have a lot to sort out here but would you call me in an hour. If I don't answer the phone, will you call the police and explain it to them. Unless of course, Colin rings them before me. He is annoyed that I got my hair styled yesterday. Very slutty of me.'

Jasper was desperate to come and check on me. Honestly, it was so reassuring to have someone who believed me AND who could actually do something about it. Don't get me wrong, once I had replaced the receiver and thought about how it could have gone, I broke down in tears.

I walked from your hallway into the living room for a paper tissue. Colin chanced his mitt and grabbed me by the arm.

'Don't you fucking dare,' I warned him and shrugged him off. I was upset but I had found my confidence again. That's when I challenged him.

'Have you always been violent to me?'

The drama queen was unleashed. How dare I make such an accusation? He had never and would never be violent to me/ you or any other woman and he was cut to the quick at such a slanderous, defamatory remark. That morning had been THE exception. It was what you were good at. Goading him. Deliberately trying to pick a fight. Then the big 'woe is me' finale. He had dedicated these past eighteen months to supporting you. By no means easy. Bolstering your school work. (Not sure how. He could hardly go in and take your class!!!) Making excuses when you were not well enough, or, get this, when you couldn't be arsed to attend family functions. There were times you could barely get out of bed. He would have to wash and dress you AND you didn't even have the courtesy to thank him. Nor did that bloody upstart in her grand mansion. Me again. He did everything. It had taken its toll on his health and on Claire's. On and on and bloody drolling on.

I was very tempted to ask, how come you had the energy to cook all those meals in the freezer and if he did everything, how come he had never plugged in the hoover since I arrived or did the ironing. But I threw in,

'So, are you calling the police or not?'

He smiled. As cool as a cucumber he bit back, 'ye may have won this wee battle but ye huvnae won the war.' He zipped up his wax jacket, slammed the door and left.

The warning was there loud and clear. He had something up his sleeve. I would have to be on my guard and be ready for retaliation.

I could hardly concentrate on my shower. Jasper phoned bang on 9.30. Again, offered to drive from Edinburgh to make sure I was okay. He lived not far from Fort Kinnaird so could be on the by-pass and in to Alderburn within twenty minutes. He wasn't on duty until the afternoon. He chauffeured special clients. Another name for wealthy, I assumed. A lot of them had something to do with the Parliament at Holyrood. I'm sure he said that he collected them from the airport and such and punted them between dinners and functions. Anyhow, he was the ideal guy to have on board.

Before Jasper had phoned, I had been looking for my handbag. Nowhere to be found. The sly little git had hidden it or taken it. After the call, I searched everywhere for a second time. It crossed my mind that it might have been stashed in his shed. That's when I found out. Bastard!!!! He had locked the back door and there was no key. A quick dash to the front door. That was locked too! I checked my two hidey holes to ensure that my money from Rory and Auntie Lisa was intact. Then I remembered your old mobile. Top drawer of your sideboard. He hadn't bothered to hide it as he thought I didn't know how to unlock it. It was one of the first things I recognised on the inside cover of your flowery folder. The password for your mobile was Alfie and Nola's birthdays. 2830. The 28th and 30th. Can I just say, why do you insist on having that wallet cover thing on your mobile? Please don't think it protects the phone. It's an old woman thing.

I texted Lisa to make sure she hadn't changed her number. A text pinged back immediately. I regurgitated the saga from the morning and within minutes she had phoned. She was fuming.

'I bloody knew it. Sleazy shite. Right, you are coming to stay with me. I'll pick you up after my work.'

Smug. Relieved. Ecstatically happy, I packed my bags. Salvaged what I could from your wardrobe and drawers (plus my money) and stuffed the bag at the bottom of the cupboard in Jade's room. I don't know why I hid it perhaps it was precautionary in case something backfired. That Lisa couldn't make it, not sure.

Next thing, there was pounding on the front door – strong enough to shake the house. I knew immediately that something was amiss. Worse than that – something had gone terribly wrong. It was the police demanding to get in. My natural reaction was to shout that I was fine. They wanted entry.

'Open the door please, Mrs Gordon,' boomed a female voice.

'I can't. My husband has locked me in.'

'Can't or won't?' a male voice shouted.

'Can't,' I replied a little perplexed.

The letter box opened and a pair of hairy eyebrows peered through. I knelt down so that I was level with his face.

'I'm sorry, I can't open the door. My husband has locked me in.'

'I did no such thing. She came out and rushed at me...well, ye can judge for yersel.'

You know that feeling when your stomach somersaults then suddenly drops? Well, mine was doing cartwheels then plunged into an abyss.

'He's locked me in. There are no keys in the door,' I screamed.

'Mrs Gordon,' a female voice called out, 'I need you to calm down. Have you harmed yourself? Do you have a weapon?'

Before I could answer, it sounded as if the roof was caving in. There were three almighty bangs. The back door was kicked open. I heard someone rush up behind me.

# TWENTY

*Rachel's flat in Portobello. Monday 6th January 2020*

Rachel soothed her throat with the palm of her hand. Long gentle strokes. Not the fierce frightening grip that Ruby had experienced. What had Colin been thinking? He had never been physically violent to her before. Had he?

Rachel uncurled from her cosy position on the white sofa and stretched like a cat. It felt good. It was 11.35pm and she was still wearing the same clothes from earlier; red leggings and a white polo neck. A quick rummage through the top drawer next to Ruby's bed, and she found a pair of pyjamas: a long-sleeved navy top and navy tartan bottoms. She washed her face in the ensuite basin; a large white glass bowl (marble effect) perched on top of a very dark brown unit. The mirror and lighting wouldn't have looked out of place in the dressing room of a movie star. Several sphere-shaped bright bulbs surrounded the tall rectangular mirror. It made Rachel smile. Everything about this beautiful flat made her smile until reality kicked in. Ruby no longer inhabited this place, this building, this life, any life.

In her bedtime attire, Rachel trudged through to the living area. Her head felt too heavy for her neck. Her chin rested on her collar bone. She felt old and done. She needed a wine and there was a Chablis with her name on it chilling in the fridge. She wrapped her lips around the top of the bottle, tilted back her head and took a large slug before filling the glass to the top.

Something she hadn't done since she was a teenager. In fact, it had been a long, long time since she had poured herself an alcoholic drink so late in the evening. When had she become so boring?

It took her a few seconds to figure out how to close the blinds until she spied the tiny handset on the coffee table. The correct silver button seemed to elude her. In the end the slatted blinds elegantly swished shut. Not that anyone could see in the big black expanse of glass, unless you were a seagull or a boat out at sea, but seeing her reflection in an unfamiliar room unnerved her somewhat.

She parked herself down on the sofa. Same spot. It was still warm and she tucked her bare feet under her bum. She sniffed the Chablis and savoured the aroma then swirled the cool liquid in her mouth. She could taste the citrus and hints of pear. Much better than the cheap muck she had gotten used to in Alderburn. She'd always had a good nose for any kind of alcohol. A friend recommended her for the sensory panel at the whisky distillery in Pencaitland, not far from Alderburn, but Colin had belittled her for having ideas above her station.

'Ye'll only make a fool of yersel an I'll be left to cope wi ye when it a' falls apart,' he'd chided.

Why had she allowed Colin to have so much control over her? She couldn't pin point an exact time. It had crept up and engulfed her. She was the mouse to his cat and he enjoyed toying with his prey. She was ashamed of herself and ashamed she had put her daughter in a precarious predicament.

She thought about going to bed but she didn't want to rush her wine.

# TWENTY-ONE

## *Ruby's Journal*

Totally surreal. I know. I've had so many already. I swivelled round on my knees. Not easy. A uniformed policeman towered above me.

He said his name was Blair. Police Constable Blair McGlashan and he asked me if I had anything on me that could harm me or him. I actually laughed. I showed him my hands. Fingers wide open. He urged me to unlock the front door. I explained that I didn't have the keys. The female officer came in the back door followed by Colin.

'I asked you to stay outside,' she scolded Colin.

'I need to make sure that my wife hasn't harmed herself.' He sounded deadly concerned.

Oh, my fucking days. The side of his faced was scraped and bruised with a huge gash on his cheek below his left eye. I looked up at PC McGlashan's stern face then whipped my attention back to Colin.

'What's happened to you?' I was still kneeling.

'I told you, Emma. She would either deny it or not remember that she done it,' Colin croaked. Emma was the other cop.

I tried to shout but the fear of what was unfolding gobbled up my words. I kept shaking my head and trying to mouth NO. I couldn't utter a syllable. I couldn't catch my breath. The policeman darted towards me. I honestly thought he was going to punch me so I cowered, lost my balance and tumbled backwards but he caught me before I hit the door and helped me stand up. He guided me through to the living room.

'He's lying,' I repeated through the tears and snot. 'He's the one who attacked me.'

'I'm no angry wi her,' Colin addressed the female officer. 'It's aye the same. She's no recollection of what she's done. Or claims no to know. I don't want her charged. She'll be fine in a wee while.'

Then Emma informed him that it wasn't only his decision whether charges would be made or not. A crime had been reported and they took domestic violence very seriously. Zero tolerance. Charged? I honestly believed that I was going to end up in jail or an institution. Colin began to cry. Real tears. God, he was good. If it wasn't so scary, I would have highly commended his acting skills.

'She's been through enough.' He came across as utterly distraught.

The female, Emma, turned on me.

'Think yourself very lucky that your husband is so understanding,' she scoffed.

The two uniformed cops walked into the hall, heads together, deliberating. In their absence, Colin raised his head and winked. It was like a bullet in the stomach. Horrible. He blew his nose into a hankie as they returned. I felt as if I looked as shifty as a serial killer.

'Can I speak with you in private?' I asked Blair McGlashan. 'Please?'

Colin had to get his neb in and urged Blair not to be taken in. However, hairy eyebrows agreed to hear me out. The pandering Emma ushered Colin through to the kitchen and gave me a look that would have sunk the Titanic.

I sat for ages wringing my hands, trying to plan a speech on your grey velvet sofa. Useless. I told Blair all about the accident and the amnesia. That the funeral was next week. A tad pathetic but I needed all the sympathy I could generate. I explained that I had no knowledge, or very little, of my life before the accident. I wish I could have but I couldn't, hence my reluctance to bond with Colin. No one, including Colin, had ever hinted that I had been violent before the crash. Anxious, yes. Depressed, yes. But violent, no. Not even Doctor Riddle had expressed concern. I knew there were two sides to a story and couldn't blame them for accepting Colin's version of events especially with the mess of his face. I asked him how Colin's injury was supposedly sustained. I had hit him with a garden spade. Lying wee gobshite. The weapon was in the garden where I had thrown it under the hedge.

I had to think. I was a crime novel junkie. All those Rebus investigations? Something must have sunk in. (Ian Rankin was a regular in Suthiez.)

I wheeled up my black jumper. I had one of those soft bras on that supported zilch and I pulled down your elasticated grey trousers to show off my hip (not a good look. You would have referred to it as your trucking-up-and-down stuff).

'Look at that bruising. Two cracked ribs.' I emphasised that by placing a finger on them and wincing.

The dark black and blue had turned a mottled green and yellow. I eased my arm out of my right sleeve. He could see the bruising stretched from the hip, up my rib cage and right over my shoulder and down towards my elbow.

'I can hardly lift a table spoon never mind swing a garden spade. Plus, I have no idea where he keeps it. If it's in his shed, I have never been there. He did that to himself.'

Then I suggested that if I had done it, would my fingerprints not be on the spade, the door handle (if it was in the shed), even the key? Blair agreed that they would be.

I allowed him to read my text to Lisa and apologised for the swearing. He did smile at that. He listened to what I had to say about Jasper and his call to me that morning. I held my throat centimetres from his face to let him examine it better. Would I have texted my (your) best friend and made it all up? It didn't make sense.

Blair instructed me to wait.

He left the room for about ten minutes. I could hear raised voices. Mainly between him and his colleague. No need to place bets on whose corner she was defending.

It was my turn to cry. Colin had done a thorough job. The thought of him re-entering the house while I was in the shower and PLANNING everything so meticulously made me wretch. Would this be the ideal scenario to have me sectioned? How would I get out?

The three of them returned to the sitting room. Blair did the talking.

There wasn't sufficient evidence – despite Colin's gash – to charge me. Blair agreed that the spade would be too heavy for me. Something Colin hadn't thought through. Lies were being told, probably by both parties. We were both reprimanded for wasting police time. However, PC McGlashan did reaffirm that it would be a good idea if I stayed with Lisa for a while to give both me and Colin some breathing space. He also agreed to wait with me while I collected my belongings.

Colin had not envisaged that I would be allowed or encouraged to leave the house. He bleated that it was madness. I was a danger to myself and others. If anything happened to me then they would have to answer to the highest authority. I was HIS wife and I should be THERE with HIM. Only HE was able to control me. Several times he was asked to calm down. Even Emma cautioned him. I willed him to carry on digging that deep hole to show his true colours.

Colin was forced to hand over a set of keys to me for both the front and back doors. Blair had to jerk them from his fist. I checked that I would be allowed back into my house at any time as it had been my home long before we were married. Bought and paid for by ME. (Actually, you but you know what I mean.) Colin pierced me with a spiteful scowl. However, I had to agree not to return to the house unless I forewarned Colin of my intentions. Nobody wanted another misinterpretation of events. What a joke!

'Where will you go? Rory's? Too far. Ben won't want you.' That hurt. A lot.

'I've already organised something. This morning. Had to,' I said not breaking eye contact. I did want to shout, 'before you attacked me' but couldn't risk the two PC's marching me out to the patrol car parked outside.

'Where to?' asked PC Blair once we were outside.

'Auntie Vera's.'

That would be my haven until Lisa was free to collect me.

*

Oh, someone at the door. More Amazon deliveries. She must have shares in the bloody place.

# TWENTY-TWO

## *Ruby's Journal*

**Monday 29th April: Annabelle's Flat.**

It was Ben!!! OMG. The two of us alone in Annabelle's flat. I know I keep saying this but to be standing so close and not be able to touch him properly. Breaks my heart. I'll tell you the outcome of THAT discussion soon.

I had to take a short walk. Clear my head and rid my senses of his smell. I'm sure if I had to smell six different men blindfolded, I could definitely pick out Ben. What was it that Napoleon used to say to Josephine? Don't wash before I get back. Well, Ben's odour does that to me. An aphrodisiac.

Right, back to what I'm here for.

\*

**Sunday 14th April.**

I stayed with Lisa and Brian until the Sunday. Auntie Lisa had forgotten that her brother and his wife from Stoke were staying with her for a week. Although she had two spare rooms, one of her sisters was planning a visit too. Wasn't a problem... well not wholly true but I was determined not to allow Colin to browbeat me. I owed it to you to be strong. Lisa begged me to move in with her Jill or Auntie Vera for the week. Not a great choice. Quick weigh up. Organic Jill – not very tidy, totally focussed on the whole recycling, save the planet thing – and vague, dull partner Andy versus Auntie Vera with more memory lapses than me. Decided, reluctantly, to move back to Alderburn. Took precautions. Colin was warned by Lisa that if I didn't contact her at given times then she would be on our doorstep within minutes to find out what was going on. (Fifteen minutes actually. From Haddington to Alderburn or forty-five minutes from her office in Edinburgh.) He got the message and I was on guard in case he pulled any more stunts.

Back to when I moved out. I stayed at Auntie Vera's for a few hours until Brian came for me. That's when I discovered Auntie Vera had a computer and Wi-Fi. In her back room!!! Beauty. Her family had set it up years ago. Not that she was all that proficient but better than most eighty-four-year-olds. Now that I had all your passwords plus my own, I was hyperventilating.

I fired off a text to all the contacts listed on your phone (not many!!!) Check the date, it is still there. I've just found it.


Hi everyone,

You will all know by now that I was in a tragic traffic accident with Ruby and my precious daughter (that's what you always call me) has gone.

Unfortunately, I have been left with extreme memory loss and I can remember very little of my life before the accident. Not only has this been difficult for me but frustrating for my family and close friends too. I am so sorry for the distress this has caused. If you see me out and about, by all means approach me but PLEASE be prepared. I doubt very much that I will recognise you or remember you. Don't take it personally and please be patient with me. I honestly wish that this were not true but it is.

Please don't reply. I will update you all again very soon.
Rachel.

I wanted to say much more but on reflection it would have appeared fuddled or smug.

Lots of replies. Should have expected that. All kind. All supportive except from Colin and Claire.

Colin:
You won't be able to keep up the pretence for long. Pack it in now before you make a complete fool of yourself.

Claire:
You are a self absorbant bitch!
(poor spelling!!)

Auntie Lisa was distraught when she realised she had boobed. Double booked. Those three days though gave me time to think and adjust. The flowery folder being the main thing. All your personal details. Having access to Lisa's computer as well as Auntie Vera's was the icing. Online banking especially. Did Colin know you could check your joint account? Joint? That's a joke. Seems that only your salary was paid into it and he organised all the outgoings. Where did his funds go? Turns out that you had a stash of ten-pound notes in an envelope in the folder. Two hundred and forty pounds. Good on you. Not so soft after all. Maybe you used it to subsidise our birthday gifts. Poor you, Mum. Having to hide some money like that. Why didn't you ask me? I'm ashamed to say that we could spend more than that on a night out.

It was at Lisa's that I first set up 'Ray of Hope' after a relaxing glass of wine, a bottle if I'm honest. It's an online forum where other abused women (anyone really) can read about me (no-one knows my real identity) and how I was coping with Colin. Then if they wanted (and they did), they could share their experiences with everyone else. It just snowballed. I was always careful to emphasise that due to my memory loss, I hadn't experienced how the manipulation had started or grown but I had no doubt that it had escalated over a period of time and it frightened me now. My lack of true historical fear allowed me to retaliate when others would not have the courage or luxury to do so. Isn't that so sad and worrying?

Change of subject. There's a great wee charity shop in Haddington and I procured a lovely black dress for the funeral. Ten quid. I'd never crossed the threshold of one before but I spent a full hour happily rummaging. I'll be back.

Lisa ran me to Edinburgh early on the Friday evening so that I could catch Ben before he headed to Suthiez. He was supposed to be taking a back seat for a few weeks but I knew his work would keep him from wallowing in grief or self-pity. Not that he was the self-pitying type. Too stoic. That is the one thing that we do have in common apart from fancying the pants off each other. Literally. God, I miss him. To see him and know that we can never be that way again is... SHITE.

I decided that Ben and Kenneth did not need to know about my domestic situation. They had enough to worry about. We discussed the arrangements for Tuesday. Not that I could concentrate. Ben wanted everyone to wear something bright. You had a pink fuchsia wrap that was perfect. After Ben left, I made tea, bathed the twosome and put them to bed. Truly magical. We regurgitated stories we had made up over the years. Alfie was amazed that his granny knew about the antics of Bogie Jim and Bogie Joe – two bogies that lived up the nose of an old tramp who 'lodged' in a shed at the bottom of our garden. Kenneth said it was the first time since he had arrived that laughter had drifted downstairs. I had to be levered out the door.

Staying with Auntie Lisa was okay but it was awkward at times. The natural banter that you two had had was missing. No matter how hard we tried I couldn't replicate it so it wasn't fair to agree to return after her brother had gone. Deep down, I guessed she was relieved when I said I would stick out Alderburn for a while longer, at least, until I had control of your financial affairs. Plus, she kept reminding me that I was staring all the time. I knew I was. Constantly analysing her and Brian. You know when you are watching TV and the camera does that amateur footage thing when the viewer seems detached from everything but can still see what is going on? It was like that for me. But unnerving for others.

As soon as I had sorted out everything with your bank and the payroll department at your work, I would look for somewhere else to stay. A permanent arrangement. Turns out that that plan was a little ambitious considering funds were a problem. Initially.

There was no grand reception at Alderburn when I returned only a flick of the eyes from Bellatrix who was there offering moral support to her father in the kitchen. Brian carried my bags into the bedroom then returned to the car for his toolbox. In his absence, I ignored their sarcastic and caustic sniping as I unpacked my case. Their faces when Brian began to fit a bolt to the inside of the pink room.

'That won't be necessary,' wailed Colin. 'She was the one who attacked me.'

Brian never acknowledged him.

'That's my daughter's room,' Claire yelled at my joiner.

'I think that you will find this is my house,' I said calmly. 'Bought and paid for by my money long before your father moved in. And if I want to stay in there, I will.' Then for good measure I threw in. 'If it makes you feel safer, Colin, Brian has a spare lock in his van. I'm sure he could fit a bolt to your room door.'

'You're a nasty cow,' snapped Claire.

I decided not to ramp up the hostilities any further. While Brian was present, I retrieved a few bits and pieces from your wardrobe. As the weight was dropping off (no appetite) more and more of your back of the wardrobe stuff was fitting me.

I asked Brian if I could make him a coffee. And I asked the Gordon partnership if they would like a cuppa too.

'What heaped wi arsenic?' Bellatrix is such a comedienne.

Brian blew up. 'Have you two no fuckin compassion? This woman is still recovering from a tragic accident. She buries her daughter on Tuesday for fuck's sake. Show some respect or I'LL smack the pair of you wi a fuckin spade.'

Even I was stunned but wholeheartedly chuffed at the same time.

All my sympathy cards had mysteriously vanished. Into the wheelie bin no doubt. That hurt as I liked to sit and read them at night. A little morbid, I know, but it gave me huge comfort. I felt closer to everyone. My big cloud of foreboding soon descended and lasted until the Tuesday and beyond.

Colin and I pivoted around each other exchanging very little. We ate separately. I stayed in my room only venturing round to Auntie Vera's for some respite. The station had paid tribute to me over the weekend, playing my favourite music. Naturally, I bubbled the whole time. Chicken hearted Jacob had trolled the archives for old interviews and relayed them on the Monday breakfast show. The one with Lewis Capaldi was phenomenal. He and I just clicked and the buzz in the station!! WOW! The phones went crazy suggesting that we were obviously an item. (Too young for me.) After I had heard him sing in Dumfries as part of the 'Hit the Road' project in 2014, I just knew he was destined for greater things. Then the craic from Big Bill and Wee Will when they had been appearing in Snow White (not sure if it was The Kings). That was wild and a trifle risky for breakfast listeners. I honestly thought I would be reprimanded (or sacked) but turns out that my producer and Big Bill go way back.

All day Monday, I willed myself to be invincible but in reality, I was wading in quicksand searching for solid footing.

# TWENTY-THREE

*Ruby's Journal*

**Wednesday 1st May. Annabelle's flat.**

The first of May already. It's five weeks tomorrow since the accident. Scary.

I've spent the last two hours sifting through my Instagram (can't help reading what my followers are still commenting about me) and updating my blog. In two and a half weeks, I've had hundreds of responses. Some caustic but the majority only want to help or be helped. I keep on top of it at Auntie Vera's. Colin is not allowed to cross her door. Haven't a clue as to why. She won't enlighten me. Only drawback is her cat. You know what I'm like around cats. Constantly sneezing. Her wee Button makes a beeline the minute I walk through the door.

Also, an Elsie Walter from a women's refuge centre in Dalkeith has contacted me offering a place to stay should I need it in an emergency. Bless her. I'm so lucky to have my very own refuge here in Pitt Street. AND I am sleeping over on Friday. A boozy, girly night in. Woo hoo!!!

Colin has been breathing down my neck wanting me to go places with him. Sooking in you would call it. He is very edgy. It has been a very difficult few days. For him too but I had to do what I had to do. (Explain later). So glad Auntie Lisa was there to support me.

**Tuesday 16th April.** Day of the funeral.

Shite. Shite. Shite and shitty shite.

Just when things couldn't get any worse. They did. Over and over and over. I'm physically shaking as I write this. The thought of reliving that day is ...just bloody awful.

Rory and Alana collected me at ten. My face was swollen with all the crying I had done. I'd listened all morning to JJ. He did more sniffling and whimpering than presenting. Wee scone. So many listeners contributed to the breakfast slot. Sharing their memories of the programme. When they had met me. How I had helped them. Wasn't ever aware that I had really. Happy recollections. JJ had insisted he would cover the morning as normal, as homage to me, but would miss the next day to nurse his long overdue hangover. He was heading to the church directly from our premises in Windsor Street. Presenters and staff from other stations had fallen over themselves to cover the rest of the day to allow all Fourth Wave employees to attend the funeral. My funeral. Ruby Martin. My head is in my hands as I write this. How could this have been happening?

Freezing cold flannels were as useless as a chocolate teapot. My eyes and face looked like the result of a serious reaction to something. Puffy and inflamed. Make-up would have to wait. I barely remember showering or dressing only the tutt-tutting from the plonker behind me as he commented on my choice of kitten heels – hardly high (borrowed from Auntie Lisa) and how I had styled my hair. Funnily enough, Colin approved of the black dress. I sat in the passenger seat of Rory's car with ice cold tea bags on my eyes. Avoidance tactics. Didn't have to justify my earlier outburst that way. Alana and Jack sat stony faced in the back. They had witnessed the fracas earlier. Jack was wearing his school blazer and the school gold, yellow and black tie. His own nod to colour. Rory was as dashing as ever, even in sombre black. He wore the same tie as Jack. A cute touch, I thought. Skinny Malinky Alana sat with her arm around wee Jack's shoulders. She had a very pretty gold and yellow corsage on her left wrist. For a woman who is so striking (the very short, black, sleek bob helps), she never looks truly well and her blotchy face was a bad as mine. Like me she was waiting until the last minute to make up her face. Shades were a must. I didn't have a pair. We were all meeting at mine. (Can I still call it my place?)

Margaret rushed out to greet us when Rory's car pulled into the drive. Immaculately groomed. Had definitely had her hair done somewhere nearby. I didn't ask. She has a gold medal in fawning and she didn't let herself down. I'm being a bitch. She has a really good heart most of the time.

'Where's the adorable Colin?' she asked in the most troubled voice she could muster.

'He's meeting me there.' No explanation given.

'Oh. Oh, I see.' She didn't but would someday. 'Come in, pet. Don't you look a sight and no wonder?' (Did I say she lacked tact as well?)

The gutless wee shitbag at Alderburn was gutted. But he was not going as my partner. End of. Wee Jack was ordered to return to the car to shield him from my profanities. Rory pleaded with me but I held firm. Alana stood in the hallway, in her black jumpsuit (she looked like a model), and didn't comment one way or another. After having been lectured by your husband all that morning about our family, why would he then want to mix with all the self-absorbed little people who had never contributed to society and never would? (Very rich coming from him)

Who lived off the back of their fathers' wealth (that one was for Ben and some of it for me and Rory) and who couldn't hold down a job that a boy scout could do with his eyes shut. He's a bitter bastard.

Rory apologised for my lack of judgement and fairness (he was slipping into that role too often) and thanked Colin for agreeing to meet us later.

'Don't attempt to sit near me or speak to me,' I lashed out. 'I mean it.' I hadn't briefed Rory about the spade incident. Yet.

The front door was open when we arrived at Deacon House and I could hear voices in our large family room to the left. As soon as my toe touched the black and white mosaic tiles in my vestibule, my grief was unleashed. Like a Mexican wave it swept over everyone in the house. A torrent of anguished wailing. I wanted to hold my Ben. Reassure him that I was there in the flesh – well your flesh – but I couldn't. Plus, he was distancing himself from me. Definitely wary. We exchanged an extremely tentative embrace. Our finger tips drummed each other's backs. Our heads leaned away from each other. 'Rachel,' he said. 'Ben,' I replied. We sort of nodded. Not good. There would be no more outbursts from me. Impeccable behaviour only. I had to focus. Be disciplined.

Perma-tanned Carrie teetered in for a cuddle. Her heels must have been five inches. Don't know how she balances with those big boobs (all her own, no implants). To be fair, her distress was genuine.

Olive Watson, the humanist, approached and hunkered down in front of me. Her face stared into mine as she introduced herself. She lifted my hand and smiled.

'Ruby was such a good friend to me. I'll miss her. I hope I do her proud.'

'You will.' I sniffed. 'You always do.'

I asked after her husband and her family. She was a little startled that I knew so much especially about her husband's Parkinson's. I realised I would have to share less with the people I knew and you didn't. As she stood up and flattened her grey woollen dress, I automatically touched her brooch.

'A present from your Ruby,' she chuckled. 'A private joke.'

It was something I had picked up in Disney. Popeye carrying Olive Oil. Olive's husband had been in the navy. No way could he carry her now. She's a chubby wee thing. But lovely.

We women put the last-minute touches to our mottled stained faces. I quickly nipped up to my bedroom for a pair of shades. Our familiar bed smell caught me out again. I buried my nose into Ben's pillow and inhaled him all the way to my feet. I felt giddy. I wanted to stay there forever.

The cars had arrived. Two Daimlers and the hearse. Festooned with flowers. A large display in red roses, RUBY, and another in white roses, MUMMY, on either side of the coffin. Mascara had been pointless. I travelled with Ben, Rory, Alana and Jack. Kenneth and his family followed on behind. Libby had collected the kids earlier and had taken them to her mother's house. They were to join us at The Vantage Hotel later.

Would you believe that there were photographers in the drive? I hadn't noticed them earlier. Jostling for the best angle. I recognised one of them. Looks like a young Adolf Hitler. Must have something to do with the station. I turned away.

As we drove slowly along the streets, I observed the vague, disinterested faces of the pedestrians and wondered what they were thinking about us as we passed. Nothing probably. I never did. Maybe briefly but nothing profound. In fact, I usually looked away if I saw a hearse and I hated if I accidentally got caught up in the procession of cars behind one. Like it would bring me bad luck. That's a joke. What could be worse than what I have now? Sorry Mum. More than you have. I AM a selfish cow!

We followed the hearse to the front of the church. I counted at least five police officers controlling the flow of traffic and the large crowd who had gathered outside on the pavement. I found out later that many were our regular listeners. A TV crew were interviewing some of the guests going into church. Or should that be mourners? Not sure. When they saw the cars, they scuttled through the large doors. I was actually embarrassed at all the fuss. Another cameraman raced up to the cars as we pulled in, and homed in on the flowers. So intrusive yet I had thrived on this kind of juicy gossip in the past and our listeners loved to hear the gory details.

Dad and Patricia were waiting for us. Rightly so. And Annabelle, Libby and Ros. Their partners had gone in ahead of them. I had a wobble when I saw the girls. My best pals. All under the impression that one of the gang had gone. Annabelle was inconsolable when she hugged me (you). We were all gently ushered in. That's when I saw Colin, Claire and Jade. Standing right at the back of the church waiting: less than two metres from us. Gallus gits. Rory instantly gripped my hand and hissed, 'DON'T' under his breath. Ben shook Colin's hand as did Kenneth. Rory was probably too frightened to let go of mine. At least they were suitably attired. No splashes of colour but smart enough. I've no idea where they sat but it wasn't beside me.

In a daze, we walked the red carpet running down the centre of the church. Somehow, I managed to put one foot in front of the other. I remembered our wedding at Fotheringham's

Estate. A beautiful sunny day. A red carpet stretched from the courtyard, right over the lush, green lawn and down the aisle between the pristine white linen chairs. The pale blue ribbons matched the bridesmaids' dresses. It stopped at Ben and Pascal. The whole congregation (not sure if that's what you would call them considering it was outdoors) turned to face us and cheered. One of the best days of my life.

No one turned this time. Sombre and rigid, black-clothed bodies stared straight ahead or at their feet. An array of scarves, all the colours of the rainbow, were draped around shoulders. As I neared the front, a hand shot out and squeezed mine. Tight. Auntie Lisa. Then I thought of you and how no one was mourning my beloved mum. You didn't deserve this but what could I do? I have mourned you, Mum. Every day when you smile at me from the mirror.

I recognised so many of the faces. Friends, family, colleagues and celebrities. Bloody hell. So many well-known Scottish faces from TV and radio all here because of me. I was as humbled as I was overwhelmed. The station crew were all there as were my pals from *Haud Yer Wheesht*. Ben acknowledged Tom Kitchin and Nick Nairn with that awkward nod that men have perfected over the years. Turns out that there were just as many guests packed into the hall behind the church. Something the clerk had anticipated. The service was relayed over to them on loud speakers. Ben, Rory and Dad made a point of going over to the hall when it was finished to thank everyone there personally.

The service. What can I say? All I could hear was the muffled sobbing from Ben. I homed in on his every breath. In and out. DEVASTATING. He did laugh occasionally when something endearing was said about me. I might have smiled then too. Not sure. I was numb.

Rory and Dad managed to speak without breaking down. Only just. Dad kept patting the head of the microphone to see if it was working. Nerves probably. Poor Annabelle crumpled after a few sentences. Libby and Ros rushed up to the rostrum to support her but no use. Each of them tried to read what was written and failed miserably. Soon the three of them had the whole place dabbing their eyes. Thank goodness for Olive. A true professional. Calming and uplifting all at the same time.

Not a dry eye when Alfie and Nola's little tribute was read out and especially when 'Let it Go' filled the church. All I could picture was their happy faces in our living room belting it out and Nola standing, so serious in her Elsa outfit, with her arms reaching for the sky. Oh Mum. How had it come to this?

HAVE TO STOP. SORRY.

# TWENTY-FOUR

## *Ruby's Journal*

Sorry about that. I've had a coffee and composed myself.

*

The service finished with 'My Life would Suck Without You' by Kelly Clarkson. The girls joined in but Ben bowed his head and cried. Heartbreaking.

The coffin was taken back to the funeral director. You were to be interred in Enniskillen in the Sutherland's family plot. I wanted you to stay with me and be buried somewhere in East Lothian where I could visit and chat. But I had no say.

Ben, Dad and Rory formed a departing line. Alana and Jack walked in front of me. I willed myself not to make a fool of myself but I'm sure I held on to Ben much longer than was expected. He prised me from him, pulled a face and passed me on to Dad who unexpectedly held on tighter than me. I felt his emotion in my very bones. Rory took over.

I stood to the side but just as many people approached me outside the church as had hugged all the men inside. One after another the procession began. Amber Rose and the valiant Jasper (he whispered he would be there for me if needed). JJ and Arjun. My girls. Annabelle was particularly hard to endure.

Distraught couldn't define her grief. And I had to stand there pretending to be you. A fraudulent SHIT.

Thirty minutes later, we entered the large function suite of the Vantage Hotel. The management had agreed, reluctantly, to allow our staff to run the show. The publicity was a convincing factor plus Ben was prepared to pay whatever was necessary.

Nola and Alfie were tearing around the hall with Libby's two. Happy as Larry. Jack joined in. Nola had decided to wear the Anna outfit. I was given a huge granny cuddle when they saw me. I wanted a mummy hug. A proper mummy squeeze.

About fifteen round tables had been set up. The centre pieces were ever so pretty and the smell? Devine. Bowls of mini scented lilies. My favourite. Larger displays were in vases on the buffet tables. The hotel staff were pouring the teas and coffees but our staff were wandering around the tables with enormous silver trays of canapés and mini finger rolls filled with mouth-watering fillings. Not that I ate anything.

I sat at the family table beside Dad and Patricia. I couldn't even engage in small talk just focussed on the kids playing. Rory suggested I mingle a little and thank people for coming. I must have shaken my head.

'Please try. It's the least you can do,' he whispered but his face was doing that squinty, disappointed thing.

I knew if I approached Annabelle first, I'd be rendered incapable of holding a conversation with anyone else so gave her a wide berth for as long as I could. I saved close friends and family til last.

I spoke with Ben's friends first. The cheffing and catering community and his cycling buddies. Slightly easier. They didn't know the woman before them other than that you were my mum so I kept it polite and brief. The cast and crew of *Haud Yer Wheesht* gushed as you would expect but again because it wasn't ME they were chatting to, they were restrained in their sharing. Kit Hendry was full of warmth and I could feel my steadfastness melt as I moved away from her and on to my station crew, especially Jacob – my JJ.

They were talking shop as always but halted when I approached. Adrian sprang to his feet and offered me his chair. One by one they took their turn to tell me how wonderful I was. Slightly two faced but I'd be the same. Sly Si and Jill from the evening slot crouched at either side of me. The nearest I'll get to them kneeling at my feet. I giggle now but couldn't then. Jill took my hand and told me I was the reason she got into broadcasting. Don't think so. She started at the station six weeks before me. Best not to correct her. I did note that drive-time Jemma was missing. Holding the fort. Aye right. She'd be grabbing the chance to hobnob with the bigger stations. Jacob hadn't moved. No surprise. He was a mess. I stood up first.

'No, no sit down.' He rushed round in his tight blue trouser suit and navy suede loafers (no socks) and engulfed me.

OMG. A tsunami was unleashed. Folk at other tables strained to ogle at us. We said nothing. Just held on. He straightened his arms, at shoulder height, and I was convinced that when he looked me in the eye, he would instantly realise it was me.

'Rachel,' he snivelled, 'she adored you. Spoke about her mammy constantly.'

Dejected, I smiled. It was JJ that called you mammy not me. 'Ditto. You were very special to Ruby.' I kissed his cheek and handed him over to Arjun. I promised I would meet him for lunch in a couple of weeks. Husband and husband sobbed in synchrony.

I was a teensier more composed at Uncle Iain's table. Seven of them had travelled down from up North. I was very touched. They would toast me properly when they returned to Fraserburgh. I could imagine. They're not shy when it comes to sinking the drink. I urged them to speak to Louisa who would wrap up some food for their journey. Invitations from your brother and my cousins were extended. Auntie Vera sat immobilised in her chair. She wafted her hand in front of her face to indicate that she couldn't find the right words and kissed the back of my hand. We should have met up more. Weddings and funerals should not have been the excuse we all needed to party. What a waste.

I swiped my wet hand on the hip of my dress and forced my legs to edge towards Annabelle.

It was actually easier than I had expected. The girls just wanted to talk about me and them and you. The nonsense we had at school and all our outrageous sleepovers at your house. Looking back, you and Dad were very tolerant. None of the other parents were as accommodating. I had to concentrate ever so hard. Too often I jumped in as me, sharing some juicy snippet that you would never say or know. The flow would abruptly stop. Confused looks would ricochet amongst the four of them

'Sorry. Ruby shared that tit-bit after one wine too many,' I tried to gloss over it.

That bit about me is very true. Loose tongue with alcohol and it has gotten me into loads of trouble and I'm worried it will again. Hannah Dunlop was there. Remember her? She used to be part of our gang at school then kind of drifted away when she went to Strathclyde Uni. Well, her and Annabelle are very chummy now since her divorce. Probably suits Annabelle too. Not much fun hanging around with us married ones.

'Dance with me, Granny.' Nola's happy faced beamed at me.

She led me to a corner near the buffet table where we birled, bounced and glided for ages. Alfie was too busy playing chasing with Libby's Mikey and Jack. A huge board, festooned with family photographs past and present caught my attention. I stopped dancing. Each photograph had a story to tell. My story. My life.

Rory and me, shoulder to shoulder, in official school poses. Holiday snaps with you and Dad. Scantily clad pictures of the girls and me on the beach in Magaluf. Our first holiday after High School. If you knew what we had got up to you wouldn't have let me out the house again. My 21st party at the Maitland Hotel. My hair!!!! Cheap perm. What was I thinking?

Then Ben. Dozens of them. With our arms wrapped around each. Always laughing. Always looking at each other. A smile that said, I know you inside out.

I just stared. Forlorn and empty and consumed with sadness. Fucking awful!!!

An arm slipped over my shoulder. I knew instantly it was Ben. God, I sobbed. Set him off too. It was Dad who rescued us, me really.

'Come on, Rachel. Let's walk.'

We walked and talked, arm in arm. Dad did all the talking. I said nothing. Couldn't. We did a great big loop around the hotel. Nice houses. We considered that area at one point. Not too far from the artificial ski slope where we take Alfie and Nola for lessons. Dad was kind, considerate, gracious. He reminisced about everything. Us as a family. We walked for at least half an hour, maybe less, until I was shivering. It wasn't cold but I was.

As we sauntered back, he apologised to you, Mum. For his philandering. Not that there was much of it, he claimed. He said that you were stunning. Always batting off compliments and admirers and that he, stupidly, felt he had something to prove so he flirted. When he told you about Pat, you didn't seem to care. Perhaps if you had reacted differently things might have been different. That was a definite cop out from Dad. I got the feeling that you two weren't very good at communicating. I reminded him that I couldn't comment as I couldn't remember the details but I asked him if he had ever loved me (you). Of course, he said but get this, he was convinced that if you hadn't got pregnant with me then you would have moved on to bigger and better things. I know he is my dad and maybe I'm giving him too much leeway but I genuinely felt sorry for him. You two should have discussed things more. Shared your feelings. Sometimes Ben and I share too much. Don't know if that is good or bad.

When we returned, the atmosphere in the hall was much more jovial. Voices were louder. More laughter. Even Ben was giggling with his cycling mates. I wanted to scream at the top of my voice that I was dead for fuck's sake. Didn't. That's what happens. Dad always used to say the difference between a Scottish wedding and a Scottish funeral is that there is one less drunk at a funeral. It appeared that way to me.

Claire approached me. All hoity toity.

'Will ye be staying at Alderburn the night?' She was very brusque.

My retort. 'I'm fine, Claire. Just... but thanks for asking.'

'This has been difficult for my dad as well.'

'Claire,' I was very restrained. 'Your dad attacked me. I did NOT attack him... and I think you know that. I have not discussed it with my family yet but I intend to. I need to return to Alderburn as I'm travelling to Enniskillen tomorrow to bury my daughter. I need to pack'

At that moment, Jade skipped up. 'Granny Rachel, can I sleep over at your house tonight?'

It was an opportunity not to be dismissed. I agreed she could sleep in the room with me. That way the weasel would have to be on his best behaviour.

# TWENTY-FIVE

*Rachel's flat in Portobello. Tuesday 7th January 2020.*

Rachel rested the back of her head on the sofa and closed her eyes.

She would have to organise a visit to Enniskillen as soon as possible. She had to visit Ruby. Why the hell did no one object to that stupid decision? Who over there would visit Ruby as often as she would? Ben hadn't been thinking straight. Surely, he would have wanted Ruby nearby unless he was intending to return to Northern Ireland at some point. But his businesses were here. Why hadn't Ruby spoken out? Then it donned on her that Ruby's protestations would have been futile. She'd have been desperate to gain Ben's trust and couldn't risk crossing him. Poor Ruby. Nowhere to turn to and nobody to guide her.

And Rob. Imagine him confessing that after all this time.

When Rachel found out she was up the duff at twenty-one, there were two options open to her; abortion or marriage. The former was quickly dismissed. For a start, she was quite far on. She'd always had erratic periods and she was eleven weeks before it twigged that she might be pregnant. By the time she had broached it with Rob another couple of weeks had passed. He was ecstatic and proposed immediately. Rachel had hesitated in giving her answer. Although, she had been more than capable of raising Ruby on her own, she wanted more for her first born. She didn't know of one other woman who had not married and brought up a child on her own. Not in her neck of the woods. A lot had changed but not marrying the bairn's dad was still deemed as unacceptable. Her mum and dad would have supported her and contributed in anyway but there would have been very little money as a single mum. Teaching would have to be put on hold. She was very fond of Rob and he was undoubtedly handsome but they had only been going out for eight months. Hardly enough time to decide if you wanted to spend the rest of your life with someone. Rob seemed desperate to play happy families. As an only child, his relationship with his parents was strained. Rachel had only met them twice before, for afternoon tea. She had blethered away, blissfully unaware of their awkwardness, until Rob nudged her with his knee. It was apparent that she had over shared. Rachel had had a happy childhood and her parents had always encouraged independence. They certainly didn't want her to rush into marriage. The choice was always hers.

In comparison to the Martins, her mum and dad seemed normal – at least normal for East Lothian.

They were happy-ish. Typical working-class folk. Her dad was a coal miner and when she was in primary seven her mum went back to work in Mitsubishi in Haddington. They worked hard through the week and went out with their cronies to the local miner's club on a Saturday night for a drink and a game of housey. Holidays were spent in a caravan park in Blackpool. Rachel and her siblings thought they had gone upmarket when they moved on to Devon campsites.

Perhaps it was the hormones but Rachel was caught up in Rob's euphoria. He treated her like a princess. Precious. He promised her and the baby everything. And he tried. They had a small, happy wedding. They bought a one-bedroom flat. He furnished it with everything Rachel asked for. Showered her and Ruby with gifts. The three R's he called them: Rob, Rachel and Ruby. He was a grafter and had a good head for business. In fact, he excelled in it.

Then three quickly became four. Rachel was stuck but she was determined to prove to Rob that he had made the right decision. She was loyal and supportive and subservient. Despite offers, she never strayed and would never have done so. But Rob couldn't sustain the bubble. He found it difficult to love. To be in love.

Rachel's wine glass was empty. She contemplated a refill but hesitated. Colin's usual undisguised disapproval nipped her conscience. She was a little tipsy after one – albeit a large one. Nothing ventured, nothing gained. She tucked the open diary under her arm and poured a half measure into her glass. Well fuck Colin and she topped it right up. After all, there was no one to judge her now. A long lie beckoned.

She smiled, switched off the lights and headed to her bed to find out what lay in store for Ruby in Enniskillen.

# TWENTY-SIX

*Ruby's Journal*

**Wednesday 17th April. Day after funeral**

Could have gladly throttled Jade. Grating, bleeping tunes on her tablet all bloody night. I was knackered. But at least she kept the wolf from my door. Literally. Though, Colin did wander in in the morning with a tray, laden with toast and a cup of tea. For his granddaughter.

My bed was covered with your clothes. Three piles: definitely, maybe and absolutely not. The last one was seismic. What to take? Sorry Mum but there was very little that fitted the bill. Enniskillen women (and men) have style, especially the circles that Margaret and Carrie frequent. Designer labels en masse.

I had made a quick pit stop at Asda, courtesy of Uncle Brian, and managed to pick up some staples. A pair of jeans and a white shirt. White trainers (even though I shot down Colin). A Breton and a casual jacket. A navy flowery dress. Had to discard a gold pleated skirt and another blouse. They looked ridiculous when I tried them on. Looked like Edna from Ad Fab on a bad day. The black dress had to go in as did your cream dress and boots. Good news. I'd lost weight. Maybe 9 or 10 pounds. Maybe more. Some of your hiking gear was acceptable. I selected your blue Craghoppers jacket and a pair of navy trousers to travel in. We were flying out to Belfast on the Wednesday and returning on Saturday. Annabelle was picking me up. Woohoo!!

Carrie had arranged a hired car for us at Belfast City Airport (George Best airport). Had no time to secure a bank card but I had ordered one to be sent to Lisa's. Enough cash though (not that I would need any).

All I could think about was how to tell Annabelle. When to pick my moment? Decided categorically it would have to be after the burial. Too dodgy beforehand in case it catastrophically backfired. Rehearsed the scenario over and over. It changed each time but there was a glimmer of excitement igniting within me.

The journey whizzed past. The chat was easy and comfortable. We talked about the funeral and her holiday in Australia. Knew I was staring again – like I was drinking in folk in for the first time. It was in Melbourne that Annabelle and Ben first met then I was thrown into the mix when he moved to Edinburgh.

Annabelle was in awe of your navigational skills given that you had only been there twice. I could have found it with my eyes shut even with my non-existent sense of direction. Take after Dad. Annabelle drove. Can never quite fathom why they have a crap rail service in N.I. and a bus service that's totally inadequate. Must be why everyone drives such fab cars. Each one better than the next.

We took the M1 out of Belfast. As soon as we reach Bally-gawley Roundabout, I always feel as if I'm en route and start to relax. I pointed out Ben's Wee Granny's house (on his mum's side). Outside Brookeborough. A row of old farm cottages down a narrow track. Few miles from Enniskillen. Wee Granny point blank refuses to move in with Margaret. Prefers her wee shack.

Two hours after landing, we parked in Kenneth's impressive driveway. Caithness House.

'Close your mouth Bella-Anne, you'll catch flies,' I laughed.

'Fucking hell. It's better than Ruby described. The photos don't do it justice. Is that all one house?' Then she paused. 'Did you just call me Bella-Anne?'

I laughed and brushed it off. See what I mean though? I constantly forget that I am you.

We stood and gazed at Lough Erne for ages. Two boats passed and waved. Obviously knew Kenneth. Most of the sailing fraternity do as he is a lifeboat volunteer. It has a Loch Lomond feel about it. Or Loch Morlich. We had great family holidays there. Didn't we? Remember that Easter at Aviemore? We had gone up for the snow and ended up paddling in the loch; it was so warm. I'm sure we skied as well. The higher runs were open.

'Does all that grassy area belong to this property? It's like a park.' Annabelle's incredulity was funny.

I pointed out the boundaries, the parts that we could see from the house that is. Kenneth's new boat was moored at the bottom of the lawn. His old one looked tiny by comparison. That's when we saw my two with their life jackets on.

'Graaannnnyyy!!'

We walked down to the jetty. Kenneth was taking them out on the wee boat. Some fresh air and breathing space for Ben.

'On your own?' Didn't trust my two to sit still while Kenneth steered. Needn't have worried. John (Kenneth's brother) popped up from the cabin.

Annabelle was itching to go out with them but I surmised (correctly) that we would sail later.

Grandma Margaret's squeal alerted us. 'You're here.' Dramatic squeeze. 'No Colin?'

'Nope. Left the arsehole at home. Brought a much more acceptable replacement.'

Annabelle was enthusiastically received. We walked up to the huge glass fronted house, linking arms with gushing Margaret. Colin wasn't mentioned until much later.

We were occupying the self-contained flat on the ground level. Private balcony and fabulous views of the loch. Annabelle was blown away.

'God Mrs. M. It's like something you would see in... I dunno... in Miami Beach.'

I suppose it does.

Ben and the kids were staying in the main house. Rory was occupying the apartment upstairs with Dad. The one that you and Colin once shared.

After a quick freshen up, we had French Martinis on the boat. Carrie and Dale moored beside us. It's a different world. Carrie's three and our two played tig with Dale on the lawn while we waited for John.

Annabelle balked, 'thought it was supposed to be casual? Do you think we should change?'

I did warn her that they would be dressed to the nines. They didn't disappoint. Mother and daughter both sported beautifully tailored trouser suits. Annabelle and I were underdressed in our jeans. But so was Ben. No surprise there. God, he was super sexy. Infinitely casual. Jeans and a smart, navy Ralph Lauren shirt. Uber cool. Sorry mum but I could have straddled him there and then. Not what you want to hear BUT it was true.

'A top up, Rachel?' asked Carrie.

I had to decline. I used to swallow a bucket load but your taste buds are so different to mine. I ended up on Morgan's Spiced Rum and diet coke.

'You've done something different with your hair,' said Carrie. 'It suits you. Less aging,'

She went to the same school of tact as Margaret. 'Mummy, I'm just saying to Rachel that there's something different about her. Doesn't she look the better for it? And I can see Ruby in you.'

Whoah!!!! I didn't know whether to laugh or cry.

Carrie is about your height, Mum, and Margaret asked her if she still had some of her early maternity outfits that might do me. Annabelle clocked my thin lips. However, I graciously accepted the offer. Beggars can't be choosers.

As soon as John and his wife arrived, we headed for Carrybridge Lakeside Lodge. Alfie and Nola wanted to ride with Carrie's gang. I urged Ben to accompany them.

'Annabelle,' he shouted, 'come with us. Better than being saddled with the oldies,' he joked.

No need to ask who I was left with.

As Dale swerved away, I was overcome with jealousy. Not one of the four gave me a backward glance and neither did the kids. The green-eyed monster felt so lonely. Dumped.

Further up the loch, the jetties were chocka. School holidays. If there was one boat there were dozens of them jostling for a space. Kenneth just slipped the boat in nae bother. As always, the Sutherlands were greeted like royalty when we entered the restaurant and a reserved alcove was pointed out to us. A cacophony of accents filled the room as we squeezed past the crowds to claim our seats.

Several voices hollered for Suthie and Ben did the obligatory high five or in some cases a familiar hug. I recognised at least two of the groups.

You have no idea what it is like to be surrounded by loved ones while you are pretending to be someone else. I wanted to scream and shout that it was me. RUBY SUTHERLAND.

Then everyone would rejoice. Ben would shag me on the table and still everyone would cheer as if it was perfectly normal to fornicate in front of your children and in-laws!

Didn't happen. Obviously. Polite banter ensued.

Annabelle was in her element. The camaraderie was infectious. I wondered how long it would take Margaret to enquire about Colin.

'He is a shifty shit,' I explained. 'Obnoxious and one hundred per cent untrustworthy.'

Kenneth blinked and swallowed a warning shot.

'Can you believe he attacked me, on Thursday? Had his hands around my throat. The police were called. (No need to explain it was for me!) I can't be certain but I'm guessing he's been controlling me for months, years even. My friend Lisa came to my rescue. But enough of that let's toast my darling Ruby.'

Talk about a bombshell. Hee, hee (too many Morgans). Just as Ben returned, the flummoxed gathering raised their glasses. 'RUBY!'

Kenneth half ushered, half frogmarched me to a corner and asked what my game was? No game. Only justice, I assured him. (Maybe revenge.) I wasn't prepared to go into detail but would another time.

'It's about Ruby. And Ben,' he rasped. Oops!! No more alcohol for me.

Three hours later, we toppled into bed half cut. Full cut for Annabelle. A quarter for me.

Next morning, Thursday, Annabelle slept in. She was on the water. Copious amounts. I was fine. She did accuse me of snoring. I have never snored in my life. Does death count? For the first time, I considered that I might actually be a zombie.

Up with the kids and the dogs. Three boisterous cocker spaniels and two excitable children. My children. Kenneth's dogs. Long walk around a nearby estate then breakfast on the decking. Alfie and Nola wolfed into the warm waffles and Nutella. Delicious chocolatey faces smiled up at me. I wanted to lick them. The dogs got there before me. Ha ha.

Later, I prepared coffee and gleefully poured each new arrival a fresh cup including Rory who had caught a very early flight. The Sutherlands tiptoed around me. Apart from some quizzical glances nothing was actually said. Ben remained blissfully unaware. Case closed. Thank goodness.

Kenneth and Ben discussed the agenda for the next day. Annabelle, Rory and I listened. I kept shtum. My chum nodded approvingly. Rory raised a couple of concerns.

How far would they be expected to carry the coffin? ... A long way.

Would he be asked to say anything? ... Absolutely not.

Rory retired to his room. Work. We spent the day wandering around Enniskillen. The castle mainly and the town centre. It is pretty. A bit like St Andrews but on a loch rather than the sea. Annabelle was suitably impressed. She spent a small fortune on crockery in Houstons department store.

You can't go anywhere without someone calling out after Kenneth. He's such a likable person and the fact that he is a BIG employer in the area helps. Kenneth's great, great grandfather (maybe another great) was a casualty of the Highland Clearances. They were gifted weavers and quickly established themselves in County Fermanagh. The rest they say is history. Sutherland's is *the* biggest wholesaler in both Southern and Northern Ireland for carpets and soft furnishings. Ben took no interest in the business, unlike Carrie, it's in her blood. Hats off. She has firmly established Sutherland's in the Middle East. Huge accolade and huge turnover.

Don't know why I had to regurgitate that. Who else can I tell?

We dined at Carrie's in the evening. Another boat trip but only around the corner to the castle again. Another jaw dropping moment for my wee pal. Carrie and Dale have a luxury, three storey townhouse, a short walk from Portora Wharf. Stunning outlook over the water. Wouldn't be my choice. A tiny garden but impressive all the same. There are wrap around balconies on two of the levels. Had to laugh. Kenneth was merry yet still drove the boat back. Ben was no better. No alcohol laws on fresh waters. Salt yes. Fresh no. Where is the logic? They rely on integrity. Hhmmmm! At least, he insists on life jackets for everyone.

I had to retire early. Totally knackered. Ben and Annabelle tackled the Jacuzzi on the decking.

*

Calling it a day. I'm preparing a lentil dhal for Annabelle for her dinner this evening and an aubergine moussaka for tomorrow. I'll take the extra moussaka to Alderburn. Doubt Colin will want my vegetarian muck. His choice. I'm driving now. So much easier and no chance of Colin following me.

# TWENTY-SEVEN

## *Ruby's Journal*

**Friday 3rd May. Annabelle's flat.**

Got to the flat early. Been listening to the breakfast slot all morning. I'm gutted. JJ has invited Jemma Courtney to host the show with him. Today, she is guesting only. Next week will be the big launch. Sly Si was on last week but there was way too much tension. Like two bucks vying for the best lines. It was cringe worthy. But another female? I've cried all morning. I know it's stupid but for a few delusional weeks, I secretly hoped that one day I would turn up (as you obviously) and JJ and I would just click and I would be back on the radio as if I had never been away.

Ah well. At least this diary is an outlet for all my negativity. Helps to keep me focussed.

\*

The Interment: **Friday 19th April**

There was no church service only a small gathering in the house for those who were unable to make Edinburgh. Forty turned up. Formal black. No colour.

Then a short drive to that cold fucking lonely place on Tempo Road, where I would have to leave you or me behind.

When Ben was called to take a cord, he had the blank stare

of the condemned man inching towards the gallows. Please don't topple in, I prayed. Same for Dad and Rory. As the coffin dipped out of sight, I felt as if I was being slowly sucked into an enormous plughole. Incomprehensible and totally terrifying. I was sure it was the end for me and I didn't want a double whammy for Ben. The mother-in –law copping it at his wife's funeral. I held my breath...until Annabelle rubbed my back. The sky and clouds raced towards my face as I fought to reach fresh air. I hit the bends. Carrie and Annabelle had to prop me up. The rest was a blur. Thank God the kids had remained at Caithness House.

Back at Kenneth's and Margaret's, I confined myself to a comfy patio chair, staring out to Lough Erne. Only immediate family had returned to the house. Margaret had hosted a proper wake the week before. Kind faces enquired if I was alright. I nodded accordingly. I remained in a strange vacuum for most of the day. Only the kids managed to penetrate it. I didn't want anyone else in. Not even Ben.

'All right Mum?' asked a concerned Rory for the umpteenth time, wrapping a blanket around my shoulders. Dad loitered nervously behind him.

I smiled or at least I tried to.

It was only when Alfie asked me to play snakes and ladders (his was dinosaurs and trees) that the barrier gently lowered. His giggling was infectious as was Carrie's Lara. Eventually, I was coaxed in to having a G&T. I stuck to one. Didn't want a repeat of the first night.

It was good to see Ben smile, laugh even. Annabelle was a tonic. Always is. Ben looked tall again. They were flicking through and sharing mobile footage of me. I could hear my voice booming over everyone else. Jeezuz, I was loud. Every so often Nola and Alfie would muscle in to see what they were looking at. Ben had needed to be in Enniskillen. Near his family. I could see that.

'You look better, pet.' It was Kenneth. 'Been a long day. A long month.' He took my hand. 'This will sound rich considering what you are going through...but will you keep an eye on them.'

He was staring at Ben and the kids. I willed myself not to cry. Difficult to smile with clenched lips. I hope I looked sincere.

No boat trip that evening. No one was in the mood plus the kids were whacked. Alfie had dark circles under his eyes and Nola had developed that monotonous 'I need my bed' whinge. She climbed on to my knee and wound her arms around my neck.

'Bogie Jim and Bogie Joe, please.'

I looked at Ben. He picked her up and walked off. 'You coming, granny?' he asked.

I had to pinch myself. Ben was actually allowing you (me) to put the kids to bed. I traipsed behind him downstairs to the bedroom area. The kids were in one room and Ben was sleeping in our room (the one that used to be ours. We even kept spare clothes in those rooms). Alfie was in the Jack and Jill bathroom cleaning his teeth. I settled down on one bed with Nola then Alfie cosied up with Ben in the other.

'Take your dress off granny. No outdoor clothes allowed,' she admonished.

My fault. My rules. Ben had already stripped down to his boxers. No scruples. I tried to distract her.

'Please granny. Mummy doesn't like it.'

I knew my silk robe would be hanging behind our bedroom door and I tentatively requested if I could wear it. Ben squirmed but Alfie had already bolted to fetch it. Awkward. However,

Ben relented. I nipped into the bathroom to change. It felt strange wearing it. Deceitful somehow but strangely comforting. Properly attired, we snuggled in.

Last time, we had left Bogie Jim and Bogie Joe tangled up on the back of a sheep that was about to be sheered. The kids loved to control the story and they love to use family names. Kenneth was the horse and Carrie the fat, orange pig. So funny. We giggled at that.

They went out like a light. I lay and listened to Ben's chest rising and falling. Gently up. Gently down. I knew it so well. He had definitely drifted off yet had denied it when his mother challenged him later. I could have lain there all night listening to the three of them breathing.

Ben had agreed to have a drink with Kenneth, Dale, Dad and Rory at the Killyhevlin Hotel. Honestly. You could walk it in twenty minutes but it's less than five by boat. It's the only way.

The upstairs was pleasantly quiet when I returned. Still in my robe and with my funeral clothes rolled into a tight bundle. Carrie had taken her brood home and Annabelle was emptying the dishwasher while Margaret put things away. I loved that beautiful open-plan house. Not as much as Dick Place but I suppose it always felt like a luxury bolt hole and to be fair to Margaret, she loved to fuss over us.

It was Annabelle who suggested we have our last night in front of the telly in the apartment. Margaret said she would watch T.V. in her bedroom where she could listen for the kids. Butterflies in my stomach kicked off. What would I say? It had to be that night. I might not get another chance.

How Annabelle didn't suss that something was up, I don't know? I was so jumpy.

'A wee wine, Rachel? I put a couple of bottles in the fridge earlier.'

I swallowed and nodded.

I changed into my jammies and Annabelle into hers. The wines were poured and she began flicking through Netflix.

'Anything you fancy?'

'A wee game,' I said.

# TWENTY-EIGHT

## *Ruby's Journal*

'What kind o' game?' Annabelle was bemused.

'A how well do we know Ruby game,' I spluttered.

I hadn't planned to say that but once I had suggested it, I found myself folding and tearing sheets of blank paper from one of the kitchen drawers.

I set a pile in front of Annabelle and one in front of me. I couldn't find any proper pens but there were some felt tips. I chose red (matched my jammies) and handed Annabelle a green one (no match, her pjs were canary yellow). A couple of cushions were retrieved from the sofa and we faced each other over the coffee table, legs crossed. Tops of the pens slapped on to the table like we were placing bets. I have to admit I was as nervous as hell. It could have gone tits up.

'I'll go first. Date of birth?' I asked.

Annabelle scribbled her answer and turned the postcard scrap over. She smiled, ever so satisfied.

I wrote my date and placed it upright on the table. 5.7.84.

'Boom!' squealed Annabelle as our cards matched.

More banal questions followed. Favourite colour. Favourite bands. When we started school. Date of my first period. Blah. Blah. Our answers were the same. Then I upped the game.

Who was my first serious snog?

Who did I lose my virginity to? Annabelle eyeballed me. But wrote the answer.

When did I go on the pill? A 'not sure if she should say' expression on her face.

What was my most embarrassing moment?

'What to pick?' she giggled.

We both wrote when I farted on my first date with Ben. He said I sounded and smelled like a hippopotamus. When the hell had he ever met a hippo? We erupted.

'Another one,' I urged.

She wrote, when I peed my pants at Nero's nightclub.

The four of us (girls) had been bouncing to the music. I suddenly needed to go but there was a huge queue at the bogs. Libby and I escaped through a fire exit but as we tried to find a discreet place in the street, I peed myself giggling. I had to throw my knickers in the bin.

'They cost a fortune from Secrets,' we screeched in unity.

'What were we dancing to... no... let me guess.' she squeaked.

Annabelle was gobsmacked as I quickly derailed her and shouted the answer. 'Don't Cha, Pussycat Dolls.'

'Now write down. Who did Ruby cheat with when she first started going out with Ben?'

I was desperate to recall incidents that only she and I knew.

'Em. How did you know about that?' she quizzed. 'That's a closely guarded secret. Even now.'

I urged her to write down the name.

'Did Ruby actually tell you? God, Mrs M. Please don't even joke about it wi Ben.'

I only did it because I had thought Ben had two timed me and I wanted to hurt him. Gaz was his Maître De. Turned out that Gaz was as desperate to keep his job as I was to keep my nasty little dalliance from his boss.

Gaz MacDonald. Snap!

'Oooooh, let's leave it there. Something light hearted me thinks,' and Annabelle leaned on the table and stretched over for the remote.

'Aww humour me. Two more. Only two. I promise.' I shuffled the remainder of the blank pieces. I dished out two to my bestie and two to me. 'Oookaaay. Write down in Euros what you had to pay the taxi driver after those two creeps from Liverpool lied about the last bus back to Magaluf.'

A very lucky escape. I was trembling thinking about what could have happened to us. We ended up in a hotel room in Santa Ponsa at two in the morning with the creeps and four other lads who were smashed out of their brains. They were baying for a gang bang. We legged it when Annabelle pretended she needed the loo. We took those stairs two at a time. From the fifth floor! I nearly broke my ankle clattering along the deserted esplanade in my heels. Had to take them off.

Twenty-Four Euros. I put my answer down first.

The dubious driver doubled the fare but we would have paid anything.

24 euros.

'Shane and Thomas,' I gloated. 'Thomas O' Malley you called him. The alley cat. We looked over our shoulders for the rest of the week terrified in case we bumped into them. You said you would never again go out with a guy who deemed it acceptable to wear a football shirt on a date.'

There were hundreds of them. Celtic supporters. They had invaded Santa Ponsa.

'Nah!' she sounded uneasy and adjusted her glasses. 'How the hell did you ken that?'

'Before I give an explanation, ask me a question that only you and Ruby would ever know the answer to.' I came across as a touch aggressive but I didn't want to lose her.

She jumped up, banging her knee in the process. 'Sorry, Rachel but I'm no indulging you. Ben warned me about your... personality change. You're scaring the shit oot o' me.'

I grabbed her wrist. 'Please, do this one thing,' I pleaded. 'Something that only you two would know. Even if it's totally trivial.'

She wrenched her arm from my hand. 'Nope. Sorry. No can do. I loved Ruby. We were like sisters... but she was a blabber mouth. Especially with a drink. She couldn't help herself.' Annabelle rubbed her face. I could tell she was deep in thought behind those hands and specs. It's what she does.

'I couldn't agree more but PLEASE. Think of one thing that you know that Ruby would NEVER tell anyone. Never ever.'

'I'm sorry, Mrs M. I'm really tired. I'm going to bed.' She filled a pint glass with water and precariously carried it to her bedroom door.

'Tenth of September 2003,' I blurted

Annabelle's legs buckled. She held on to the handle of the door. She half turned. Water splashed down the front of her yellow top. The colour really did drain from her face. With her long dark hair, she looked like a ghost. She said nothing. That look of disgust and contempt. It was dreadful.

I barely whispered, 'It was a Wednesday. We were supposed to be going to Glasgow but...'

Her hand shot up. Palm facing me. 'Don't say it... I'm begging you.' She tentatively edged away from the door and balanced on the arm of the chair. I was still on the floor. 'I can't believe Ruby would tell someone that.' And she started to cry.

I crawled on my hands and knees and knelt in front of her. I had been so anxious to unburden myself that I would have raked up anything to convince her. Suddenly, I was afraid to say the words. I held her hands in mine. She was freezing.

'Look at me. Tell me honestly. Do you truly believe that Ruby would ever have divulged that to anyone? Especially to her mother.'

She shook her head. Her shoulders heaved and shuddered.

'Not on her life. Not on Alfie and Nola's life.' I took a deep breath. 'I know what everyone has been saying about me. Nut job. Trying to persuade anyone else who would listen that I was Ruby. Post traumatic stress or whatever. Well, I'm going to let you be the judge.' I had to get a cushion for my knees. You are not good at kneeling.

'I'm not going to talk about it. THAT. I won't say it.' I promised her but I needed to point out other things that were pertinent to that day. 'You bought a black hoodie and trackie bottoms from that cheap sports shop in Tranent High Street. You said that after that day you would dump them in the nearest skip as you would never be able to wear them again. No reminders, you said. I agreed to do the same. I wore an old pair of grey jogging bottoms and a pink sweatshirt. The next day, I chucked everything into a skip at the back of my dad's shop. Even your canvas shoes. Who else would know that, Annabelle?'

'I dunno.' She shrugged. 'Do you think I've been punished for making that decision?'

'You?' I said. 'Who would ever punish you?'

'God.'

'No. Whoever, whatever is out there spared you that agony? Mother Nature intervened and took it out of your hands.'

We sat for a while, both revisiting that terrifying day.

'Remember when we were in primary five?' I pitched in. 'We stole a packet of mints from Mrs Munro's bag. Then about a week later we took a pound coin each from her purse.'

'She was a crabbit bitch,' exclaimed my wee pal. 'She deserved it.'

'Yeah, but poor Jimmy Latto got the blame. His dad battered 'im. We were too scared to confess after that. My mum would have gone ape shit.'

'Jimmy Latto. Whatever happened to him?' She was coming round.

'Married an extremely rich cougar in L.A. So I was told. A kept man. He went out on a holiday visa and hasn't come back. If he flies back to Scotland, they'll no let him back in again.'

'He wasn't that good looking. Had a big nose.'

'Big nose. Big dick,' I chuckled. We both did.

Annabelle sat up straight. 'Be honest. How do you know all this?'

'Cos I'm me. Ruby Roo. Or as you liked to tease, Ruby Roo, drag race princess.'

'I'm not convinced. Maybe... just maybe, Ruby let the cat out of the bag.'

I could feel the anger bubbling. 'NO! Absolutely not. I swear on my kids' lives, I would never divulge what happened to you in 2003. How would anyone else know what we were wearing? It was only important to you and me. And Gaz MacDonald? Could you imagine what Ben would think of me? Even now after all this time. And Thomas O'Malley? Okay, the girls probably could recount that one... but to my mum? I might have mentioned stealing from Mrs Munro but not the other stuff.'

'Aarrrghhhh!' She ruffled her hair roughly with her hands. 'I want to believe you but it's not possible.'

It was my turn to cry. Oh aye, still had plenty on the tearometer to use up. 'I don't want it to be true either. Look at me. Stuck in my mother's body for fuck's sake. Do you think that Ben would take me seriously looking like this?' I swept my hands over my hair and the rest of my body. (Sorry Mum but it was a fact.) 'I'll NEVER be with Ben again. I can't be with the kids. I can't go back to the station. I don't sound like me. No matter how hard I try. I don't have any money. Anywhere to stay.'

'You own your house in Alderburn.' She was only trying to be kind.

'It's my mum's house, Annabelle. And that fucking twat. He is a nightmare. Why in God's name would I put myself through that?'

'He is a bit of a twat,' she agreed.

'Mum came to my house that horrible day for a Mother's Day treat. You recommended The Copper Bowl. You booked it for me and sent me the booking code and reminded me there was a free glass of prosecco for mums. You were going to go to that new place in North Berwick on the Sunday with your stepmum and granny for afternoon tea and you were miffed that your Auntie Doreen had invited George. It was supposed to be women only. What grown man plays BitFit games on his mobile phone? Bell-end, you said.'

We both laughed.

'God, Bella-Anne. I could go on and on. I don't know what

more I can say to convince you. Honestly? I feel like throwing myself under a bus. Or swimming down to the bottom of that loch where no one will find me. Wrapped up in reeds. At least I'll be here with Mum. But then the two of us will be gone and Alfie and Nola will have no one.' More tears.

'NO. No, no, no. Don't think like that?'

'Then tell me,' I simpered. 'If you woke up in hospital one day and realised that you were in your stepmother's body, what would you do to convince me that it was you? Because I'm at a loss.'

She took an eternity. Eventually, and it was a drawn-out eventually, she spoke,

'Same as you probably.'

'Exactly.'

We must have exchanged memories for the next two hours at least. No wine. Only coffee (decaf).

'Right. Bed time,' she yawned.

I tidied the coffee table and washed our glasses and cups. Annabelle waited. I headed for my bedroom door.

'Hey,' she cried. 'Where are you going?'

Ever since we were little, if we stayed over at each other's houses and there were no men present, we always shared our beds.

'Don't you dare put your cold feet on me. And keep to your own side. Half way line.'

She drew an imaginary line down an imaginary bed. She hates having her space invaded.

At long last, someone believed me. I knew she would.

# TWENTY-NINE

*Ruby's Journal*

**Saturday 20th April. The day we returned from N.I.**

As I neared Carberry Crescent, despair engulfed me.

'You okay, Rachel?' Dad drove me back from the airport so that Annabelle didn't have to. Pointless, he had said and it was true.

'It's not easy,' I confessed. 'For me or Colin. I can't remember anything about our lives together. Honestly, I'm shit scared of him.' Tears raced down my face but decided to cut out the dramatics.

Up until then, our conversation had focussed on the funeral and Ben and the kids. Dad took my hand.

'For fuck's sake, Rach, yer trembling. I dinnae ken what to say. Would you like me to come in?'

'It'll only make him worse,' I said.

'For what it's worth,' Dad said, 'Rory thinks that Colin's a decent guy. It cannae be easy for him either. You two are good the gether. Don't push it. Gie him a chance, eh?'

Dad was only trying to humour me. Very frustrating. I did suggest that he could give me a call in a couple of hours to make sure I was still in one piece. Think that spooked him – the thought of me being cut into pieces!!! Dad insisted on carrying my bags to the front door. I called out to an empty lobby that 'it was only me' when I turned the key. Half expected it to be locked. There was no response. But boy, when Dad shouted his goodbyes, Colin sprinted out of the kitchen and stumbled out the door and on to the doorstep.

'Colin,' shouted dad and he shook his hand. 'Good to see you. Sorry you couldnae make Enniskillen. Neither could Patricia. Look after her (he motioned to me), she's had a rough few days.'

Poor Dad. He had no idea that he had stoked the fire. When he mentioned Patricia, Colin's nostrils flared. Practically flapped.

'Will do. Will do.' Was all that Colin could manage.

He stood with my bags in his hands until Dad's car pulled away. He had a washed-out grey tracksuit on. Must have felt dull and dowdy next to Dad,

'I'm no yer bloody lackey,' he growled and launched my bags up the hall.

Here we go, I sighed. The onslaught began.

No Patricia. How convenient.

How long had it taken for Rob to get into my knickers?

No doubt that lot encouraged it. (As if that would actually happen).

Giggling behind his back.

Did we shag on the boat?

I did remind him that we had all been at a funeral. And that Rob was married. And that I had no feelings for him in that kind of way. Nor him for me (you).

'Look at ye. Mutton dressed as lamb. (I was wearing jeans and a white shirt and trainers). You're right. Why would Rob try it on with a pathetic, fat whore like you when he has Patricia at home?' He was full of rage. 'I should have been there. As your husband!!'

He rushed to my holdall and started to shake everything out onto the floor.

'What are you doing? You'll break things.' There wasn't a lot to break... but still.

'What's this?' He held up an expensive bottle of wine that Carrie had given to me. She had given one to Annabelle too. 'Why is it wrapped up in your clothes? To hide it from me?'

'It's for you,' I shouted. 'From Kenneth.' Didn't know where that came from but I had hoped it would placate him.

'That's my consolation prize? A measly bottle of wine. Well, you can shove it.'

He plonked it on your console table and made a grab for my handbag. I held on with every ounce of strength I had. Couldn't risk him finding my purse (with all my money) or confiscating my phone.

'PLEASE, STOP IT!' I was bouncing off the walls as he tried to wrestle it from my grip.

The doorbell rang.

Whoever it was, allowed it to drone on. Colin staggered to the door. It was Dad. All agog. He had to have heard the commotion.

'Rob?'

'Colin?' Dad stared at the mess on the floor then at me. 'Rachel?'

'Welcome to my world,' announced Colin. 'Not two seconds through the door and all this chaos.' God, he was calm.

I began to laugh. A laugh that came across as erring on hysterical.

'That was NOT me,' I insisted. But guess what? Dad didn't look convinced. 'He accused us, you and me, of sleeping together. In Enniskillen.' My finger was centimetres from Colin's nose.

Colin shook his head. His squint eyes and tight smile were squashed together – resembled a bulldog. 'I merely asked how the two of you got on. There was no hint of impropriety. She hit the roof.'

'LIAR,' I screamed. 'You fucking lying shit!'

Colin shrugged. Resignation written all over him.

'Who do you believe, Dad (meant to call him Rob)? Him or me?'

'You left your jacket in my car,' he said. His lack of empathy said it all.

'Thanks a bunch,' I snarled sarcastically and snatched it from him. 'And thank you so much, ROB, for assessing my situation. It's so reassuring to know that you have my back.'

At that precise moment, I was more angry with Dad than I was with Colin. I left them whispering on the doorstep while I gathered up my belongings scattered on the floor. I tossed them into my bedroom (the pink one) and bolted the door. Was aware that my sides didn't ache as much.

When Dad left, Colin chuckled and whistled like the cat that had got the cream.

'How does it feel, Rachel?' he cried as he prowled up and down the hall. 'Your whole family thinks you're off your bloody heid. They're all talking about you. Well now you know how it feels.'

I double checked the bolt.

Annabelle got it all first. Then I regurgitated the whole nasty episode to Lisa who threatened to drive over to Alderburn and then to Dad's.

I emptied my purse and stuffed some of the money under the mattress, behind the wardrobe, in my boots again. Small amounts here and there. Suddenly, I was bursting for a pee and gasping for a coffee. No way would I have contemplated going to the bathroom. I can't believe I did it but I rigged up a plastic bag in a shoe box. Didn't have to use it. The phone rang.

I put my ear to the door to listen. I could hear Colin bleating then his footsteps stopped at my door.

'Rachel,' he grunted. 'Rob wants to talk to you.'

'Minute,' I shouted. Then I pretended to phone Auntie Lisa.

I walked out simulating a conversation. Colin wholeheartedly believed it as he called out to Lisa that there was no need for this. Once I confirmed it was indeed Dad, I hung up.

'Yes?' I was very dry.

'Rach, it's me. Look I'm sorry I scarpered earlier. You okay?

'Would you care?'

He cleared his throat. 'Lisa and Brian called me. Put me in the picture about what happened before.'

'Do you believe it?' The long silence confirmed it. Probably not. My laugh was laced with contempt.

'Look Rachel, I heard you. Screaming and cursing at Colin. When did you ever swear like that? It's not you. You're not yourself.'

Well, he got that right.

'You heard what you wanted to hear,' I snapped. 'And you saw what you wanted to see. I'm so disappointed. I expected more.'

'I know it hasn't been easy. Brian said they said some vicious stuff when he was there.'

'Vicious? He had me by the throat.' I stared directly at Colin as I said it.

The vulture jumped in, sharing the mouthpiece space with me. 'She's the violent one, just ask the police.' His forehead was grinding into the side of my temple. I turned my back on him.

'Sorry Rach, I don't want to make matters worse for you.'

'A bit late for that.'

Dad mumbled some kind of apology and hung up.

Colin was desperate to find out what had been said.

'Why did he phone?'

'Guilt maybe. Patricia wants to call me later. That'll be interesting.' I shrugged. She didn't but I always felt (still do) that he had to believe that others might contact me at any moment.

Returned to my room with coffee, snack and plastic mixing bowl. Saved me trekking to the bathroom in the middle of the night. When my ribs have fully healed, I will definitely be tackling your pelvic floor muscles. Way too slack. I'm never away from the toilet.

Was about to nudge the door with my bum, when he had to get that last dig in.

'Nobody's taken in by you, Rachel. Not Ben. Not Rory and certainly not your ex-husband. Time to pack in the act.' He forced a false hearty laugh.

I slammed that door but you know me I couldn't let him have the last word. 'You may have won the battle but not the fucking war.' His quote from before.

'It's called annihilation,' he sneered.

Honestly Mum, the way he said it. Full of menace.

Undeterred, I had to lash out. 'You are a bully. A nasty bully. Not big enough to take on a man so you pick on a vulnerable woman.' At that, I started to cry. I was fed up with it all.

A floorboard creaked. He was directly opposite me, outside my door. I could feel his breath penetrate the thickness of the wood. His tone shifted.

'This is silly, Rachel. You and me, like this. This is no how we work. Come on love. Let's get back to how things were. Let me look after ye as I've always done.'

I wanted the hostility to slow down. It was tiring. 'That's the point, Colin. I don't remember how we were,' I whined. 'I didn't ask for this memory problem. It's a horrible predicament...for everyone. But you haven't exactly been patient or supportive.'

'It's been worse for me. I feel rejected. You huvnae given me a chance to be yer husband.' The frustration was creeping in.

'I can't. I don't know you. I'm sorry but you're a stranger to me.'

He thumped the door. 'You must remember something or are ye enjoying all the attention? The doctors said your memory would return once you were home. Familiarity they said.'

'Well, they got it wrong.'

'Just open the door, Rachel. We can talk properly.'

I tried to negotiate with him. 'We can talk tomorrow morning when we are both calmer.'

'Open the fuckin door!'

'Please don't force me to call Rob. We can speak in the morning.'

Not what he wanted to hear. 'Rob? Fuckin Rob? He dumped you. Found something better. What the hell do you want to call that useless bastard for?'

'Because he was my husband and I was married to him for nearly thirty years.'

He body slammed the door. Nearly took it off its hinges.

'BITCH!' he screamed. 'You are RACHEL GORDON. And don't you forget it.'

# THIRTY

*Rachel's flat in Portobello: Tuesday 7th January 2020*

Rachel woke with a start. Pools of sweat had gathered under the flaps of her breasts and in the small of her back. Her first thought was Colin. Subconsciously, her legs and arms flailed beneath the duvet searching the space beside her. Empty. She couldn't work out where she was. The squawking and screeching of seagulls outside the apartment helped her to readjust. Portobello. Ruby's flat. Relieved, she melted into the deep mattress again. The rumble of thunder could be heard far off. She tucked the duvet tight around her.

She'd had very disturbing dreams. Mainly about Colin and Ruby but Ruby was always a little girl in them and Rachel was trying to rescue her; climbing on to wardrobes and kicking holes in ceilings to haul Ruby up through them or precariously balancing on planks of scaffolding as they made their escape. It had been exhausting.

Rachel admonished herself. Why the hell had she allowed Colin to have so much power over her? And poor Ruby bore the brunt of it. Rob was no surprise. He could project manage huge building developments (for the electrics) and the men in his employ yet he was hopeless with women and family affairs. Looking back, he lacked the balls to kick Patricia into touch. Rachel had made it too easy for him – she hadn't put up a fight. At least Rob was never abusive; either verbally or physically.

She made herself a coffee. She couldn't believe it was almost quarter to ten. It had been an awfully long time since she had risen so late in the day. She switched on to STV and was pleased to find that Lorraine was still airing. Mark had bagged some fantastic bargains in the sales. She liked Mark. Normally she would watch with envy as he enthusiastically introduced each model, especially the older ones, knowing that his collaborations were off limits. But now, after having salivated over all the clothes in Ruby's wardrobe, she wondered if she could put together some of his suggestions. Lucky Lorraine, to have Mark's advice on tap and of course the gorgeous Doctor Hilary.

There was Philly in the fridge and Rachel slathered it on a bagel. No Colin to chastise her for wasting the cheese. She stepped on to the balcony for a moment but quickly retreated back into the warmth of the lounge and to the remainder of her bagel and coffee. A gale-force wind had whipped up since yesterday and heavy rain clouds hovered slap bang in the middle of the Forth. They were heading her way.

She double checked the contents of the fridge and their best before dates. A tub of olives that had been opened was thrown into the white metal pedal bin, in the cupboard, beneath the sink but everything else seemed fine. She would have spicy parsnip soup for lunch and an omelette for tea. She wasn't in the mood for anything fancy. There were plenty crisps and biscuits to snack on. She had spied them last night as she was fathoming the layout of the kitchen cupboards and drawers.

Whether it was because of the proximity of the sea or the fact that Ruby's flat was an unknown entity, it made Rachel feel as if she were on holiday. The apartment had a holiday feel to it; albeit it an upmarket one.

Hailstones battered the patio windows. They were bloody

huge. Rachel hoped the glass wouldn't crack. Surely, they could withstand the intensity? Chairs from the balcony below Ruby's were dragged in the wind; clattered and smashed against something – the railings probably. She checked there was nothing on Ruby's that could cause damage. A green tarpaulin was draped over some furniture. The legs were peeking out the bottom and the structure was strapped to the balcony railing. Seemed secure enough. Rachel put all notions of going out for a newspaper aside. No point in getting soaked.

After replenishing her coffee, and resisting the temptation of a chocolate biscuit, she curled up on the sofa with Ruby's journal. Showering could wait. It was not as if she was expecting visitors. Plus, the nurse had suggested she should wait at least 48 hours before attempting to wash her hair in case her stitches opened. Another few hours would make little difference. When the doctor had asked when she had last had a tetanus jag, she hadn't a clue.

She brushed her arm. It still ached.

# THIRTY-ONE

## *Ruby's Journal*

**Wednesday 24.4.19.**

Nothing much happened on the Sunday. I spent most of the day at Auntie Vera's. Same with the Monday. She has been great. I turn up at her door and she smiles. No awkwardness. No questions. I'll always be indebted to her. I think Colin knew where I had been slinking off to but after Saturday's confrontation, he had said very little. The fact that people kept checking up on me helped.

All day Sunday, Monday and Tuesday, I trawled through the contents of the locked grey box checking everything that was in it. Yep. I broke in. Wasn't hard. A three-year-old could have forced it. Switched all the documents with old newspapers and placed the box back in your sideboard. Thought I'd been detected though. Colin had gone out for his usual constitutional hike but nipped back for his gloves as I sat shaking the contents on to my bed. The dresser door was wide open as I had intended to return the box once I had completed my subterfuge. If he had gone into the living room, he'd have noticed it immediately. I sat listening to his every move. It was a long minute. The second he had gone, I scurried to the living room to shut that door.

Found your passport and driving licence. All the mobile contracts were there too. Colin's was all singing and dancing. Bloody typical. Bloody cheek.

He had no idea I had ever emptied the box, although, he must have known I had read everything or I wouldn't have been able to alter/cancel the direct debits and standing orders.

After devouring the information in your insurance policies (at Auntie Vera's), I intended to change them all but only after your own account had been set up. Had you two never heard of switching providers? I saved you a small fortune. I'm not joking. Well over £800 for the year. I thought Colin was the type to be well up on all that stuff. Forgot. He wasn't paying for it!! A quick call to your lawyer was required. I had to make sure that that slimy sod had no claim on your house. (He didn't) Life assurance policies were also on my radar.

I had an appointment with your bank in Haddington. 10.30am on Monday. To open an account solely in your name. I'd missed the boat in having your salary paid in to it but as soon as it appeared in your joint one, I transferred it. Colin and his entourage would no longer be subsidised by me. Plus, I wanted to have your name taken off the joint account. The balance in which was only eighty-three pounds. Not much if you needed money in a hurry. Where did it go? That's rhetorical, by the way. It was in black and white. You footed the bill for EVERYTHING. Nearly all your bills and utilities were paid by monthly direct debit. Good budgeting, mum, but what did Colin pay for? He must get benefits of some kind. You paid for Claire and Jade's mobile contracts. What the fuck for? Taking the piss, that's what for. Well, no more. The bank of Rachel Gordon was firmly closing.

At one point, the business manager poked his nose in and asked if Colin should be informed of my intentions. He spoke about my recent tragedy and that Colin had popped in to warn them that I might appear confused. He appeared to know you.

A youngish guy with short, blond hair (looked dyed). I asked him if I looked confused. NO? He emphasised he had a duty of care. He could stick his duty of care. I left him under no illusion what I would do if he breached my privacy. Backed down.

Bless you, Mum, you'd opened junior savers accounts for Jack, Alfie and Nola. Deposits had dwindled since February 2018. I'm assuming Colin put his oar in. If I needed to, I would be able to withdraw those savings. Haven't so far but good to know.

Anyway, I asked the clerk if I could take my name off the joint account. Not without consulting with Colin BUT get this, I could close the account without informing him. Either or survivor it's called. I made out that the two of us wanted to have our own accounts and save jointly in another. Don't think I raised suspicion. AND once an account is closed, the direct debits don't have to be honoured by the bank. Bonus for us. Meant that Colin, Claire and Jade would have to pay for their own mobile phones. Plus, smart bastard Colin had the electricity and gas bills in his name only. Well, he could bloody well continue to pay for them. AND even bigger bonus, he was on YOUR insurance for your car as a named driver as was Claire. No insurance of his own. Guess what? Correct. Removed both their names. He would no longer be legally insured to drive your car. Direct Line was informed that no one else would be allowed to drive your car unless I added them to my insurance. Oh, the power. Felt so good.

WEDNESDAY – used a key to enter Annabelle's flat. Unbelievably exciting and an overwhelming sense of relief. I know, I use overwhelming all the time but there is no other word to describe what I have gone through, am going through. Nerve wracking maybe?

The weasel had no idea that I had a bolt hole in Edinburgh. I will always be grateful to Auntie Vera and to Lisa but I couldn't impose myself on her long term. She is YOUR best pal and I needed mine.

I felt stronger. My ribcage didn't ache as much. I could walk further, a lot further, before feeling washed out but most of all, for the first time since the accident I had motivation. Positivity. A sense of purpose. My biggest priority, after solving your money problems, was focussing on rebuilding a relationship with Ben – mainly for the kids. While we were in Enniskillen, he never allowed me to be alone with the kids. Always encouraged someone else to accompany us.

I was realistic. Even if Ben were ever to believe that I, Ruby Martin (or Sutherland as he liked to emphasise) truly existed, we could never be THAT way again. Although I dreamt about it every night (and conjured up scenarios in my deluded daydreams constantly).

I walked around the flat and smiled. I dug out my notes from my handbag and wrote that first letter to you. Did you notice the handwriting? I was shaking, I was so nervous. I bought the notebook from Paperchase. I love that beach scene. Typical me, don't you think?

\*

It's bizarre. Writing to you and not knowing if you will ever read it but it gives me huge comfort to unburden all my thoughts and worries to you. I feel you here beside me, guiding me. Oops, getting all sentimental.

I love you, Mum. I hope that wherever you are, you know that.

# THIRTY-TWO

## *Ruby's Journal*

My weepy waver is over (for a wee while). Procrastinated. Gave the flat a quick tidy. I'll scrub her bathroom later. Put champagne in the fridge. Well, it is a celebration. Was sorely tempted to have a wee sample of wine but reneged especially as I'm about to write about our binge last Friday.

*

**Saturday 27th April.**

Sore head. Too much alcohol. Actually, now realise it's too much for your body. Lightweight!! In the past, Annabelle and I could have sunk two bottles of wine each without blinking. After downing only two between us, I was slurring my words and reluctantly had to call it an evening. My bus wouldn't wait. Before I left, Annabelle phoned Ben, (gulp), and asked if we could take the kids out on the Sunday. Bloody hell. He only agreed.

I had arranged for Auntie Lisa to meet me at Carberry Crescent at noon. I had forewarned Colin the night before that I wanted a meeting with him and Claire to discuss my finances. If they weren't there, they could not blame me for not being kept in the loop. That caught his attention but I avoided answering the bombardment that followed.

I hadn't the courage to face Colin alone. Fortunately, Lisa was well up for it. When her white BMW cruised the corner, I sprinted out to meet her. Claire's car pulled up at the same time. Her jaw dropped to the floor when she clocked Lisa. She nearly knocked us over in her rush to overtake and clipe to her dad.

'Whit's this,' growled Colin, 'an ambush?'

I prepared coffees. The Gordons declined – again.

We three women sat at the kitchen table, less informal than the living room. Colin leant against the worktop, arms folded, suited and booted for a long country walk. Actually, he wasn't quite. I could see a white polo shirt peeking out from his green ribbed jumper. He had an air of bravado about him but we both knew he was bricking it.

I had chosen the navy, floral dress I'd bought in Asda. I had spent a lot of time on my make-up and hair. I was determined to look my best. Lisa was as elegant and effortless as ever: short green leather skirt with a pale green sweat shirt tucked in. Claire? Jeans. Grey, dull and bland. I actually felt sorry for her.

I launched in. I wasn't nasty, at least I tried not to be but there was no cushioning either. I placed my hands flat on the table.

'I've cancelled our joint account and set up my own. I transferred my salary into my account on Thursday then closed ours. I will take over the payment of most of the direct debits but not them all.' I blurted it out much faster than I had planned to.

Waited until it had sunk in.

'You can't do that,' wailed your man. 'The bank would've informed me.'

'I can and I did and they didn't have to,' I informed him. 'From now on, you three will have to pay your own mobile phones and sorry but you are no longer on my car insurance. Cancelled as from twelve noon today.'

'Dad! Say somethin,' demanded Claire.

The commotion had alerted Jade and she wandered through from the living room to find out what was going on.

'Your greedy granny has decided that she doesn't love you anymore. She's not going to pay for your phone.'

Poor wee Jade burst into tears. Lisa waded in.

'No. No. No. Nobody said anything about no longer loving anyone. Tell the girl how it is. You two have sponged off Rachel for the past two years. You've ground her down. Well, no more. Pay for your own bloody phone and your daughter's. She is YOUR responsibility. Not her granny's.'

Claire screamed and yelled for a couple of minutes. How unfair. You promised. Your idea. Not theirs. Thought you loved Jade as she certainly loves you. What were they going to do? When was the next monthly payment due? They needed more notice. You can imagine. Colin remained very quiet.

'Why?' he asked as if an explanation was required.

'Why?' said I. 'Because you are a nasty piece of work. You wouldn't give me money when I needed it. You deprived me of a bank card and my phone. There wasn't a smidgen of sympathy for Ruby. She is DEAD. And you couldn't give a fuck.' I looked at Jade. She was distraught and my cursing didn't help. I decided to choose my next words carefully. 'You told a blatant lie to the police. I could have been charged with assault when I had done nothing.' My voice was breaking up.

There was a long silence. I eyeballed Lisa and we understood that Colin would have to speak up next. We waited.

He staggered to the table and collapsed onto the spare kitchen chair. He overlapped his arms on the table and rested his head on them. Nothing was said but his shoulders were shaking. Not violently.

Jade and Claire scurried to his side. The three of them were cuddling and only two of them shed real tears.

Lisa shot me a 'don't be taken in' warning.

'Look what you've reduced him too,' whimpered Claire.

'I'm sorry,' he whispered. He repeated it another three times and each time was a teensiest bit louder than the previous simper.

Jade buried her face into her grandad's shoulder.

Lisa fired another dagger so I waited until the theatricals tailed off. Once he was calmer, I asked him,

'Sorry for what?'

I could hear the cogs whirring. What would he say? He sat up. Eyes totally dry and stared at the table.

'The accident floored me,' he said. 'I'll admit, when the doctor explained about your memory loss, I was terrified you wouldn't remember me, us.' He elongated a sigh and stretched the skin on his face downwards with the palms of his hands. Scary. An Edvard Munch portrait sprang to mind. (The one that looks like the Scream mask.) He continued, 'What if you couldn't remember how we met and or what we meant to each other. Okay, I apologise. I was impatient. Angry. Bitter. But only because I was desperate not to lose what we had.' (Maybe not all in that order but more or less what he delivered.)

Lisa laughed first. It was more of a guffaw. I pulled a bemused face.

Then he snarled at Lisa, 'Oh you can laugh. You were jealous of what we had.'

Auntie Lisa's turn. 'I wasn't jealous. Far from it. When Rachel met you at her night school, I was genuinely chuffed for her. She was happy. She was excited. But once you got your feet under the table, everything changed... for the worse.'

'Rubbish!' he yelled. 'She wasn't well. None of you wanted to admit it. You were happy to leave me to cope.'

Claire chipped in. 'Dad was struggling and none of you cared.'

'Rory cared,' I reminded them. 'Not only did he pay for my care but he funded a holiday in Spain for the three of you.'

'He did what?' gasped Lisa.

'Paid for them to go to Benidorm.'

'You can remember that,' scoffed Colin.

I kept my voice level. 'No, I can't, I'm afraid. Rory confessed that little gem when he visited me in hospital a few weeks ago.'

I scrutinised Colin in a way I hadn't done before. Huddled around your table, I wasn't frightened of him but understood that Lisa's presence had given me Dutch courage. He wasn't a big man. Probably underweight. Gran would say he had a lived-in face. A polite way of saying 'not very bonny' yet I could see how you might have found him attractive. Not that his hair helped. Curls of steel wool. He did have a presence about him though and I remember thinking that I had always assumed he was a learned man. Self-taught. Ben enjoyed his company. A mutual interest. His knowledge of East Lothian and Edinburgh walkways and cycling routes was impressive. He could be a bit gruff (his broad dialect didn't help) but then Dad could be like that too. Why had we never considered that he might be lazy? Happy to leech off you.

The way he was with me, Mum. From the very beginning, he was oppressive. Not kind or tolerant and that hadn't happened overnight. That was standard behaviour. His behaviour.

I imagined him settling into your home. Slippers and a mug of coffee. Smug and entitled. Belittling you until you believed you were to blame for his failings. I'm disgusted that I refused to see him for what he was. By condoning what he said about you, his distorted interpretation, I contributed to your unhappiness. I am so sorry.

'That is utter bollocks and you know it.' Didn't give him a chance to respond. 'Do you have a bank account, Colin?' I enquired.

No comment.

'You don't work so you must have a pension or benefits of some kind. You paid the heating from your account.'

More silence.

'You had access to everything of mine. My passport and driving licence were locked in a box, for God's sake.'

I had impressed on Lisa earlier that there would be no knee jerk reaction from me yet I could sense that I might be losing it. Change of tact.

'Let's be clear. If you want cooperation from me, I want to see your current bank account statements for at least the past six months and perhaps some sort of negotiation can begin. If not, I will fund nothing that I don't have to. You, on the other hand, will have to pay for gas and electricity as the account is in your name. I've cancelled Sky Sports. You can't drive my car and I will pay and prepare my own meals from now on. You can get your own.'

I reiterated that I didn't want a battle or a war but I did want respect from both of them and to feel safe in my own house.

His smirk was menacing. 'Coffee?' he asked Claire nonchalantly and rose to make it.

Lisa waited until I had packed an overnight bag. I walked around the house surreptitiously filming every room, talking quietly the whole way through. This was something I would do (if possible) every time I left Carberry Crescent. My little piece of evidence that all was intact when I left. I slipped Jade a tenner and told her I would always love her (that was for you). I hovered the camera over Colin and Claire. Both intact. Free from injury.

Still recording, 'Thank you for having this meeting with myself and Lisa. Please think about what we discussed. You've had full access to my personal details and banking. It's only fair that you share your income and outgoings with me. I look forward to continuing this amicably tomorrow.'

Nowt said to me. They replied goodbye to Lisa.

Head thrust forward, I marched out the door with dribbles of pee dampening my knickers.

# THIRTY-THREE

## *Ruby's Journal*

**Sunday 28th April.**

It's the first time I'd felt lonely. Really alone. Not sure if the adrenalin had kept me company (or alert) in Alderburn but there was nobody to talk to or to avoid in the BnB.

I stayed the Saturday night in Gifford: in my room all night with a sandwich, packet of crisps and the complementary coffee tray for sustenance. Not too far to drive back in the morning. I didn't want to intrude on Auntie Lisa as I might have needed a bed another night, another time. I had taken the car. A wee bit uncomfortable but okay for a short journey. It's my neck more than my ribs. After a very early breakfast (couldn't sleep), I wandered to one of our old family haunts down by the river. Fab play park nearby. So much choice. I don't know why we had never taken the kids there. I'd forgotten it was such a lovely spot.

I had dreaded seeing Colin again yet he said nothing when I returned. Never even acknowledged I was there. Seconds before I left to meet Annabelle, I enquired about his bank statements.

'Won't be happening,' was all he said.

'Suit yourself,' said I.

I took that to mean there was no way he wanted me to know how much money he received on a weekly/monthly basis. I surmised that he had a lot more cash than you had ever envisaged.

Crafty wee git. Well, let's see how long he could manage without you propping him up.

I parked your car around the corner from Pitt Street. No spaces near her property. Annabelle drove us to Dick Place in her wee Micra. As she had no child seats for my two, we would have to take the bus to the soft play centre. I made a mental note of checking out Halfords the following week.

Alfie and Nola were so happy to see me. Not nearly as ecstatic as I was. When I see them it's as if a golden glow envelops us. Not so my husband. Ben's greeting to me was lukewarm. A cuddle would have sufficed but, no, he flashes that tight – I'm-only-tolerating – you smile. God, he can be so rude. He was much more receptive to Annabelle. He kissed her affectionately on the cheek. Sometimes I forget that she was his friend long before I met him.

Nola's hair was a mess. All tangled and had more knots than Auntie Vera's cat. I scooshed some leave-in conditioner into it. It helped a little. She loves having her hair brushed. It was one of our bonding routines. She would do my hair and I would return the pleasure. Sometimes, in her hypnotic state, she would nod off. Not that Sunday. She was screaming in agony. It was one of the many tell-tale signs that Ben was not coping. The place was a bombsite.

'You know, Ben, I'm free every day. I'd love to help out with the kids and around the house. It wouldn't be a problem.'

'I'll think about it,' he said with very little conviction.

I decided not to push it.

Once rounded up, we headed to Minto Street, in Newington, for a bus. The kids were jumping. They hadn't been at the play centre for weeks. Both of them have a yearly pass as we are (were) there so often. Ben hadn't a scooby where their passes were. I had to pretend that I'd found them by accident, in the basket on our kitchen workshop. Where they have always been!!!!

The staff at Portobello know them so well. Both go to gymnastic classes on a Friday.

'Hi handsome boy,' shouted Mandy as we walked in. Well, he is. Alfie beamed at the compliment.

The minute we were in the cafe area, the kids kicked off their shoes and my two wee blondies were off. Nola followed Alfie like a puppy dog. Usually, he couldn't give a toss about her but on Sunday he waited for her to catch up and patted her hair and back a lot. God! He was genuinely looking out for her. My wee mannie being protective of his little sister. I was off again. Annabelle passed me the napkin from under her coffee cup. The last thing I wanted was for this to be a teary day out. The kids deserved to be surrounded in happiness and laughter.

Nola asked me to play with her. Alfie had spotted one of his nursery pals and poor Nola had been punted. I managed for a wee while but Annabelle had to take over. Funnily enough, it was sliding down the big chutes that was harder than scrambling over all the obstacles. Every time I landed at the bottom, a jolt travelled from my bum to my ribs. It stole my breath each time.

We had lunch and another short session before heading for the promenade as I had promised the kids an ice-cream from the café at the bottom of Bath Street. There was an old man watering his plants on his balcony in a block of smart new flats right on the promenade. Nola asked what he was doing and they chatted for ages.

It wasn't that warm but the kids insisted on a quick paddle. Annabelle and I were coaxed in too. The water was bloody freezing. I had to sprint up to the cafe for a quick pee. I grabbed fistfuls of paper and stuffed them into my bag for their feet.

I had my usual boring ice-cream; vanilla flavour. Annabelle and Alfie chose chocolate mint and Nola eventually plumped for strawberry. Four happy bunnies tucked into our cones sitting on the wall watching the world go by. The prom was packed. What a transformation in the last ten years. Portobello has a real buzz about it. A quick trip to the toilet and we headed up to the High Street for a bus. Day over. Too soon. Too short.

Then disaster. Honestly, you couldn't make it up. A fucking eejit on a skateboard (he was about fifty by the way) was exercising his dog. A totty teeny thing. Nola didn't realise the dog was on a lead (the length was far too long), she ran in between them and tripped over it, walloping her face off the ground. Blood gushed from her mouth and soaked her pink sweatshirt covering the white unicorn in red gunk. Instinctively, I scooped her up and ran all the way to the sports centre. There was bound to be a first aider. Poor wee munchkin had split the inside of her bottom lip.

'Always looks worse than it is.' First Aid man tried to reassure us. 'Best to check with A&E to be on the safe side.'

Mandy at reception called us a taxi. One arrived within minutes. Nola was chalk white. Alfie's frightened face was as pale as hers. Annabelle carried her out to the car. My strength had dissolved into jelly legs syndrome. Nola sat on my knee the whole way there. Alfie hugged my waist. It wasn't fair. They'd had enough drama lately. Annabelle contacted Ben. I was too scared. No blooming wonder. He went ape-shit.

The A&E department was quiet and Nola was seen quickly, thank goodness. Alfie waited with Annabelle. Nola was so brave and remarkably calm. Shock probably. She was to have a scan to make sure there was nothing untoward.

We could hear raised voices in the corridor. It was Ben. Knew it would be.

'What the hell happened?'

The nurse explained that as a precaution, Nola would require an x-ray to check the area around her mouth and nose. Her lip was twice the size and her wee nose was all scraped and bruised.

I began to stammer. No use. The palm of his hand was shoved close to my face.

'Forget it. Help ME with the kids? You can't be trusted to take them for a simple day out. Not happy that you destroyed Ruby's life, you want to ruin my daughter's too.'

Mum, it was like a sledgehammer to the soul. I wasn't even given a chance to defend myself.

'Just go,' he snarled 'and don't you dare wait for us.'

I don't know how I made it to the waiting area. It was like wading ankle deep in melted toffee, the floor tugged at every footstep. Annabelle rushed towards me mumbling her apologies as she wrapped her arms around me. Ben had ripped into her too. Hey, at least she was being allowed to remain with Alfie. It should have been me.

Don't know what other folk must have been thinking when they saw me. I was inconsolable. Once outside, I was flummoxed. What to do next? I leaned against a wall and dialled the only number that might come to my rescue.

'I'm so sorry to bother you. I'm outside A&E. Could you pick me up?' I hoped that through all the sobbing and nose wiping, I had made sense.

Fifteen minutes later, the smart black car swept into the pickup point. Jasper rolled down the window and with a sympathetic smile summoned me in.

I sunk into the big soft seat and began to cry. He pulled into a parking bay and let me wallow in self-pity until I was ready to speak.

'I can't thank you enough for coming. I didn't know who else to call.' More blowing and snot.

Not exactly true. Me, Ruby Martin, knew dozens of people who would have dropped everything and driven out to pick me up. But me as you? Not so easy. Jasper knew all about my memory loss so I didn't have to explain why a fifty-six-year-old woman had no one to turn to other than a stranger she had met on two occasions only. Although, he had texted me a few times since then.

'Where to?' he cajoled.

No way was he allowing me to drive back to Alderburn. I was in no fit state. Couldn't believe it when he said he would drive me home then return the following morning to take me for my car at Pitt Street.

'Are you sure?' I asked. 'Why?'

He shrugged. He had nothing else on. As we drove to East Lothian, I tried to work out how old he was. Amber Rose had to be ten years older than me so forty-five or thereabouts. He was older than her so he could have been around fifty. He was pretty fit for his age. Probably worked out and he was easy on the eye. He had that silver thing going on at the temples. I've always found that quite sexy.

He jerked his neck and stared right at me. 'Are you checking me out?' he chuckled.

I actually felt the heat flare up my neck and radiate from my face. I shook my head rapidly. Mortified.

'Sorry. I was trying to work out how old you are.' It sounded too coy and flirtatious even. Jings, what an idiot.

He just laughed. 'Had the big five O in December and you?

I coughed nervously and double checked my calculations. 'I'm fifty-six but if I'm honest, in my head I feel much younger.' Then I interjected quickly,' I know I don't look it but I'm working on it.' Sorry, Mum. Didn't mean to be derogatory.

'Personally, I've always been more interested in what someone is like in the inside.' He laughed heartily. 'Is that me being in touch with my feminine side?'

God, he chuckled at that for ages. I ended up joining in. Not sure if I was laughing at him or with him but it was a tonic at the end of a rotten evening.

All too soon, he pulled up at the front door. The curtains twitched so whoever was inside, had heard the car engine.

'Could you be ready for 7.30am? I have an airport pick up at 10am. I like to be early.'

'Oh, where do you park?' Had no idea why I asked that.

'Pals have the Park n Fly. Usually have a coffee with them.'

'That's handy.' WTF??? 'I'll be ready.' I smirked.

'First time I've seen you smile. Suits you. See you tomorrow.' He was so matter of fact; he threw me.

'Um yeh, great.' I fumbled with my seat belt. 'Tomorrow's fantastic.'

He gave a little toot and was gone.

My heart was thumping and my head was all over the place. Was he flirting with me? Or worse. Was I flirting with him?

Nah! I'd gotten it all wrong.

*

My hand is aching. Not used to holding a pen all day. Massaged it for ages and hasn't made a blind bit of difference. I can type much faster than I can write but don't want to switch now.

Looking forward to my first sleepover with my oldest (longest) friend. We can get absolutely bladdered without having to worry about the following morning as neither of us has anything to get up for. I've almost caught up with everything that has happened to me so far. The next time I write in my diary will be the last snippets of the past and hopefully years of a future.

Am I being too optimistic?

# THIRTY-FOUR

## *Ruby's Journal*

**Tuesday 7th May. Annabelle's flat.**

I'm going to try and bring you up to speed. Everything that's happened since Jasper dropped me off on Sunday evening (28th).

*

**Monday 29th April.**

I heard Jasper's car at 7.25am. Guessed he would be on time.

'That's yer fancy man outside,' yelped Colin.

'Don't be ridiculous.' I explained everything last night. 'Why do you have to be so ungracious all the time?'

'I'd've come up to the hospital in a taxi. I could've driven you home once we'd located the car. Nah, nah. Chauffeur man looks better for the neighbours.'

Honestly, does he not get it? One minute he is refusing to share his bank details (and his money) with me and the next he is offering to fork out for an expensive taxi fare. No way will he find out where Annabelle lives nor that she is giving me sanctuary.

Then with another shift in gear, he asked as casual as you like, 'What time will ye be back? I'm making a Thai green curry for tea. I thought we could eat together. Be civil for a change.'

The man is not right in the head. But neither am I.

'I'll be back for teatime. Let's see. Maybe. That might work.'

Playing along with him might be beneficial for me too.

Jasper opened the passenger door for me. He was impeccably dressed. Expensive grey suit, white shirt and a grey and pink tie. Not your typical chauffeur. In fact, he looked as if *he* was the businessman most likely to be collected at the airport. I felt significantly underdressed in my jeans and your green shirt and brown jacket. It fits so much better now. I can almost close it. Two corners away, he stopped the car.

'You can jump in the front,' he grinned.

I decided not to stay too long at Annabelle's. Just enough to catch up with writing and an obligatory tidy. We'd chatted for ages on Sunday night. Consoling me. Bless. She had given Ben what for after I had left. Nola didn't need stitches and nothing was broken but she had given herself a nasty whack. Ben had decided not to send her to nursery. Wise decision. He doesn't work on Mondays anyway.

I updated my blog and googled the services provided by Women's Refuge and City's Women's Aid. I want to provide accurate information for anyone who needed their help. Gave them a call and alerted them to my blog. I was known to them already. Imagine that. So arranged to visit them as soon as I am able to.

I wandered around Annabelle's flat to see what she had. I wanted to buy her something that she needed, as a thank you, but hadn't a clue what. It's a smashing wee pad. Tastefully decorated and furnished. Fifty shades and textures of grey. Mainly from Ikea but it all blends really well. She has a decent size living room and separate small kitchen. Her bedroom is as big as the living area and her computer desk nestles in a small alcove. The spare room is small but very long. I love the bathroom. Unusual tiling – courtesy of Jim, her dad. It's what he does. Not sure how well you know him. Think you may have met her mum before she died. He remarried years ago. Really nice woman. Anne.

The only thing I don't like (and it is minor) is that her tallish furniture is not tall enough. Don't mean to sound bitchy. Like Deacon House, she has high ceilings with deep cornices. The wardrobes are lost against them.

I decided on either a double hanging planter, with plants obviously, for the corner of her living room to break up the wall space or a copper kettle. She'd admired the one I had bought Carrie when we were over in N.I.

No sooner had I sat down at the computer desk, cup of coffee in hand, when the doorbell rang. It would be an Amazon delivery. Annabelle and someone else in the stair are Amazon junkies. If the outside door buzzes it's either for her or M. Fascia on the top floor.

My outstretched hand was ready to accept the brown parcel. Never in a month of Sundays did I consider it would be Ben. 'Oh!' was all I could manage.

'Can I come in?' he asked meekly.

'If you're here to tell me what a crap human being I am, then no.'

'I come in peace.' He failed if he thought that was funny. It's what he does when he is nervous. Cracks inappropriate jokes. 'Sorry. I think we need to clear the air.'

I stood back to give him space.

'Erm, living room,' said I. He knew the way. We were regular visitors. 'Coffee? I've just made one for myself.'

'Thanks.'

A strong black coffee, level teaspoon of sugar and the froth from hot milk (same as me minus the sugar) was placed on the coffee table in front of the fireplace. Ben was staring out the bay window on to Pitt Street. He'd lost weight. His jeans were sagging at the bum. Same with his black and white rugby shirt. He sat on the only chair. I sat on the three-seater sofa and waited. Wasn't going to make it easy for him. At that point, he could have been there to apologise or to stick the knife in deeper.

'Is Nola okay?' My first and important question.

'She is. Shaken. Sore face but she'll bounce back. About yesterday. Sorry. I was bang out of order.'

'You're not the only one who is suffering. I've been to hell and back. In fact, I'm not back. I'm still there.'

I did my usual. Opened the floodgates. He was all flustered, sat down beside me. Leaned in for a cuddle. Withdrew. Changed his mind and rubbed my shoulder as if I were a stranger. I cried harder and louder. I needed a hug. From him! Will it ever get any easier? My turn to apologise. I wiped my face with the palms of my hands. Dried them on my jeans and sat bolt upright. It was my way of saying that I could cope with his proximity.

He gave an odd cough. 'You've smudged your mascara stuff.' And he waggled his finger in front of his own eyes as if it was on his face.

I'd forgotten I had applied it for Jasper. Not that I was trying to make an impression but it was kinda satisfying to make an effort again. Plus, when my face was healing, I couldn't be bothered. A dab of kitchen roll did the trick. I went for the jugular.

'Nola tripping was not my fault or Annabelle's. How dare you accuse me of that.' I mulled over my next words. 'As for the accident...' I couldn't finish. I chose the mirror above the fireplace to focus on, as I fought to control my rapid breathing.

'Please don't.' His eyes filled with tears. 'I'm an arsehole. As I said, bang out of order.'

He swiped his tears. I tore off more kitchen roll. For him and me. I was incapable of saying anything. The whole bloody 'it's me, Ruby' speech was sticking in my throat. If that escaped, it was goodbye to the kids indefinitely. He gathered his composure.

'Annabelle gave me a right bollocking. No more than I deserved.'

He had more to say. I can always tell. Unlike me, he is usually more calculated. Sunday was an exception.

'It's been hard since, you know, since Ruby. We haven't been coping. She organised everything. The kids, their nurseries, their clubs, meals, work, our lives. I didn't need to think about any of it. I can't find a fucking thing. All I get from the kids is *Mummy doesn't do it like that.* It's not their fault. I know. It's mine.'

Perfectly true. I'm the spreadsheet poster girl. There's nothing I can't fit on a grid. When the kids were born, I even had a column for pee and poo. (Times, colour, amount, smell.) Ben was happy to leave it all up to me. I should have involved him more. You were like that, mum. The family wall calendar was always jam-packed with information. Dad went with the flow.

'I'm more than happy to help. What else is there for me to do? I can't work.'

'I know and I appreciate it.' His brain was whirring. 'But I don't think you are able. Physically or mentally.'

I sighed. 'I did have two cracked ribs and massive bruising but I'm getting there. I managed to carry Nola to the sports centre. I'd say that that was a feat in itself.' I acknowledged that an adrenalin surge must have played a part.

He shifted from one bum cheek to the other and rubbed his hands on his knees. 'But mentally? That nonsense in the hospital freaked me out. Rachel, you thought you were Ruby.'

'I can't explain that.' What else could I say? 'But look at you. You're not in a good place either.'

'That's different,' he scoffed. 'I'm grieving.'

'We're all grieving, Ben, and I'm fucking terrified. My memory hasn't returned. I live with a man I hardly know. Can you truly say that you would be happy waking up one day and forced to live a life that was unknown to you?'

'That's exactly what I mean. You don't know me and you don't know the kids. So, what's the difference?'

My calculated thoughts were doing somersaults in my head. I tried to articulate. Here's the brief version.

'I can't explain it but I do know you and the kids. I dunno, it's as if my brain is trying to protect Ruby's memory for me. Like I don't want to forget her. I can remember lots of things about my life from years ago and lots of things about my family's lives, especially Ruby's, but I can't remember current things. I've forgotten how to teach but not how to cook, read, drive, work a computer. God, facing a bunch of kids in a classroom would freak me out.' We both giggled at that. 'I can negotiate the streets in Edinburgh. I think I could easily drive to London and I remember everything about the kids. (didn't want to include Ben.) What they eat, who their friends are, their favourite toys and songs but I remember bugger all about Colin. And HE does not like that. I can't blame him. But at this moment in time, he is a stranger to me.'

Without going into any great detail, I explained how my memory loss had affected my relationship with Colin. It was difficult. For both of us but Colin more so. His frustration often verged on violent, mainly verbally. I did ramble. Nerves probably.

'Mum and my Daddy said that the police had been called out.' He always refers to his dad as Daddy. A Northern Ireland thing. Carrie calls them Mummy and Daddy.

'Neighbours. They'd heard us shouting and were worried.'

He grimaced. Don't know how convincing I was.

'Until I am sure that you are able physically for the kids and... sorry, mentally, I'd prefer you not to take them out on your own. Just for now. It's a fuckin liberty, I know, but I have to be sure. I think Ruby would agree if she was here.'

My first reaction was, stick your gesture up your ungrateful arse. BUT, it's exactly what I would say. I would insist that my two were safe before anything else. Especially with someone like me (post-accident).

'That's fair,' I said. 'I can help get them ready some mornings (didn't want to say every). Do some light housework. I take it you still employ Joyce? (He nodded. She cleans twice a week.) I could prepare some simple family meals. I'm happy to babysit but appreciate that might not be on your radar yet.'

He was still juggling night times. Some of his young staff stayed with the kids while he was at Suthiez. He looked knackered. His rest at Enniskillen had slipped off his face. Sunken cheeks. Dark circles under the eyes. Unkempt. Christ, he could have been a junkie.

Suddenly, I had an image of Nola home alone. Who was looking after her?

'Libby's mum. She's been great but I can't rely on her all the time.'

Absolutely. She has Libby's two twice a week and must be seventy. Not as young as you. I mean me. Fifty-six.

I am a fifty-six-year-old. Scary. I want to be thirty-four again.

We chatted about bits and pieces. The kids. How I was coping. Told him that Colin was a fucking nightmare. He was shocked at hearing you swear. He'd never heard you curse. Ever (apart from the hospital outburst which we are disregarding). We both laughed. It felt good.

He wasn't sure why Annabelle and me (you) had struck up this friendship.

'She's helping me out short term, that's all.'

'You can make a grand mug of coffee. This is good. Almost as good as Ruby's.'

The elephant in the room was aired again. Not that Ben was ever that forthcoming in thrashing out problems. I was always the instigator.

'God, I miss her, Rachel. I can't believe she's gone.' More tears from him this time. Lots of them.

We hugged for a very long time. I willed myself to behave like the mother-in-law. Guarded my every move. Terrified that I might touch him in an intimate way. My way. The Ruby Martin way.

'Every morning, I inhale her.'

I pulled away. What did he mean?

'I kept our bedding. Bundled them up and bagged them. Her pillow cases are on top. She's in a black bin bag. The other day Alfie asked *What if I forget her.* The three of us sat on our bed. Close your eyes and when I say sniff, breathe in deeply. I held the bag under their noses.

MUMMY! They shouted together. So, I said to our wee mannie, if you ever have trouble thinking about what Mummy was like, we can do this together.'

FUCKING HELL!!!!!!!

# THIRTY-FIVE

## *Ruby's Journal*

My bedclothes might have given the kids comfort but Ben's delicious bodily odour only served to set me off on one. In that instant, I wished I hadn't survived. I felt so guilty. Did I want to live that much that I had ousted you out of your body and taken over? God Mum, am I pariah? Sacrificing my own mother, for what? Cos this is not the life I want.

Do I write to you out of guilt, pretending that I am writing this journal because you might come back? Or am I writing it to me in case I wake up tomorrow and the whole bloody process begins anew? I am fully aware that two of us cannot co-exist. My shell is six feet under in Enniskillen. Empty. I can hardly dig my way out.

FUCK!!!!!!!

After Ben left, I had to get out for fresh air. You always used to say that it's the ones who are left behind that suffer. They are, I am and I can't do anything about it other than witness their anguish and live with mine on a daily basis.

I gave myself a thorough shaming as I roamed the cobbled streets. Enough of the woe is me. I'd been given a second chance. I owed it to you to grab life with both hands and embrace it. See the positive in every situation. I was determined to try. Give something back. I would help Ben and the kids and throw myself into aiding those unfortunate women (or men) who are trapped (in a different way).

I did have something to eat with Colin. See. Optimism. Thai curry from a jar. What happened to his crap trash morals? Pissed in the wind when he had been left to fend for himself, that's what. AND he had poured it over chicken breasts that I had grilled and hidden in the freezer. Did not cast it up. I did, however, switch the plates after he put them on the table. It amused him.

'D' ye think it's poisoned?' he chortled.

I smirked, indicating that I wouldn't put it past him.

'A truce,' he hailed and poured us both a glass of wine. Again, he found it funny when I switched them. He raised his glass, 'to the woman I knew and loved. Hope she finds her way hame soon.' I actually struggled to toast that. I didn't want you to be found, mum. Not yet, not ever. I took that back. Not until my family were ready. But I didn't want them to be ready without me. What a bitch, eh? However, I did croak, 'to a truce.'

I had one glass. Colin had two. We rubbed along in guarded harmony for the rest of the evening. Doing dishes. Tidying the house. I even watched T.V in the living room for half an hour before going to bed. Still bolted the door. And double checked it. A little basin was bought to replace the mixing bowl. Not leaving my room to pee.

Next morning, (Tuesday 1st May) I was up with the larks. Actually, the dawn chorus kicked off long before my alarm. You forget how loud they can be. Colin was in a good mood, whistling away while, I showered. A lot more ominous though than the orchestra outside.

'Enjoy your day with your grandchildren,' he sang after me as I closed the front door.

I kid you not. I checked my car over. Kicking each tyre in turn. When I glanced back over my shoulder, I glimpsed a shadow stepping back from the living room window. I'll never be able to trust him. How do you trust a man who was willing to crack his face open with a spade to prove a point? The optimistic new me isn't able to reconcile with Colin. Not yet. Probably never.

Being with the kids in the morning was the best thing I had experienced in weeks. We slipped into a pre-nursery ritual with ease. You have to remember that I hadn't done the nursery run in years. Ben did mornings and I did afternoons and evenings. Thank you for helping out every second Thursday, Mum. My late night. We were like ships in the night. Instead of making time to chat, we left notes for each other, rapidly barking instructions as I came in and you left. What a waste. I understand that now.

Anyway, I was as chirpy as our garden birds. We sang songs, laughed a lot, although Alfie is not a morning boy, and caught up on all the nursery news.

Megan had got engaged to her girlfriend and Elloise had brought in homemade cupcakes because it was her birthday and popular wee Arthur was leaving. He was one of Alfie's besties.

'She is twenty-three,' emphasised Alfie as if the next birthday meant drawing her pension.

Too soon, they were all out the door and the house was empty. Ben surprisingly complied when I suggested that I tidy the house and sort through the washing – something I always did.

What a mess. Baskets, and any receptacle that could be used, stuffed full with clean washing. I sifted with great delight (simple pleasures) through the mountains. Ironed what was needed and put away everything else. Obviously, I pawed everything that was in my bedroom. I felt like an intruder in my own home. Fully aware that I had an ear on the front door the whole time I was there. Terrified that Ben would catch me.

Oh Mum, all my lovely clothes. Believe it or not, I found some cardigans that fitted you (well me) at a push. I reckon I have lost well over a stone. No exercise as such, apart from walking, but I have not eaten many biscuits or nuts and crisps. I know you had a taste for Pringles.

Guess what? I tried out some of my toys. OMG!!!! Orgasm after orgasm. Definitely missed those wee pals. Ben loved using them on me and sometimes I reciprocated. So, I stuffed one at the bottom of my bag. He would never know. There were so many!! Jeepers, I'm actually sharing that info with my mum!

I contacted JJ and organised a brunch date. Woo hoo!!!

Time evaporated and before I knew it my two munchkins blasted through the door.

'GRANNY!!!' They were unequivocally happy to see me. As I them.

Meatballs and spaghetti were simmering on the aga. Beer battered fish and chips and peas for Ben. He was impressed. Long may it last.

Repeat Wednesday and Thursday.


**Friday 3rd May.** Wine o'clock at Annabelle's. Or should I say champers o'clock.

On that Friday morning, my car didn't start. There's a surprise. So I phoned Jasper. He drove me to Dick Place. Have to stop depending on him to bail me out. Dad organised for my car to be towed to a local garage (thought I had AA cover). Turns out that there was diesel in my tank. No way. It had to be Colin but I had no proof. I knew I had been complacent but decided not to share my concerns yet with the wee weaselly shite. Kept shtum and coy.

I spent the morning at Deacon House. I had a real sense of accomplishment as I breezed through the door. A clean, fresh, tidy home welcomed me unlike the cluttered shit hole I had had to wade through on Tuesday. The vestibule had been crammed with discarded coats, foul smelling shoes (Ben's trainers), bags and anything else that could be dropped at the door. Joyce, our cleaner, was capable enough. Not brilliant but reliable and trustworthy. She was not, however, employed to pick up after us and rarely had to.

Kids were up and dressed in the clothes I had laid out on their bedroom chairs. I could smell eggy bread wafting from the kitchen. Ben looked better. His lycra confirmed his weight loss but he was keen to get back out on his bike, something he had not done since the funeral. Perhaps I'd imagined it but there was renewed positivity in the air – for all of us. A local taxi was dropping the kids off at nursery before his school run. He was lifting the child seats from his boot as I walked them to his car.

'Hi, its Patrick, isn't it?' Of course, I knew. Patrick used to collect me every morning at 4.30am. What we didn't know about each other...!

'Aye,' he confirmed in his Slovakian accent. 'Children look happy today. Happy to be with Grandmother.'

'Hope so,' said I. 'Thank you.'

Ben peddled off shortly after. I did my chores whilst listening to JJ and Jemma. I know I shouldn't have taken any pleasure in it but the posts were shit hot with listeners moaning about Jemma. Her grating voice. Her unendearing laugh. Full of self-importance. Lack of rapport. Nothing like me. There were a few kind words (probably from her mum and dad. Ha, ha). The same things were said about me when I first joined so I knew the hullaballoo would die down and before long Ruby Martin would be piously acknowledged now and again.

Housework done, I headed into the city centre. I wanted to search John Lewis for that kettle. Dad texted to say that my car had been returned to Alderburn. He had taken care of the garage. Thank you, Dad.

I was like a kid on Christmas Eve. A coiled spring. So excited about my sleepover.

I had ordered food to be delivered from *Heavenly,* a fantastic Chinese restaurant in Dublin Street Lane. The absolute best. I had set the table. Quality paper napkins. Bumble bees. New champagne flutes (from moi) and an elaborately wrapped copper kettle.

Annabelle was impressed. We had a ball. Both hammered before the food arrived. Hee hee. We reminisced, sang and danced. Ate, peaked then drastically dipped. Markings of a fabulous girls' night in.

We paid for it the next day. Emerged from our cocoons after 2pm. Can't remember the last time I did that.

**Saturday**. Dragged my beleaguered body into Carberry Cres at teatime. Used an Uber. Jasper had done his share. Couldn't face anything to eat. Crawled into bed and conked out. At two in the morning, felt marginally better and in need of sustenance. Sneaked into the kitchen to make toast and tea. A huge hangover learning curve for me. Normally, I could have sunk a whopping amount before it impaired the following day. This was my new norm.

**Sunday**. Colin was distant. Was he ever close? I felt fine. Bustled about totally ignoring the muttering.

'Are ye walking or no?' he barked.

'Yeah. Fine.' Oops! 'Where about?' I'd forgotten I had agreed to walk with him on Sunday.

'Cockburnspath,' he shouted.

Meant nothing to me. I made sandwiches and a flask of coffee. I drove. No alternative.

We walked for miles. All very civilised. I listened to him harping on about Bass Rock and the ins and outs of the mating rituals of the gannet. Marvellous. Not. A gannet can live for 35 years. Same as me (minus 2 months). Who would've thought? They go blind from diving too often. Gobsmacked. Thought it was wanking. There were loads more. Riveting stuff. OMG! How did you remain sane?

We made a couple of pit stops. Walking for a bit then driving again along single-track roads. We stopped at Pease Bay for our picnic. It was a beautiful day. No need for jackets but I wrapped my fleece around my waist. We passed a sign for Drysdale something or other and parked the car. There was an information board which Colin read aloud as if I were incapable of reading. 1km to Siccar Point and we had to walk. Great. Through fields. I was sorely tempted to cop out but Colin would have had a meltdown. He was sure I would have some kind of epiphany and my memory would be restored. A geological rocky promontory lay beneath our walking boots. The intricate layers of the 4.5-billion-year-old Siccar Point beckoned to be admired.

'You have to be joking. I'm not going down there,' I was indignant.

'It's where the spark was ignited. I thought it might trigger something.' He seemed perplexed.

What was I thinking? Not enough. Before I knew it, I had

grass burns on the cheeks of my bum. It may have been beautiful and sunny at the top but as I slid towards the bottom there was nothing sunny about it. The waves were crashing onto wet rocks. The sun had disappeared to God knows where. A freezing cold spray slapped my face. Thank God for my fleece. Colin had an inflated elation about him. I was grappling at the bottom of a very dangerous slope. Between me and several metres of grey ribbed rock was the deep, dark ominous North Sea. Fuck! The perfect place for me to disappear.

There was a rope-wall secured to the cliff face. Hoping it reached the top, I made my ascent. Don't know where the strength came from but I heaved on that coir.

'Where the hell are you going?' yelled Colin. 'I wanted to take your picture.'

'Take my arse,' I thought.

I dragged myself up. Searching for a foothold with each step. Not easy. Shale and dust clouded behind me. Thought my lungs would burst with the exertion. The leather had rubbed off my gloves. Any second a hand would grab my ankle and yank me down.

At the top, I collapsed onto my back. The sky and the clouds rushed to meet me. For several seconds we were at one. The ground, me and the sky. Inhaling and exhaling painfully. I staggered over those fields in a blur on auto pilot. I heard him calling your name over and over. He sounded far away and that suited me fine. Not once did I look over my shoulder. I was focussed on reaching the car.

I emptied my guts all over the grass behind your wee grey Corsa. An elderly couple were parked close by and ogled me suspiciously. Managed to text Annabelle, stating my presence and my lucky escape.

Colin was visibly stricken when he reached me. 'What the hell?' he blurted.

'Sorry. The sea freaked me out.' I could hardly say that I thought he had lured me to a second death.

The journey back was awkward. He prattled on about how I had deliberately thwarted the opportunity of rebooting those precious memories. He had been so looking forward to witnessing the look on my face. What? When he pushed me in to the sea? And the biggie, he had not gone to his only granddaughter's birthday celebrations as he thought it was more important to be with me. Holy fuck!!! I remained silent, reflecting on my close call. Although, I can never be sure, I won't put myself in such a precarious predicament again.

On Monday, I was back at Deacon House. I sifted through new and old mail and put them into piles labelled – bills, personal, junk and not sure. I opened those that I could easily reseal. Shit, I accidentally ripped one. Read it. Not that important so I scrunched it up and hid it right at the bottom of the kitchen bin before Ben got back from his run. He would have perceived it as crossing a line if he thought I had tampered with his mail.

Did I mention I had found my phone? I've been meticulously checking all my conversations and deleting anything that could be taken the wrong way. Then replacing it in Ben's bedside table.

The kids' drawers and wardrobes were reorganised. I labelled the insides to indicate what should be stored where and on the wardrobe doors, the order of how their clothes should be hung: – school, sport, casual and dress. I even put little drawings on them to help Alfie and Nola. Same with all their toy storage boxes. Little pointers that would make everyday life a little easier.

It was hugely comforting to be pottering around the house while Ben caught up with his work in his office. It was an effort not to wander in too often. He gratefully accepted the coffees I made. Pleasantries were exchanged. Teeny, tiny steps, I reminded myself.

I made mild chilli mince for tea, liquidising the sauce for Alfie. He had become really fussy of late. No visible bits in his food. He had gone from a little boy who would eat anything to a pernickety wee picker who sifted his food with a microscopic eye. A phase, I'm sure.

I set the table. Alfie's bowl of chilli and a chunkier version for the rest of us. A large dish of rice and a green salad each for the adults. Slices of yellow and orange peppers along with strips of cucumber on side plates for Alfie and Nola.

Ben made no comment when I joined them at the dinner table. I won't do it every time but at least it was a start.

# THIRTY-SIX

*Ruby's Journal*

**Tuesday 7th.**

I took Jade out for her tea on Tuesday to a McDonalds on London Road. We met there. She bussed it. A post birthday treat. You would've done something. I gave her vouchers for Primark. She was dead chuffed. Her mother had paid for her to have pink streaks in her hair. Bloody mess. Every alternate nail had been painted black then purple. A present from her pal's step-mum. She has a pretty face and good skin so I was pleased to see that it wasn't caked in make-up like the last time we met.

'What was your granny like? Your mum's mum. You must think about her on your birthday.' Felt rotten taking advantage of her.

'Not really.' Through a mouthful of Big Mac.

'You were probably too little.'

'She cried a lot, I think.'

Did she now? 'Oh, I'm sorry to hear that. Was she ill?'

'Don't think so......but she was odd.'

'In what way?' I tried to be ever so nonchalant.

'Her eyes always looked funny.'

'Must have been hard for your mum.'

'Actually, I remember a caravan holiday. Just me, Mum and Granny. We laughed a lot. A seagull pooped on Granny's head.

Hope it brings me luck, she said.' Podgy fingers dipped a fistful of chips in a BBQ sauce pot.

'How old were you?' She could only have been a toddler.

'Seven. Maybe eight.'

'Oh, I thought your granny died a long time ago.' Hoped I didn't sound as shocked as I was. You had said that Colin was a widower when you met.

'She was in that special home for a while until she died. Mum was sad but said she had lost Granny years ago.'

At that, I assumed she meant a hospice but no.

'So how long did they live apart, your granny and grandad?'

She took a never-ending slurp of banana milkshake. 'Dunno. I can't remember how long Granny was in the home for.'

'Before that,' I said nodding with encouragement.

'Granny and Granda lived in our house. The one we're in now. (I'm taking that as Northfield.) We moved in with Granda when Granny was put away cos he was lonely. Now we pay rent to Granda but cos it's Granda's we get it cheap.'

Put away? Honestly, between the excruciating slurping and me trying to calculate dates and figures leap-frogging in my head, I knocked over my bloody coffee cup just missing Jade's brand new, black hoodie and black jeans. (She is turning into her mother, poor soul.)

'Careful, Granny Rachel.'

'So, your granny didn't have a house of her own?' I asked, drying up the spillage with whatever napkins I could find and chucking a couple her way.

'No...Granda hoped he'd have better luck with you cos Granny bled him dry.'

She asked if she could have an ice-cream. 'Are you going to get better?' she enquired when I returned.

'I hope so.' What else could I say? 'When did your granny die again?'

'Do you remember that first time Mum and me came to your house for lunch?'

'Nope. No memory, remember?'

'Oh, yeah. Sorry. When we got back to our house, the hospital phoned to say she had died.'

She opened her mouth and spooned in an enormous dollop of soft ice cream. Then another. I could only stare. It was if she was talking about someone she vaguely knew. Like announcing that their guinea pig had passed away. There wasn't an ounce of compassion.

That night, she shared my room and Colin drove her to school next morning. It was hard to believe that in seven weeks' time her primary education journey would end. She didn't seem mature enough yet I bet she's more street wise than my two will ever be at her age.

**Wednesday 8th.**

I blitzed the house. Very cathartic. Colin has been avoiding me. He is up to something. AND he has acquired a car. A SAAB. Oldish hatchback but in good condition. Very cocky about it too.

Bellatrix senior was at pains to emphasise that she prefers driving it to mine. She had been on to thank me for treating Jade.

'Just as well.' It was a sarcastic reminder that she was no longer on my insurance and never will be.

Back to Colin. Been acting shifty. Shiftier than normal. I don't think he stayed in the house on Wednesday night. I couldn't sleep so up early. Thought all night about not being able to be with the kids for a whole week. Sutherlands coming. The house was quiet. 6.00am. Too early for Colin's morning walk. I pottered around for a while. Had breakfast. Checked over my to do lists. Showered and still no sign of him. I pressed my ear to his door. Silence. For a split second, I wondered if he was dead. That tiny moment of elation was immediately replaced with 'shit, I'll get the blame.' So I knocked on the door. Three quiet taps followed by three loud ones. Called out his name then recalled he had done this before. Last Wednesday when I had been too preoccupied to notice or care. Gently eased the handle and pushed the door open. His bed had not been slept in. Hhmmm! Definitely up to something. Gave me a chance to rummage in your wardrobe for more clothes. When I questioned him about his walk, he claimed he had left while I was still in bed. I didn't mention I had risen early. Two can play at his wee games.

**Friday 10th.**

Accompanied Colin on his walk. From Longniddry to Cockenzie and back, with a coffee stop. My way of making amends for Sunday although got the impression he wanted to be on his own. All very amicable on the surface. Took us about three hours. My energy levels have surged of late. Hardly notice my ribs now. Weight loss has helped. Quizzed him about his first wife. Liz.

When did they meet? They were childhood sweethearts and married in 1981.

Were they happy? Very. (Not according to Jade.)

How long were they married? Him – *why did I want to know?* I wanted to know more about me and him. He accepted that. He did not reply immediately (obviously working out the finer details). Up until she died. Thirty odd years.

'Same as Rob and me.'

'Oh, ye remember that?' he snapped.

'No. I've been trying to map out my life. Understand myself better. (half-truth)

What did she die of? Cancer. He responded immediately.

'I'm so sorry. And I never met her?'

'How could ye'ave? She died long before we met.' Now that was NOT true.

I asked him to explain how me (you) and him met. Holy Moley! Mills and Boon eat your heart out. Only the romance of the decade. Was tempted to ask why he had been so nasty to me since the hospital. Decided not to scupper his fantasy. Let him have his moment.

He asked me not to quiz Claire or Jade about his late wife as they find it too painful. Oh, I'm sharpening my tongue already!

Should be jumping with excitement but I'm in two minds whether to go at all. The girls are having cocktails and nibbles at Ros's tonight. Annabelle assures me that they are delighted that I'm going. Really? I wouldn't have been enamoured if you or Libby's mother, Irene, gate crashed one of our nights out or in and I get on well with Irene.

I'm desperate to see them all but apart from Annabelle and tentatively Libby, Ros didn't have much to do with you so it would be difficult for me to engineer a meet up with her.

I have given myself a get-out card.

# THIRTY-SEVEN

*Rachel's flat in Portobello. Tuesday 7th January 2020.*

Rachel slotted the photograph of her with Ruby's family into the journal. She closed the book and stared at the front cover for several seconds but her mind was elsewhere: Colin and his wife.

His script had always been the same. Never deviated. He and Liz had lived apart; leading separate lives until she passed away with pancreatic cancer. She died within weeks of her diagnosis. Claire was bereft and rarely spoke of it because she and her mother were estranged when Liz died. Now, it seems that Liz lived her final months (hopefully not years) in a home or, God forbid, an institution.

He rarely mentioned his wife. The relationship had been strained for a number of years before they separated and Colin refused to dwell on it. Rachel enquired only once about Liz and was instantly shut down by Claire. She never asked again.

Why had he lied? Rachel felt sick. While she had been 'entertaining' Colin, his poor wife had been languishing in surroundings that were not her home. She sincerely hoped that Liz had spent the remainder of her life being cared for in a hospice by compassionate staff but an uncomfortable truth contaminated the air; Liz had been abandoned.

Rachel shivered. She whipped off the throw and checked the thermostat on the remote control. 17.5 C. She turned it up.

The rain had stopped pummelling the window. It was still very grey outside. Obviously, not evening dark but daylight seemed to have forgotten to make an appearance. Black clouds hovered ominously above Portobello.

Rachel swithered whether to remain in the flat or make a dash up to the supermarket – not that she needed anything in particular but she longed to clear her head.

She selected an ankle length, camel quilted coat from the first peg in the hall cupboard. Ugg boots were on a low shoe rack and a selection of hats, gloves and scarves were folded neatly inside clear plastic bags in a wicker basket. Rachel chose the black set.

A quick recce of the fridge and she was off: on a mission.

The promenade and the streets were quiet and bitterly cold. Rachel pulled the woollen beanie down over her ears, it hid her unwashed hair, and tightened the scarf around her neck ensuring all her flesh was protected from the biting wind. Schools were back tomorrow yet there were no youngsters milling around. The cafe on the first floor of the sports centre seemed busy. Rachel could see it clearly as she neared the corner. It overlooked the beach and the Forth. Where else would families go in such miserable weather?

Rachel scoured her surroundings as if she would recognise the blood-stained spot where little Nola had tripped over the leash. She even rubbed a few discoloured patches on the gritty paving stones with the sole of her shoe. The strong gales had carried swathes of sand on to the promenade. What had she been hoping to find? Poor Ruby. It was one thing after another.

Why had she never considered opening a bank account in her own name again? Thank goodness Ruby wasn't as intimidated by Colin as she had been yet, deep down, it was what she had always wanted to do. Demand her own account again. When they married Colin insisted that they should have a joint account. No secrets. What's mine is yours; he was at pains to point out. She wholeheartedly agreed. What he really meant was, what was Rachel Gordon's was his. He invariably made excuses as to why his benefits hadn't been paid into their account. They were recalculating underpayments due to him; better to leave his current details on their system until the problem had been rectified. The longer it went on, the harder it became to challenge him. When she did, he would moan that she was accusing him of lying.

'You phone them,' he would scream. 'It's hard enough without you accusing me of not trying.'

Eventually she gave up – on everything, including herself. Colin convinced her that she wasn't coping and she began to rely on him to make decisions. One day, she found herself sitting in her doctor's consulting room begging for something to help her cope – preferably tablets. Colin squeezed her hand as she cried. Antidepressants were prescribed. Over the months their strength increased as did her dependency.

Rachel crossed the High Street and marched into Aldi. She stuffed her gloves into her pockets and grabbed a sturdy, black plastic basket. What to buy? A bag of rocket, a pepper, a cucumber and a bunch of spring onions. Definitely needed bread. Rachel chose one that Colin would have turned his nose up to. Ciabatta with olives. Nor would he have condoned dried peppers in garlic oil. That was dropped in too. Moroccan couscous, milk and a small pack of Pringles rounded off her purchases.

The young lad at the checkout smiled and acknowledged her. 'What's up, Rachel?'

'Oh, I fell and bumped my head. I've lost my memory,' she stammered. She didn't know him from Adam.

'No way,' He was shocked.

Rachel didn't realise that his *what's up* was more of a statement than an actual question.

'You okay?'

'I'm getting there. Thanks for asking.'

'Were you able to find your way here?'

She pulled a face and packed her bag quicker than she might have. She couldn't cope with intrusive questioning and made a hasty exit.

Once outside, she gulped the fresh air she had longed for earlier. She understood now what it must have been like for Ruby. Strangers grilling her about what she could or couldn't remember.

Rachel pulled the scarf up over her face to avoid further recognition and scurried towards the prom. In less than five minutes, she reached the sanctuary of the apartment.

Was it too early for a wine?

She thought not.

# THIRTY-EIGHT

*Ruby's Journal*

**Sunday 12th May.**

I was dreading facing Annabelle after Friday night. It was horrible. Wish I'd never gone. Cried all night.

It kicked off okay. The girls scrubbed up well even though the dress code was casual. Always is. Each and every one of them looked glamorous compared to me. Great hair, nails, make-up, lash extensions. I had spent ages on my hair and face. Wore jeans, white shirt and white trainers. Waste of time. I felt your age. Looked frumpy. Felt frumpy. Felt old and fat. Sorry, Mum. Not your fault.

Ros and Annabelle both wore black jeans. Ros's were suede affect. And they both had cream silky tops. Annabelle likes to cover her arms unless we are abroad. Ros's was short sleeved. She's dead skinny. Always has been. Suits anything. She has grown her hair lately. Suits it. Nearly at her shoulders. Shiny blonde.

Annabelle brought a bag of vegetable crudités to nibble on and a vinaigrette dipping sauce. Forever on a diet. Does she not get it? She is drop dead gorgeous. Inside and out. She has a fabulous hourglass figure. I wish she could see what I see.

Libby and Hannah (yeh she was there) both chose floral dresses. On seeing them, I wish I had put on my navy one from Asda. Hannah's was too short (I'm being bitchy) with thigh length boots which she did take off thankfully. Her thick thighs let down what could be a decent figure. I'm ashamed to say that I'm jealous Annabelle has rekindled a close friendship with Hannah and yet I can't blame her. Both are single (since Hannah divorced) so why not? Cos I'm now single and can't have what they have. Kindred spirits and young men AND SEX!!!! I've never gone this long without sex, apart from when the kids were born. Ouch! Alfie with his big napper. Never missed it then. Too effing sore.

When I was with Ben and building my lucrative career (what a joke) I was happy that Annabelle had Hannah to hang around with. Saved me worrying about her. Hell, they had a fab holiday in Dubrovnik last September thanks to me. I recommended the hotel. There was a photo of them at night in the pretty harbour area. Ben dared to suggest that Hannah resembled me, slightly. I have NEVER needed hair extensions. And my shoulders are not as broad. Nor is my nose or fake smile.

It's like wearing truth glasses when I'm with family or friends. Like I'm looking at everyone for the first time. I focus on their flaws. Flaws that I had never noticed before.

At the beginning, the girls were so pleased to see you (me), all very nicey nicey, just like at the funeral. Hyper. Giggling. Crying. Recalling silly things we did at school but very quickly, I was on the outside looking in. I caught them rolling their eyes when I tried to join in. A quick, witty comment that they would normally have chuckled at made them visibly cringe. Even shut me down on a couple of occasions. My friends treating me like that. I was embarrassed – for them more than me. Would I have been as disparaging to one of their mums? Probably.

We had two shots each of cherry gin, on the bounce. Within minutes, I was giddy.

Annabelle was desperate to include me.

'Oh, don't apologise. (When they cussed or let a crude comment slip.) Rachel's thick skinned like Ruby.'

'Honestly, I'm fine. Say what you like.' I backed her up but that only served to confirm that I was shutting down their banter.

There was a silent sigh of relief all round when I made my excuse to leave. Early start in the morning. Had to be fresh. Typical justification of an older woman.

'Please don't go,' begged Annabelle as I slipped on my jacket at Ros's front door.

'I'll be fine, really. Enjoy the rest of the night. I'll see you on Sunday.' I hugged my dearest friend in the whole world (my only friend) and kissed her cheek.

I found myself sobbing outside on the pavement in Trinity Grove. SHIT! I leaned into a privet hedge and toppled right through the bloody thing. Feet over arse. Thank God, nobody saw me. Leaves fell from my hair when I shook my head. Felt even shittier. So, I did what I always do and reluctantly called Jasper. He couldn't come. Had an important airport pick up. He apologised profusely. Was he letting me down gently? Is shittiest the superlative? I was at my shittiest low. Not true. This was only one of my shittiest lows. Marched towards Ferry Road and jumped on the first bus I saw. No idea where it was going but recognised the Botanic Gardens so buzzed the bell for St Bernard's Row. Suthiez was less than 10 mins away. Should I or shouldn't I? Should won. I actually crouched down in the street and reapplied my mascara and lippie in the wing mirror of a parked car. Sprayed a little perfume. Not for Ben, he would be working but it felt like the right thing to do.

I stood outside that familiar frosted door and hesitated. I

was about to turn and run when the door opened and a smartly dressed couple slipped sideways to let me in. The heat, the smell, the atmosphere enveloped me. Our Suthiez. Helena (learned her name later) rushed forward, a no no. Never show you are flustered. She was so sorry. Last orders had been taken.

'Not to worry,' I assured her. 'I was hoping to catch my friend.'

Did I want to look for her? Nope cos I had no idea why I had even come in. I pretended to text. Helena left. Suthiez was mobbed. And loud. Good to see. And so it should be. Ben deserved his Michelin star. I knew each table off by heart. Starting with table one on my immediate left. When we refurbished, everything was chosen by me. From the beach washed tables and chairs, right down to the salts and peppers. Casual but smart. We had fifty-six covers and from what I could see it was a full house.

I was about to leave when a familiar voice squawked, 'Rachel?'

WTF! It was Patricia. I knew what to expect. She ushered me through to their usual table. Number twelve. Tucked in at the back. Tad dah!! She presented the catch of the day. Me.

I had not expected to see Ben sitting with them in his chef whites. Immediate reaction. Who was looking after Alfie and Nola? Didn't say it. Didn't dare. Would've been the guillotine for me.

The shock on their faces. Priceless. I had rumbled them. Sorry Mum. This was something the four of them did when the senior Sutherlands were in town. I didn't tell you because I wanted to protect you. Now I wish I had. I could sense they had been discussing you the moment I approached the table. They were guilt ridden. Patricia looked smug.

Kenneth rose first and embraced me. Margaret leapt up. Hers eyes apologised to Patricia before she moved in for the hug. Dad remained seated and nodded. I had jumped from one group who clearly didn't want me into another who were embarrassed at being caught out. Talk about frying pan and fire.

'Why are you here, Rachel?' Ben asked. Why indeed?

I explained that Annabelle had invited me to supper with Ruby's friends at Trinity. Probably out of sympathy, I laughed. I left early because I was as welcome as a damp squib. Not fair on them. With no knowledge of the bus routes (true for me), I recognised I was close to Suthiez so disembarked. Was hoping to meet a friend here but he was unexpectedly called away.

A table called over to Ben. Wanting a selfie.

'Dad, get Rachel a drink.' And he was off.

I declined. I'd had two shots and two Espresso Martinis at Ros's. More than enough for your body.

'How's it going with you and Colin?' enquired Patricia with an injection of feigned interest and sympathy.

Not, how are you coping without Ruby? Or are you feeling better? Got stuck right in. Bitch.

'Colin is a cocky, conniving, cunning, coercive little shit,' I replied. 'I could easily use another apt C word but I'd upset Rob.' That wiped the smug smile off her face.

'Oh, what do you mean?' She stuttered.

'Well, when I was being bounced off the hall walls by Colin because he believed I had been shagging Rob in Enniskillen and, get this, with the approval of everyone there. Rob was a little shocked at the expletives exploding from my mouth while it was all happening.'

Wish I had taken their photo. They looked like they had been snapped at the end of the Pepsi Max ride in Blackpool.

'Did you hear it?' Margaret asked looking directly at Dad.

He cleared his throat nervously but I spoke first.

'What would you say, Patricia (I almost called her Pat), if Rob rattled you off the four walls because he suspected that you were shagging Eric when you had merely been attending Emily's funeral together? And bear in mind, I hadn't the strength to fight back.'

She looked stunned. Using her family names hit home. But good on her,

'I would definitely have used the C word,' she laughed.

'You must have been terrified,' sympathised my mother-in-law.

'I think Colin has controlled me for a long time. I suspect he was extremely adept at playing the concerned husband. I can't prove that he was ever violent towards me before, but I do have proof that he withheld my money.'

'Why are you still there?' asked Patricia.

'Where else can I go? I don't know anyone well enough now. Plus, it's my house.'

Margaret ordered Kenneth to fetch me a chair. The women tutted and offered their sympathy. Female solidarity. '*Me too*' eat your heart out.

The mood at table twelve had definitely plummeted. My fault.

'You know what?' I interjected. 'I may have forgotten huge chunks of my past but I am so so lucky. I remember everything about Alfie and Nola and Rory and Jack (had to include them). Perhaps the brain is mightier than we think. It preserves our happiest memories. Seems that way to me anyways and I am grateful for it.'

Margaret actually clapped. 'Oh, pet,' she enthused, 'are you sure you won't be having that drink?'

Pat insisted that the extra chair be placed next to her. Christ, don't suggest I move in with them!! Margaret proceeded to tell the group what a grand impression I had made on Deacon House. It was clean, tidy and organised. Labels everywhere. The kids were happier and Ben was less frazzled.

When Ben managed to shake off table three, he seemed pleasantly surprised to see us women laughing and joking. 'Who is this friend then?' he teased.

I could feel the blood rush to my cheeks.

'Is my mother-in-law blushing?' he cajoled.

'Jasper,' I blurted, flapping my hand in front of my face. 'Sorry, hot flush.'

'Who's Jasper?' Ben was intrigued.

'Amber Rose's brother,' I explained as if it were perfectly obvious.

'Amber Rose as in the hairdresser?'

'The very same.'

'Jeezuz, Rachel,' he laughed, 'you don't hang about.'

I could have kissed him. The others were gagging to find out more. Too bad. I politely excused myself. Wished them a pleasant evening and fastened (woo hoo) your brown jacket.

'Where are you heading?' Ben asked.

Alderburn obviously. Needed to catch a bus on Princes Street or London Road.

'Rob and Patricia can drop you off.'

Patricia was driving. Thought I detected a flinch. Thank you, Ben. Forget a kiss. I could have fucked my husband there and then on the table (done that plenty of times when the restaurant has been locked for the night). Dad smiled and nodded. He could hardly say no.

I ordered an Appletizer.

Margaret and Patricia may have been sitting pretty in their expensive Ralph Lauren and Jigsaw dresses but my mum (okay me as you) in your Asda shirt and jeans had the two older men drooling into their malt whiskies as I coyly told them how Jasper had come to my rescue.

# THIRTY-NINE

## *Ruby's Journal*

On Saturday, I met Jacob for Dim Sum near Colinton. Best in Edinburgh as far as I'm concerned. We used to bring the kids with us, more often than not on a Sunday. We'd have breakfast then head to the zoo or to the Royal Botanical Gardens. But guess what? You didn't have a taste for it. Dim Sum. The texture in my mouth. I could hardly swallow it and that is not like me. (There's a joke there somewhere!!)

It was so good to see JJ. We chatted away about everything and anything. Even he remarked how well we got on. God, I miss him. Miss the show. I wanted all the gen. Some of which he was reluctant to share cos he thought I was you. Can't blame him. It's such a back stabbing environment and there's always someone ready to tittle-tattle back to Adrian or Connor (big boss).

'So how are you getting on with Jemma?' First big question. We had slipped in some family stuff prior to that. And me of course.

'So, so. Not as well as Ruby obviously.' That was a given. 'But better than I expected.'

That was what I did not want to hear.

'The JJ and JC show?'

'That was not my idea. She won't drop it.' He did seem miffed.

'The hyena laugh doesn't grate?' I asked.

'Ha, ha. Ruby hated it.'

'So do the listeners. And Adrian. Or is she sitting on his face?'

The green chai tea in his mouth showered his napkin. My turn to laugh.

'I couldn't possibly say.' Suggesting that she might be.

'I'm sorry. That was despicable of me,' I said.

'You know Mrs. M, (he called you that too) you sound just like Ruby. It's spooky.'

I really have to be careful. The *despicable of me* was something we both used after the MSP Andrew Dreyton had been on our breakfast show. He was/is a first-class arsehole. He had used his parliamentary privilege to dob on a fellow MP who was having an affair with his wife. He apologised on air. *It was despicable of me*. Bollocks. He had no remorse. Just wanted payback for the man who had run off with his wife. You would know him, Mum. Combs his hair over his bald bit. Looks ridiculous. Far better if he shaved the lot off. Would take years off him.

'Is he still cheating on his wife?' I was referring to Adrian. JJ's eyebrows hit the ceiling. 'I'll take that as a yes,' I laughed.

'Did Ruby share everything with you?' he asked.

'No. Not serious stuff like secrets, only light-hearted stuff. She may have had a big gob on her but she was extremely loyal to her friends.' I had a few things on Jacob that I would never have shared with anyone and him on me.

JJ nodded in agreement and the worry lines on his forehead relaxed.

'Tell me about your loft conversion,' I said.

He was off. It was his second love. Sorry third. Arjun Singh was definitely his first.

Did I tell you that they had bought the top floor of a disused warehouse near Ocean Terminal? The plans are amazing. The penthouse bedroom will have open views across the Forth. Full length and breadth glass windows and a balcony to die for. I pleaded for a peek when it was all finished.

Two hours whizzed past. I was made up when JJ agreed to allow me to sit in on a show. I had to promise to be polite to Jemma. A reasonable compromise.

Before I forget, Colin stayed out all night again on Friday. Patricia followed me into the house. Think his antics have genuinely shocked her. She, not me, called his name several times. We checked all the rooms. Empty. Wasn't happy going to my bed knowing that he could creep in in the dead of the night so when Pat left, I locked the doors and left a key in the locks. I double checked the windows. Didn't want him climbing through them. Got to be vigilant. Left the living room lamp on all night. I waited up for another hour then bolted my bedroom door.

I think he has a woman!!!!

**Sunday.** I rang the doorbell even though I have a key. I would never use it knowing that Annabelle was in.

'What the fuck! You have a key,' she declared when she opened the door.

'Amazon,' I hollered, holding up a brown paper bag. We both laughed.

I handed her our breakfast. Croissants and coffees from the wee deli on the corner of Ferry Road. Not cheap but worth every penny. Almond for me and raspberry for Bella-Anne.

'You look... fresh,' I said.

'He didn't stay over but..'

'You fucked,' I blurted.

'We did,' she whooped.

'Shut up! Spill,' said I, barging in, 'all the horny details.'

Annabelle had dated a bloke she had met at a gin festival she was working at. Andy somebody. She's a brand ambassador for MeanKelpie, a gin distillery in Perthshire that specialises in flavoured gins and he was one of her punters. Oh, they are so good. Ben stocks them and Annabelle has held tastings in Rubiez.

He's asked her out before but she always turned him down. The trouble with Annabelle is, she is looking for Mr Perfect. A cross between Jason Statham and Aidan Turner who will be good in the sack then bring her tea in the same bed in the morning. Won't be happening but can't deny she deserves it. She is a loser magnet. Attracts bad uns without even trying. She assures me that this guy is not that good looking. Andy Fenton, that's his name!

We sat on her thick grey carpet and set our goodies on the coffee table.

'Leave my bloody carpet,' she scolded. 'You'll wear it away.'

I can't help it. It's so soft and deep. Love it. I had one last feel between my fingers before tearing into my pastry.

'So?' I urged.

'He was nice.' I looked at her. 'Okay, better than nice. I really like him.'

I did a drum roll with my hands on her table. I was genuinely pleased for her AND it was so good to be listening to cheerful news for a change. Made me feel normal.

'And how long did it take to get down to BUS-I-NESS?' I wanted to hear all about it.

'We had a quick drink in Mullen's then on to Rubiez. Where else? Then we walked to his place. He has a second floor flat at the bottom of Leamington Terrace. Very nice.'

'Not far to walk then?' I said.

'Not far at all,' she giggled.

'And?'

'We had a couple of glasses of wine.' I must have appeared too eager to hear the juicy bit. 'God sakes Roo. We were at it before I finished my second glass. Okay?'

I was so jealous. 'Bedroom or floor?'

'The sofa actually and yes...he was good.'

Annabelle is acutely aware that her fertility clock is ticking. She has seriously considered using a sperm donor. Fingers crossed for Andy Fenton.

A big drum roll from me and an equally louder one from her. It was funny. Uplifting and drummed home that my chances of shagging anyone remotely young and interesting was zilch. BUT didn't spoil it for my pal. Remained upbeat until

'Why did you bale out on Friday night?'

# FORTY

## *Ruby's Journal*

**Thursday Evening 16th May.**

I'm staying over at Annabelle's tonight. I'm knackered. Needing an early night. Colin stayed away again last night. Spent the night listening for him. Totally denied it when I tackled him this morning. Claimed he came in during the night. He didn't. I had the keys in the locks. Set my alarm for 5.45am and removed them. I heard him sneak in around 6.30am. Claims he has a job and his shift finishes at 1.30am. Refused to tell me where he works. Cos it's not fucking true. I let him think that I believed him. However, I told him that I would not be home tonight. He thinks I am staying at Deacon House. No need to correct him.

On Monday, I had an update with the insurance company. Progress slow.

I took the train to Glasgow on Tuesday. Dr Riddell had arranged for me to meet Professor James Warnock (her godfather). She was at pains to emphasise that consultations with him were like gold dust. He was doing her a huge favour by seeing me so soon. It's a private clinic but he does NHS work too. Relieved that Kenneth and Margaret are still here to look after the kids. I don't want to let Ben down when I've only just got a foot in the door. He might find a replacement.

I can drive around Edinburgh with my eyes closed but for

some reason I can't navigate Glasgow city centre yet I've been plenty times. I love the shops. There's a buzz about the place that Edinburgh seems to lack. Hence the train.

When I stepped off at Glasgow Queen Street, I was an hour early. Didn't want to risk a coffee stop so walked in the general direction of Argyle Street. Knew I could have walked it in time but flagged down a taxi. Found a lovely wee cafe two minutes away from the Inglis Trust. Had an Americano with a little hot milk on the side. I'm trying to educate your taste buds!! You can't cope with as strong a coffee as I did.

The building was very impressive from the outside. Built in the same style as the Art Gallery round the corner but much much smaller. Still a little intimidating. There was a white modern extension at the side of it. Wish I had taken the car as there were plenty parking spaces. Deep down I knew that I would have been bricking the drive. As you know, I have no sense of direction. I once took the wrong turning leaving Glasgow Airport and ended up crossing the Erskine Bridge. I only realised my mistake when I was reading signs that Loch Lomond was nearby. What a tube!! Ben couldn't believe it. No, actually he could.

A huge part of me was wishing I was somewhere else. I only agreed to do this to placate Eleanor Riddell. Keep her on my side.

I could've had a coffee of choice in their ultra smart waiting room. And a dinky piece of millionaire's shortcake.

James Warnock was not as I imagined he would be. Old, bushy hair, eccentric. Instead, he was drop dead gorgeous. A little older than you maybe. His dreamy brown eyes were mesmerising. He looked Scandinavian but had that posh Scottish boarding school intonation that so many of our neighbours at the Grange have. Very calming as was his room. More comfortable than clinical. He asked me to take a seat. I sat in one. He sat in the other opposite me. Two large grey tartan tub chairs. A glass coffee table separated us. An assortment of large pebbles filled a wicker type plate. Maybe trying too hard. I was pleased I had chosen the navy floral dress. I bought rose pink suede sling backs to wear with it. The weather outside was glorious for May and his French doors opened out onto a lovely well kept private garden.

'I'm NOT having hypnosis,' I blurted.

All he had asked me to do was take a chair.

'Why would that be, Rachel?'

What could I say? Because you'll have me sectioned if you discover that a fifty-six-year-old woman truly believes that she is her thirty-four-year-old daughter.

'I'm too frightened that I might subconsciously reveal something that you warrant having me put away for.'

Fucking hell, I started to cry. It was only then that I realised how nervous I had been about the consultation.

He smiled and assured me that that would not happen.

We chatted for a long while. Mainly about what I could remember and what I could not. Not always about my life but things in the news, historical events and my reactions to them. Honestly, I was exhausted guarding every utterance that came from my mouth. I refused to have our conversation taped. That had to arouse his suspicions that I was holding something back.

Soon we were on to the nitty gritty stuff. What had my relationship been like with my family members? My/your mum and dad. Me and Rory. Rob and Colin. He had to have noticed that I squirmed when Colin's name was mentioned. Yet he was gentle in his questioning.

At one point, I asked him if he believed me or did he think that I was putting it on?

'Are you?'

I shook my head. 'Do you honestly think that I want to be like this? My whole world is upside down,' I could feel my anger bubbling away. 'I don't remember the relationship that I had with family and friends. Or with Colin. And I don't ever want to rekindle what I had with that man. Never. I'm one hundred per cent certain that it was an abusive controlling relationship.'

I can't remember exactly how I phrased it all but I did let him know how lonely it is not having access to everything in my memory bank. Haven't a clue if he believed me.

'Perhaps together we can unlock them,' he slipped it in.

'That would mean hypnotising me,' I said.

'Maybe, maybe not.'

'What then. Electrolysis? A lie detector? That won't be happening.'

'Let me tell you about the brain,' he said very matter of factly.

I have to say it was fascinating. He showed me diagrams of the brain and pointed out the hippocampus where the memory is stored. In my case, there were no obvious signs of physical damage or injury but stress, anxiety and depression, even insomnia can cause trauma leading to memory loss. He asked about your depression and anxiety.

I could only repeat what others had told me but I felt compelled to say that at this moment in time I sensed that Colin had engineered it. I wasn't suggesting that it hadn't manifested into me (you) requiring medication as I had to admit that after the accident, I was grateful for them. They calmed me down. Gave me clarity but I had been weaning myself off them.

'With Doctor Riddell's assistance?' he asked.

Oh, he could tell that it was not the case. I apologised for doing it behind her back.

He talked about psychogenic amnesia where the patient, or in my case me, had gaps in their memory and loss of personal identity. We are profoundly unable to remember personal information about ourselves and can fail to recognise close family members, friends and colleagues. Matched me perfectly. I was nodding at anything that would logically fit my profile. Not my real profile obviously but one that would on the surface satisfy the professionals. Not that I was naive enough to believe that James Warnock could be duped but let's face it, he would be hard pushed to give any credence to my explanation.

I scribbled my notes as did he (felt rotten about that) and underlined psychogenic focal retrograde amnesia as that seemed to pinpoint me to a T.

Apparently, truth drugs and hypnosis don't always give the results expected as the information they illicit is often a mixture of truth and fantasy. Ooooooh, imagine the fun he'd have trying to work out what was true about me.

In most cases, people like me were more than likely to recover of our own accord. Familiar surroundings and routines should help.

I asked if Colin could be taken out...of the equation. He illicted a little laugh at that as did I.

And that was it. Over and done. Would I be willing to see him again in twelve weeks say or earlier if there was a significant change?

Of course, I would. Needed to keep on Eleanor Riddell's good side. I walked back to the train station. Took me forty minutes. Took a couple of wrong turns!!

Yesterday had my wee rays of sunshine. I was allowed to pick them up early from nursery (but not in the car, had to walk there) and take them for an ice-cream in the palace courtyard.

We cut through Holyrood Park. Nursery almost backs on to it. Fabulous weather. Hundreds of tourists and students enjoying the sunshine just like us.

Talking about rays, I'm visiting a woman's refuge centre next week. My Ray of Hope blog has taken on a life of its own.

So humbling yet exciting at the same time. I am actually reaching out to hundreds of women. Why did I waste so much energy on Instagram and Snapchat? Always assumed it was part of my job to keep my followers happy. Futile vanity!!!!!!!

Yet have to admit, I'm addicted to checking up on Jemma fucking Courtney.

# FORTY-ONE

## *Ruby's Journal*

**Friday Morning 17th.**

Had a great night's sleep. So good not having to have an ear on sonar alert. Annabelle left sharpish. She has a stand at a Gin Festival in Newcastle and won't be back until Monday. I can come and go as I please and stay any or every night if I choose. Not sure what I'll do. There's no real need for me to be at home (my house at Dick Place) all day. Not enough for me to do to justify me being there. Don't want to piss Ben off. Garden needs attention so that could be my future excuse.

We have always taken the kids out of nursery early on a Friday for gymnastics and quality family time. They have been desperate to see the new 'How to train Your Dragon' and Ben has found a cinema that is still showing it. I would have loved to have been invited, instead I'm bulk cooking for the freezer. Mainly for the kids but I'll prepare a few meals for me and Annabelle too.

**Saturday.**

Yesterday evening (Friday) had fish and chips with Auntie Vera. Hadn't seen her properly for a while. Was forced to watch Emmerdale, Coronation Street and East Enders back to back. Not seen any of them in years as it's the kids' bedtime routine from seven to eight thirtyish. Bath, chat and stories etc. Had to keep asking Auntie Vera who was who. I honestly think she was getting them mixed up though. Definitely no Dingles in Corrie!!!!! I had to be aware of the main storylines of all the dramas on TV and radio, especially if I was interviewing any of them. Facebook and YouTube kept me abreast of any gossip or poignant story lines.

Claire and Jade stayed over. Decided not to object. Jade in with me and Claire on the settee. Something was up. Claire had a face like fizz. Jade told me that her mum and granda had words. Interesting.

Now back at the Pitt Street flat. Billy no mates.

**9.00pm.** You'll never guess? I was flicking through Netflix in my jammies when a text popped up. Bloody hell. Only Jasper asking if I fancied a drink or a coffee later. He will be dropping his last fare off at the North British Hotel around 9.30ish. No probs if I can't.

First time I've heard from him since last Friday. I thought I'd been given the big E. Like he thought I'd been using him. Which I had been but not in a selfish way. At least, I hope it didn't seem that way.

**9.45pm.** I'd brought nothing with me to wear so I hauled out half of Annabelle's wardrobe. Plumped for a pair of black stretchy trousers and a loose-fitting shirt. Black with white polka dots. The trousers are those that one size fits all. Seems to work as they fitted you. Not bad, I think. Thank God you two have size 5 shoes. Found a pair of black ankle boots with a decent heel. Jasper is quite tall. Jeezuz, I hope he doesn't think a shag is on the agenda. By pure chance I had packed matching bra and knickers. Don't go there I hear you shout. I won't.

I'm actually shaking as I write this. Sorry. You'd think a chicken had scratched the words on to my diary.

I must pick up some eyelashes the next time I'm out

shopping. Your lashes are minute and so fair. I'll get them dyed too. And what the hell have you done to your eyebrows. Thin or what? Sorry, I'm criticising again. Don't wish to be mean. It's nerves. Please God, no expectations of sex. I'm not ready. I have missed it... but with Ben. Not craving cock anywhere else. Oops. Rude crude.

OMG. THE BELL!!!

**12.55am.** Back already. You know what? I had a very pleasant evening. We went to a SleepEEzzy Hotel near Corstorphine. NO, not for sex. I'd heard of it but never ever thought of going there. It has a smart lounge bar-cum-restaurant on the top floor. Never expected a budget hotel to be so nice. Elegant, comfy seating and chairs. Colours were a bit zesty but it suited the place.

Jasper ordered a charcuterie board for us to share. I wasn't hungry but nibbled on it to appear amiable. Again, surprisingly good. We do a seafood sharing platter at Suthiez and Rubiez. I miss my old life. We chatted away like we'd known each other for years. He had been in the marines for twenty years then worked in security for six. Protecting vessels and tracking pirate ships in the likes of the Gulf of Aden and the Gulf of Guinea. Pretty scary stuff. He said the pirates in the South China Sea were the most vicious. I was amazed how sympathetic he was about the Somalians. For many it's the extreme poverty that drives them to it. Bear that in mind if you are staring down the barrel of one of their guns!!!!!

He is actually looking good. Still had his suit on when he picked me up but ditched the jacket and tie. I did have a little flutter in my stomach when I was chatting with him.

'I take it you are not married?' Felt I had to ask.

'Married at thirty. Short lived. One daughter. Nearly

eighteen. Lives with her mum in Liverpool.' He smiled broadly. 'Anything else?'

I shook my head. He has lovely white teeth. I like good teeth.

Not a lot to tell about me (you) that could match his exciting life. Spoke a little about me (Ruby) and Rory. That's what mothers do. Boring the pants off others while extolling their children's virtues.

To be fair, he kept steering the conversation back to you.

'What's next for you, Rachel?'

My memory loss fascinated him. Reinvent yourself, he said. He was so sincere. You can now do or be anything you want to be.

A tiny flame flickered somewhere. I suppose that's all that was open to me. A new me.

The staff definitely knew him. Every one of them acknowledged him as they passed and he had a bar tab.

'Do you come here a lot?' I quizzed.

He laughed again. 'I stay here regularly. They do me a good rate. It's cheaper than the airport hotels and I can be at the airport in less than ten minutes, especially at five in the morning.'

He had an early pick up. My face flared. Honestly Mum, what is wrong with your metabolism? I never blush but you do constantly. It's hugely embarrassing. I rightly assumed that he had a room for the night.

'Don't worry, Rachel. I'm not making a move.'

Oh, my days!!! He leaned in and kissed me. A little more than a peck. Soft juicy lips kissed mine and I blushed again.

'It's the wine.' I said patting my face. Who was I kidding?

Funnily enough, the conversation continued to flow. No more kissing until he escorted me downstairs for my taxi. Asked me to check I had enough money for the fare home. He'd had too much wine to drive me back.

It certainly wasn't a snog but longer than a goodbye kiss that two friends might exchange.

In the taxi, my head was all over the place. I felt as if I had cheated on Ben. Jasper is a handsome guy for fifty. I'm sure many women of my age would find him attractive and I'm pretty certain that he could pick and choose. So, what the hell was he doing with you/me?

Home. I mean Annabelle's. No sex. Fair enough yet mildly disappointed. I'm away to retrieve Boner Man. A girl has needs after all. I can hardly stash it at Carberry Cres. Ben bought me Boner Man for a joke on Mother's Day when I was pregnant with Alfie. But it is the best sex toy ever. Supersedes most of the other dildos in my collection. See you in the morning.

# FORTY-TWO

*Rachel's flat in Portobello. Tuesday 7th January 2020.*

Rachel had sudden dread. What if she and Jasper had actually had a relationship? And what if it was still happening now, at this moment in time? Surely, he wouldn't turn up in Portobello expecting anything? Her eyes scoured the smart room as she tried to imagine Jasper and her shagging on the white leather sofa or stretched out naked on the shag pile rug. Rachel's cheeks burned and she automatically apologised to Ruby for her red face syndrome; she'd had it since she was a teenager. Her pals ribbed her constantly about it. Life seemed simpler then. Then it donned on her; she missed Lisa and she needed to talk to her to get her take on the mess that she found herself in

Annabelle had been too quick to text everyone urging them not to contact. She meant well and Rachel had gone along with it only because she was still trying to make sense of it all. But she is not Ruby and what she needed now was her own friend. It had been a long time and she feared Lisa might tell her to get stuffed. Maybe not in as many words but it's no more than she deserved. And yet Lisa had reached out to Ruby when she'd asked for help. Rachel had been an idiot. A stubborn idiot. Mother and daughter had a lot in common.

She had a quick sniff under her armpits. Ooooh! Whiffy! A shower was required but before that she typed a short text to Annabelle.

Daft question

Is there any chance that at this moment in time Ruby was in a relationship with someone and could that said someone have a key to this flat? Xx"

The reply was instantaneous. She couldn't possibly have had time to read or type, thought Rachel.

'Ha ha. No worries bbz. I'm only one with key. See you on Thursday"

Followed with several emojis of laughing faces with streaming tears and beating hearts.

Rachel stepped into the spacious, cylindrical shaped cabinet and allowed the hot water to massage her shoulders and back. The large shower head ensured that 'tropical' spray covered every inch of her body. Bliss. She tried not to dwell on the sex thing. Gently, she worked the shampoo into her hair and scalp, carefully avoiding her stitches. The lather was silky soft. More quality products courtesy of her Ruby. And the smell? Honey and something else. Rachel was determined to pinpoint it before checking the label. She caressed her body with the foam from her hair. Nutmeg or cinnamon. That was the 'what else' she could detect. She sneaked a peak at the bottle. Yeh, nutmeg. Feeling terribly smug, she let the hot spray work its magic as she closed her eyes and smiled.

Once she was thoroughly dried, (she hated dressing while her body was damp) she slipped on Ruby's oversized white towelling robe. Bathroom scales had been tucked in behind the laundry basket. Rachel wondered what she weighed. The robe slipped off her shoulders and dropped to the floor. Steam clung to the full-length mirrored tiles on the wall opposite the shower cabinet. She swept her hand back and forth to take the worst of the water off then buffed the square mirrors with her towel. She studied her naked body as she had done before in the hospital, only this time she wasn't as shocked so she took her time. She surmised she had lost somewhere between three and three and a half stones. Bloody hell, she was nine stone and eleven pounds. A loss of almost four stones. She weighed just under nine stones when she was twenty and even then her mother claimed she looked gaunt. Rachel had always been heavier than she looked. Heavy bones her old granny would say.

With a chirpiness that had eluded her for a long, long time, Rachel blow-dried her hair on a cool heat. The area around her wound was itchy and she didn't want to aggravate it.

Darkness had descended. The promenade looked empty and Rachel closed the blinds. She was a little peckish. She'd skipped lunch but had demolished the small packet of Pringles she'd purchased earlier and was annoyed with herself. Ruby had obviously worked hard to shift the fat and must have exercised regularly to achieve the level of energy that Rachel could feel that she had – in spite of her sore head. Thinking about food, she reflected on Rob and Patricia having cosy restaurant meals with the Sutherlands. Why had Kenneth and Margaret never invited her and Colin to join them: in anything? They did used to spend quality time with her when she was on her own and single. Zoo trips and picnics at the beach or park with their grandchildren. Perhaps Colin hadn't disguised his dislike for them as well as she had hoped.

It was 7.00pm. Lisa would definitely be home and have had tea.

She hesitated. Why was she so nervous? In for a penny, she rang her friend.

'Rachel?'

'Hi Lis, it's me.'

Rachel cried quietly.

'You okay, honey?' asked Lisa. More muffled sobbing. 'Rachel? You're worrying me.'

'I'm so sorry, Lisa, for everything,' sniffed Rachel.

'What do you mean? What's happened?' There was an anxious tone to Lisa's voice.

'I should've listened to you.'

'What d' ye mean like?'

'Colin... and everything else. I'm so sorry.' She sniffed louder this time.

'What's happened? You sound different.'

Rachel composed herself. 'I've got my memory back. Well, sort of.'

'What? You can remember everything?'

'Not everything. Nothing for the last nine months but everything before the accident, I think.'

'Oh my God, that's fantastic. Weird but fantastic,' enthused her pal.

'Scary weird. Oh Lisa, I need to see you. My Ruby has gone.'

The grieving erupted. Firstly, from Rachel quickly followed by her childhood friend.

'I'm so sorry, Rach. I'd come over if I could but I've got wee Oscar for the night and the wee bugger won't settle with Brian. I can't leave him.'

Eighteen-month-old Oscar was Lisa's only grandchild. Unconditionally loved by his grandparents and unconditionally spoiled to boot.

'Tomorrow maybe? I know I don't deserve it but I'd really appreciate it.'

'Of course I'll come...if I can get past your Rottweiler,' scoffed Lisa.

'Christ! Do I have a dog?'

Lisa laughed. 'I'm talking about your new best pal.' Rachel didn't reply. 'Annabelle!'

'I'm so sorry Lisa. I can't explain that.' She could but chose not to. Rachel fully understood the need keep the contents of Ruby's diary confidential.

'I'm being a bitch. How about I come to you after work tomorrow? Say six?'

'Do you know where I live?'

'Oh aye, I know. Yer fancy wee pad in Porty.'

'Oh, it's fancy all right. What wis I thinkin?' mocked Rachel. 'Will you be driving? It would be nice to have a wee drink. And I'll cook us something. Nothing fancy.'

'Now I know you're back. The last time ye had me for dinner, I thought ye were auditioning for MasterChef,' Lisa chortled.

'God Lisa, I've missed you.'

'I've missed you more my lovely. Tomorrow it is then.'

'Love you, Lisa.'

'And I love you, Rachel.'

# FORTY-THREE

*Ruby's Journal*

**Sunday Morning 19.5.19.**

Sweating like a pig!! My first run for me as you. Knackered. More walking than running but it's a start. I'm cutting out the croissants and lattes in the morning so after my shower, it's avocado on toast with a teensy sprinkling of chilli flakes and a squeeze of lemon. Grabbing some water first.

**10.40am.** Aaaahhhh, feel normal. Ran, washed and fed.

I've been thinking about what Jasper said and it's time to think about my future so here goes.

I can't be me and I haven't a clue how to be you so I do have to reinvent myself. Thought I'd start with a list.

God it's so hard. Do I do pros and cons? But not sure what my pros and cons would actually be about.

*What I want to be. What I don't want.*

Nope. Don't want that.

I'm going to list what I can do or can't do. Jeepers, how hard can it be?

1. Can't be a teacher. Wouldn't know where to start.

2. Good news – I still get paid. Full pay for a while yet. BUT can't take on another job. Bummer.

3. Can't be a radio presenter. Actually, I could but not while I'm getting paid from school. No point in not taking advantage of that.

4. Can still see the kids THANK YOU SO MUCH (if that's God I've to thank) but have to be careful or that could be whipped away from me.

5. Can't be with Ben. Has to be the saddest bit. I'm heart-broken again. Not fucking fair!!!

6. Be positive, at least I can look after him. DON'T SPOIL IT!!!!!

7. Need to be fitter and healthier. Starting now.

8. I still have Annabelle. Thank you again for that. I should have put that nearer the beginning.

9. I have to be rid of Colin and that will mean leaving Alderburn. Sorry Mum.

10. I must be more proactive on the blog. So many women seeking help and advice.

11. Need to build new friendships or I'll get bored. Can't expect Annabelle to carry the can all the time.

12. All those years of networking down the bloody drain. No use even trying with the girls. Can't blame them. I'd be the same.

13. Will try and maintain some kind of friendship with Auntie Lisa but others of yours will be left behind. Sorry.

14. Perhaps I could go back to my roots. Events Management. Or wedding planning. I could do that with my eyes shut.

15. Maybe Ben would let me be the kid's nanny. That would definitely be the dream job.

16. Must must ensure that my funds are as good as they can be.

17. Wean myself off diazepam.

18. I mentioned it earlier but being as fit as I can be.

19. Don't piss off Annabelle or Ben. EVER!!!!

20. Finishing on twenty. Stop being scared because I'm still shitting it.

Plenty to be getting on with. Maybe should have said something about getting Ben's affairs in order and I want to sort through all my belongings at Deacon House and at Carberry. And need my hair done soon.

**1.10pm.** Blog updated. I'm really getting to know some of my ladies now. Not personally as we don't use our real names nor do we ever name our tormentors. The risk is too great. The women (it's mainly women) are from all walks of life. From obscenely wealthy to church mice poor and from all colours, creeds and ethnicities. Yet our problems are the same. We live or used to live with nasty controlling bastards. Some of those pieces of shit are so vindictive they are desperate to hunt down their previous partners and track sites/blogs like *Ray of Hope* looking for clues to their whereabouts. My ladies who still live with their abusers are terrified that someone, anyone, might inadvertently tell their partner that they have read something about them. They live in fear and are controlled by fear.

Advice is given by those who have lived it. Walked the walk and felt the punches yet the sad thing is – too many of them go back to the abuser either for the sake of the children or the misplaced belief that he (sometimes she) has changed. Far too many have been hospitalised and still return to the family home. Often it is the threat to the children that gives them the courage to leave. Desperately heartbreaking stories and not enough support from society in general to tackle and thwart these bullies.

There's Laura. Has no friends. Her family have disowned her (or maybe she did them). She's had umpteen miscarriages which her partner thinks is something she has engineered. She is a successful accountant. He is a surgeon. Beats her severely at least twice a week then doesn't touch her for months. When he is remorseful, showers her with gifts and holidays that she hates. The waiting she says is often worse than the beating phase. My team of readers try to give her the tools to cope and to prepare for escape.

Betty. Bless her. Think she is older as she has chosen an older name. Madly, deeply in love with a younger man. He started to fleece her ages ago. Now he is borrowing and not paying back. So far never violent but you can tell she feels intimidated. I've lost count of the number of excuses she makes for him. We need to build her confidence.

Zena. Very much emotional abuse. Makes her do and say

appalling things. Often sexual. Not violent but deviant. Can hardly write this. He encourages the pet dog to mount her. No penetration, thank Christ. It hardly bares thinking about.

God there's more. Tons of it but those three are regulars.

I'm going back to Alderburn tonight. Having tea with Lisa and Brian. See Mum, making an effort. Plus, I like Auntie Lisa. She's a sensible sounding board.

# FORTY-FOUR

*Ruby's Journal*

**Wednesday 22nd May.**

Where to start? Sunday night after I had had tea with Lisa and Brian.

I'd let my guard down. It had been three weeks since I had confronted Colin about my banking and four since returning from Enniskillen. You would think that my blog would have kept me focussed. My senses alert. No!! Let's be honest, four weeks isn't a long time but such a lot had happened to me in the weeks that followed it could have been four years ago.

Got in from Lisa's around 9.30pm. I had dropped my stuff off earlier but he wasn't at home. Alarm bells should have been ringing. Every light in the house was on when I got back. Ben and I were always leaving lights on, much to your consternation, Mum. Like Blackpool Illuminations, you would bleat. We would just laugh. BUT Colin is usually more frugal. I didn't call out when I entered and I certainly didn't sneak in.

I caught him in my room. Foraging in my drawers. My wardrobe door was wide open and boxes from under both beds had been pulled out.

'What the fuck?' I screamed.

He sprang up. I'd startled him and he'd been rumbled. Standing bolt upright, he faced me. 'Where's my fucking money?' he demanded.

'What money?'

'Ye ken fine. It was in my room. Where is it?'

I laughed and gave him one of my notorious put-downs 'As if I'd take anything that belonged to you?'

I ambled through to the kitchen, for nothing in particular, to gain composure before returning to my room. He was still raking.

'Are you still here? Could you please leave my room?' I could feel the hairs on my arm stand up. Domino effect in reverse; straight up my arm to the base of my neck.

'What do you call this then?' He emptied the contents of a plastic River Island bag. 'Where did you get the money for this shite?' The shite was all my new running kit.

'That's the money I save not having to fork out for all your mobile phones.' I understood immediately the scorn in my tone.

Within a split second, he had his hands at my throat and steered me backwards on to the bed. I could smell alcohol on his breath. It was strong. Whisky rather than beer.

I screamed that I knew nothing about any money. I hadn't been in all day.

'Liar!' he roared. Spittle covered my face. 'I need that money!'

Then I did remember I had been in. Dumped my bags on the bed before setting off for Haddington. He took that momentary glance at my belongings as an admission of guilt. His face was puce. Scrunched up and plain horrid. Horrible and ugly.

'You're a dirty slut just like your dirty snob of a daughter.'

Next thing, he wedged his left forearm under my chin and began tugging at my shirt and jeans with his free hand. FUCK! His unshaven chin was scratching my face. I was wriggling beneath him with all my strength. My knees constantly shrugging him off. Jade's soft toys kept toppling on my face. He would not have me without a fight. I thought about head butting him but with him on top, he might have done the same to me with considerably more force. Then I remembered an article I had read on-line about pushing your fingers up an assailant's nose. So I did. I wriggled my right arm free from under his body. I shoved, with all my might, my forefinger and middle finger straight up his nostrils. AND it bloody worked. His nose erupted and saturated me with blood. He was writhing in pain. You have always had thick strong nails. I inherited them too. They say fight or flight mode can kick in. With me it was fight. I kneed him right in the balls, grabbed my bag and ran. I was tempted to leg it to Auntie Vera's but hit Dad's number instead.

'He tried to rape me.' Was all I managed to blurt.

Next thing, the young guy next door leapt the fence and was fussing over me. His heavily pregnant partner waddled round and down your path. I was more worried for her at that point than me. She was shaking. I remember they sent a lovely sympathy card when I died. Sean, (young guy's name) rushed in the front door. It was ages before he came out. Or it seemed ages.

'Tried to mak oot that you attacked him. Aye right!' acknowledged Sean.

Anyone with half an eye could tell I had been attacked. The buttons had been ripped from my open shirt. The zip of my jeans was down. I had to look dishevelled. The blood alone must have been frightening.

Huge pregnant belly wanted me to go to their house but I insisted on waiting for Dad. And I begged Sean not to call the police. Truth is if it was Blair and the unsympathetic Emma, we might both be lifted this time. Kind of explained this to Sean. He was appalled.

'I'll gie him a doing for ye,' he offered.

I thanked him. Maybe next time.

'If there's a next time, he's fuckin deid,' insisted Sean. I like him.

Dad and Patricia pulled up. Dad took one look at me and barged through the front door. The three of us were hard on his heels.

'COLIN!!' hollered Dad. 'Fucking show yersel.'

Colin was bending over the kitchen sink. Cold tap running hard. His head at an awkward angle. The water flowing over his oversized beak.

Dad gruffly pulled him by the scruff of the neck.

'It wad Rachel,' he snivelled through a blocked nose.

'Ye got away wi it last time, mate, but not this time,' Dad warned him

'Deck im,' sang Sean dancing on the spot, in his bare feet. His jeans were hanging off his skinny bum. He looked about sixteen. We were all hyper.

'No!' It was Patricia. 'Let the police sort it out.'

I tried to remonstrate but Patricia was having none of it. 'Don't let him off again,' she said softly. She wandered into the living room to make the call.

I started to cry. Relief probably. Colin was ranting that it was me who had flown at him. It wasn't fair he yelled. Same script as before.

At one point, Colin tried to leave the kitchen but both Sean and Dad blocked the exits. He slumped onto one of the chairs at the table to await his fate. There was an eerie calm in the house. Patricia draped a throw over my shoulders and made us teas and coffees. Colin got bugger all.

Get this, Patricia whipped out her phone and took

photographs of me and the bedroom. Evidence should I need it. I felt guilty that I had thought so little of her in the past.

In less than 10 minutes the police were at the door. Sean had gone to check on Tanya but raced back round when the patrol car parked at the gate. Dad had to explain why Sean had suddenly reappeared.

Fortunately, it was two different uniformed officers. Both male. I can't remember their names. Only that one was blond and the other jet black, as in hair. Maybe I was in shock or truly grateful that Patricia was doing a lot of the talking but it all seemed to wash over me.

Colin ranted. Blamed me. Over and over until the blond one told him to shut up or he would be cuffed and put in the car.

They asked me if I could talk them through what had happened. I showed them the bedroom. There was blood everywhere. All over the pillow and duvet. It had splashed on to the headboard and large splodges were on the carpet. Jade's teddies looked as if they had been mutilated.

'Accused me of taking his money,' I said, explaining why the room was in such a mess.

'Did you?' asked black hair.

'Nope,' said I, 'was in and out again in five minutes. I wouldn't even know where to look for his money. Plus, would be too frightened of getting caught.' Held up my hands as if to say, 'can't you tell?'

Sean, Dad and Patricia gave their statements. Sean, bless him, was very animated. Kept saying what a kind, decent neighbour you were. His mum knew you and thought the same. Kept referring to Colin as 'dodgy though'.

Another police car arrived. A woman constable and an officer in plain clothes. Never did I think that I would have to go to the station. Patricia insisted on accompanying me. The woman PC, Susan, suggested I pack a change of clothing. Colin was put in the other car. Dad said he would lock up with Sean.

To be fair, I was processed reasonably quickly. I wouldn't say I was interrogated but they were making sure my answers were consistent. I had to be photographed. The lady photographer was kind, gentle and efficient. She explained everything she was doing and why it was necessary to do it. I was covered in fresh bruising. There were large whelps where Colin had pinned me down, on my arms and huge ones on my legs. I was stunned when I saw them. My neck had a deep red indentation under my chin. Even though I insisted that I had not been raped, photographs were taken of the bruises between my thighs. My clothes were bagged. I refused a shower. I preferred to shower at home. Overall, I was shown more kindness than I had been after my previous run in with the police.

Colin was kept in overnight for questioning. I was allowed to go home.

There was no way that Patricia was letting me stay on my own. I had to go to their house. Was actually grateful. Had a hot bath and Horlicks and toast. Two paracetamols and two ibuprofen. Big comfy bed. Slept like a log.

Next morning Patricia ran me home. We stripped the bed and washed the stains on the carpet. Nothing fazed her. I genuinely meant it when I thanked her and hoped we had turned a corner. I wanted to be able to visit Dad without Patricia wishing I was somewhere else. I'm fully aware that my relationship with Dad will mirror the one I have with Ben – walking on eggshells. But any relationship is better than nothing.

Imagine my surprise when the doorbell rang. I thought Pat had forgotten something. It was Claire.

'What the hell do you want?' I spat.

'I'm here to collect some clothes for my da.'

I was trying to think of something sarcastic for my retort when she asked politely if she could come in. Then it spouted.

'How is the wife beater?' I asked.

Claire made for his bedroom, said nothing, and began throwing shirts, pants, socks and trousers into a large black holdall. She worked quickly. I asked my question again.

She let out a huge sigh and plonked her bottom on the bed. I actually felt sorry for her. She looked done. Years older than her... How old is she? Forty? Forty-five? I'm not sure. It's the navy hair – ages her. Too harsh for her pale white skin.

'Look Rachel, I know my da is no angel.' Didn't expect that. 'But he hasn't been right since your accident. It freaked him out. He's been drinking more and that's no him.'

'It hardly been a bag of laughs for me,' said I.

'I get that. An I get that you needed to sort out yer money. I'm no daft. I suspected Da had made you pay for our phones but he's always made out it was his money. I didn't question it. I was just happy that someone was paying the bill.'

Made me feel a wee bit rotten. Was well aware that Claire and Jade lived on or pretty damn close to the breadline.

'Has he been violent to me before?' Had to be asked.

Here response was for real. 'Not that I'm aware of.'

'Then why now?'

Claire assumed it was my memory loss that threw him. Plus, I was different. Feisty. Answered back. He probably concluded that I would start asking more probing questions, especially about money. And you had always been compliant.

'Did we (her and you) get on before the accident?' I had wondered.

'You were good to Jade. She adores her Granny Rachel. You treated her with respect. Spent a lot of time with her. Her confidence has soared with you in her life.

'And now?'

She gave me a look that suggested that Jade had regressed. More pressure.

While we were in sharing mode, I asked her about her mother.

'Sorry to ask this but I need to get my head round it. Why did your mum and dad separate?'

She laughed (more of a scoff). 'Mum had been in and out of care for a while before you came along but once Dad took an interest in you, I knew she would never be out again. She had fathomed it out too. Stopped eating.'

The look on my face must have said it all. My insides were in turmoil. Poor woman.

Then she dithered. 'It could have been anyone. If not you then somebody else. My da had set his sights on a new partner for a long time. Can't blame him. Mum had depression for years. He was miserable. She held us all back. Jade never really had a granny. Wasn't able to help out like she done before. Had some periods when she was happy. Didn't last though.'

I reminded her that people with depression aren't able to help others. It's them that need our support. Had she always been depressed?

Claire's face lit up when she talked about a childhood filled with happy memories. Her mother was very hands on. Picnics everywhere. In the garden. In the park. On the beach. She made up for their lack of family holidays.

'Was money tight?' I asked tentatively.

She laughed again. It was laced with spite. Regret maybe?

'My da couldn't hold down a job.'

She jumped up. The sharing was over. More bits and pieces were shoved into the bag.

'Is he staying with you?'

'Nope, thank God.' She was about to say where but stopped in her tracks. 'He hasn't been charged with anything, Rachel.'

I was stunned. 'Look at me,' I shouted, pointing to my neck. 'He ATTACKED me!'

She screwed her indifferent face and shook her head. 'Not enough evidence to charge him. It wasn't your blood. He had bruises too. Claims you enticed him in to your room then called rape when things got heated. Not the first time.'

I couldn't believe it. The wall was holding me up. I could feel my words choking me.

'Do you believe me, Claire?'

She shrugged her shoulders. 'My da likes to be in control... of everyone. You disappointed him. He doesn't like to be disappointed.' She was back on team dad.

'Was it you who took his money?' She didn't deny it nor confirm it, merely raised her eyebrows then smirked.

She's as menacing as her dad.

# FORTY-FIVE

*Ruby's Journal*

**Tuesday 21st May.**

Had a meeting with a Sheena Levigne from City Women's Refuge.

The moment I walked through the door, she clocked the bruising around my face and neck (beneath all the makeup!). Suppose she is trained to notice. Said nothing. A true professional but I had to blab it all to her. I apologised for the mess of my skin.

She frowned. *Why did I need to apologise for someone else's lack of self-control?*

True. I apologised for apologising. Then she smiled.

'I'm one of the lucky ones,' I said. 'I've found the courage to fight back.'

I gave her my (your) background. Felt I needed to explain the amnesia and why the abuse seemed new and alien to me.

We chatted about my blog. She followed us regularly. I explained that I wanted more guidance. I was fully aware that there were more professional sites than mine but I had set up my blog as an outlet for me and hopefully to help others along the way. I didn't want to give false hope or unhelpful advice to those women who depended on true, hard facts. She was lovely. More than that, empathetic and enthusiastic, often in the face of unfair bureaucracy.

I was given contact numbers that are manned 24/7. Callers should always hear a sympathetic voice at the other end of the line. Although, through my many contributors, I understood the stages of help available, it felt worthwhile to have it all confirmed. Many refuge centres operate under strict secrecy but there were some that are known to regular returnees and unfortunately their perpetrators. These centres are fairly secure and vulnerable families can be transferred to more secure sites if deemed necessary. Unfortunately, some women (or their children) were forced to reveal where they had been hiding and that information was often shared with other abusers on unscrupulous websites.

I asked Sheena about my own predicament. She wasn't surprised that Colin had walked away scot-free. Domestic abuse is often hard to prove and harder to generate real sympathy within certain establishments. The abuser is often very convincing and, like Colin, portrays themselves as the victim. Distance yourself from him was the advice I was given. My situation was most unlikely to improve. On average, it takes seven attempts before a woman finally leaves her abuser.

I emerged from that building with remarkable positivity, armed with more information than I had hoped for. I felt sure I could make a difference.

Something else I hadn't expected that day. Ben insisted on paying me for helping out with Alfie and Nola.

He was appalled when I admitted that it was Colin who had caused the bruising to my neck and face. Bless my Ben, he offered me the spare room at the other side of the house. It's the one we keep for guests who may wish privacy away from the main house (and the kids). It's a lovely space with an ensuite and a pantry kitchen just outside the bedroom door. French doors open onto our garden. I was sorely tempted to accept it but deep down knew that I would interfere too much. Wouldn't be able to help myself. I would say something I shouldn't and Ben would retaliate. He doesn't back down easily. Stubborn, like me. I assured him I was sorting things out but if an emergency arose then I would move in for a few days at most.

'Is money a problem?' he asked.

I replied that I was trying to get on top of that too.

'You've been great, Rachel. The kids need stability. I don't want to go down the route of having a full-time carer for them. If you're happy to help then I'm happy to pay you. I think Ruby would approve.'

I could sense a but was coming.

'But...I want you to be honest with me. If you feel ill at any time, sore heads, or your memory puts the kids in any danger you have to say. PLEASE.'

I would NEVER do that, I promised. I told him I was thrilled to be given the chance to look after the kids and would consider his generous money offer.

I'm sure you would never have accepted payment, Mum, but I had no knowledge of what was round the corner for me. At the end of the day, it was my money too. I requested time to think about it but my mind was already made up. I needed all the money I could get my hands on for a future I wasn't sure I would have. A nanny would not be cheap and there was no way that another woman was going to play Mummy to my babies. Jeezuz, could you imagine a young, frisky nanny playing happy families with Ben and my two? I might normally have said 'not over my dead body' but since I'm already dead it will have to be 'not if I have anything to do with it!!' Can't believe I made a 'dead' joke about me and you. Ah well, life goes on.

It would have to be cash up front. Or he could pay some of my expenses (nails, hair and the like). I couldn't risk your salary being stopped because I had another job. I would work out something fair.

Slowly but surely, I have been unobtrusively sorting through my clothes and paperwork. There are piles of clothes in my cupboards that I will never wear again. Some clothes that may fit and suit you/me when I am slimmer, fitter. That depends if Ben will allow me to take them but like most men, he doesn't have a clue what I have in my wardrobes.

There were texts from Kit Hendry asking me what I thought about Best Scotland's offer asking me if I would consider taking over permanently from her on *Haud Yer Wheest*. (I found my work phone!!) She wants to concentrate on writing and producing more plays. I had already deleted emails regarding all job offers.

Two major radio stations invited me for talks. One in Scotland, the other down South. That would have meant a semi-permanent move to London. I could never have done that to Ben but, on reflection, maybe I would have contemplated it. Oh, my days. Would I have jeopardised my life with Ben and the kids for a glimpse of fame? I'm mortified that I might have done. And now all I want is to be with them. Night and day and every minute in between. You don't appreciate what you have until...

Ben's unable to open my business mail as I never gave him my access code. Says it all really. I'm an untrustworthy bitch. I knew all his passwords.

Being with the kids is the best thing ever. I'm sure I've said that before but it truly is. When they run into my arms, my heart bursts with love, pride and enormous sadness for what will never be.

There was a reminder in Alfie's nursery bag that there will be a graduation ceremony at the end of June, a little leaver's do, for all those moving on to Primary school after the summer holidays. Whatever next? Parents or guardians can attend. If the weather is good, it will be outside in the garden. Normally, I would have jumped right in and volunteered Suthiez to do the catering but not now. I hope Ben lets me go.

We had a family tea together again. I'll only do it twice a week. I know it's only eating together but I love every moment of it. I watch every mouthful they chew and savour their every swallow. It's pathetic. I wonder if this is how other people who have been given a second chance behave. Like cancer survivors or those who have escaped from war zones. Do they, like me, devour everything their loved ones do?

A police car was waiting at Carberry Crescent when I turned the corner. My stomach flipped. I needn't have worried; they were only there to reiterate what Claire had told me on Monday.

I invited them in and made us (Blair McGlashan and the blond one this time) a cup of coffee. They couldn't charge Colin with assault as the evidence was inconclusive. It was my word against his and given what happened the last time. I think PC Emma what's-her-name put her oar in. A pattern was emerging, exclaimed PC Blond.

I nearly choked on my coffee. 'Funnily enough, abuse is about identifying patterns in a perpetrator's tactics.' I told them all about my visit to the Women's Refuge Services earlier.

They listened and nodded as I lectured them on identifying coercive and controlling behaviour. Maybe it was like trying to sell snow to Eskimos but I felt compelled to say it anyway.

Blair piped up. 'I'm sorry Rachel but it would have been blown out of court. A decent lawyer would blame you. Have answers for everything. Colin was covered in his blood. He had bruises consistent with being punched. His story was believable.'

'And mine wasn't? Did you see me?' I argued. 'I am a normal, respectable teacher. I led an unremarkably quiet life until my accident unveiled some pretty disturbing stuff. All I want is a quiet contented life.'

I asked them if they would be happy to leave their own mothers in my predicament. Forced to live with a lunatic. To the outside world perfectly plausible but a nasty piece of work all the same. That's what they were doing to me.

Blair confirmed I would need irrevocable proof that Colin was targeting me. Did he mean video evidence? Because I knew a man. (Derrick from Fourth Waves.) They looked at each other and did that squint eye thing. I took that as a yes.

Meantime, be careful he said and rubbed my arm.

Well thanks a bunch to my local constabulary.

# FORTY-SIX

## *Ruby's Journal*

**Wednesday 22st May.**

So that was my last two days. Hey, life as you, Mum, certainly can't be described as uneventful.

Ben is going to put my name (yours) on the insurance for my Audi A4. He feels it's been nearly eight weeks since the accident and since I'm allowed to drive your wee Corsa he doesn't see why I can't drive the kids in my Audi. Car seats are already in place. It makes sense. And I can drive the kids to nursery and collect them. Gives us the opportunity to go places when the weather is nice.

I popped into the station today. Felt strange, surreal, sad and exciting all at once. David on reception buzzed me in. Can't just wander in anymore after the brush we had two years ago. Some nutter (maybe not a fair description) wanted his five minutes of fame and five minutes of airtime over a grievance he had with a house builder and the architects. Neither were admitting liability for building his house in the wrong place. But he was armed with a knife and frightened the life out of poor Arlene on the front desk. She never came back.

I'm sure you've been to Waves before. Just off London Road. On Windsor Street. Lovely building. Especially since it was sandblasted. Reception isn't a big area. For the number of times I had passed through the entrance, I had paid scant attention to the space. It could do with more plants and a lick of paint. Isn't very inviting. Not that many people sit there. We have a small meeting room/staff area. Most of us tend to go straight to our studios or to Adrian's office (he's our programme director/ controller).

It was almost 9am and the show had been running since 6.30. There was an hour left. I told David I knew the way. I counted my steps from reception to the studio door. Eleven. Same as always. We are studio 1 (obviously). There are floor to ceiling windows on two sides of our cube. JJ sat in his usual chair but Jemma occupied mine. Different mic though. Thank you, JJ. I had a psychedelic head but immediately noticed Jemma's was orange. Matched her nails and lipstick. In contrast to our casual clothes (I had beige cropped trousers and a cream tee-shirt. JJ was similar to me only he had cream tight fitting jeans), Jemma looked like she was heading off to a wedding. Pink and orange floaty dress and pink heels. Her long brown hair was salon perfect. Jeepers, I usually tied my hair up. Minimal make-up, if any. Comfy gear had always been our preference.

I waited to be summoned by JJ. I would never have sauntered in uninvited. He smiled his big welcoming smile as I paused at the glass door. They had switched from manual back to queue (on our broadcasting screen) for the news. Always on the hour. That meant I could enter and they could take their earphones off. Those few seconds before crossing the threshold were an eternity. I was stepping into a huge part of my life that I could never reclaim. 'Be grateful, be humble,' I breathed. JJ's embrace was as warm as his smile. Jemma was OTT gushing. Better than being dismissive.

You never think about your own room having a smell but ours did. Irrefutably, Jacob Johnston. (Tom Ford *Ombre Leather*. I bought him TF's *Fucking Fabulous* range for his 40th. So JJ.) I pulled up the stool we keep for guests and sat on the other side of JJ away from gushy knickers. Honestly, it felt so good. Jemma ran through my dos and don'ts. Was tempted to show her the palm of my hand but thanked her profusely instead. No gritted teeth (ha ha).

I looked at the timings. 'We've got three minutes. Anything I need to know?'

JJ laughed, 'Like daughter, like mother.' Then his face dropped. Full of remorse. I patted his thigh to reassure him. 'Are you up for a wee chat?' he asked, nodding at the mic.

'Absolutely.' Jemma's face was like thunder.

After the news and our jingle, actually theirs now, Jacob introduced me as his guest. I thanked him and all the listeners for their generous condolences. It was a huge comfort to me and the family. Two more tracks were played then he accepted phone-ins for the *Stop the Bus* challenge.

The caller has to name seven different items/places etc beginning with a letter of the alphabet. It's the best of three. The first one, a man, had to name a collection of things beginning with H.

'Name a city beginning with H.'

'Holland.' There's always one!

His other attempts were just as dismal. Why do they come on? To win the prize of course. A trip around Edinburgh on an open-top bus with lunch for two at Hangman's in the Grassmarket. Rubiez have donated lunch in the past as well.

The third caller did really well and trumped the other two by miles. As Jemma chatted to her about her win, I suddenly recognised the shy wee giggle.

'Ashlyn is that you? Ash from Ashford?' I interrupted. She was one of my regulars.

'Yes,' she giggled nervously.

'Have you had your baby?' I immediately regretted the question in case anything had gone wrong.

'A baby boy. A wee heifer. Ten and a half pounds.'

'Ouch!' I laughed. 'You wanted a boy.' She had three girls. 'Aww, I'm made up for you honey. I really am.' And I was. We used to make a joke that if anyone tuned in to Fourth Waves and waited long enough, they would eventually hear Ashlyn whether it was a competition or just a request. I would make a point of sending a gift to her.

'I am so sorry for your loss,' she whimpered. 'Ruby was a great girl. I loved listening to her cheery voice in the morning. No offence, Jemma.' She threw that in as an afterthought.

'None taken, Ashley. We all miss her,' insisted Jemma and she flashed her insincere grin in my direction. A straight line caught between taut cheeks.

Ashlyn coughed. 'It's Ashlyn.'

Jemma, completely oblivious to her error, wound up the conversation and introduced her next track *Old Town Road* by Lil Nas X. I prefer the new collaborated version with Billy Ray Cyrus. Love it.

The hour whizzed by. I felt that JJ and I fell in to that easy-osey banter that we've always had. He did too as he said as much when we parted.

I left them to it. They would be meeting with Adrian immediately after to discuss the morning's broadcast and to run through the following day's programme. It was only when I was at the end of Windsor Street that I remembered about asking for Derrick Smith's mobile number (telecoms guy) so I nipped back. David gave me the thumbs up and the door swung open.

I was typing in Derrick's number when I heard the raised voices coming from the boss's office. I guessed it was about me.

'She was in for too long,' snarled Jemma. 'She was taking over just like her bloody daughter.'

'It's a one off,' JJ snipped back. 'Look at the feedback. The listeners loved her. No harm done.'

Must admit, Instagram and the rest of the social media was shit hot with comments about how well JJ and Rachel got on.

'Get shot of Jemma and bring on Ruby's mum,' requested one of the punters. Can't deny that I felt well chuffed.

'I don't understand why you are so loyal,' moaned Jemma, 'when she was about to shaft you.'

'So you keep saying. Ruby would never have done that.'

'Tell him, Adrian. Ruby was being offered the morning show as a solo gig.' Jemma was enraged.

'Er, she hadn't officially accepted it,' answered Adrian weakly.

'And she wouldn't have.' JJ was emphatic. Good on him. I had NEVER even been asked to do the show on my own. Nor would I have done. Please, let me believe that.

'You keep thinking that way if it makes you feel better but other stations were sniffing around too,' huffed my replacement.

'Why do you have to be so vindictive? Ruby was one of my closest friends. She was good to you, Adrian. Good for the station.'

'Good to herself. She was a selfish cow. Everybody knew. What Ruby wanted; Ruby got. Tell him how it was Adrian.' I could visualize Jemma's contorted face.

Don't know what kind of body language Adrian was giving off but it was not the backing Jemma was hoping for.

'Honestly? Look at the pair of you. She only had to bat those artificial eyelashes.'

'If you hadn't noticed, I'm gay and married.' I could hear the revulsion in JJ's voice.

'Me too,' mumbled Adrian. 'Not gay!!'

Jemma guffawed. Must admit, I had to stifle mine. Adrian couldn't keep it in his pants. I heard a door bang. I didn't wait to see who had come out the office so I darted out the door and marched round the corner to check if JJ's car was in its usual parking place. It was.

I used to get a taxi in the morning and make my own way home around lunch time. I would take a nap in the afternoon ready for the kids later. At least once a week, I would grab some lunch with Ben at Suthiez or we would head down the coast to Gullane for lunch with our friends who have a little bespoke restaurant there. JJ liked taking his car – a yellow Toyota Supra but it cost a small fortune to park it. At least, three mornings a week he would bring it to work.

I knew he would be at least two hours. I slipped a note under his windscreen wiper and sat outside a popular coffee bar on Leith Walk with a book. Two hours later, I sauntered round. Sure enough, I clocked him strolling down the street. He was surprised to see me. Had to mention that I had recognised his car earlier.

I explained that I had overheard the racket and I wanted to reassure him that Ruby had NOT been offered anything from the station. She would have discussed it with Ben or myself. Plus, I threw this part in, Ruby had assured Ben and the family that she would never move away from Edinburgh. As far as she was concerned, Ben's career came first. Maybe not true a few weeks ago but now I would want that before anything else so now it was the truth. I had to convince JJ of that (and me if I'm honest).

He did raise his eyebrows in surprise. 'I always knew the bigger guns would come for Ruby. *Haud Yer Wheesht* propelled her to a new level. People were asking about her constantly.'

'Well, it was a level that flattered her but it was one she was prepared to turn down. She told us all, she had everything she needed in Edinburgh. Ruby's family meant more to her than fame.' Again, those bushy eyebrows twitched. And I had to pray that JJ would never raise it with Ben. No, I'm pretty sure that would not happen.

'Thanks, Mrs. M. I'm grateful. Thanks for waiting.' He hugged me tightly.

'Ruby loved you like a brother. You were a loyal friend and I know she was loyal to you.'

His bottom lip flopped. He's a big wimp really. I hugged him then we parted but I had a sinking feeling that neither of us would call each other again. I'd never see that new penthouse suite.

# FORTY-SEVEN

*Ruby's Journal*

**Monday 27th May.**

At Annabelle's before I go to Dick Place. Not much has happened. Quiet weekend. No sign of Colin at the house, thank goodness. Was on edge the whole time. Although, Lisa and I did tail him on Saturday morning!!! Can you believe we did that? When I told Auntie Lisa that I suspected that Colin had another woman, she was determined to play super sleuth while Brian was left to change the locks on your doors. Colin is a creature of habit so I was betting that he might go to Aldi in Tranent and he did.

We took Lisa's Jill's old banger so we wouldn't be spotted. Don't those eco-warriors realise that an old jalopy is worse for the environment than a new car. An electric one would be even more efficient. Anyway, I was gobsmacked when I saw him sitting in his white SAAB. Paper draped over the steering wheel. We pulled in a good bit away from him but from where we had a good view of the car. Then bloody hell, a woman about your age wheeled her trolley up to his car and started loading her bags into the boot. She resembled you, sort of. Short brown hair, similar height and quite plump (sorry, he must go for the same type). Lisa was flabbergasted.

'What if you had bumped into them?' she said to me.

I told her that I would never go back. Too many people

acknowledged me (you) there and I didn't have a scooby about them. It was exhausting having to explain myself each time. I refused to enter that shop again.

Honestly, I don't know how Colin didn't detect us. It's not as if we had decent disguises. I wore a cap and huge sunglasses. Lisa hadn't even tried. Twice we lost him and once we ended up in front of him. Wee Oscar was in the back. Slept through the whole pursuit. If you could even call it that. I don't know how he didn't wake up with us hee-hawing all the time. Anyway, we ended up in Prestonpans. Bottom Pans Auntie Lisa called it. She used to date someone from there apparently.

He drove into an opening (archway) in the middle of a block of flats and parked round the back of them. The flats were on a long road that stretches down to the High Street. The surrounding area looked nice enough. Well-kept grounds and gardens. We couldn't see which block they went in to but at least I had my suspicions confirmed. He was seeing someone else. What's the smarmy git got? Surely not a big dick. (He is one!!) I don't see the attraction but you must have, Mum. It's not as if you're a poor judge of character. Dad was a good catch... I think.

Auntie Lisa was furious. If Oscar hadn't been in the car, I'm positive she would've been ringing doorbells.

Now that I know where she lives, I WILL be paying his new buddy a visit. We had a quick coffee in Cockenzie House before I picked up my car at Lisa's place. I almost swung by Dad's when I was in Haddington. Keep forgetting I'm you, not me.

Meant to say that Dad and Patricia have been looking at a house in Pathhead. Some sort of steading that needs gutted. How many times have they moved? Itchy feet.

Talking about an itch, I have one that needs scratching. Presenting. Ever since I popped into Fourth Waves, I can't stop thinking about it. When I was passing through Cockenzie with Lisa, I twigged that there was a local charity/community radio in the area. A quick google and I found it. Harbour Radio. Owned by a guy called Charles B. Rioch. I've emailed him. No reply as yet. With it being a charity, I won't get paid so it shouldn't interfere with your salary from the school. That's if I'm allowed. Fingers crossed.

**Friday 31st May.**

First of June tomorrow. The weeks are flying past.

I'm having a night out with Annabelle tonight. We are actually going to Suthiez. A treat from Ben as a thank you for all our help. Annabelle was trusted to sift through my mail and emails (with input from me). There were hundreds of them. The majority of them were dealt with swiftly or deleted (and many by me previously). A short direct reply was all that was needed. Some had to be left for Ben. Annabelle red flagged a to-do list for the ones that required urgent attention. We put the rest into my different folders (family, work, personal etc) so that Ben could find everything quickly. He is not an IT buff. I could have done it weeks ago but couldn't risk Ben's wrath if he thought I had been interfering. I had already sorted and filed my paper post into folders for my hapless husband. Annabelle gave him the extra nudge to do something about them.

I love checking in with Ray of Hope. It practically runs itself now. I would love to meet everyone but that's impossible. It's the anonymity that allows us the freedom to express ourselves without being caught out.

I had a meeting with our lawyers this morning. Aitken & Aitken. Their office is at the West End of Princes Street in Coates Crescent. Remember the street where your pal Lesley's mother worked for the Scottish Country Dance Society? Well, it's there. The big crescent shaped one. Looks as if it could be used for the setting of a period drama. They are dealing with the insurance claim for both of us. I wasn't happy with Colin trying to muscle in so I handed it over to our lawyers as they were dealing with my estate and my claim (as in me Ruby).

Had to answer lots of questions about my amnesia. Obviously. Having Professor Warnock on board was a huge plus. I met with Shirley, wife of John, who is the most senior partner. Know them well so had to control my urge to enquire about the family. They don't frequent Suthiez much but their sons and their partners do. I get on really well with Shirley's daughter-in-law. At least, I did. It's all those casual friendships that I miss just as much as my old girlfriends.

I have to meet with an assessor for young Rhys Jones's work's insurers. Should be straight forward but they may ask me to be examined by a psychiatrist/psychologist of their choosing. Hopefully not. Finding one that would be willing to contradict the eminent professor would be pushing it, according to Shirley.

Annabelle peeked over my shoulder the other day while I was busy writing.

'Bloody hell bbz, talk about War and Peace. Why the screeds?'

It's in case I have a Groundhog Day. I'm terrified that one morning I might wake up to find out that I'm in your body for the first time all over again. This way I'll know what I've been doing. In detail. Same goes for you, Mum. Jemma was right about one thing. I am a selfish cow. I love writing this and it makes me feel closer to you but do I want you to be able to read it? Unequivocally not. I miss you, Mum. I miss your honesty and no-nonsense approach when it comes to giving advice, especially to me. Just wish I had opened my eyes to your problems. I'm making up for it now. Or maybe you think I'm making a pig's ear of it all.

Annabelle is in love!!!!

She has been seeing a lot of her new bloke. Andy Fenton. Typical Annabelle. Falls head over heels in a very short time and convinces herself that he is THE ONE. He's been staying over a fair bit that's why I've not been hanging around in the evenings and giving weekends a wide berth. This weekend he is in Krakow. Stag do. Can't pretend I'm not jealous. Not about her having a man but that I can't spend as much quality time with her as I would like. Conscious of maintaining a healthy balance.

On the way to Aitken & Aitken, I bumped into Fraser Gibson. Literally. Outside the Caledonian Hotel. He's our advertising manager at Fourth Waves. He's renowned for giving away more prizes than any other Scottish station. Bloody good at his job. Generates loads of business for us. Keep saying US!!! I gave him a big wrap around hug. Squeezed him hard. Told him that it was so good to see him. Bless him, he froze then answered me as if he knew exactly who I was. Didn't. Said I looked well and that he couldn't stop. Was in a rush. We did that whole bravado thing. Silly, loud, embarrassing goodbyes and dashed off in opposite directions. I didn't even look back. Keep forgetting I'm you.

Haven't heard from Jasper again. Not even a text. Not sure if he is playing games or I'm reading too much into it. I suppose I could text him but don't want to appear desperate. If we do meet up, I'm going to ask him if he objects to me texting him now and again. Is that being needy? God, I'm not looking for a physical relationship but having a friend of my own (the new me). There's something reassuring or liberating about it.

I'm away to pound the streets of Newhaven. I can actually jog without looking as if I'm holding up my right breast. I really enjoy it. Clears my head.

OMG!!! An email from Charles Rioch. I'm scared to read it.

# FORTY-EIGHT

## *Ruby's Journal*

**Tuesday 4th June.**

We had a lovely night on Friday at Suthiez. The food was great as always. Ben received his first Michelin Star three years after Suthiez opened and he works incredibly hard to maintain his standards. Curtis Stone was one of the first to congratulate him. Their paths had crossed lots of times due to mutual friendships in Australia (Melbourne). We knew we were being assessed. We had two AA Rosettes but it's the Star that's the coveted prize. Rubiez only managed it last year. Maybe because we were experimenting more with the menu there. Scotland meets Japan. Exceptional products, locally sourced (if we can), prepared with a Japanese influence. Cannae beat it!!! Okay, it's pricier than Suthiez but the interior is stunning. It has to be Edinburgh's ultimate dining experience.

I had the Orkney scallops to start followed by roasted monkfish. So good. Annabelle's not so keen on sea food (unless it's from a chippie). She had the cheese soufflé and fillet of roe deer. Honestly, the soufflé melts in the mouth. Absolutely delicious. And it was so good to be sitting with my best pal and my husband. I had to stop myself dissolving into tears because I was so happy to be sharing a table and drinks with them. Ben joined us for a full hour then had to leave to take over from Katie, one of the sitters.

We finished as we started, with a Caipirinha cocktail. So chuffed that you enjoy Cachaca, Mum. Probably because it's a Brazilian rum and you do like your rums. James behind the bar makes the best Caipirinhas in Scotland. Without a doubt. I just love them.

Ben asked if I would like to do some night time babysitting as the two young girls that share it at the moment are keen to do less. I jumped at the chance. Later, Annabelle warned me not to take on too much at Deacon House. 'You have your own life remember'. I was a little peeved at that.

I stayed with Annabelle on Friday night but declined the offer to go out with her and Hannah on Saturday. No interest in rekindling a relationship with Hannah. Have always been wary of her. Opted to sit in with Auntie Vera instead. Woo hoo! NOT!!!!! How times have changed. Left early doors. Was meeting Lisa early in the morning. I am definitely going on Tinder soon. Better than what I have at the moment.

Also, mother. What is going on down below??!!

As you know, I never sit on a toilet seat outside my house (I always squat) and I'm ashamed to say not even in some of my friends' homes. I did in yours obviously. You were as fastidious as me. Well lately, I have been aware that I have been dribbling down my leg. When I was at the loo at Suthiez on Friday, I noticed a wee pool of pee on the floor when I wheeked up my knickers. Naturally, I mopped it up and scrubbed my hands. The next time I went. No pee on the tiles. BUT after I had peed there was a wee puddle on the floor again. So, I have been studying my waterworks or more to the point, how it flows. You pee squint. Not all the time but enough that I now have to pay close attention to what I'm doing. Plus, I tend to fart now while peeing. Mortifying. It must be an age thing. Well, now

I'm doing pelvic floor exercises constantly. Hope it works.

Best bit of my news (apart from being given more access to the kids), I spoke with Charles Rioch at long last. Several emails had passed between us and I had to fill in a strange and detailed questionnaire about why I wanted to work at the station. He sounded lovely on the phone but there was something about him that I couldn't quite put my finger on. I've to go to his house on Thursday. That's where he broadcasts from. I've tuned in quite a lot to Harbour Radio since last Saturday. It's okay overall. Charles does four weekly shows in the morning. Not always the same times which I find odd. Sometimes he does the early morning from six til nine or he does the next one, nine til noon. I have no idea what times I'll be given. If I get offered anything. There's a young lad, Robbo, who does the charts on a Saturday. He is actually a natural and quite funny. Wasted there. Surprised he hasn't been snapped up by another station. Perhaps he has a full-time job.

I googled Charles again. Seems he is off aristocracy. His father was a Baron but Charles refuses to use the title. He is loaded. Apart from inheritance, he made his money in designing computer games in the nineties and early noughties then seems to have retired and vanished altogether. No personal Facebook page. Has been married but divorced. Set up Harbour Radio nine years ago. Promotes and supports several local charities, especially for disadvantaged children and mental health. No children or siblings as far as I can tell. Only personal photo on Harbour website is one from 1999. Looks normal enough and good looking (tall, jet-black hair) but you can never tell. Please don't let him be sleazy. I can cope with odd but not sleazy odd.

I heard next door's front door slamming at five this morning, followed by the car engine revving. It raced off. I'm sure I could smell the rubber from my bed. Presume Tanya has gone into labour. For a first baby, she was huge. All bump on a skinny body. I wonder if any of her family will come over from Estonia?

I'll cook them a batch of food while I'm doing everybody else's. Annabelle loves that I prepare four meals a week for her. She more or less gets what we are eating. Who needs Hello Fresh or Gousto when Ruby Martin is around? I prepare plainish food for the kids and spicier options for the grown-ups. Believe it or not, Ben loves home-made beef burgers (typical chef) as do the kids, except we adults have fabulous toppings. I do a vegan version for me.

Can't wait to be part of the bedtime routine. Only wish I was part of Ben's too. But as me, not you. Obviously.

# FORTY-NINE

*Rachel's flat in Portobello. Wednesday 8th January 2020.*

Rachel bustled about. She was excited and nervous in equal measure. It had been a long time since she and Lisa had socialised; she was looking forward to it. When was the last time? She racked her brain. They had exchanged Christmas presents but that would be 2018. Rachel had driven to Haddington to deliver them personally yet didn't even accept the offer of a coffee. Why ever not? Must have felt like a right slap in the face for Lisa. The last proper time, therefore, must have been in August a week after she returned from Abbotsford Priory.

Lisa handed in a birthday present for Rory and wee Jack. The friends perched awkwardly on rattan chairs in the back garden in Carberry Crescent chatting about irrelevant rubbish: the weather, the garden, work. Anything, other than the retreat. Rachel had fired her friend that knowing steely stare – begging her not to interrogate her about her stay, as Colin might overhear. He was adamant that it was nobody's business but theirs. When the flow dipped, they would smile in the silence while their body language screamed at the futility of it all. Fat chance of having any kind of private conversation even if they had wanted to; Colin hovered constantly. If Lisa began to question her pal about anything, Rachel immediately shut her down. Her fear had extinguished all rational means of deduction.

*No dwelling on the past. A new start*, she kept reminding

herself today. If it hadn't been so close to Christmas, Rachel would have cooked a roast chicken dinner: Lisa's favourite. She prepared pot roasted pork instead; a dish that was often served by Rachel's mother on a Sunday. The pork joint was covered with dry mustard and simmered in milk for two hours in a deep pot. It's important to keep turning the joint for an even cook. When the meat was ready, it was transferred to a plate to rest while a heap of gravy powder was stirred into the mustard juices. Great on cold winter nights like today. Peas, carrots, broccoli and creamy mash potatoes were on the stove ready to reheat. Rachel realised she was hungry. Apart from her curry on Monday night, she had only been nibbling on bits and pieces.

Rachel gave the place a last-minute tidy. The glass dining table had been set in the afternoon. Rachel wanted perfection. More than that, she wanted a happy, cosy night in with her best pal.

The main door buzzer sounded and Rachel's stomach plummeted to her knees. She pressed the button allowing Lisa entry to the block. Rachel stood at the door and waited, listening to her friend's soft footsteps on the stairs. The moment Rachel registered those warm, welcoming, familiar eyes, the tears started. The two women embraced.

'Oh Lisa, what am I going to do now? Without Ruby?' blubbered Rachel.

When she was reading the diary, she felt as if Ruby was with her but once the book was closed, reality kicked in. Ruby was gone.

'Come on,' Lisa reassured her, 'you'll be absolutely fine. I'm here.'

They hugged again. Rachel couldn't help thinking that she no longer dwarfed her pal as she wrapped her arms around her.

She had always felt like a sumo wrestler cuddling a child before. Now, Lisa's body didn't feel nearly so fragile. Rachel assumed it must be something to do with her own dramatic weight loss.

'Okay?'

'I am now.'

She helped Lisa off with her navy, wool coat. It weighed a ton.

Lisa kicked off her nude court shoes and wandered into the open–plan space. 'I have to admit, Rach, this place is bloody impressive.' She handed Rachel a plastic box full of goodies.

'I know. I don't know how I managed it.' It was a white lie but what else could she say? *It was Ruby's choice.* No. Ruby would have to remain in the navy book beneath the beach scene.

Rachel proffered her chum a glass and filled it to the top with chilled chardonnay. She poured a generous measure for herself.

'To friendship.' And they charged their glasses.

'No more tears, eh?' said Lisa as Rachel's bottom lip quivered, knowing full well there would be many floods before the evening was out. 'I'm glad to see you've got in a decent wine for a change. You kept bringing me Sauvignon or Rioja.'

'Blame my memory,' laughed Rachel.

They sat on the sofas where the questions and explanations began.

'So, what do you actually remember?' asked Lisa.

Rachel explained that she had regained all her memory from before the accident but could remember nothing about the last nine months. She told Lisa that she had kept a diary but not that she believed Ruby had written it.

'What did you write?'

'Everything that had happened since I woke up in hospital in March,' Rachel confessed.

'Why?'

'I think I was scared that I might lose it all again. I needed a detailed reminder.'

'Good on you. You were always well organised. It really disnae surprise me,' admitted Lisa. 'What did I used to call you?...Perfectly Practical Rachel. So, aye, a diary is right up your street.'

'I've not read it all yet. Bloody hell, it's been eventful.' Rachel laughed then proceeded to choke on her wine. Lisa fetched a wad of kitchen roll to dab her face and clothing. When she regained enough composure, Rachel continued, 'I'm up to June last year.'

The mood dipped while the two women recalled their feelings after the tragedy and discussed Ruby at great length. They talked about the funeral and Ben and the kids. How they had all coped in the aftermath. There were more tears which was to be expected.

'You were a great help to them, Rachel. You should be really proud of yourself.' Lisa stretched over from the other sofa and patted her friend's knee.

'You'd've done the same. Anyway, what do you think of my weight loss?' pressed Rachel.

'You look great but it's your clothes that make the difference,' acknowledged Lisa. 'No offence, Rach, but you started dressing like my mother. Plain woollen jumpers and elasticated waist trousers with seams down the front. And don't blame your size. You've been big most of your adult life but never resorted to the *auld wummin* look.'

'They were comfy,' she teased.

'They were fit for the bin,' insisted her pal. 'Look at you tonight. You exude elegance.'

She did. Rachel wore smart navy trousers and a shirt, a shade or two lighter than her trousers, over which, she wore a navy sleeveless long cardigan with a navy and biscuit geometric pattern on the front panels. Very Jaeger.

'I hadn't a clue what to wear. I can't believe I have so many clothes. Did I win a make-over?' In another world, it would have taken something like a make-over on *Lorraine* to entice Rachel away from the drab outfits she felt obliged to wear. Colin used to accuse her of flirting when she dressed up.

'Now I know where to come,' laughed Lisa.

That was a huge compliment indeed. Lisa was a walking clothes horse. She rarely dressed down. Dresses, smart or casual, were her preferred go to. Today she had on a pale pink, light-weight jacket (influenced by Chanel) over a matching shift dress. She had come straight from work.

'Hungry?' asked Rachel.

'Could eat a scabby horse,' chibbed Lisa, laughing.

The women talked about their childhood and teenage years. Brian and Rob. They had all been good mates and Brian and Rob hit it off at their first meet up.

'You and Rob should never have split up,' quipped Lisa, slurping on the creamy gravy. 'He adored you.'

'Oh aye, adored me enough to shag anything in a skirt,' Rachel reminded her pal.

'He had a wandering eye but you know what? I don't think he took things that far.'

'He did with Pat the Rat.'

Lisa laughed. 'I forgot we used tae call her that.'

'I'm sure it was you that coined the phrase,' chortled Rachel.

'I've coined plenty for Colin. Best thing you ever did.'

Rachel raised her eyebrows quizzically.

'Kicking that wee bastard in to touch. For good.' Lisa confirmed.

'Haven't got that far in my diary yet,' Rachel informed her.

'Then I won't spoil it for you but suffice to say that you spectacularly put him in his place.' Then her friend's voice adopted a more serious tone. 'Don't want to alarm you, Rach, but you need to be on your guard. It's not that long since Rob and Brian paid him a visit but keep vigilant.'

Rachel shivered and decided more wine was required. She opened another bottle.

'That mustard sauce was fabulous,' said Lisa, 'I've tried and tried to get it right but never tastes anything like that. Honestly, better than your mum's. Plus, it beats that jackfruit concoction you made me last time.'

Rachel visibly cringed. So typical of Ruby. 'Hey, you can't be good at everything,' she teased, referring to Lisa's baking skills. She produced sweets and puddings that Suthiez and Rubiez would be proud to serve.

The conversation inevitably drifted back to Colin and Abbotsford Priory. Lisa had raised it with 'Rachel' on many occasions but because Ruby had no knowledge of it, there had been no point on pressing her. This time it was different.

'I'm so sorry I shut you out, Lis. It had to be the drugs fogging my brain. And Colin.'

'I didn't see it happening at first. He wasn't number one on my list but he made you happy and that was good enough for me. But you changed. Became secretive. Defensive. You refused to even contemplate that Colin was ostracising you from family and friends.'

'Why didn't you make me see sense?' Rachel pleaded.

'Jesus Christ, I tried. Ye didnae want to know. I knew if I

pushed too hard you would shut me out permanently and I couldn't risk it. I'm no joking; the number of times I was sobbing into Brian's knee!' Lisa braced herself for the next part. 'I'm sorry to say this, but Ruby was too willing to believe what Colin was feeding her, and Rory was too far away to grasp what he wis like.'

Rachel rubbed her face. She loved her son and daughter but reading between the lines of Ruby's journal, she had more or less come to the same conclusion.

'I'm not blaming them entirely. He was bloody good. My Brian was sucked in. Kept saying that I was imagining it. Looking for the worst in folk. But there was somethin shifty about Colin from the very start. Same wi his daft daughter. What did you start calling her? Bellatrix.'

They had a giggle about that and all the other names they had for people they used to go to school with. Lisa helped clear the table while Rachel made the coffee. Two slabs of Lisa's legendary Christmas cake were put on to side plates.

'Half for me please. I'm stappit fu,' puffed Lisa.

Rachel was stuffed too and sliced the huge piece in half. And she was feeling the effects of nearly two bottles of wine.

'Why do you think ye had the courage to tackle him after the accident and not before?' pressed Lisa.

Rachel contemplated her reply. 'Honestly? I think it's because I wasn't afraid of him. Like, historically afraid. He scared me shitless but it was different from a fear that builds up over months if that makes sense. See when I read what he did to ... (she nearly said Ruby) to me. I can't believe I plucked up the courage to confront him.'

Lisa hooted, 'Ye did more than that, girl. God, ye ken how to pick them.'

'What do ye mean?'

'MEN! Out of the frying pan and into the fire!'

'What? With Rob then Colin?' asked Rachel.

'Them too. Naw, Colin then Jasper.' Lisa blew a long whistle as if to imply something substantial had happened there. 'Oh, and not forgetting your other wee dalliance.' This revelation was followed with a cheeky wink.

# FIFTY

*Ruby's Journal*

**Friday 7th June.**

Yesterday went better than I could have expected. Charles Rioch is a really interesting guy. He is agoraphobic. I've never met one before.

The broadcasting set-up is in his house. A beautiful modern building. A stone's throw away from Cockenzie Harbour. When I rang the doorbell, he called out for me to come in. I opened the door and entered a porch a little bigger than ours at Deacon House. His flooring is slate whereas ours has Victorian mosaic tiles. He stood behind a glass door. As he opened it, he politely requested that I close the other one and beckoned me in. I never thought anything about it.

'I'm an agoraphobic,' he apologised. 'For my sins.' And he smiled.

No wonder he is in radio. He has the most calming, velvety voice. I could happily drown in it. It's not posh but it reminds me of an Inverness accent. Scottish with all the harsh gruffness filed away. Very refined. White-grey, wavy locks (very distinguishing) have replaced the black. First impression – he looks like a retired pop star or musician of some sorts. He is tall, slim and his skin tight jeans were fashionably torn. He had on a green cotton shirt with pink flecks. The cuffs and collar were pink. The whole ensemble suited him. Only his old-man slippers let him down. I doubt he cared less. I felt over-dressed in my navy jumpsuit and pink heels. A pair of trainers next time.

He led me into a large sunny lounge and this lovely old lady brought us a tray of coffee and biscuits. She left it on a large oval coffee table.

'Isobel, this is Rachel. She will be joining our team, if she decides we are good enough,' he said.

How cool was that? So kind. He immediately put me at ease.

'You might not like me,' I suggested.

Then Isobel piped up, 'You wouldn't be here, dear, if he didn't already.' So very matter of fact without a smidgen of malice or sarcasm.

Turns out that Isobel was his childhood nanny. When he was in his late thirties Charles discovered she was living on her own in a rundown flat in Fort William. His father had dismissed her without a backward glance. No redundancy or handsome gratuity. Thanks but no thanks. She had raised his only child and stayed on as housekeeper for a grumpy, thankless git when his second wife had run off with her tennis coach. The third wife insisted on having her own staff. Isobel was given 24 hours' notice. She had worked for the family for twenty-seven years for a pittance. It was her love for Charles that had kept her there. There was no love lost between him and his father (and I'm assuming 2nd and 3rd wives) BUT following tradition his father left his entire estate to his only son. For that he was eternally grateful. Rioch is his mother's name so have no idea what the family name is. Yet.

After coffee, he showed me the studios. There were two. They were on the first floor and each room (formerly bedrooms) overlooked the Forth. Large windows let the light flood in. A bit bright and open for an agoraphobic, me thinks. The equipment wasn't nearly as sophisticated as ours in Fourth Waves but was perfectly adequate. Two screens and a mixing deck in the middle plus the usual other bits and pieces. Easy peasy for me. Studio One was empty. A woman about my age, Maria, in Two, gave me a wave and a thumbs-up when we looked in. Both studios were set up like small offices. There was the presenting desk, an office desk and two wing back chairs at a coffee table. A succinct kitchen area with a sink, kettle and microwave was in the corner near the door. Cosy, practical and comfortable. I loved them.

Charles asked if he could talk me through what they do. Instead, I talked him through everything I would do. From the moment I would be sitting down at the presenting desk until the end of the show. Looking back, I was over excited and far too keen. I had to re-familiarise myself with the older system (our news and weather reports are automatically updated whereas I would have to manually replace the old reports with the new ones that came through) but apart from that I could do it with my eyes closed. He was impressed but puzzled. How could someone who had never actually presented be so knowledgeable?

I confessed that I had sat in regularly with Ruby. Obviously, you hadn't but I had to offer a plausible explanation.

He showed me the rest of the first floor. His office. A bathroom and a separate shower room (for the presenters use). Upstairs was his and Isobel's private quarters as were the downstairs. Didn't go up there. Charles suggested we should return to the sunny lounge to discuss my options. As we reached the bottom of the stairs, young Robbo skipped in. He was a handsome boy with a shock of red hair. He was full on animated. All arms and gesticulating. Immediately, I clocked that he was on the spectrum. He gave me a high five. Spilled what he had been doing before he arrived then took the stairs two at a time to start his new slot.

'That was our exuberant Robbo,' laughed Charles. 'Once he sits at his desk and is ready to begin his show, calm descends.' The palms of his hands smoothed an imaginary horizontal line.

It must do. I'd heard him several times. He was good. Witty yet completely in control.

Isobel appeared again. This time with a tray of sandwiches and home-made scones. Charles sat opposite me at the coffee table, leaving the long sofa empty. The chairs were similar to the ones upstairs but the lounge ones were larger and more luxurious. Yellow and red chintz with generous red velvet cushions to support our backs. Sounds hideous when I try to describe them but they complemented the room beautifully. Like something Carrie would have chosen for one of her grand hotels. (Maybe not the Dubai ones. More like the country hotels down South.)

'Indulge me, Rachel. What is it about Harbour Radio that intrigues you?' he probed.

As I had explained on the telephone, following the amnesia, I had a desire to reinvent myself. Reconnect with people again but from a safe distance.

'Does that sound weird?' I asked.

'Not at all. It's the same with my agoraphobia. I invite people into my life, into my living room and I don't have to leave the house.'

I asked him how long he had been like that. Too long, was all he would say.

Then I asked the question that I had been putting off.

'Can I use a different name? I don't want to be broadcasting as Rachel Gordon or Martin. I don't want your listeners to know who I am.'

'Am I permitted to know why?' (He is ever so polite.)

I wanted to be free. I didn't want to be judged as Rachel Anybody. AND I couldn't risk Colin finding out about me. I didn't want anyone knowing who I was.

He asked how I would achieve this deception.

'I want to be known as Reya. I will be from Northern Ireland.' I looked him directly in the eye and waited for the scoff.

'Do you think it will work?' he enquired. Face devoid of mockery.

I put on my fake accent. As strong as I could. I've mimicked Carrie and Ben on numerous occasions so I'd plenty of practice. 'Charles, pet. I could fool my own wee granny, sure I could. But the big test will be duping the rest of my family and I wouldn't be suggesting this if I had any doubts.'

He slapped his knees and laughed. 'You sound completely and utterly convincing. Younger, if you don't mind me saying. Well Reya, do you fancy joining me tomorrow morning on my show?'

And I did. This morning at ten. After I had dropped the kids off at nursery. I stayed over, as Ben now wants Thursdays to be his chill night. To grab a drink with staff etc. It's the etcetera that bothers me. I could hardly say no.

Honestly, Mum, it was great. Charles and I just clicked into place. Maybe not straight off but definitely after an hour or so. Think he was pleasantly surprised at my slickness (is that a word). Anyhow, we were slick. Loved it. Have no idea as to what kind of programme I want to present but I'm sure it will evolve. So exciting. I'm working with him again on Sunday afternoon.

One thing that Charles was serious about was the wellbeing and safety of his staff. We were not allowed to disclose or discuss personal details about each other that were not already on our website pages. Many of the staff had difficulties of their own and sharing those idiosyncrasies outwith the station was frowned upon. That suited me perfectly.

Buoyed by my new adventure, I texted Jasper.

Hey Jasper

Rachel here. Hope all is well with you. I'm good. Have started with the reinvention. Things looking up. Hope you don't mind me texting. Just wanted to thank you for the push I was needing.

Take care.

Finished with some smiley faces. No kisses. Didn't want to appear desperate.

Five minutes later, my phone pinged. Did I want to meet him tomorrow for a drink?

We arranged to meet in Musselburgh. The Creel at 7.30pm. Fine by me. Neutral territory. Ten minutes later, he suggested something to eat.

Colin and Claire are coming tomorrow to collect more things. Lisa's Brian volunteered to chaperone me. I texted Colin last Sunday to let him know the locks had been changed. Not a happy bunny. Sean next door caught him trying the doors and windows on Tuesday. Sean was convinced he was ready to break the kitchen window.

'She's out mate. Better to come back when she's in.'

Colin called him a turncoat and marched off.

# FIFTY-ONE

## *Ruby's Journal*

**Thursday 13th June.**

This is the first time I've been back at Annabelle's since last week. She's been busy entertaining. Didn't want to intrude. We still phone or text every day so don't feel as if I'm missing out.

I bought myself a laptop at long last. Should have done it earlier but Colin watched me like a hawk. Saves me having to go round to Auntie Vera's all the time. Hide it in my bedroom. Still not convinced that he won't gain access to the house when I'm not there, that's why I won't take this journal to Carberry Crescent until I'm certain that he will NEVER return.

Derrick Smith put up a security system in and around the house on Monday. Relieved. Especially after Saturday. There's a camera in the hall. One at the front door and one at the back. The amount of area the lenses cover is amazing. You can see the whole of the front garden and most of the back and I can hear what's going on too. Not sure if I want to though. I could actually hear everything Sean and Tanya were saying on their doorstep the other day. Will make a point of not ear wigging on them. Not fair.

Last Saturday Weasel Colin and sidekick Bellatrix rocked up. Bang on time. 3.00pm. Jade was with them. She looked miserable. I felt rotten when she asked if she could stay the night. I was meeting Jasper later. I promised she could stay next weekend as long as I didn't have to babysit Alfie and Nola. She offered to help me out. Eh, awkward. I said I would check with Ben. Also reminded myself to check in with wee Jack more. Again, keep forgetting I'm now his granny.

I sensed Colin was about to launch into a vicious verbal lecture. It was the way he pulled himself up and puffed his chest but he stopped before he had even begun. He spotted Brian in the kitchen.

'This isn't right, Rachel. Putting me out. This is my home too,' he moaned.

Jade and Claire stood and gawked from the living room.

'I think you'll find that you left of your own accord and haven't been back. Plus, let's not kid ourselves, you have somewhere else to go.'

'I can't stay at Claire's forever,' he snarled.

'Oh! Since when did Claire move to Prestonpans?' I asked.

His body jerked upright. It was if a rod had been rammed up his arse. 'What do you mean by that?' he snapped and threw a quizzical glance at Claire.

She put her hands up in defence. Poor Jade glowered at them both. He knew perfectly well what the question implied but I wasn't about to play his game.

'Take what is yours and nothing else,' I stated. 'The furniture and everything else belongs to me. Unless you can prove that you have paid for it, it stays here.'

Claire jumped in. 'He's due more than that. He's lived here for about three years.'

'And for three years, he has sponged off me. I couldn't find anything that he had paid for. (Then I kinda lost it.) Not ONE fucking thing. So, keep your nose and mouth out of my fucking business.' I stabbed the air with my finger. I'd had enough of her.

Brian came in to the hall to check I was okay. Claire shuffled back into the living room. I'm sure she was poised to lunge at me but I was ready for her.

'Colin is just collecting his belongings. Aren't you, Colin?'

He pushed past me and made to close the door of your bedroom. That was not going to happen. My bum held the door open. My arms folded across my chest. I was in no mood for his nonsense.

He stuffed drawers full of clothes into black bin bags. He had a lot. He was wearing smart beige shorts and a pale green, polo shirt. No walking gear. Seems he has ditched that period. Several white T-shirts, shorts and trainers were retrieved from the wardrobe. He's switched sports!!!!! He has taken up badminton. Explains the new, squeaky trainers in the hospital. He lifted your jewellery box. I was right in there.

'What are you doing?' I grabbed the box.

'Looking for my watch.' Don't think so. It wasn't there and he might've pilfered something of yours. 'Do you mind? I'd like some privacy,' he huffed.

That would not be happening. 'I can stay or you can go and I'll pack everything for you and send it on. Your choice.'

He chose to stay and pack. As each bag was filled, Claire and Jade humped them to his car. Jade was a mini-me of her mum. Black vest and short grey leggings. It was roasting outside. I had on a light weight, blue shift dress from the White Stuff. If I say so myself, it was very slimming. I've lost over two stones. Since jogging, the weight has been dropping off. My eating regime helps. I try and follow the Beach Body diet through the week. For four days, I stick rigidly to the plan and my protein shakes. I tried it for six days but I was starving. Too restrictive. So now I do it for four. For the rest of the week, I eat sensibly. Usually vegan on weekdays with zillions of vegetables. At the weekend, I allow myself some treats (wine) and meat. It's working for me.

It's stupid, I know but I made a huge effort with my hair and make-up. Not that I want to make Colin jealous but looking and feeling good gives me confidence to face them. Is that daft? I got my hair cut in Haddington in the morning. Couldn't face going back to Amber Rose. If I had gone there, I might have had an ulterior motive. Jasper Thistle Christie.

Back to Colin. He rummaged in the wardrobe, kitchen cabinets, the hall cupboard and took coats and wellies from his shed. He sifted through the living room drawers too. Kept a beady eye on everything he was doing. He must have shifted ten bags at least out to his car.

'I'll need to come back and check the loft,' he said.

'Not a problem. Let me know when you want in. If you don't forewarn me there will be no entry,' I warned him.

'I think you will find that I can enter my house if and when I choose. So don't push it.'

I wasn't that sure of his rights so I didn't. Nor did I remind him that the locks had been changed. Actually, I was surprised that he was willing to go so readily. His next abode is obviously more appealing.

'Can I still come and stay next week, Granny Rachel?' Couldn't believe that Jade would still want to come. Of course, I agreed. Felt sorry for her.

Within an hour they were gone. Though he did leave me a little parting gift. Just as he was about to pull away, he jumped out of his car. 'Rachel' he yelled.

When he was certain that he had my attention, he did that thing with his two fingers. Slowly and controlled, he pointed them at his eyes then pointed his forefinger at me. The 'I'm watching you' warning. Then he did it again. Real menacing like. Admittedly, I was unnerved yet again. He is a NASTY piece of work.

So happy that the security system is up and running.

**Saturday Night.** My date, if you could call it that, with Jasper went well. I took the bus as did he. I got off at The Hayweights and walked the last 5/6 minutes in the direction of Portobello. He was there before me, nursing a pint of beer at a pavement table. He looked very relaxed and handsome. I'm sure I've said it before – he IS a good looking guy – in a not pretty but something about him way. Tall, dark and he has a body that most forty-year-olds would die for. Don't know if it was because of our close proximity to the sea but there was a real holiday vibe in the air. The warm, sunny evening helped. Jasper exuded charm. He rose and kissed my cheeks and asked if I would like a wine. I declined and asked for a cider instead. It was nice to see him in jeans instead of a suit. A white cotton shirt hung over his hips. The sleeves were turned up. Very casual. Very nice. I plumped for the navy jumpsuit and pink shoes again. He did comment on his return that I was looking well. I accepted the compliment with a flare of pink in my cheeks. I had to constantly push down the feeling that I was two timing Ben.

He had little Scotch eggs as a starter (I had one of them) and we both opted for fish n chips for our mains. We shared a bottle of wine. The conversation was easy. We finished our bottle of wine out at the front of the building. Before we knew it, it was time to go. He had said right at the beginning of the night that he had a very early start next day.

We had half an hour to spare and had a wee donder along to the harbour. There were a few smoochy pecks. It was a great evening. Couldn't fault it. Do you sense a BUT?

When the bill came it was nearly £60 including the drinks before the meal. Not bad at all. A fraction of what it would have cost at Suthiez. He put £35 on the plate (actually counted it out). It's not that I wasn't happy paying my share. If I'm out with the girls or folk from work we always split the bill equally. Unless Fourth Waves is picking up the tab (or Ben). I kinda expected a discussion beforehand, that's all. I thought your age group frowned on the woman going Dutch. I'm obviously mistaken and out of touch but he was the one that asked me out. At least, it seemed like that to me. Haven't been on a date in donkeys. Since before Ben. Not going to let it spoil my memory of the night. It was so good to be out on a Saturday and with an easy-going companion.

I refused a walk to the bus-stop. However, we did kiss before we parted. Nothing exciting but a little hint of more to come. I asked earlier if he objected to the odd text now and again. He was fine about it.

Don't know how I feel about him. He seems more guarded now than he was when we first met. Rushing to my aid when I needed it. Maybe I'm out of practice or he is playing hard to get. Can't read the signals as well as I used to.

**Sunday.** Did an early show with Charles. Heaven. I WANT MY OWN SLOT. Actually, I'm getting it. Start on Friday. 9.00pm til 11.00pm. After eleven the station switches to continuous music only. No presenter. Sooooooo excited. Not sure how I'll play it. Will select the playlist and take it from there. Love the idea of being in control of selecting my own songs. Adrian usually selects them for everyone apart from the late-night slots. The bigger stations have one person who programmes the whole day. Saves repetition. Nothing worse. Though Christmas season does my head in. The same tedious songs and jingles dominate the day. By Christmas you could see them and adverts far enough. Fortunately, I can view the history of what has been played before by everyone else for that day or even weeks ago.

After the broadcast, I headed for Deacon House. Ben was in charge of Rubiez (only for lunches) and I promised to take the kids out for the day. Karl had put in for eight days holidays. As you know, our chefs rarely take time off in July and especially August. They wouldn't dare. Festival Fever. The Fringe events kick off on the Sunday at the beginning of August in Holyrood Park. Last year was particularly good. You were there Mum, with Colin. Remember the guy juggling with those swords? Colin volunteered to lie under his tightrope. Pity he didn't drop one on his nuts. Now that would have been something to celebrate. Looking back, you were very subdued. Now I know why. Still, it gives a flavour of what's on offer at the Fringe and the official Festival events. I'll definitely be taking the kids to see Julia Donaldson and the *Gruffalo* this year. Alfie and Nola love her books. *Stick Man* must have been watched fifty times last Christmas.

I just love spending time with them. Although I love Ben being there, I'm not so guarded if he's not. I know that one day I'll do or say something that will put me back to square one. Please, don't let that happen.

# FIFTY-TWO

*Ruby's Journal.*

**Sunday 16th June.**

Popped into Annabelle's to update my diary. Was going to take my babblings back to Alderburn but decided against it. If I do then I might not make the effort to see her as much. CANNOT allow our friendship to slip. Need her too much. Love her too but need her more. She is my only true link to me. And keeps me sane.

Friday night was amazing. Nothing extraordinary but oh so good to feel that mic brush my lips and chat to complete strangers. Liberating and exhilarating. Charles hovered protectively outside my room. Popped his head round the door during songs to give the thumbs up but his huge grateful grin said it all.

Quite a few responded during my slot. Wishing me well etc. I asked them for suggestions on what they would like to hear. So funny. One person said I should do the show in the nude!! On a radio show?? S'what I get for asking. Most sounded down beat. Don't want that really. Want an uplifting gig. I know it can't be all and out party though some did say they were getting tanked up for a night out. Gave me a lot of food for thought. Obviously more local East Lothian listeners than my usual city dwellers but I'm up for the challenge.

Talking about a challenge. Ben dropped a bombshell. The kids are spending the summer with the Sutherlands. I am beyond gutted. Six whole weeks without them. I honestly thought I was having a panic attack when he told me. Small consolation, I am being allowed to go out with them for two days to lay flowers on my grave (or is it yours?) for my birthday. So, we take the ferry on Thursday 4th July, lay the flowers on the 5th then I'm being packed off on the plane on the 6th. I feel so useless and isolated. Over and over again. Will it ever get any easier? Think not. At least I can help with the journey and pack their cases. Not Ben's. Jeezuz, could you imagine? Normally I would select what he was to wear but this time I'm hoping he packs all of his shit shirts and tees. Less chance of some tart getting their claws into him.

Nola clings to me like a limpet. She misses the real me, wee soul. They enjoy their 'granny' in their lives and I try to keep their routine pretty much the same as it was before. Bedtimes are the best. We talk about me all the time. Funnily enough, not in front of Ben. They intuitively understand that he is just not ready. He does say things like *Mummy liked it done that way* or *not that way* when they are pushing it. Sometimes he says things that are just way off the mark. He cranked up the radio recently to a seventies tune, *I Love to Love* by Tina Charles and claimed that I would dance around the kitchen to it whenever it was on. Eh. NO!! He encouraged the kids to jump around the island waving their arms. They loved it. He stood still. Not surprised. Ben is a watcher, not a dancer. He only gets up for smooches or when he is pissed. I don't dislike the song but definitely not a fave. Plus, it continues *but my baby just loves to dance*. Obviously, I didn't correct him.

I have arranged to visit Rory and Jack when the kids are in Enniskillen. Haven't been to Brentwood for three years. Looking forward to the distraction.

## Saturday 22nd June.

Annabelle is out setting up a gin tasting in Victoria Street. I can hear Andy Fenton snoring like an old man from Annabelle's bed. He is more often than not here at Pitt Street than at his own pad which means that I don't hang around for too long. He is a really nice guy but not sure if he is the one for Annabelle. I want someone who will care for her and truly love her as Ben did for me. She smothers him (as all her past others) and worst of all he lets her. Bless her, she tries so hard then they begin to lose interest.

I hear him at the loo.

We have just had a coffee. Him in his boxers. Took me all my time not to check out his credentials... which were almost dangling out by the way. He said I remind him of his mum. Thanks for that.

I'm going to slip out while he is in the shower.

Everything else going okay. Starting another show on Tuesday, same late slot and another on Monday morning. Ben likes to take the kids to nursery on Mondays so that works for me.

No word from either Colin or Jasper. Relieved and miffed in that order. Jade stayed over on Saturday. Spent most of her time on her phone. Is that the norm for youngsters? We made a unanimous decision to keep Alfie and Nola away from computers and games for as long as we possibly could.

She was no bother. Happy to have a Chinese carry-out for tea while I binged on Peaky Blinders. Believe it or not, I haven't seen one single episode of The Crown. Annabelle and Libby devour it. I have so many good series to catch up with.

Jangly Balls has finished in the bathroom. I'm going now.

**Tuesday 2nd July.**

Another busy and emotional week.

Alfie graduated from nursery last Thursday. All the parents decided that the 27th was the better date. I was a blubbering wreck. Honestly Mum, I willed myself not to make a fool of myself but couldn't help it. I did hover at the back when the tears started as Ben can't cope with my/your emotions. He was so different with me. Not that there was ever much dramatics with us but when I did cry, he was sympathetic. Unless, I was crying from frustration, especially after a blow up. Very little sympathy then.

Alfie's little face. He was so proud of his graduation medal and certificate. Thought Nola was going to explode when his name was called. She clapped and grinned as if he had received an Oscar. I wasn't sure if Ben would allow me to attend but Alfie insisted I should be there. After nibbles and a chat with the staff, we drove to Dunbar Leisure Pool. Alfie's choice. Neither of them have any fear. They love the slide and the waves. If I say so myself, I looked reasonably good in a swimsuit. We stopped off at the Italian in Tranent. Alfie loves it there. They make such a fuss over kids. The staff were excited to see Ben. Even the chef came out to have a selfie with him. Fortunately, Ben praised the pizza.

It was my night for babysitting. Ben changed to go out. He looked delicious as always. Not fair. On occasions like this we would have sat in the garden and polished off a bottle of champagne or two after the kids had gone to bed. Then found our private spot, overlooked by no one, and made raucous love or not so raucous if we had had too much to drink. Yep, so not effing fair!!!!

**Sunday 30th.**

Auntie Lisa organised a surprise birthday party for you in her garden. Oh, my days, I couldn't cope. Niagara Falls. Fucking fraud doesn't begin to explain how I felt. Ben sent his apologies but Bella – Anne brought the kids. I had had no idea. Thought I was having lunch with Brian and Lisa. Annabelle had claimed she had a prior engagement when I asked her to spend the day with me and to be fair, it's not as if the date of your birthday was a priority for her. There must have been about thirty folk and I hardly knew any of them. Auntie Lisa had invited who she thought should be there. Difficult, she had confessed, as I couldn't remember them. A small screen had been set up (courtesy of the Civil Service). Rory FaceTimed and gave a wee speech about what an exceptional mum you are. He asked us to raise a glass to me (Ruby) during it. Tears from everyone present. Exchanged a 'fucking hell' glance with Annabelle. Thank God, she was there. Wee Jack made up a limerick about you and performed it. Had everyone in stitches.

'You might have forewarned me,' I huffed at my best pal.

'I was sworn to secrecy,' she hissed.

Then Lisa brought the cake out while Alana giggled nervously on screen. A great big R shaped lawn surrounded with little cupcakes that resembled flowering plant pots. Lisa had excelled yet again. The candles, digits 57, flickered for me. I felt like the big bad wolf that had run out of puff. Despite the air in my lungs, a pathetic poofff left my lips. It was Lisa who blew them out.

Nola was totally enchanted with Auntie Lisa's grandson. What is Lisa's Jill like? The complete opposite to her mum. Eco princess versus materialistic queen.

I surveyed the 'happy' gathering.

I would never again be surrounded by all MY mates and colleagues at my own party. Ben would never kiss me affectionately and wish his wife a happy birthday in my ear and hint of better celebrations awaiting. Very sobering.

# FIFTY-THREE

*Ruby's Journal*

**Friday 12th July.**

Can't believe it's been so long since I put pen to paper. Where to begin?

Finished my morning show two hours ago. Did two extra shows this week as I'm flying down to Brentwood this evening. Love Harbour Radio. Everyone is so friendly. Isobel leaves a small treat (usually tray bakes) on our desks before our broadcasts. How sweet is that?

Annabelle and Andy flew out this morning to Paris. Long weekend. For her birthday. Still loved up. At least she is. Jury's out on him. Nothing from Colin. Yippee!!! Nothing from Jasper. Jury out on him too.

I'll start with Enniskillen. I stayed over at Deacon House on the Wednesday night (3rd July) and we drove to Stranraer for the ferry. The kids were excited. Ben got fed up explaining to Nola why Granny could only stay a few nights at the beginning of their holiday. I eventually rescued him.

'Granny has to spend some time with Jack. It's only fair.'

Ben was grateful. He didn't say it but I knew.

The ferry and the drive from Larne to Enniskillen went smoothly. Unbelievably so. We sang our usual songs and played our habitual games of 'I spy' and spotting the first red car etc. Several times I caught Ben eyeing me suspiciously, especially when I pointed out landmarks that were only important to us.

Honest to God, it took every ounce of concentration not to reach out and touch his face or ruffle his hair like I always do when he is at the wheel. At one point, I nodded off. You know when you're in that dreamy state when your surroundings are warm, happy and hazy and you are trying to stretch yourself to wakefulness? Well, I could hear my three chatting away and giggling. I smiled a thoroughly contented sleepy smile and was centimetres away from squeezing Ben's thigh (often too close to the crotch) when Alfie hollered,

'GRANNY you were snoring!'

I jumped. They erupted into hilarious giggling. I laughed too but I was shaking with what might have been.

I must have gone really quiet for a while because Ben asked if I was okay then he said something that made me happy and sad in equal measure.

'Ruby did that shivery thing when she woke up in the car. Same as you.'

I asked him what he meant.

Apparently, when I stretch out after a nap, my body shivers from top to toe. Now that I think about it, it's true.

'Sorry,' I said.

'Don't be,' he replied. 'It's those things that I don't want to forget.'

Bloody Hell, Alfie jumped in. 'Remember when Mummy pumped? She blamed Daddy.'

And my beautiful wee Nola said, 'Mummy's pumps smell like roses.'

We hooted at that.

Ben launched in. 'Your mummy farted on our first date.' He

made a loud trumpeting sound with his lips. 'Sounded like a hippopotamus.'

'And it was very, very smelly,' laughed Alfie.

They had heard that story before.

'Was not,' shouted Nola and her wee lip wobbled. 'It was beautiful, wasn't it Daddy?'

'Well, it didn't stop me asking her out again so perhaps it was beautiful and smelly at the same time.'

Nola was appeased and for a few minutes we were all lost in our thoughts.

When I shouted, 'Wave to Daddy's wee granny,' as we drove past Brookeborough. On cue, the kids cheered enthusiastically. I thought Ben was going to choke.

'Jeezuz, Rachel, how the hell did you remember that?'

'Not the foggiest,' I lied.

Can't deny it. The kids love it at Lough Erne. As soon as we arrive, they dash to their grandpa's boathouse to find their life jackets. Alfie is desperate to learn how to wakeboard or ski. Ben and Carrie are naturals. I'm okay if a little hesitant. They didn't disappoint. Kenneth stood at the open doors of his big wooden shed waiting for the twosome and they rushed to him. With his big arms he scooped them up and embraced them. I know Dad adores all his grandchildren but Kenneth is far more demonstrative. You always won hands down in the cuddling department, Mum. God, I miss your reassuring hugs.

That evening, the kids put their finishing touches to the cards we had started in Edinburgh. More heartache. I slept in beside Nola in the twin room and Ben shared his bed with Alfie. Margaret felt we should all be in the main house. I was grateful for that. Every Sutherland had an early night.

Next morning, we were up at the crack of dawn. After

breakfast, Ben, his dad and the kids went sailing. It was cold and blustery. Not a good day for visiting the cemetery. Margaret and I took the dogs for a walk in the nearby wooded grounds of a huge country house. Three hyper cocker spaniels and two unusually quiet mothers.

'You're looking well, Rachel,' said Margaret. 'Ben says you've taken up jogging?'

There was a little bit of incredulity in her tone as if Ben may have been mistaken. She just can't help it. A filter malfunction. Though some would say I had the same fault. Your body has now shed 29lbs. So much more energy.

'A near-death experience gives you a jolt. A reality check.' I had more of a lecturing tone than planned!!! 'I want to be as fit as I can be now. Especially for Alfie and Nola.' Wanted to say Ben too but that might have sounded a trite incestuous.

She grabbed my hand and kissed the back of it. 'Aww, pet,' she whimpered.

We talked about me, as in you, and how I was coping and how Ben was coping. Then she asked about Colin. I could sense it was coming.

'He is living with his new woman.' I looked at her speechless face. 'New sport. New love interest and I hope a new life as far away from me as is humanly possible.'

'Oh Rachel, as if you haven't been through enough.' She stopped abruptly for a bear hug. The dogs reacted by jumping in on the act. Wet and dirty trousers!!

'Don't feel sorry for me. I'm relieved. He is a snivelling wee bastard,' I spat. 'He's been controlling me for years. I'm sure of it.'

I gave her the quick version of what had happened the past few weeks.

Then she asked about Jasper. Nothing wrong with her memory!!!! Again, I brushed him off. Actually, what is going on with Mr Jasper T. Christie? I had the stupid notion that he might be a government spy. Well, he does hang about the parliament buildings and drives the top brass. Now that WOULD be something.

After coffee and a snack, the four of us freshened up to visit my/your grave. No black today. Summer outfits for everyone. Nola wore a lovely pink Laura Ashley style dress that I had bought her from John Lewis. Alfie and Ben had long, grey shorts and lemon and grey shirts. I had on a pink dress, paler than Nola's, three quarter length sleeves and the pink shoes I bought ages ago. It suited you, Mum. I slipped a pair of canvas shoes into my bag for the grass.

Kenneth dropped us off and waited outside Breandrum while we filtered in. FUCKING HORRIBLE YET AGAIN!!!!! At least it wasn't raining and the wind had definitely dropped.

The headstone is beautiful. White marble and gold lettering with a black outline. Everything was written inside a great big gold heart.

Ruby Eleanor Sutherland
*Age 34*
*5/7/1984 to 28/3/2019*
*Beloved wife of Ben Kenneth Sutherland*
*And beautiful caring mother to Alfie and Nola.*
*Taken too soon.*
*No doubt, Scooby Doo, you will be controlling all the broadcasts*
*in Heaven. Love you to the moon and back.*

I'm crying as I write this.

Oh Mum, was I such a bad person to have ended up like this?

Nola and Alfie set their cards against the headstone. Inside a plastic wallet to protect them from the elements. They each had a little plant pot of white roses and Ben brought white lilies. The smell was intoxicating. I planted some plants from my garden at Deacon House and some from yours in Carberry Crescent and the Pinks from Dad's garden. I buried the little St Christopher you and Dad gave me when I was christened, under the Pinks. Hope it keeps us both safe.

I had prepared myself once again for the dramatic switch when I touched the cold marble. Eyes tight. Held my breath. It was surprisingly warm. Nothing happened. Thank you so much.

Alfie opened the container he had been carrying ever so carefully. It was a cup cake with a single candle on it. The kids belted out *Happy Birthday*. The words couldn't make it past Ben and my lips. I couldn't even conjure the tune. They sang their end of term nursery songs with all the actions and oodles of gusto. All about sunshine and scarecrows. They were bursting with pride. I led them to Kenneth's car and left Ben. His sobbing rippled along the grass and seeped into my soul.

Margaret and Kenneth had booked a late lunch at the Killyhevlin. Carrie, Dale and the kids joined us. Alfie and Nola adore their cousins. It was a welcome distraction and light relief.

I put the kids to bed. Won't see them for six weeks. How will I cope?

The kids crashed within minutes of going to bed. Ben suggested a night cap on the veranda immediately outside the bedrooms.

It is so beautiful and peaceful looking out over the water. It was dull again but I had a blanket wrapped around my legs. Ben talked about me for well over an hour.

About how we met in Belfast when I chummed Annabelle over to meet up with him and Pascal (worked with Ben in Melbourne). Pascal was a great chef too yet he deviated into food photography. He is freelance but prepares and arranges food displays for all the top magazines and chefs. They are amazing works of art. NOT always for eating unfortunately as they are sprayed with all sorts of non-edible varnishes. Must be well paid as he and his wife, Cherish, live in a mansion house in Surrey. I would love to have caught up with him this weekend but I can hardly rock up as you!!!!

Ben was the most handsome man I had ever met. Intriguing, shy but funny. We clicked straight away. I thought Annabelle and Pascal were well matched but she thought differently. I was in bed with Ben less than three hours of meeting him. OMG!!!!!! AMAZING SEX. Sorry, Mum, but totally true. We couldn't keep our hands off each other for the rest of the weekend.

'It was June 2006 when I saw Ruby for the first time,' said Ben. His beautiful blue eyes glazed over. 'Jeezuz, Rachel, lightning struck. She left me speechless. I was spouting utter shite.'

'Didn't put her off,' I laughed.

'I couldn't leave her side. I returned to London to work but I knew I had to try and make it in Scotland.' He twisted the malt whisky in his hands. He does that when he is nervous or deep in thought. 'Chef at the Dorchester recommended me to Andrew Fairlie at Gleneagles. How lucky was I? A legend. Great chef. Great boss. Now that's the two of them away.'

Think he meant me and poor Andrew. More twisting of his glass.

'She was so grateful you did all that for her. So was I.' Tried hard to react as you.

'I would never have been able to open Suthiez without Ruby. She truly believed in me. Kept pushing me. Boosting my confidence. I was that close,' he held his thumb and forefinger in front of his face, 'that close, to pulling out but she wouldn't hear of it.'

I was focussing so hard not to be me that I couldn't think of the right words.

'She was so proud of you,' was all I could muster.

'D'ye think I held her back? In her career?' I did not expect that.

'Absolutely not!' I cried. 'You, the kids, the restaurants were enough for her. It's all she talked about that day. The day of our accident'

'Why?' he asked.

'Why what?' I queried.

'Why did she bring it up?'

'Cos I did. I asked her if she was happy. I knew Ruby. I knew she would be weighing up what was going on in her life. Especially with the success of *Haud Yer Wheesht*.'

'What did she say?' he asked hesitantly.

'She said that she would never move from Edinburgh. She loved it there. It's where the restaurants were. It's where you all belonged.'

'But she loved her job. Her face lit up whenever she talked about it,' he was at pains to point out.

'She did and she admitted that too. But she loved her family more. She said she would rather flourish here and have her five minutes of fame than crash and die in London.'

Ben swallowed but I could tell his mouth was dry. 'Well, she crashed and died on a street in Edinburgh.' Tears streamed down his face. And mine.

'You know, Ben, she loved and was loved back unconditionally. Ruby knew that. Some people, like me, never find that truly compatible partner. You two were lucky.'

Sorry, Mum but from the wee snippets I glean from Lisa, Brian and Dad, I think you and Dad were never truly content with what you had. Even Auntie Vera opined that 'once you had made your bed, you had to lie in it.' What a waste!

He swiped his arm across his eyes. 'Think my luck has run out.' And he downed a large Macallan.

# FIFTY-FOUR

*Rachel's Flat in Portobello. Thursday 9th January 2020*

Rachel's head was pounding. Oh, my word, how much wine had she and Lisa polished off last night? She can vaguely remember opening the door to Brian but at least he was laughing when he half carried his wife down the stairs.

Her mobile pinged. A WhatsApp from Lisa.

Fuck's sake, Rach. When was the last time we had a session like that? Extremely delicate this morning but totally worth it. I've had to reschedule my work load today.

Catch up soon xx

PS glad to have you back. xxxxxxx'

Rachel smiled. It was good to be back. Not without Ruby, naturally, but good to be back on speaking terms with Lisa. She had missed her oldest friend.

Rachel brushed her hair, ever so lightly with her middle finger. Ouch! That hurt. It was as if each stitch had a direct link to the centre of her brain or the centre of her headache. The realisation of having her stitches removed, with a hangover, was daunting. Too late, she could hear the key ram into the lock.

'Only me,' shouted Annabelle. 'Jeezo, Ruby, I mean, Mrs M...

You look rough.' Then the penny dropped. 'I take it you had a good night with Lisa?' she laughed. Annabelle had been addressing Rachel as 'Ruby' for months. She, too, was not finding the readjustment easy.

'Too good,' replied Rachel. But she couldn't disguise her pleasure. 'Thanks for agreeing to take me this morning. Not sure if I could have done it alone.'

'Course you could've,' chastised Ruby's pal. 'But I'm glad you asked me.'

Rachel had never met Eleanor Riddle before – at least not as herself, although Ruby seemed taken with her.

'Good morning, Rachel. Take a seat. Normally the nurse would have done this but I wanted to see you for myself.' Doctor Riddle assessed the wound. 'That's a nasty gash. What on earth happened?'

Rachel explained that she wasn't sure. She could only repeat what passersby had seen.

'I have no recollection of the last nine months. Since after my accident with Ruby.' Her face quivered as tears filled her eyes. She hadn't discussed the accident with outsiders yet; only Annabelle and Lisa. 'This is the first time I have met you.'

Eleanor dropped to her seat again – the surgical scissors still in her hand. She shook her head.

'You never fail to amaze me, Rachel... and I'm rarely lost for words. Do you remember your life before the accident?'

'Every bit of it,' Rachel confirmed, 'and if I'm honest, I have no wish to return to it. Well, to Colin if I'm being honest.'

'Ah!' said her doctor. 'I think that horse has well and truly bolted... at least I hope so. For both our sakes.'

'You?' Rachel was surprised.

'Yes me. For some reason your husband thought I was some

sort of conspirator or collaborator. Favouring you over him. He no longer attends this surgery, thank goodness.'

'I haven't got that far yet.'

Doctor Riddle looked quizzically at her patient.

'I kept a journal of everything that had happened to me since I woke up the last time. It's very detailed.' Rachel's face flushed. 'I'm only as far as July.'

'Gosh, you have a lot to read then.'

'Actually no. I'm about two thirds or three quarters of the way through it. Life must have been fairly uneventful after July.'

'I doubt that very much,' laughed Eleanor. 'You have to be one of the most intriguing patients I have ever met. A journal? Good on you.'

'I can't believe it either but I am so grateful to... me for having the foresight.' She almost thanked Ruby.

Rachel chatted about her stay in hospital – her second stay – as her stitches were removed.

'It was a neat job. I'm pleased with how it looks.' Eleanor was referring to the excellent stitching technique. 'There's no sign of infection but keep the area clean for the next week or so and take extra care when brushing your hair. I shouldn't need to see you unless you want to discuss anything with me.'

'I honestly can't think of anything right now but that could change. Thank you for keeping me on. After me moving away, I mean.'

'Well, technically you still reside at Carberry Crescent. You have only moved temporarily to allow your neighbour's family to live there.' Rachel remained blank. Eleanor laughed. 'Not read that part yet?'

Rachel smiled. 'Obviously not.'

'You are a very kind lady, Rachel. Please do not hesitate to come and see me should you have any concerns as regards to your wellbeing. If it's any consolation, you have been in very good health as of late. A healthy diet and exercise have helped. Keep it up.'

Rachel had one question. 'Do I take medication for depression or anxiety?'

Doctor Riddle laughed again. 'No, you don't, considering everything that has been thrown at you. You have been coping remarkably well without them.'

Rachel thanked her doctor profusely and joined Annabelle in her car.

'Well?' asked her young friend.

'All good. I just need to catch up on that bloody diary. What has Ruby been up to?'

'You sound just like her you know. It's scary. I have to keep reminding myself who I'm with,' remarked Annabelle.

'Before we go back to Portobello, would you drive past my house? I'd like to take a peek.'

# FIFTY-FIVE

## *Ruby's Journal*

**Saturday 20th July.**

So much time lapsing between my entries but you know my reasons. However, I might now be hanging around here (Pitt Street) more often.

Annabelle's in 'mourning'. She found out that Andy had been sexting his ex while they were in Paris. Took a picture of his erect dick next to a postcard of the Eiffel Tower and told her to expect a big French surprise when he got back from his conference. Classy. If it hadn't happened to Bella-Anne we would probably have found it hysterical but I had to side with her and express my horror at his crassness.

One bonus, I have someone to go out with at the weekends again.

Kenneth drove me to Belfast for my flight home. Ben wanted to spend as much time with Alfie and Nola as he could before travelling back. Don't blame him. Five weeks without them. He returned on Saturday while I was at Rory's.

Brentwood was okay. It was good to catch up with Rory and Alana. Not so good playing Granny Rachel to Jack all the time. Was wee Jack always so needy? He wanted my attention constantly. That's a rotten admission but I did try. You must have had the patience of a saint, Mum. Actually, I'm being unfair. Jack is obviously very fond of you and you must have played lots of games with him. He did say your computer skills had massively improved. I was able to give him a reasonable run for his money on some of his games. Well, kind of. He's an utter genius for a ten-year-old. Much better than Rory – much to his consternation. Hee hee.

They've had a huge extension built. A lot cheaper than moving apparently. They had a decent sized garden before so not made a huge dent in their outside space. Being an end terrace helps; all that extra land at the side. Their kitchen now incorporates a dining area and family room. Can you guess the value of their house? Not much change out of 900K or more, I would think. Good on them. I know, I know. We are very fortunate to own our house at the Grange. Don't think we would ever have been able to afford it without Kenneth's dad's generosity. That's not a dig at you or Dad by the way. You two have always given way more than was necessary but Ben's granddad left all his grandchildren a substantial inheritance. Felt his immediate family didn't need any more money. Probably right. Carrie bought a second home in the south of Tenerife near Adeje with hers. Only been once but it is very nice. Near the beach. Private swimming pool.

I'm sure I saw Rylan Clark get into a car on the same road where Alana's parents live. Moved from Lewisham three years ago to be closer to Jack.

Anyway, back to Rylan. Remember him? Tall guy. Big white teeth. Was on the X-factor a few years ago. JJ and I interviewed him once. He was really nice. Much more genuine than you would think. Dad can't stand him. Don't know why? But then Dad is uncomfortable around gay men full stop. See what he's like with JJ and Arjun. He got annoyed when I told him that he can't catch homosexuality by shaking hands or receiving a man-hug.

Rylan was the only celebrity I saw. It's nothing like what you would imagine when you see *TOWIE* on the telly. The centre is okay but I was hugely disappointed the first time I visited. Think I expected a miniature Hollywood Boulevard. Daft, I know. Every second shop, however, is a hairdresser, beauticians or offers some kind of therapy service and the women (and men) are very well groomed. Alana fits in perfectly.

Jack and I did a heritage walking tour around the city centre. Neither Rory nor Alana had ever heard of it. It was actually quite interesting. Even big Jack and Fran were impressed by our knowledge when they had us over on Sunday evening.

I came home on Tuesday. I know I should have stayed longer. Maybe when I'm more used to being you, I will.

In fact, as a result of that weekend, I decided to drop your family and friends a letter updating my status and how I was fairing generally. I was really requesting more time and space to adjust to my new world and would appreciate their cooperation and understanding.

And that is the crux of it, Mum. It's tiring and depressing playing you ALL the time. It's so much easier with people who never knew you although I suppose I'm getting used to Lisa and Auntie Vera... just.

Kind of cheated as it was a typed generic letter but I added a footnote at the bottom of each one. A wee bit more personal. I included your Fraserburgh crew and Auntie Lillian in Canada. Your two cousins that you used to meet up with and Dad's parents (I know you didn't have much time for them or them you but they were nice to me and Rory). I found the address of your young teacher pal, Sarah, in your teaching folder so kept her in the loop. AND I posted one to Claire. Just added that I was so sorry that her dad had had his life turned upside down by it all but sadly he is a stranger to me. Now that he has found someone else (should have put in long before the accident!) it was perhaps time that we all moved on. I wrote that I would still be happy to see Jade occasionally if she wanted but (dropped this in) that I understood she would probably be developing a new relationship with Colin's new woman. A tiny bit sarcastic but did end with *I wish you all well. Take care.* Thought 'love' would be pushing it.

Ben has asked me to 'attend to the house' on Wednesdays only until the twosome return. Feel he is distancing himself from me a little. Knew this would happen. He opened up too much in front of his 'mother-in-law' in Enniskillen and now he is being all professional about our arrangement. He can be such a twat. But it will pass. It always does. I'll just have to make the most of it and him while I'm there. PLUS, I know how to play his games better than himself!!

I had a great show last night (Friday 19th). Feel as if I'm finding my feet at HR. Had to work hard to steer things away from the Agony Aunt route. Christ, it was depressing. So many sad stories and negativity. It was wrist slashing stuff!!! Now, we are focussing on positivity. Not quite a wellness advice programme but certainly giving out upbeat vibes and boosting our confidence with well-meaning anecdotes and information. And for those in need of more help, I've put together an information package that is either emailed or posted out. Who would have thought eh? Little ole Ruby Martin dispensing so much wisdom.

Charles is really pleased with how things are turning out. For the first time ever, he has had advertising enquiries for a night time slot. One was from a small shop in North Berwick that up-cycles clothing and accessories for resale or the rental market. That was a result of us sharing tips about getting ready for a night out. One female texted in saying that she had stopped going out because she doesn't have the right clothes to wear. Hell, we were inundated with help. Folk were offering her dresses and shoes they no longer wore or saying that she should just accessorise what she already had. The buzz was amazing. So I'm going to try different themes to see how it works BUT I've told my listeners no doom and gloom – it's all about positivity. Being the best we can be. Having fun and a bloody good laugh. AND, fantastic music, obviously. The Monday morning broadcast has definitely boosted my evening ratings. More listeners are joining me because of it. If it wasn't for the kids, I would volunteer for more mornings but I won't jeopardise my time with them. EVER.

# FIFTY-SIX

## *Ruby's Journal*

**Monday 22nd July.**

Can't believe I'm about to write this. SOOOOO embarrassing. Or should I say ashamed? God, I'm so mixed up. Don't know how I feel or how I should feel but can't shake off the sense of disgust with myself. Not that I did anything disgusting. Not really.

I HAD SEX!!!!!!!!

Too much alcohol involved or that's the excuse I'm sticking too. Annabelle is made up for me even though she said that it's a sad day when a fifty-seven-year-old gets laid when she can't.

We went out on Saturday night. Unusually early for us. After a nice meal that I had prepared at Pitt Street. First chance we'd had to celebrate her birthday properly. She is 7 days younger than me. Started walking up to George Street. Succumbed and flagged a taxi. Had a couple of drinks in Tigerlily's then headed up to the Grassmarket. It's funny but when I'm with Annabelle, I totally forget I'm in your body. We're exactly as we used to be. All touchy feely. Leaning in. Wee pecks on the cheek. Some men asked if we were lovers which we found hilarious. But I suppose from the outside looking in, it could be perceived that way. We've made a wee pact. If anyone asks, we are ex colleagues that still enjoy each other's company. We got fed up having to answer questions about my 'daughter' plus it puts a damper on our days/nights out. So, I am Rachel Martin who used to organise events. True of me so not difficult to hold a conversation if questions become invasive.

Anyhow, we did a pub crawl from one end to the other. The ones that we could get in, that is. Not a hope in Hell will anyone squeeze past security if it's bulging. The whole area was bouncing (fab weather). Some of the guys on the doors were a bit heavy handed. Not with us but there's always crowds of lads, especially on stag dos, who over react when they are refused entry. The bouncers do their best to restrict large groups. Easy to get round though. All they do is go in twos or threes and meet up at the bar once inside. Sometimes their accents are a give-away.

We had a great laugh. Lots of the dads and uncles were chatting me up. I had on white jeans with a colourful jazzy blouse. Really suited your skin tone and hair. Bella-Anne looked stunning in a fab wee dress from FatFace. She has such a good body. Just wish she could see what everyone else sees. Annabelle thought it would be hilarious if she got off with a groom and me with his dad. I said it would be even more hilarious if I got off with the groom and she ended up with his dad. Then we agreed that shagging a groom would be extremely poor taste.

At around 10.30 we decided to head for Gene Genies in the Cowgate. It used to be a haunt of ours years ago and neither of us could remember the last time we had been there. So off we staggered down the darkening cobbles. When you're wasted you don't notice the dark as much. No way would I walk there on my own at that time of night even though there's plenty folk milling about on Saturdays. Genies was hoaching. A real festival vibe. The outdoor lights helped.

Couldn't believe it, the first person we bumped into was Hannah fucking Dunlop. She was there with two of her pals from work, sitting at a table in the courtyard. Naturally, Annabelle made a beeline for her.

'Don't be rude, Ruby,' she warned. 'She's been a good friend to me.'

I left her to it and went to the bar for a drink. Not like me normally, but I didn't even ask if the others wanted anything. Took me over half an hour to squeeze through the throngs there and back. Older faces are totally overlooked at the bar. Deliberately ignored!! I had to sound truly pissed off before a young girl was willing to serve me. Plumped for longer serves. Prosecco with Aperol. No sooner had I plonked down beside Annabelle than I was smothered by Hannah proclaiming that her and I were the best of mates and how much she missed me. What could I say? Annabelle had begged me to try.

The whole tone of the evening changed immediately. Annabelle and I HAD to be more guarded. I knew I had had too much to drink as I couldn't sober up. We were lucky if we'd had two slurps of our drinks when one of Hannah's pals (the loud, gobby one) suggested we all go to Sam's Jazz Bar. Everybody knows that Sam's is notorious for those who are on the pull. The staff at Fourth usually head for Toreador's.

'Drink up!' yelled Gobby. 'We might beat the queues if we go now.'

They'd never make Rose Street before midnight. I'd made up my mind already: I was going back to Annabelle's. I'd call an Uber but the girls ganged up on me.

'Nah, nah, Rachel. You, my honey, are coming wi us,' and Hannah slipped her arm into mine and guided me out the gates.

Why didn't we hail a taxi or phone an Uber...? Every one of us had heels. Something I never wore as I hated towering over folk, especially Annabelle. You, Mum, are barely two inches taller than her. So there we were, teetering and tanking over uneven streets up to South Bridge. Thank goodness I had lost weight as it was heavy going. We were about to turn down Cockburn Street when Annabelle collided with a smart, suited man. She bounced backwards but his quick reaction saved her from a nasty fall. He grabbed her wrists and held on until she had steadied herself.

Fuck me!!!! It was Jasper.

'Rachel?'

'Jasper?'

The girls stood. Wide mouthed and smug. Their eyes pinging back and forth.

'This is Jasper,' said I. 'Amber Rose's brother.' My face was burning.

'So, you're Jasper,' sang Annabelle, slurring.

That tone told the others all they needed to know (Jasper included). Plus, it wasn't hard to deduce by our body language that something was going on.

'These girls are Ruby's friends,' I gulped. The words were sticking in my dry throat. I think you need HRT.

'And Rachel's,' chipped in Annabelle trying to give me some sort of street cred.

'You MUST come with us to Sam's,' rasped Hannah in his ear. 'We won't take a NO.'

Jeepers, she is something else. When did she ramp up the vamp? Though, she was wearing a tight red dress. Pity about the fat thighs.

Jasper did actually stutter. He had been well and truly hijacked so I did my best to rescue him.

'I think Jasper has just finished his work. It's probably the last thing he wants.'

He nodded and pulled that wide mouth awkward grin that people do when they're not quite sure what to say.

Then my big gob lost control. 'Why don't you go on and Jasper and I will have a nightcap before we both head home?'

There were ooohs, nudging, giggling and winking from the others. Cringe. But they/we were rat-arsed.

Jasper visibly relaxed. His whole demeanour emitted, 'thank you.'

The girls clip-clopped down Cockburn Street as we tried to gauge what we should do next.

'I'll call an Uber,' I said. 'Would you mind waiting with me?'

He pulled his neck in. 'Thought we were going for a drink?'

I was only giving him an out. Didn't actually think he would take up the offer. Or maybe I did. Or hoped. Not sure.

'Oh! Only if you want to.' I think I used a ridiculous husky tone similar to Hannah's. It was meant to sound funny but may have erred on desperate. Double cringe.

Before I had time to take stock, Jasper had phoned an Uber.

'SleepEEzzy, Corstorphine.'

Five minutes later, a car rolled up. Punters were pouring out of the pubs and there's always one smart arse that tries to nab your taxi. One look from Jasper though is enough. Especially when he pulls up to his true height. Streets whizzed past my bleary vision.

'Would you like a nightcap here or in my room?' he asked when we stepped into the tiny foyer.

I replied in a voice that resembled a blackbird being throt-tled. 'You choose,' I tweeted.

We went to his room.

It was reasonably big. The room!!!!

He pulled off his tie and threw it along with his jacket on to one of the red bucket chairs. I shuffled to the other chair and sat down. He placed two fat glasses on the round coffee table in front of the chairs. Honestly, I felt as if I was watching it unfold on the telly. He poured a generous measure of malt in each glass. I nodded when he asked if I would like ice.

'Relax, Rachel. We're only having a drink. If you'd rather we sat upstairs, (the lounge bar) it's not a problem. Honestly.'

'Sorry,' I said. 'It's me. I'm not used to going out on my own, never mind having a drink in (I was going to say a stranger's) a man's hotel room.

He chuckled. 'I'm not in the habit of asking women to my room.'

Somehow, I doubted that.

Then, as if a switch went on, calm descended. We both chilled.

I smiled at him. He grinned at me. 'Cheers,' said I. 'Slange,' he replied.

He had one more before he made his move.

Ever so slowly, he took my hands in his and pulled me to my feet then softly kissed me. Oh, it was so so nice to be kissed. I just melted and let it all happen. He met no resistance. Nothing.

He undressed me. I had to undo the button on my jeans but I was beyond feeling embarrassed. All my clothes lay in a heap. I pushed his shoulders and he sat on the bed. I undid the buttons on his shirt, flattened my hands against his chest and he eased backwards. Oh, my days, without speaking, I straddled him and nibbled his nipples. When I was sure he was responding I upped the ante. Not a word was spoken between us until we were both naked and beneath the duvet.

'I never expected this,' he murmured.

'Nor me.'

Then we went for it. Truthfully? I wished it was Ben but that was never going to happen so as drunk as I was, I was determined to enjoy it. I did try. Think he did too. We didn't use a condom!! Something I would NEVER have done in my own body but wasn't sure what you oldies do. Maybe I should have done. Too late now.

Before I fell asleep, I had the sense to warn Annabelle that I was staying over!!! And with whom and where.

I'm not a total eejit.

# FIFTY-SEVEN

*Ruby's Journal*

**Sunday Morning 21st. 5.30 am** (not when I'm writing but when I got up).

I couldn't work out, at first, where I was when I woke up. Totally starkers. Mouth like a badger's bum. Yuck!!

Jasper was still stocious. He'd knocked back another before he stripped me. Dutch courage, he had mumbled.

Stripped me!!! OMG!!

I couldn't face him so took the coward's way out. Dressed as quietly as was possible. Barely breathed. Tiptoed out. Had to pass reception to get to the lift. The eager beaver young lad on the desk was obviously fed up as he perked up when he caught sight of me.

'Checking out?' he chirruped.

'No, I'm not,' said I, 'but could you call me a taxi, please?'

'Not checking out?' Maybe he was deaf or just thick.

'Nope. A taxi would be grand, thanks.'

He dialled the company asked for the taxi then the wee gobshite asked for my room number.

'Be sure to tell the driver I'll meet him downstairs.' I was very gruff but he got the message.

I went back to Carberry Crescent. Couldn't face going to Annabelle's flat. Couldn't face the interrogation.

I scrubbed myself in the shower. Didn't want Jasper's smell

on me. Honestly? I felt a right slut. Not Jasper's fault. He didn't force me. I was more than a willing partner. But I was consumed with guilt. Never ever ever had I cheated on Ben while we were a proper item (apart from that one time way at the beginning but that doesn't count). Never wanted to. I'm five minutes in your body and desperate for a shag!!!! What is wrong with me?

I found Horlicks in your cupboard. Took me right back. Remember when I was in the middle of exams and I had panic attacks at three in the morning? You would make us Horlicks and toast. We would have a chat then you would cuddle me in in bed. Thank you, Mum. You were so kind and patient.

I had a mug. Thick butter on my toast and crawled, literally, into bed. Zonked. I never moved until I was aware of the ping, ping, ping from my phone. Still ignored it until it rang. Left it to ring then checked it. It was Jasper as I had expected.

Rather than try to recount what happened, I'll copy out our texts.

(HIM) Rachel, Are you okay? Where are you

(HIM) Rachel? I'm really worried please let me know if you are safe.

(HIM) I've tried calling. Please, where are you?

(ME) I'm fine. Home safely. Sorry I bailed out. Very cowardly. Sorry. Shouldn't have happened. My fault entirely. Xx

(HIM) Nothing to apologise about. Two consenting adults. I had a great time. Didn't you?'

(ME) I was drunk. Gung ho!!! Sorry. Won't happen again! X

(HIM) Really? Was it that bad?'

(ME) You are my only friend since the accident. The only person that I truly know and who only knows the new me. I DO NOT want to jeopardise that friendship.

I could have mentioned my colleagues at Harbour Radio (nobody knows about them) or the staff at the cafe close to Pitt Street but surely the latter don't count?!!!!! Pretty pathetic admission that cafe acquaintances count as friends.

(HIM) Don't be daft. I value your friendship but we are two friends who had sex. No big deal if it doesn't have to be. Can I call you?

(ME) No. Please don't. I'm not ready. I know I'm overreacting. You have no idea how bad I feel. Sorry. Can I contact you when I'm ready?

(HIM) Okay but only for a few days then I'll be in touch.

He was true to his word. Haven't heard a peep since.

Annabelle's interrogation was fierce. No stone unturned. She turned up at my house in the afternoon when she could be certain that she wouldn't fail a breathalyser.

'Did you give him a blow job?' she asked. See what I mean?

'Truthfully?' I stumbled. 'Can't be certain.' I threw my head back in defeat.

It was true. I was that drunk I can't determine what I actually did from what I might have done. If that makes sense? Now, Ben and I rarely had sex without a little fumble of tongues or full-on oral sex. I'm blushing as I confess this but only because the thought of you reading this one day appalls me.

'Who made the first move?' she asked.

'Him.'

'Who was naked first?'

'Me.'

'Knew it.' She slapped her thigh.

'What does that mean?'

'Eh... it's Ruby Martin we're talking about. Sheds her clothes like a cat sheds fur.'

'I do NOT!!!!' I did. I like being naked when my partner is fully clothed. Don't know why all my friends needed to be in on this deviance. But I am a big mouth.

After she had dissected every move, she slumped into my big chair satisfied and chuckled.

'So, what now?'

Indeed. What?

I'm giving Jasper Thistle a wide berth.

Next door's baby was in their back garden. We had to have a look. She is adorable. Ayesha. And I've been invited to the Christening (25th). Also volunteered my spare room for some of Tanya's family. I am now in your room, Mum. New mattress, naturally, and new bedding. Totally gutted the place. No hint of Colin's rancid stench or presence.

Let Annabelle in on my secret. Had to tell someone. Asked her to tune into Reya's breakfast show on Monday morning.

'Why? What is Harbour Radio anyway?' she asked.

'Just tune in, please. You'll love her. Be listening 8.00am after the news. You'll get the shock of your life.'

My morning show is a hoot. Full on fun and laughter. A wee bit like my evening show but with much more content. Same kind of themes. Revolves around wellness tips whether it's fitness, sleep, make-up, fashion, diet or mental health. Plus, everything green and eco-friendly. Anything goes and it does. I have been inundated with requests from all sorts of gurus and nutters (unfortunately) who want to enlighten us with their knowledge or experiences. Harbour Radio has a rule – no visitors to the studios – and I'm happy to comply. I've rejected all face to face interviews and online meetings too. I could never be bothered with Teams but at least you only had to concentrate on your top half. I have never yet done it in my pants or pj bottoms. A girl has standards you know!!!!

We don't do live phone interviews either. All my guests (only had two) have been pre-recorded. It's something Charles can control and edit accordingly.

8.15am on the dot. Monday morning. A private message from Bella-Anne.

'What the fuck??!!!! Is that really you?'

I played a request especially for my best chum. The morning we started High School together this song was belting out from the radio as my dad checked the knots in our school ties before we left my house.

'Mysterious Girl' by Peter Andre.

Annabelle was so nervous she puked all over her shoe at our front gate and I had to find her a pair of white ankle socks. I doubt any first years now would be seen dead in white ankle socks with a lace trim.

I was asked today why there is no photograph of me on the website. I brushed it off claiming personal reasons. Someone wrote on our Instagram page that I was the victim of stalking.

That has now gathered momentum. An Elaine Penman asked if she could interview me on the subject. She has a podcast 'Why Us?' All about women. From their rights and safety to everything else that impacts us. Politely declined. Got enough with Ray of Hope.

Ran ten miles today. Managed fine. Get me!! Get you!!!

Think I'll join a Zumba class. Somewhere where nobody knows us.

# FIFTY-EIGHT

*Ruby's Journal*

**Sunday 28th July.**

FaceTimed the kids this morning when they returned from church and before they headed out for lunch with the Sutherlands. They never question why they go to church in N.I when they don't here. We're too lazy and not all that religious yet fully appreciate that we would be amongst the first to moan if all the churches closed. No happy medium.

Reminded them to send wee Jack a birthday message. I will send a gift from all of us.

Three whole weeks without them. Sure, it's flown by. Ben has settled down again. Knew he would. I had a sandwich with him on Wednesday before he dashed off to meet up with Alex and Karl to confirm everything is in place for August. Festival madness already. We usually reduce the menus over August as it's so busy. We also have quicker turnover times. Have to, to accommodate demand. Kenneth and Margaret have taken the kids at the beginning of August since Nola was born. You used to take Alfie, Mum, but you claimed that two of them was too much. Now I understand that buggerlugs would have put a stop to it.

Talking about the weasel, haven't seen him for weeks but I've had an uneasy feeling, on several occasions, that someone was watching the house or me. Sure enough, Annabelle and I reviewed the security images and we're certain that Colin has driven past the house in his Saab. Can't see his face. Worse still at very odd hours. From very early morning til late at night. Kinda freaked me out.

Ever since starting at Harbour Radio, I NEVER take the same route home but I'm going to make sure my arrival journey is varied too. Sean next door repeatedly reminds me that he is less than a minute away. That's okay if he's at home!!!!

Jasper contacted me on Wednesday. He texted while I was eating with Ben. Ben asked if everything was okay because my face was beaming. A mixture of guilt and embarrassment. I nearly fell off my chair when he asked if it was Jasper. How the Hell did he know? But we used to do that all the time. Say something at the same time, think something at the same time or just know what the other was going to say or do. Like we were connected spiritually. Unnerving but comforting too.

Jasper came to Alderburn on Thursday evening. We had chicken asparagus risotto for supper followed by a walk round the village. Sean and Tanya clocked him. Big, enthusiastic wave from their living room window. At least it made us laugh. I pointed out Auntie Vera's. No, we didn't go in.

When we got back to the house fully expected him to head off. But no. He produced a bottle of Chateauneuf-du-Pape. My favourite red. Pleasant mellow radio in the background, courtesy of Alexa, and what can I say. Had it off on the rug in front of your fire. Me fully naked. Again. Less than fifteen minutes after the first drop bleached my lips. Confirmation. Ruby Martin has no moral compass.

Not sure where we go from here. Confused. Confused. Confused.

On Friday, Annabelle stayed over. Same with Saturday. She stayed in the house and tuned into my show.

After a morning jog (Annabelle wants to lose weight), we spent the Saturday in Dunbar then North Berwick. It was fab. Great weather. Great craic and a found a smashing wee pub on the main street, around the corner from the beach. Really good fish n chips. Back to Alderburn for too many wines then fell, together, into my bed.

'Don't you be thinking I'm Jasper,' she cackled. Nudge, nudge, wink, wink!!!!

On the Sunday we checked the security footage on cloud before heading to Edinburgh. NOOOOOO!!!!!

Colin drove past the house 30 seconds after Jasper and I walked up the path. Then twice more on Saturday while Annabelle and I were in North Berwick.

Decided to pop into the Police Station in Dalkeith (fully manned there). I had also emailed in advance. Not convinced they took me seriously as it was and probably should still be his house after all. Their words not mine. Hey, at least they have a record of my concerns.

Shattered. Morning show tomorrow and Tuesday and Wednesday. Covering for Maria.

**Saturday 3rd August.** Festival has kicked off. Holyrood Park closed to traffic. The Meadows was mobbed. Event tents, people, food stalls. I love Edinburgh at this time. I know lots of locals loath it. Too many cars parking illegally in their streets but for a presenter it is Heaven. A buzz like no other. Annabelle has a gin bar at George Square, up from McEwen Hall where you graduated. She shares it with a couple of small breweries, taking turnabout. I said I would keep her company and help out.

OMG!!! It was so busy. I'm knackered (now 11.30pm).

What a laugh though. We finished at 9.00pm and one of the guys from Plimsole Real Ales took over. Annabelle will be on duty tomorrow from 9.00pm til 11. The bar is a converted horse box. So cute but oh so practical. We decorated it with fairy lights and ivy. Made a huge difference. Thought moan a minute from Plimsole's was going to take it all down but the other guy with him persuaded him to leave it. Annabelle had concocted seven cocktails (with my help), using MeanKelpie gin as her base. We named them after streets or areas in Edinburgh. *Pitt Street Zing* is our favourite. Really simple. A rhubarb gin (not overpowering) served with ginger ale, lots of ice and wedges of lime, garnished with a mint leaf. Absolutely moreish.

OBVIOUSLY, we had a few before staggering back. Sorry about the drunk handwriting!! Hee hee.


**Sunday 11th August.**

Oh, my days. Went to a show with Annabelle yesterday. 'Showstoppers'. I interviewed them last year. They are A-MAZ-ING. How can I describe them? A drama company but their whole show is improvised. They specialise in musicals. It's a mixture of music, comedy and drama BUT the whole show is based on themes/titles suggested by the audience. Then they make the whole shebang up. Songs, script, everything. Outstanding.

Anyway, they asked the audience, as usual, for ideas. One guy shouted out 'My big, fat, ugly cousin's wedding'. That got a laugh and a huge cheer but they plumped for, wait for it, 'Inside my Mother's Head'. Annabelle said the colour literally drained from my face. However, it was fantastic. It was about a mother called Josie who had dementia and it was all about her life from the past to present day. Honestly, there were so many moments that I could identify with. A bit spooky but surprisingly uplifting.

Kids are home next weekend. Can't wait to see them, apart from the fact that Kenneth and Margaret are returning to look after them for another week or so. WHAT THE FUCK!

I could easily have done that. What is Ben playing at? A huge kick in the teeth after everything I do for him. What can I say? Absolutely fucking nothing. That's what.

Phoned Rory yesterday to wish him Happy Birthday. Included his gift with Jack's parcel. They are in Majorca. Missing my whole family today. Just feeling sorry for myself.

Nothing from Jasper. I'm convinced he is playing games. Annabelle agrees. When I am keeping him at arm's length, his interest peaks. When I comply, his interest dwindles.

As for Colin, still driving along your street. Pretty sure that two days ago, it was him in a hoody actually walking past. Hood pulled right up over his head. I think he knew I was out. Sneakily, stared into the window using his hand to shade his face from the camera.

I'm shivering as I write this. I'll have to be on my guard.

# FIFTY-NINE

## *Ruby's Journal*

**Sunday 18th August.**
Had lunch with the kids today. Couldn't keep my sticky paws off them. Felt as if it took a good couple of hours before they properly settled and relaxed with me.

We had a long walk through the Meadows investigating everything on offer from snippets of Fringe shows to funfair rides. Naturally, I was on my best behaviour with the Sutherlands. Margaret enthused over my weight loss and insisted I had a sparkle that suited me. Had I considered Botox? No self-respecting woman over forty in Enniskillen would be seen in public without it. Ruby had had it done!!!! No, I bloody well hadn't but Margaret was adamant that I had. She has some gall.

Told Charles about my concerns with Colin. I have to text him when I arrive home after my late-night shows and only once I'm safely inside with the doors locked. He even offered to have someone drive me home if I wanted. He is a really decent guy. It's such a privilege to work there.

**Monday 9th September.** WHERE HAVE I BEEN?
Where have I been indeed and where the hell do I begin?

I've had pneumonia. Exactly??!!!!!! At least that's what they suspected. Your body has been in the best shape in years yet I succumbed to this crippling infection. Totally floored me. But that wasn't the half of it.

Colin made an appearance. OMG!

On the 22nd August my big boy (but will always be my wee mannie) started school. George Heriots. He looked so grown up in his uniform and blue school blazer. To be fair, Margaret was snivelling as much as me so Ben could hardly scold me and not her. We waved him off at the front door of Deacon House and I dropped Nola off at nursery. Opposite ends of Edinburgh. Not sure how mornings will work but we'll manage.

**Saturday 24th August.**

I met Jade at a bus-stop in Tranent, in the morning, not far from Aldi. She was staying the night. I hadn't been able to see her on the day she started High School but I did buy most of her school uniform. I parked in Aldi car park with the nose of my car facing the street so that I could watch for the bus further along the street.

I never gave it a second thought that Colin or his new woman would be there. Too busy thinking about how I could entertain Jade for the day. I walked towards the town centre to meet her.

It was a pleasant day, not raining and not too cold. Jade was dressed for the winter. In black, like her mother, and her hair had a navy tinge save the two pink streaks at either side of her head. I had on white, cropped jeggings and a navy Breton top. As we approached my car, she yelled,

'That's my granda's car!'

And she was off. I scurried behind her. Don't know why as I sure as hell did not want a confrontation. Thank God, it was empty.

'Do you think he will be in the shop?' she asked.

I explained as kindly as I could, that given our circumstances, I would prefer not to have to meet him. She shrugged and reluctantly followed me back to the car.

BUT NO!! No such luck.

'There's a woman breaking into the back of Granda's car.' Then she bolted.

I knew it would be HER.

His new bit nearly shit herself when Jade demanded an explanation.

'My car's in the garage,' she blurted apologetically, clearly shocked at being hijacked.

I felt I had to wade in and explain who we were.

'You're Colin's wife?' She went chalk white. 'I thought you were... have they let you out?'

She had the cheek to back away. Her eyes darting everywhere for an escape route.

'From where?' My turn to ask a question.

Her eyes were like saucers. You could tell she was struggling with how to phrase her next words.

'What the fuck are you doing with my granda's car?' Jade the diplomat as always.

'Your granddad? I thought she was your granddaughter?' She stared at me for confirmation.

'This is Jade,' I said. 'Claire's daughter. Colin's granddaughter.'

'Jade?'

Honestly Mum, we were like something from a sitcom.

Jade threw her arms up. 'So, who the fuck are you?'

One week at High School and she was behaving like an aggressive seventeen-year-old.

'Glynis,' answered the woman who appeared really frightened now.

I calmly introduced Jade to Glynis and Glynis to Jade. It was transparent they had never met.

Glynis looked at me then Jade then back to me again. 'Why are you two together?' Then obviously feeling a little more in control, she asked Jade, 'Does your mother know that you are with Rachel?' She knew your name.

My turn. 'Hey! What exactly are you inferring? Of course, her mother knows. We spoke last night.'

Jade whipped her phone out and rang Claire. She regurgitated our conversations, hardly stopping to draw breath. Jade handed the phone to Glynis. The corroboration was short. 'H.. hmm. H...hmm'. Defeated, Glynis handed the mobile back. It seemed an age before she spoke.

'Where do you live, Rachel?'

I told her.

'You haven't been...in the care system... recently?'

'Nope.'

I could tell that Jade was hindering what she wanted to say or ask. I gave Jade a fiver to buy some goodies for our movie night.

Glynis put her shopping in the boot and we got stuck in. I deliberately kept my true opinions about Colin to myself. I portrayed us both as victims of my memory loss.

'It can't have been easy for him,' I stated, 'but I honestly don't remember very much about our time together. He is a stranger to me.'

I did say he'd had some aggressive outbursts (probably toned it down) but I understood where he was coming from. (Did I hell.) Didn't condone it as he frightened me at times and I was relieved when he left.

According to her, he'd had to leave me because of my

aggression AND my addiction to gambling. Scratch cards to start with then on-line gaming machines. I'd spent all our money. When I started to laugh, well guffaw, she added that the cost of private health care (to pay for my failed rehabilitations) meant there would be no money left when he sold HIS house.

You would have been proud of me, Mum. I could have said much more than I did, especially about all the threats and attacks, but I suddenly felt very sorry for her. She looked totally dejected. Another older woman who found him beguiling. She didn't have much going for her in the looks department. Probably couldn't believe her luck when Colin came knocking.

I was aware she was assessing me – my hair, my clothes.

I tried to be kind.

'The house is mine and only mine,' I said. 'I have lived there for years. Ask my neighbours. I have NEVER gambled although I do believe I have suffered from depression since I met Colin (didn't actually say that he was probably the reason) and although I don't ever want him back, I wish you both good luck in your relationship.'

Turns out that Colin had pulled a muscle in his neck at badminton and was resting in Glynis's or he would have been there with her. I bet he would have been. Watching her every move and counting the pennies too.

Cue the return of Jade. I asked Jade in front of Glynis if I had ever been mean to her or if she was afraid of me. Bless her, Mum, she wrapped her arms around me and kissed my cheek. She said that you had been the best granny a girl could wish for. She did drop in, 'except when you cancelled my phone.' Oops. We didn't dwell on that.

'And before my accident, had you ever heard me shouting

at your granda or anyone else for that matter?' I asked, praying that she would say no.

'Granny Rachel,' she laughed, 'you're scared of your own shadow. It was my granda who kept losing his temper. Same with me and Mum.'

'What accident?' Glynis asked.

'Granny Rachel was knocked down crossing the road. Her daughter Ruby was killed. You would know Ruby Martin off the telly. Long blonde hair. Very beautiful.' Jade was devoid of emotion. She should be a newsreader.

'Was this recent?' she sounded genuinely concerned.

My lips actually started to quiver when I realised how long I had been in your body. I could only nod. I didn't want to say five months. I apologised and intimated we were going.

Glynis asked Jade what she would be up to later on.

'Sean and Tanya's baby is being christened tomorrow and I've been invited. They're really nice. I'll be looking after Ayesha when she starts to walk.'

I doubted that very much but let Jade have her moment of delusion.

We exchanged polite goodbyes.

'Who was she?' demanded Jade as we made for my car.

'She plays badminton with your granda. He let her borrow his car.'

'She's bloody lucky,' she laughed. 'He moans when Mum asks to borrow it.'

'Lucky?' I thought. 'We'll see how long her luck lasts.'

As soon as I switched on my engine, I knew there would be repercussions. It was inevitable.

# SIXTY

## *Ruby's Journal*

**Saturday night (24th).**

It's spider season. Great big hairy feckers. One hurdled across the carpet when Jade and I were sitting on the floor watching TV in our bare feet. Scream? I'm surprised next door didn't hear us. We trapped it under a glass. Kid you not, an even bigger tarantula appeared from nowhere. Circumnavigated the tumbler trying to get at the trapped one. Arachnid fight!! Sorry Mum, I should have put them both outside but Jade whacked the big one with a slipper, knocked the glass over and we had to flatten the other one too.

I slept in the spare room with Jade as Tanya's sister and her husband had my room (arrived late Thursday night). They were lovely. Very appreciative. Allowed the two of us to have our movie night before coming back through. Tanya's mum stayed next door.

**Sunday 25th August. The Christening.**

We had a really pleasant day apart from my thumping headache. Was worried that Colin might show up and spoil things. The minister at Alderburn church did them proud. Sean had erected a gazebo in his garden. Apart from a drizzle of rain when we walked back from the church, it was warmish and the sun shone occasionally. Tanya's mum prepared a feast. I handed in several tray bakes for a sweet treat.

Jade looked fabulous in a short, black flowery dress I had bought her. I pinned up her hair. She soaked up the compliments given to her by everyone. A nice young couple offered to drop her off in Edinburgh on their way home. Yippee. Meant I could have a flute of Prosecco. Unfortunately, only managed one.

**Thursday 29th August.**

I was clearly unwell. Felt it festering all day Monday. Started with what I thought was indigestion. A tightening in my chest. Kept apologising to my listeners for my intermittent coughing. Shouldn't have gone to Deacon House on Wednesday but you know me. Too stubborn for my own good. Stayed away from the kids but did the housework. Was thankful that Kenneth could collect Nola as I didn't want to share a car with her.

Don't know how I managed to drive home. I ached from head to toe. Went straight to bed with two hot water bottles. One minute I was shivering uncontrollably, the next I was kicking off the duvet soaked in my sweat. Thank goodness my Estonian guests had left on Tuesday. My usual hysteria kicked in – was this it? On my way out?

On the Friday morning, I could hear banging at my front door but couldn't work out if I was hallucinating or not. Wasn't. Every bloody window in the house was pummelled. Then the back door. Instinctively knew it would be the wee gobshite. He must have realised that my curtains were shut so he started hammering on my bedroom window from the front garden. I was too poorly to be frightened. If he'd managed to get in, there was nothing I could have done. I was too weak to care.

I heard him shouting at someone.

'Mind your own fucking business. It's my fucking house. Get back to your own fucking country.'

It must have been Tanya in his firing line. She might be a skinny wee thing but she ain't no pushover. The bawling seemed to move away from the house then it ceased. I could hear a door slamming, a car revving, followed by the screeching of tyres. My mobile rang. It was Tanya. I had to strain my voice to be heard.

She wanted to come round but I persuaded her not to. No way did I want Ayesha to catch whatever I had.

She was fuming. She warned Colin that if he didn't leave immediately, she would call the police. It put the frighteners on him as he marched straight to his car, cursing her the whole way.

'He called me a Nazi cunt,' she laughed. 'We'll see who the cunt is when Sean gets hold of him.'

'Aww Tanya, are you okay,' I gasped. Felt as if I had breathed in pins and needles and they had stuck in my lungs.

'Mum's still here. I'm not afraid of your weestel,' she scoffed.

Tanya suspected that Colin might have been at the house on the Monday while her sister was at home. She'd said a man was enquiring about me but wouldn't leave a message. She had forgotten to mention it.

'You sound terrible, Rachel. I hope you've called the doctor.'

I really didn't want them involved and she was right, I needed to phone the surgery. It must have been early as I had to leave a message on the answer machine. I left a croaky plea.

Eleanor Riddle was at the door within the hour. She'd collected a key from Tanya and let herself in.

She was very thorough. Felt all my glands. Neck, armpits and even my groin. Wasn't happy with my chest. She scrunched her nose at the gunk in my tissues. Prescribed antibiotics and she would hand them in personally. I was beyond caring but asked her to take the other spare key and pop one back to Tanya.

I texted Annabelle, not that she could help, she was in

Amsterdam with her work. I copied in Ben, Lisa, Rory, Auntie Vera and accidentally included Jasper, who offered to come over. 'Please don't,' I replied. I just wasn't able.

I apologised to Charles and asked him to cover my Friday evening shift. He dared me not to return until I was well enough.

Auntie Lisa rebuffed my request for no fuss and no visitors. She was at the door later in the evening with home-made soup, Granny's recipe, plus 6 tins of chicken soup and plenty of bread should I require it later. She is a good friend, Mum.

I vaguely remember Doctor Riddle holding me up while I swallowed some tablets. Must have slept until the following morning. Heard someone rustling outside my room. It was Auntie Lisa. She had warmed up some soup and spoon fed me. Wiping the dribbles from my chin.

'Doctor thinks you have pneumonia.' She shot me a warning look. 'So no trying to be a martyr. There's nothing to do here. Stay in that bed until you are well enough to get up.'

Tanya had obviously filled her in about Colin. I'd give her my account of it and the Glynis episode when I had regained my strength. Couldn't be arsed at that point.

'If that bastard comes back, dial 999. You've put up with enough. He better hope that my Brian doesn't see him first,' she spat.

She popped in later that day as did Eleanor who felt I didn't need hospitalised but she would monitor me carefully. Another locum called in on Sunday.

**Monday 2nd September.**

Although my chest and body ached, I felt marginally better on Monday morning. At least I could sit up unaided (only just) and I was starving. Managed to shuffle to the kitchen and struggled to open a tin of chicken soup. It was still in the pot when I heard Eleanor Riddle's voice. She admonished me for getting up. I sat at the table while she gave me the once over.

That's when it all kicked off. Bedlam.

Eleanor had gone to the loo and I was sipping my soup when Colin barged in. Eleanor hadn't locked the front door. He was like a bloody rhino in heat. I could hear him charge up the hall. He nearly took the door off the hinges. If anyone had been behind it, I'm sure the force would have knocked them out... or worse.

'BITCH!! FUCKING LYING BITCH!!'

He swiped my bowl from my hand, leaned over the table and grabbed the front of my dressing gown. The bowl hit the wall. There was creamy gloop everywhere.

'How dare you accuse me of all those things?'

He pushed me back into my chair then stormed round the table obviously to get a better grip. He wound his hand around my hair and dragged me to my feet. I honestly thought he was capable of murder. I'll never forget those eyes. Full of hate.

Eleanor Riddle's scream filled the room and bounced off the walls. She was loud.

'MR GORDON!!! Don't you dare!'

Somehow, she got between us, trying to prise us apart. All the time that he was throwing his punches, he was yelling that I was poison. Not happy that I had evicted him but had now ruined his relationship with Glynis with all my lies. Fucking Hell, he only turned on Eleanor. Blaming her for turning me against him. Total drivel. He rammed her against the cooker. She was having none of it. When he swung round to face me, she walloped him on the back with the soup pot. Right between the shoulder blades. In that split second, I knew he was making for my knife rack. Then down he went. He'd only slipped on the bloody soup. Karma.

Eleanor Riddle gently manhandled me out to the lobby. Not easy. It was pandemonium and we were terrified as Colin scrambled to his feet.

If you thought Colin had charged in like a raging bull, he was like a lamb compared to Jasper. You couldn't make it up. I had no idea he was coming. Poor Eleanor, it took all her negotiating skills to convince Jasper to leave Colin to the police. They didn't take long either.

Tanya had heard all the screaming and dialled 999.

I was sitting on a chair in my garden wrapped in a duvet. The whole street was out to see what was unfolding. The blue lights were flashing. Another panda car pulled up. Officers and Eleanor were inside with Colin. Jasper stood at the front door, his suit was covered in what looked like baby sick but must have been the soup. All I could think about was that I hoped he hadn't an airport pick-up.

Tanya's mother brought us a cup of tea. Baby Ayesha slept obliviously in her buggy on the other side of the fence. Tanya was regaling the story to all the neighbours when a young guy sheepishly called out,

'Is this 21 Carberry Crescent?'

'Aye,' chorused the gathering.

He wandered up the path with a huge bouquet of flowers. They were absolutely gorgeous. A rainbow of colours. Tanya's mother handed me the small envelope. I looked at Jasper and could feel my face flush.

'They're from Annabelle,' I lied.

# SIXTY-ONE

## *Ruby's Journal*

Jasper had actually finished for the morning. Instead of going home, he chose to call in on me. The police wanted to speak to all of us anyway so he hung around for several hours.

Colin remained in the house for some time. The snippy Emma was one of the police officers on duty. She deliberately tried to avoid me but when I did catch her eye, I gave her the look that meant *who do you believe now?*

Eleanor Riddle approached me. She pleaded with me to go to hospital to get checked over but I knew within myself that Colin hadn't landed any significant punches. Most were lost to the air or to Eleanor. However, my head ached where he had pulled out tufts of my hair.

'I don't want you here on your own, Rachel. You are not well enough.

Jasper immediately volunteered. Doctor Riddle peered into my face and raised her eyebrows to question his proposal. I bobbed my head indicating that it was okay.

'I need someone to be here over the next 24 hours, at all times, to keep an eye on her,' she warned him.

Jasper said he would need to go home for an hour to collect clean clothing but would stay overnight. Tanya was happy to sit with me while he was away or her mum would do it.

'If there is any change, even a slight deterioration, I want to know.' We all nodded as if we were still at school. Tanya draped one of her own throws around my legs.

Just then PC Emma appeared at your front door. 'Doctor Riddle? You're required. Now.'

More tea and biscuits arrived courtesy of next door. I owe them big time. Jasper disappeared to his car to change his jacket and make a few calls. I had a sneaky peak at the small square card that came with the flowers.

*Look after yourself my dear friend*
  *Regards*
  *Charles xx*

I smiled and tucked it into my dressing gown.

The tom-tom drums had reached Auntie Vera. Aww, Mum, what a state she was in. Once I reassured her I was fine, Chrissie, three doors down, took her home. That's when a shocked Jasper ran through the gate.

'Are you okay?' he shouted.

An ambulance had pulled up. Emma beckoned them into the house. 15 minutes later, there was Colin being wheeled by two paramedics out to the ambulance. I swear to God that he eyeballed me menacingly as he was being hurled past. Even when everything appears to be against him, he has to steal the limelight. The ambulance sat for at least half an hour before pulling away with Colin still inside. Patients must be stabilised and assessed on site apparently.

That's when I was summoned in by guess who? Yep. The helpful Emma (not).

'Stay where you are,' demanded my lovely doctor. 'My patient will need to be carried in.'

A flustered Emma and one of her colleagues wrapped the belt of my robe around my body and secured me to the chair then hoisted me, chair and all, into my bedroom.

A detective sergeant and Emma interviewed me while I lay in bed. By that time, I hadn't the energy to sit up. Eleanor Riddle refused to leave, at first, then insisted she would be in the hallway should she be needed.

I answered all their questions as honestly as I could. I told them about Glynis too (Jade would confirm) and the security camera footage. Emma reminded her sergeant about the other incidents. Vindictive cow!

'Oh, there's more than that, Emma, but I was too scared to report them.'

The older man asked me why? 'In case officers like your young Emma here, believed Colin rather than me.'

They exchanged looks. He didn't comment but her face was burning.

He's a barefaced liar,' I said. 'But a very, very plausible one.'

Couldn't force my eyes to stay open a moment longer. The interview was terminated. They had no alternative. I didn't surface until 9.00pm that evening to what sounded like a party coming from the living room.

I phoned Jasper. Hadn't the energy to shout.

A minute later, three bodies squeezed into my room. Jasper, Lisa and Patricia. Then I clocked Dad's voice.

'Who else is here?' I probed.

'Only Rob and Brian. Your Auntie Vera left half an hour ago,' Lisa informed me.

'Good craic?'

'Trust you,' she giggled. 'We've had a good catch up. Haven't we, Jasper?'

She's a wee minx is Auntie Lisa. I mouthed 'sorry' to Jasper but he gave me a wink and a grin. Once I had assured them that I felt better, Jasper and Patricia snuck out leaving me with Lisa. She wanted to know if I was comfortable with Jasper staying overnight. I confessed he had stayed before.

'And ye forgot to mention it to me?' She was perplexed.

I keep forgetting she is meant to be my best buddy.

'Good on you. Ye deserve it. He'll huv more energy than Colin,' she sniggered, 'and a bigger tadger, nae doobt.'

I keep forgetting what filthy minds older women have. Anyway, you know what Auntie Lisa is like? A rota was drawn up for everybody who had been roped in to babysit me for the next two days.

The living room entourage filed in one by one to say their goodbyes. I started to cry when Dad came in. To me, I will always be his wee princess and what girl doesn't want her dad? Don't know what Patricia makes of me but I keep reassuring her that I have no interest in Dad, in that way, whatsoever.

Poor Jasper, thrown in at the deep end.

'I'd like to get up please. Just for a little while.'

He scooped me up and carried me through to the living room. He asked why I was smiling. I was thinking about when Ben staggered with me to the toilet mirror in the hospital. That's when I realised I was you. It's funny what I find amusing now that I didn't then. God, it seems like a million years ago.

'Did Lisa leave a spreadsheet?'

Jasper rolled his eyes. 'No but the rota is pretty detailed. No room for manoeuvre.'

I apologised again for him having to face my lot, especially Dad. He shrugged. Didn't seem at all fazed. He made me a coffee (he was coffee'd out) and we tucked into Auntie Lisa's millionaire shortbread. I had three bits!! He dozed while I watched an old episode of New Tricks. He stirred during Taggart and I hinted it was time for bed. Jasper slept in the spare room. I didn't smell too good. Hadn't showered for several days.

Have to admit, the following morning, felt as if I had been in the ring with Tyson Fury. Throbbed all over. Lisa's rota was in full swing. Dad took over from Jasper. He was still in the house when Eleanor Riddle popped in. Only for five minutes. What must she think about me with all these different men?

Colin had been admitted to hospital but because I was still legally his next of kin, I was given all the ins and outs. Western General. Severe palpitations. Blood pressure shockingly high. Possibly stress related. He was undergoing more tests.

'Can you fake a panic attack?' I jested.

Regardless of his present condition, the police were taking the assault seriously and Eleanor Riddle was adamant that she would be seeking a restraining order to prevent him from approaching her and urged me to do likewise. She hadn't reached the end of the gate when I hit speed dial for our lawyers in Coates Crescent.

I could sense that Dad was on edge being alone with me (you) so I suggested I would shower before Patricia came. Felt unbelievably refreshed afterwards.

Patricia arrived laden with hot creamy coffees and a selection of pastries for the three of us. Gratefully devoured. Dad left for work.

The doorbell rang. For longer than was necessary. We assumed Dad had forgotten something. Nah. It was Claire. With a face like thunder.

'If you are here for a fight, young lady, then turn around and leave. Or trust me? I won't hesitate in calling the police.' Patricia left her under no illusion.

I shouted to let her in. I was stretched out on the sofa. Claire stood in the middle of the room. She had obviously rehearsed a speech.

You could tell she was nervous. Her right heel kept rubbing against the inside of her left foot.

She started off with, 'No that you'll be in the least bit bothered but ma da had a heart attack in the early hours o this mornin...and he's still alive, by the way.'

I did say that I was sorry to hear that. Not that I was but there's a time and place.

Then the rant began to roll.

Why was I not happy with everything I had ended up with? The house, the car and all the money. But no. I had to poison Glynis with my lies.

'Er... because they were all mine.' I pointed out. 'I paid for it all. And let's not forget that I did not seek out Glynis. It was Jade who approached her.'

Quoting the gospel of Claire Rennie, 'what her dad hadn't contributed in money value he had more than made up for it in other ways. I, of all people, should know that.'

'Like what?' I was intrigued.

'SUPPORT!' she spat. 'He did NOT have an easy life with you. It put a huge strain on his mental health and obviously his heart.'

'Well, he's been very unlucky,' I pointed out, 'cos his first wife went the same way as me. Funny that.'

'You leave my mother out of it and Jade. She's just a bairn.'

I informed Claire that Glynis told me that Colin had said that not only was I very aggressive but had gambling problems, so much so, he was having to sell his house to cover all my so-called stints in rehab. A downright lie. What part of that was I not supposed to defend?

'Okay, he exaggerated a wee bit. He never thought the two of you would meet.'

'She shops in Aldi's! How the hell did he assume that we would never meet?' She clearly hadn't grasped my side of it. 'Claire,' I sighed, switching to a more sympathetic tone. 'Your dad had already been seeing Glynis before the road accident so we have to conclude that he had been preparing to move on. You must have been aware of how controlling he had been. Of me. Your mum. And I think Glynis would have been next.' I was going to include her but I could feel that conscience hammer thumping a warning – don't go there.

'Well for your information, Glynis is there as we speak. In hospital, holding Dad's hand. Where you should be. You are *supposed* to be his wife!'

I looked at Patricia for some kind of confirmation that I was processing the conversation correctly.

Patricia sprang to my defence. 'Claire, your dad forced his way into this house and attacked a woman who was ill with pneumonia then attacked the local doctor for fuck's sake. That is not normal behaviour.'

'He was at his wits end. He thought he was going to lose everything AGAIN,' she screamed.

I was, according to Claire, a spiteful, vengeful bitch. I wouldn't be happy until I had broken him completely. If her dad died because of me, I would have her to deal with. She was actually foaming spittle as she said it.

Patricia piped up, 'Your dad hasn't given a fuck that his wife lost her only daughter in a tragic accident. Imagine if that had been you, and Rachel had not supported your dad.'

Oops, my words to Patricia that night in Suthiez had obviously impacted her.

Claire began to cry. Great big heaves. She sat down on one of the chairs.

'He's still my da,' she wailed. 'An I love 'um. He's always been there for me. He's a better person than you are making out.'

# SIXTY-TWO

Rachel closed the diary. Never mind Colin, she was having palpitations just taking it all in. She wondered how Colin was. Even now, she wished him no real harm. Claire was right in some respects; her dad did love her and Jade. He hadn't always conveyed it as well as he should have but he put his daughter's wellbeing and welfare before his wife's, more often than he ought to have.

Yet, it was true; he had never been physically violent to Rachel before the accident. That might not have lasted because there had been noticeable discord in his attitude towards her of late: late being nine months ago. She irritated him – big things, little things, everything. It was his vicious tongue. Stung like a viper.

Now armed with all this new information, she concluded that the accident prevented Colin from playing the woe-is-me card. He could no longer be assured of the sympathy vote if he'd wanted to have her put away. People would have expected him to give her more time to recover. Time, he didn't want. Colin had been desperate to get his smarmy paws on her estate to oil his new life with Glynis but he needed Rachel out of the way and with power of attorney to boot. Rachel had been ever so close to signing her home over to him. His whining had worn her down. Why on earth had she never discussed her predicament with Ruby and Rory?

She had been fully aware of Colin's control; especially with whom she associated and what she wore. She'd kept a small case of clothing in a cupboard in her classroom that he didn't know about. Every morning, she kicked off her sensible loafers and slipped on a court shoe with a two-inch heel. There was a smart blouse, soft woollen blue jumper, navy trousers and a beige jacket that she could change into for seminars or meetings. Not forgetting a make-up bag and perfume. As she was leaving for a parents evening, not long after he had moved in, Colin accused her of flirting with the dads. A ludicrous notion but one he wouldn't drop unless she dressed more appropriately; or in other words, dowdier.

There was no one to hear the audible sigh of relief that whooshed past her lips as she contemplated what might have been. She was indebted to her Ruby for standing fast.

Rory would be in Portobello on Friday. She couldn't wait. She longed to hold and be held by one of her children. She would prepare the master bedroom for him. A unicorn palace, in the spare room, hardly seemed fitting for a six foot, thirty-three-year-old businessman.

And she had had sex with Jasper! Rachel blushed from head to toe and up again. She had no idea if she was still seeing him. Annabelle only confirmed that he didn't have a key to her flat.

Rachel flicked through the bits and pieces at the back of the navy book for anything that might shed some light on her current relationship status. There were photos of the kids – Alfie in his blue Heriot's uniform. George Heriot had been born and raised in East Lothian. Gladsmuir; not far from Alderburn. Ruby and Ben probably hadn't even considered the connection.

One particular photograph brought tears to her eyes. The

one of her two grandchildren reading birthday cards aloud at their mother's grave. How on earth did Ruby cope with that?

She shuffled through tickets and receipts (to be digested later) and stopped at a photograph with her and another man; tall, grey hair, distinguished and eyes that enthused kindness. Sort of dishevelled in a bohemian, chic way. Had to be Charles. The scribble on the back confirmed her presumption.

*Rachel and Charles 16.11.19 Birthday.*

Rachel studied his features and smiled. His was a face that you wouldn't get fed up with.

The rest of the photos were mainly of the kids on holiday in Adeje, including a couple with Ben and Annabelle.

'That's interesting,' thought Rachel.

There was a snap of Ben and Annabelle playfully toasting the photographer (presumably Ruby) with their holiday cocktails. Annabelle's right hand was resting on the table while Ben's left hand was placed on top. They looked incredibly comfortable with each other. Rachel dismissed the silly notion immediately. Ben and Annabelle had been friends for years. It was Annabelle, after all, who had introduced him to Ruby.

Rachel tried to picture Glynis, her adversary, but the only image she could conjure was one of herself; drab and grey. She thanked her dead daughter for her transformation. Glynis must have kicked Colin into touch and he had reacted by storming into Carberry Crescent. Imagine if he had managed to reach the knife rack. Surely to God, he wouldn't have used one. Rachel shuddered and automatically rubbed her arms to warm them up. And to think Glynis may have taken him back. Had she no common sense?

Rachel's tummy was rumbling. She'd had nothing since

7.30am. She fancied some soup – anything but cream of chicken – then she would nip up to the butcher's to buy a nice steak for her and Rory tomorrow.

# SIXTY-THREE

*Ruby's Journal*

**Thursday 5th September**

I was savouring the peace and quiet. I had persuaded Auntie Lisa that I could cope perfectly well on my own. The antibiotics had well and truly kicked in as I was feeling so much better. Annabelle had seconded that as she called me a nippy sweetie the day before. She'd flown in from Amsterdam and driven straight to Alderburn on Tuesday afternoon. Needed to see me for herself. Think Lisa was pissed off when my bestie cancelled my 'carers' for the rest of the night and the Wednesday. Annabelle had cleared her diary to concentrate on me. Only I understood her neuroticism.

Jasper seemed relieved when Annabelle offered to stay on Tuesday night. He had been scheduled to pick up a V.I.P from Inverness on Wednesday morning – early doors. Meant he could travel up the night before.

Anyway, was busy listening to JJ and Jemma (can't help myself) when I heard a knock at the door.

'GRANNY,' beamed my wee angel, holding up a home-made card.

'Thought you might need cheering up.' Ben kissed my cheek.

Floodgates opened... but only for a little while. I'm getting better at regaining composure. Sometimes.

The Sutherlands had caught the ferry on Tuesday morning.

They had stayed on an extra few days when I texted to say that I might have pneumonia. Libby's mum chipped in too. I am truly grateful to all of them.

Ben looked really good considering he had worked flat out in August. It had been their busiest Festival yet. Takings were up twenty percent on last year. So, he had a little proposition for me.

'We're going on holiday, Granny, to Auntie Carrie's villa and you're coming too,' blurted my excited daughter.

Ben clasped his hand over her mouth and mocked her for stealing his lines. It was true. I had been invited to join them in the October break. Ben's treat for everything I've been through and for everything I do for them.

'Auntie Annabelle's coming too.'

My stomach plummeted. Not that I didn't want her to be there but it was a timely reminder that I would never be Ruby Martin. Wife of Ben Sutherland. We never shared our precious family time with anyone. Holidays were sacrosanct. Only for the four of us. Not now though.

'Annabelle's become very fond of you since Ruby... you know... and I thought it would be nice if the five of us...'

'Absolutely. Great idea. Thank you.' I plastered my face with false enthusiastic pleasure.

Ben looked relieved. We chatted nonchalantly over coffee. Nola played with Jade's soft toys. What's left of them.

The conversation drifted to Colin. Annabelle had brought him up to speed. He shook his head. Ashamed that he'd actually liked the shite. Offered me the spare room again. As previous, had to decline.

We agreed, I would try out next Wednesday but only if I felt strong enough.

Hugged my wee honey bun. Nursery beckoned. Restrained myself from snogging the face off my husband. Pecked his cheek instead. Wept when they left. Pulled myself together then wept for another half hour!!

The rest of my time, I spent researching ideas for Ray of Hope and my station. I want to drop in wee snippets of advice during every radio show about being good to ourselves. Plus, I jotted down ideas for competitions, games etc that haven't been used before. It was exciting!!

I've also enrolled to help at a local food bank. Get me. Mrs Humanitarian.

I log into Ray of Hope most days to read or comment on what my flock are saying. (Is that patronising cos that's what they mean to me?) There is a lot of positivity, although, I suppose to outsiders, it must read like doom and gloom. It's uplifting and reassuring to discover that someone had the courage to break free. Our Zena has finally fled her husband. Now pioneering Women's Refuge Centres. She has moved to a new city with her children, starting a new job but sadly the rest of the family have disowned her. It's the Ray of Hope family who now have to continue to support her.

Laura, the accountant, is pregnant. Fingers crossed for a safe pregnancy.

And our Betty, still madly in love with her money draining man.

Elaine Penman, the podcaster, contacted Charles requesting both of us to speak on her show. Charles declined but asked if I would do it instead. Reluctantly, I gave her a phone. She was actually really nice. Fortunately, I don't have to reveal my face to her listeners. She set up her podcast after suffering years of hidden abuse from her partner (Susan). She didn't hold back and it was an awful story to tell. Imagine her surprise when I confessed that I was in a similar relationship with Colin AND the Ray of Hope blogger was me. She was flabbergasted and fully supportive that my true identity not be made public. Guess what? I'm appearing as Reya. Next week. Yikes.

Tanya has been a regular visitor. Think I'm breathing space from her mother who seems to want to stick around rather than going back to Estonia. Apparently, her sister (not the married one) would like to come here to study.

It got me thinking. Maybe I could rent out the house to them and find somewhere new for me. A fresh start. Won't say until I'm sure.

Had dinner with Charles on Sunday evening (8th). He sent a taxi for me. Oooooh.

He can cook. Not as well as Ben, obviously, but he specialises in Asian food. We had little tapas-styled dishes. It was lovely to sit down at a table and not feel rushed. At Annabelle's, 9 times out of 10, we sit with a plate on our knees or bums on the floor around her coffee table, scooping it in.

I was warned not to dress up. Charles prefers casual.

He had on tight faded denims with a cream, collarless shirt hanging over them. I chose white jeans and a soft denim shirt. My jeans were loose. I'd lost a lot more weight because of my nasty bout of flu or whatever it was. My appetite had not fully returned so I picked at the food.

The only time we saw Isobel was when she poured our wine. We had two each and a liqueur with our coffees. She brought the bottles in, poured the drinks then took the bottles away with her. Odd!! But I never asked.

Shit. Charles clocked my interest. I was mortified that he felt obliged to explain.

'Please don't,' I protested. 'None of my bloody business.'

He just laughed.

Turns out that he was addicted to drugs for years. Isobel rescued him and nursed him for as long as it took and still looks out for him today. She is the mother he never had.

Although, he never abused alcohol, the temptation was always there.

'Addicts are always addicted to something' he said. 'They replace one thing with another. Zealots!' And laughed. 'For some it's religion. Others it's a cause. For me it was the station and agoraphobia.'

Not sure about him attributing his fear of the outdoors to that but could see why broadcasting could be addictive. It was the same for me.

Isobel controls his consumption of alcohol by being the provider. He has no direct access to it and it doesn't bother him one little bit.

'It's moments like this,' he explained, 'when I could drink more that I ought.'

'Sharing a meal?'

'Being in the company of a beautiful woman,' he said.

Oh, my days. My face burned. I was dead chuffed for you, Mum, being described as beautiful because you are but I haven't been given many sincere compliments lately.

I unburdened myself. Probably the alcohol (and lack of food) but Charles is a real gentleman and so easy to talk to. Obviously, I didn't tell him about the switch – too much even for him but I did explain how difficult it was not knowing who I am and that I was frightened that one day I might wake up and everything had changed again.

He said that for fifteen years drugs had blighted his memory.

Huge chunks of his life were missing too but he didn't want to relive them because it wasn't a life he wanted to remember.

'I was a most unsavoury character,' he acknowledged. 'Or as they would say in Cockenzie, a twisted bastard.'

I doubted that but he was adamant.

'If it hadn't been for Isobel then I wouldn't be here today.'

'I thought you had rescued her,' I said.

'I had underhanded reasoning. I was a nasty bugger. I knew she would be the only one who could keep me on the straight and narrow. I needed her more than she needed me. Same applies today and I am so grateful she remains with me.'

After dinner in the lounge downstairs, he invited me upstairs to his drawing room for coffee and liqueurs. A modern, chic room with fabulous views overlooking the Forth. We sat on midnight blue comfy sofas. The cream carpet was almost white. A large glass table balanced on an exquisite piece of driftwood. I liked his taste.

'I'm surprised you have such big windows given your agoraphobia.' It sounded like I was challenging him but I was just curious.

He never takes offence. Tiny steps, he said. He used to close his vertical slatted blinds all the time but gradually opened them a little wider when he felt braver. The first time he opened them fully was at night. He would stand for hours and stare out to sea. Daytime is slightly different. Less bravado. He keeps his distance from the window but at least the light floods in. However, there are still some days when the blinds remain closed. That's when he told me about his modern gaff on Portobello Promenade with huge patio windows. He rents it out.

'Oh, I'm hoping to rent out my house,' I blurted.

'Why?' he looked perturbed.

I regurgitated the Colin/doctor saga. He was disgusted. You know, it spouts from my mouth as if it were a common everyday occurrence for the majority of us. The Ruby of old would have been distraught at the thought of her mother enduring all of this. I'm so sorry, Mum. Charles agreed that a change of address would be advantageous.

Hell, he only went and offered me the apartment on the prom. The current occupant was vacating at the end of September and it was mine if I wanted it. For however long I wanted it and he wasn't joking.

'How much do you charge?' I asked.

'What can you afford?'

Jeepers, I hadn't a clue. I hadn't thought what I would charge for your house plus couldn't be sure Tanya's relations would be remotely interested. He suggested I think about it.

As I sipped my Amaretto, he sat next to me on the very long, four-seater sofa.

'Too close?' he asked.

I shook my head and rested the side of my face on his shoulder. We listened to Bob Dylan who was playing quietly in the background. Tears leaked into his shirt but he said nothing. Somehow, we ended up spooning. Him with his back to the sofa, me facing the darkness as the light outside faded.

Soft, white cushions supported our sleepy heads.

# SIXTY-FOUR

*Ruby's Journal*

**Monday 9th September**

Just returned from a long walk. No jogging today. Lack lustre energy. I've been writing all morning and needed a break. Achy fingers. Stopped off at my 'local' cafe on Ferry Road. Treated myself to a latte as it's been Americanos since my serious attempt at eating more healthily. Lemon chicken is defrosting on Annabelle's worktop.

Right, back to Harbour Radio and Charles!!!!!

*

Gentle hands shook my shoulders. Apart from a dim table lamp somewhere, the room was dark. Charles's attentive face leaned in.

'Taxi's here.' He spoke very quietly. Isobel smiled behind him.

I sat up, apologising and asking for the time.

'It's 11.30. You've had a little sleep but I think you would rest better in your own bed.' There was a hint of a tease there.

In that split second, I prayed I was fully clothed. Quick check under the throw. Everything intact. I apologised for nodding off and stood up. I needed the bathroom. Red, puffy eyes stared back in the mirror. Really? I have to stop making an exhibition of myself.

Isobel had her jacket on.

'No please, I can manage on my own. It's kind but no.'

Well, that fell on deaf ears. Charles insisted as did Isobel. He kissed my cheek and Isobel accompanied me home. A quick recce of the house.

'He's still in hospital as far as I know.' My attempt to reassure her.

She patted my hand – the same one she had held in the taxi as we sat in the back in complete silence. Satisfied, she left. No wonder Charles is in awe of her.

As I lay in bed last night and ran through the evening in my head, I actually thought I had dreamt it. It felt as if I was drifting gently on an airbed, on a calm sea, and the sun was warming my skin. Everything had gone so smoothly. The meal, the drinks, the music and coffee. Me melting into Charles on the sofa. Sleep quickly engulfed me again.

First thing this morning, I phoned Annabelle and invited myself over for the day and dinner (previously prepared and frozen).

'Ruby Martin, how many men are you juggling?' she chuckled.

DON'T. Mortified doesn't even justify my conduct or how I feel.


**Saturday 14th September.**

Tanya and Sean are delighted that I've agreed to rent out the house to Rina (her mum) and sister (and her boyfriend!). It's all happened so quickly. I've only asked for £425 per month. That's a snip by the way. I could get a lot more considering the proximity to the enormous science research centre up the road. I'm just grateful that the house will be looked after properly. We have tentatively settled on a six-month let that could possibly be extended to a year. Tanya's dad seems to have a good job in Tallinn and the sister's boyfriend will be contributing too. Tanya wants to return to work and will pay her mum for caring for Ayesha. It's a win win.

I had to fight with Charles to let me pay £800 per month for his place. He would have been happy with what I'm getting for Carberry Crescent. No way. I'm pretty sure he could get £1500 for it. Honestly, it is fabulous. Annabelle chummed me to inspect it yesterday. It's right on the sea front. Two huge balcony windows overlooking the promenade and the Forth. Beautifully furnished. We have very similar tastes. Apart from some bits and pieces and redecoration, I can move in on the first.

My salary (I mean yours, Mum) will be reduced to half pay soon but with what I'm earning from Ben, I should just about make it. Plus, I have £12,000 in an account that Ben doesn't know about and I'm embarrassed to admit this but I've never declared it to the tax man. I'd completely forgotten that I had it and when I did find the book a few years back, I decided I would use the money to treat Ben and me to a late honeymoon without the kids. Never happened and won't now. So, I'll dip into it and hope I don't get caught. I'm hoping that compensation for the accident will eventually come through. If not, I'll seek early retirement on medical grounds and find employment elsewhere.

I did my radio programme on Tuesday evening. Thought meeting Charles and Isobel would be awkward but no. Both were as natural as could be. Charles admitted he had had a really pleasant evening and would I like to do it again. I nodded. Probably too enthusiastically.

We broached renting the apartment. He was delighted although we did disagree on the price. Chose to compromise. If

Tanya's family hadn't wanted mine, I would have handed it over to an agency to find a tenant for me.

For the first time in a long time, I have things (opportunities) to look forward to. Even the food bank is uplifting. I can't give the time it deserves but I'll do what I can.

Annabelle is on a mission to lose weight for our holiday. I'll be sharing a room with her. I have very mixed emotions but don't want to be separated from the kids for one day longer than necessary. I missed them so much in July and August, can't bear to be apart for another week and as much as I love Bella-Anne, I'd feel resentful that she was spending a week with my kids and my husband without me.

Colin is out of imminent danger. Wouldn't wish him dead (wouldn't wish anyone dead, not now) but incapacitated with occasional long spasms of pain would suffice.

He has been charged with assaulting our lovely doctor. He totally denied attacking me, claiming self-defence once again. You have to laugh. Dr Riddle witnessed it all. Unfortunately, all statements, given at the time, claimed that she was out of the room when he initially barged in. In theory, I could have reacted first despite suffering from suspected pneumonia. We will have to wait until the trial. Meanwhile, he was allowed home as he posed no immediate threat to either of us. At least he has been warned not to approach or contact us. Not exactly an injunction (for me) but a serious caution. A little consolation.

Saw the kids on Wednesday. Bliss. Can't deny that I felt tired but I just pottered about. Slept over on Thursday. Ben had a night out. I think he is seeing someone. It's too soon but he was shifty on Friday morning and kept dodging the kid's questions. PLEASE, don't let him be dating. Which is rich coming from me but the circumstances are different. Aren't they?

During the day on Thursday, I travelled out to the Gyle to do the podcast with Elaine. I had NEVER considered teaming up with a female before. What a laugh. The overall theme revolves around domestic violence or coercive control yet between us we managed to inject some humour into the programme. This week it was about airing your problems (tactfully) within your working environment and how to tell your boss without putting your job at risk. Elaine had done her research. Boss's responses ranged from downright diabolical to hilariously absurd. If you didn't laugh, you would cry. It's hard to do her show without tears but she is also there to raise hopes and inspire. She always winds up her podcast with an inspirational story. I love it. Her listeners do too. Many of whom have contributed to the discussions. They range from the homeless to well-known celebrities. The list of who's who is endless. A couple of years ago, I had always been wary of podcasts. Saw them as amateur rivals to our radio work. Not now. It's a huge platform with huge potential. Love it.

Met up with Jasper on Friday afternoon for a quick coffee. He has been a really good friend to me and an ally but I don't want a physical relationship with him. Nothing to do with Charles. Should have been open and direct about what I want. Wasn't. Bottled it. Played on the pneumonia. Feigned tiredness. Said nowt!! We parted on good terms on the premise that we would meet up soon.

Oh. Nearly forgot. He asked me about my insurance regarding the accident and when I thought it would be awarded. When I asked why? He said he knew someone who had been pushing for settlement for years and he didn't want me to get lost in the system. Fair enough.

You'll never guess who turned up at my door on Friday

evening. I had finished my tea and was tidying up before leaving for my show when there was a knock at the door.

Bloody Hell, only Glynis standing sheepishly on the step.

She asked to come in. I asked if she was on her own. Was, so let her in. While she stood in my hall, I positioned her in front of the camera and instructed her to wave. I texted Tanya explaining that Glynis was in my house and would she come round in 15 mins.

I carried two chairs from my kitchen and we sat in the hall. Why? So that we would be in full view of recordings at all times. I had no desire to be accused of something I hadn't done. She thought it was extreme. I had every reason to be paranoid. She accepted a coffee.

'You have 15 minutes,' and tapped my watch to indicate the clock was ticking.

Can I say, she'd made no real effort to impress me with her clothing. Dull grey trousers and a purple crew neck jumper. Very mannish and not a dapper man like Dad. I know, I'm a bitch. But if I had been confronting my rival, I would have put more thought into what I was wearing. At Harbour, we dress for comfort yet I looked as if I was going out for the night. Cropped jeans and a black shirt tucked in. Okay maybe just to the pub but I had done my face too.

'I'm not here for a brawl,' she said. 'Not my style.'

Bless her. Style isn't part of her DNA.

'Nor mine,' I added. She was nervous and I didn't want to make her worse.

She confirmed that she had allowed Colin to return to her home, temporarily, as he had nowhere else to go.

I could have suggested his daughter's but kept my mouth shut.

She reiterated what she had told me in Aldi car park. That

Colin had said I gambled away all his money and my aggression frightened him. I couldn't hold in my chuckling.

She claimed that Colin was only trying to pacify me a fortnight ago and unfortunately the doctor got in the way when he was trying to calm me down.

I asked her if she truly believed that explanation. She bit her lip.

I started by saying that I didn't want to instigate her and Colin splitting up. Quite the opposite. As long as he was happy with her, he was leaving me alone.

As far as my gambling was concerned, there would have to be proof. There was none. EVERYTHING was paid from my teacher's salary; bills, food, heating and even his family's mobile phones. It was all in black and white if she wanted to see it. At the end of each month, there was very little left for me and not enough to fritter on gaming sites. I had never seen Colin's bank statements or how much money he earned from wherever. He had access to everything that was mine. My generosity was not reciprocated.

She was appalled that I rarely had enough money in my purse to buy a coffee. When I came home from hospital, he had hidden my phone, my bank cards and had withheld passwords and codes. I had amnesia and felt totally isolated. Empathy from him or Claire was nonexistent. Sympathy for me having lost my precious daughter? Nothing.

'What would you have done?' was my question to her.

The front door opened. It was Sean asking if it was okay if Rina stayed instead of him and Tanya.

'Bairn's playing up,' he laughed.

I motioned Rina to sit in the living room. She had an Ipad for company.

I apologised to Glynis. I had somewhere to go.

I urged her NOT to discuss our conversation with Colin. He would only deny everything and retaliate and I couldn't take anymore abuse. Anyway, I said, I'm moving away. For my personal safety. I'm not sleeping at night. Too frightened. Not entirely true but tried to convey, I'd had enough.

She appeared flustered. I felt obliged to say what I did.

'If you are truly happy with Colin then who am I to say? BUT if I were you, I would walk away while you can. That's the best advice you will ever be given. He will worm his way into your life and you will trust him unconditionally. You will be under his control and he will bleed you dry. Financially, emotionally and physically.'

# SIXTY-FIVE

*Ruby's Journal*

**Wednesday 2nd October**

I'M IN! BELVEDERE BEACH APARTMENTS 1F2 PORTY!!!!!!

Can't believe I'm here. Diary has a new home too. Dad organised a small van (someone he knew) to move my belongings from Alderburn yesterday. I've left most of my house intact, just brought all my personal stuff and other bits and bobs. Mounts up.

Oh, my days. So much to do. It looked perfect when I first saw it but as I cast around, there are things I need to change.

Fortunately, Charles has had it thoroughly deep cleaned for me. I ordered a new king-size mattress and bedding. (Arrived as I was unpacking.) Not prepared to sleep on something all sorts of bodily fluids may have possibly soaked in to. Yuck.

I'd been soooooo busy preparing for my move. Drawing up contracts. (Felt rotten about that but must watch my back.) Contacting the utility providers. Notifying anyone who needs notifying. (Remaining with my GP.) Packing. Buying. Cleaning. And still juggling all my jobs. It's been manic and magical at the same time.

Rina is like a pig in shit. She thinks the Carberry house is 'most beautiful'. Tanya's sister, Sofia, flew over last week. She is completing her studies remotely but is hoping to get work while she is here. Not sure how that fits in with the Brexit rules. Didn't delve. Her boyfriend should be here by Christmas.

Elaine Penman has asked me to join her Podcast once a week. She does two weekly broadcasts but enjoyed our banter so much (as did her regulars) that's she's offered me a permanent gig. Can't get paid but other rewards in the offing.

Best bit. The kids are staying with me this weekend. I'm collecting them from school. Ben is covering for Karl who has his brother's wedding. Annabelle's staying here to babysit on Friday while I do my show. Haven't discussed that part with Ben but will figure something out. Can't wait to have them all to myself.

Things progressing nicely with Charles. When I say nicely, I mean friendly. We've had lunch and supper since my 'sleepover'. Unless he is on air directly after me, we will have a coffee and a chat upstairs although we don't flaunt it in front of the others.

**11.00pm.** Knackered. Been at it all day. Got kids tomorrow so have to be away early. Night night.

**Friday, Midnight.** Kids are zonked. Annabelle not long gone. I was tempted to have a small wine but talked myself out it. They were in bed before I left, having cuddles with Auntie Annabelle. Told them I had to nip to Alderburn to sort something for Rina. Not comfortable with lying. Won't do it again but can't tell Ben about my show. Kids were sound asleep before my programme started.

**Saturday 10.00pm.** Two wee munchkins out for the count. Had a fab day. Long welly walks along the front. A short stint in the amusement arcade. This won't be happening every time. Then two hours in the soft play centre. We met with Libby and her two for a play date. That was so good for me too. I miss my old pals. Happy, happy twosome. Very, very happy Mummy who has to pretend to be Granny. I'm off to bed.

**Monday 7th Oct 10.00 am.** I had two missed calls from Shirley Aitken (our lawyer). Charles was on after me so gave him a wave before leaving.

Rhys Jones's insurers want me to meet with one of their own doctors (psychiatrist probably) to discuss my amnesia. A date had been pencilled in for the 17th October. No can do. In Tenerife. Shirley called back. Could I make Friday 25th? Glasgow. 10.30am. Could hardly say no. I was allowed to bring a friend. She would email all the details.

Who should I take? Annabelle was the sensible choice. I called James Warnock instead. If you don't ask you don't get and he is in Glasgow after all. Bloody hell, he only agreed. I read out the email from Shirley. He had a little chuckle.

'Desmond Reardon. This will be amusing.'

I phoned Eleanor Riddle. Had to tell her about my impulsive request.

'We were discussing you only last weekend,' she informed me. She too had a wee giggle to herself.

She and her partner (she never gives a name) had had dinner with her godfather and she had told him about her altercation with the shitebag Colin. (Not her description but I'm sure it's what she would use given the chance). He asked about me. Said my case had had him bamboozled so no doubt he would have been delighted to hear from me. Made me feel much better.

Jasper has been texting. As I've said before, when my interest decreases, his ramps up. It's not that I don't like him but there's something that I can't put my finger on. He is a handsome guy choosing to hang around with me. Sorry Mum. No disrespect but he could be dating women half your age. Okay, I have lost a fair bit of weight. Over three stones and counting and looking good for fifty-seven. Very little of your old clothes fit. Even the ones hidden at the back of your wardrobe. My energy levels after the pneumonia, if it was that, are returning. Slowly. Beauty is only skin deep, I hear you say.

That said, I do enjoy his company. Not forgetting the sex. Pretty satisfying. Not that I can remember the first encounter but the second one was vivid enough. I'm blushing. You and your bloody hormones!!!!

**Sunday 13th October.**

Annabelle and I had dinner today with Ben and the kids at Deacon House. Roast beef and Yorkshire puddings and luscious lashings of gravy. Prepared by me and deliciously scoffed by all.

Ben had asked us to help pack away my clothes and belongings. Shit show. Tears and belly laughs in equal measure. There were five piles. Clothes bank, charity shops, one for me, one for Bella and the last for selling. Monies to go to Maggie's Centre. Several times Ben couldn't choose a pile. Too painful. Too many memories. Like the T shirt I often wore in bed. Or the dress I wore on the night he proposed. He is so sentimental. That's why I love him. A sixth pile evolved.

Alfie and Nola had to have an input. Both tried on lots of my stuff. So funny.

At one point Ben mouthed aside, 'Do you think he could be gay?' Referring to Alfie strutting around in one of my cocktail dresses.

'So, what if he is?' I gruffed back. 'Ruby would love him whatever.' My bottom lip quivered but I recovered quickly.

'What's not to love?' he agreed affectionately as we giggled at their antics.

Unlike the dithering pair, I selected piles quickly and efficiently. Ben kept repeating himself.

'Thank goodness you're here. Sure, you're so like my Ruby.'

It's times like these that I can't cope. Close intimate contact with Ben. When I'm doing housework, I kind of mooch around in a businesslike manner but rummaging through my personal belongings and reminiscing about good times is hard, especially when he picked something up that I knew meant a lot to us and only us.

Pieces of my jewellery were put aside for Nola and Alfie. I chose my watch and a bracelet that would be gifted back to the kids anyway. I gave Annabelle my gold necklace that I bought from money you and Dad had given me for my thirtieth. She sobbed for a minute until I gave her a sharp nudge. Couldn't decide what to do with the rest so boxed them with other items that were in limbo.

Bless him, Ben had put all my 'toys' into a box. Annabelle told me later.

'You should have kept them for me,' I teased.

'Oh yeah, like I'll take those vibrators for your mother-in-law.' We did hee-haw.

We cleared what we could and filled my car with black bags for various destinations.

I began stripping our bed. Ben's bed. Hadn't been changed for a while. Ben disappeared with Alfie and Nola.

I froze.

A pair of skimpy knickers shook free from the bottom sheet. I looked at Annabelle. She feigned stunned. She knew something. She fucking knew.

'What? Who?' I held them gingerly by my nails.

She shook her head. Too vigorously. Hiding something.

'Nnnn no idea,' she stammered.

Didn't buy it. I've known her for too long.

'ANNABELLE?'

She hid her face in her hands. 'Don't ask. I can't say'

'Can't or won't?' I prodded.

Fucking hate her. Not Annabelle. Hannah fucking Dunlop. Judas. Didn't like her before, hate her more now.

I actually staggered when Annabelle spoke her name.

She pleaded with me not to say anything. Ben would go ballistic if I (you) knew. It was a mad moment. Poor judgement. Too much alcohol. Etcetera. Etcetera.

'When?' I demanded. 'When?' Women always ask that question, don't they?

'The weekend you had the kids,' she blurted.

WHAM!! A sucker punch directly to the guts. Then a second explosion was detonated in my heart. I'll fucking kill her was my first reaction quickly replaced by hyperventilating. I knelt by the bed and buried my face in the duvet. Ben's smell choked me.

'Please don't,' pleaded my distraught pal. 'It was nothing. It won't happen again.'

'You sure?'

She wasn't. She was only trying to placate me.

We both understood that I would have to pull myself together. I wasn't in a position to challenge my husband. It was none of his mother-in-law's business. I couldn't jeopardise our new friendship and trust (or the pending holiday). I had to wait until I was alone with Annabelle to extract all the gory details.

When Ben saw my tearstained face, he assumed the clearing had become too much for me. He hugged me tightly and urged the kids to give Granny a cuddle. I wanted to knee him in the nuts.

I was giving Annabelle a lift home. We made it as far as the Meadows when I hit the brakes.

'Spill.' I was in no mood for half-truths.

'If you use this information to compromise my friendship with Ben then on your head be it. Neither of us will be allowed in the house and where will you be then?' she spat.

Ben and Hannah had gone out for an Indian on Thursday last week. Not a date as such but a catch up. Hannah had enthused to Annabelle about how well they had got on and that Ben had enjoyed being with someone who didn't object to him bringing Ruby in to the conversation all the time. He arranged a taxi home for her. On Saturday night, Hannah had been in town with friends and they'd finished their night in Cameron's (close to Suthiez). How convenient! So as any concerned pal would, she popped in to say goodnight to Ben. Bet she fucking did. One thing led to another and she ended up sharing a taxi with Ben to Deacon House. It was only supposed to be for one drink. You can guess the rest.

'She orchestrated that,' I sneered.

Annabelle was convinced otherwise.

I let rip. Moaned and groaned and swore like a trooper.

Annabelle's hand shot up to halt my disgusting profanities (and they were).

'Pot calling kettle black, Ruby,' she yelled.

That hurt. My situation was completely different. He was supposed to be mourning me.

'He does. Every fucking day but life has to go on Roo.'

That hit much harder.

'Ben will never love anyone as much as he loved you.' She was much more sympathetic now. 'But he deserves happiness, honey, and so do you.'

I had tested the waters. It was only fair that Ben could too. Deep down, I understood that. I just don't want him to be with Hannah Dunlop. Anyone but her. Anyone but me I meant.

'If it's any consolation, he won't be seeing her again,' she said.

'How do you know?'

Annabelle twisted her mouth. Ah huh. Ben had obviously confided in our mutual pal. She wouldn't divulge any details only that he wasn't complimentary. Good.

'I honestly don't know if I can continue like this.' Then I broke down.

Annabelle drove my car here to Portobello. We parked round the back of my apartment and braced ourselves for a biting walk along the prom. It was a bitterly cold wind. But hey, it cleared my head.

I was being selfish. I had reinvented myself but I wanted Ben to be miserable without me. Not fair on the kids either. They deserved to see Daddy flourishing. I had deliberately chosen to stay and be Granny. I knew it wouldn't be easy but had persuaded myself all those weeks ago that it was a price I was prepared to pay. I stumped up daily.

I scoured the stormy, barrel-grey skies hovering over the black menacing waves. Summed up my mood succinctly. I took three long deep breaths and expelled my anger with each outward blow. (One of my recent wellbeing anecdotes). Needed another three.

It was hard granting Ben his freedom.

# SIXTY-SIX

*Ruby's Journal*

**Tuesday 15th October 5.00am**

Up early. Driving to airport. Picking up Bella-Anne en route. Meeting Ben and the kids there. I packed Alfie and Nola's cases last week. Nothing changes! Fingers crossed. Thoughts guarded. Mouth zipped. Fuck!!! I am so nervous.

**Tuesday 22nd October 11.30pm.**

Dumped my bags into the hall and headed to the shower. Feel as if we have been on the go all day.

The holiday was okay. Sunshine and sea and good food. Kids had a ball and that's all I'm bothered about. Not wholly true but to see the kids laughing and giggling every single moment of every single day was an utter joy. To be fair, we bumped along reasonably well. There were no cross words but pretty sure I had little skin on my lips by the end. Nibbled to bits. Avoiding confrontations. Would I do it again? At the moment, absolutely not. Next week? Probably yes.

Carrie's villa was beautiful as you would expect given her background in soft furnishings. It had had an upgrade since the last time we were there. She's obviously mirrored the opulence of the hotels in Dubai and Sharm-El-Sheikh. Absolutely breathtaking but practical too. Annabelle loved it. We swam every day. Morning, noon and night; in the sea and in the pool. Actually, we did very little apart from eat, swim and sleep. Occasionally, we ventured into Playa de Las Americas (only ten-minute walk away) for long strolls and a late lunch. Ben cooked simple meals but mainly we had barbeques. Very leisurely. But I felt old. Ben constantly called out 'be careful with Granny.'

Three days in, it hit me like an avalanche. Would I look after the kids to allow Ben and Annabelle to hit the nightlife? What could I say? Annabelle was apologetic but she still went. Ben knew someone who owned a bespoke restaurant in Adeje. He was in semi-retirement but opened his house (veranda) three times per week to guests who could afford (willing to pay) his exuberant prices. In a former career, he had been awarded two Michelin Stars.

'SSSSHHHH.'

They sneaked in, all giggly and childish, at four in the morning, pissed as farts. NOT amusing. I was cuddling Nola who had had a bad dream.

I could barely look at them the next morning (afternoon), let alone speak. Ben was oblivious to my contrite retorts. He had a new recipe for Suthiez – Iberian pig cheeks in a sherry jus. He talked about nothing else. We'd had them before but NOT like this. Annabelle was hung-over. Thank goodness the water park outing was the following day as neither of them could have coped.

I managed to nab her around 4.00pm.

'Don't give me a hard time, Roo. All he did was talk about you. We had a very pleasant evening but stayed on with Jorge and his wife after everyone else had gone. Too many cocktails and shots. Sorry.'

She lay back down on the sun lounger in the shade of the huge palm tree. She looked fab in her crimson red bikini and golden tan. The sun just has to glimpse at her and her olive skin glides into a darker shade. Was I jealous? Absolutely. Not of her but her youth and of what she had yet to experience. I'm an ungrateful bitch.

The water park was hilarious but some of the rides? OMG! We girls were bricking it. On one flume ride we lay back in a round dinghy and plummeted into a black dark, vertical canyon. Honestly, I had to walk behind Annabelle to check her costume. She was adamant that she had had a wee follow-through.

Our last evening was shit for me. Once again, the two 'young' ones walked down to a beach bar for a night cap. Actually, on reflection, I'd rather take the kids on holiday on my own.

**Thursday 24th.**

I'm over my huff. Just. Did a four-hour stint at Harbour Radio yesterday morning from eleven til three. Got my fix!! It's like I immerse myself in my own wee life-suspending bubble and for a few magical hours I am Reya. Witty, young and happy.

Not staying over at Deacon House tonight as Ben not going out after work. Relieved.

Meeting with Professor Warnock tomorrow!!!!!!

**Friday 25th October 1.30am.**

Charles and I blethered for ages after my show. Apparently, our profile has gone through the roof since I arrived. Don't know how! Charles says I've spurred young Robbo to up his game and he has had enquiries from other stations. Aww, I am so proud of him. We agreed he is not quite ready to move on. I'm going to have a long chat with him and his parents, hopefully prepare him for what might be in store. Unfortunately, I have no clout with Adrian or JJ anymore as I could have smoothed the way for Robbo. Fourth is only one of the three stations who want to poach him.

Charles and I had several smoochy kisses tonight. So different from Jasper. I can wholeheartedly say that I could easily fall in love with the guy yet the prospect scares me more than the black canyon. I MUST be fairer to Ben.

This morning was something else!! Thank God, James Warnock was with me.

I met James (didn't call him that) in reception at the Inglis Trust. I would never have found my way to Gartnavel Hospital. Rubbish sense of direction. James drove. Desmond Reardon has a small, mainly private clinic near the Gartnavel: an environment, nowhere near as plush or welcoming as the Professor's. Too clinical for my taste.

We sat for at least 45 minutes before a receptionist invited us to go in. As far as we were aware, there was no one else with Doctor Reardon before me. I wondered if it was a ploy to unnerve me.

OMG. His face when he clocked the eminent Professor. Another black canyon moment. Pure brilliant. The thought of skid marks on the pants of the immaculately suited Desmond cheered me up no end. James was casually dressed, yet smart, by comparison. I wore a black dress with red cherries on it and black boots.

'Professor Warnock, how are you?' Desmond shook his hand firmly if a little too long. 'Is this an ambush?' He half joked but the chortle stuck behind his prominent Adam's apple.

James Warnock assured the doctor that his capacity was as a friend and not as my physician although I was under his care at present. The formalities began.

The insurers of the Elwyn Edwards University who employs Rhys Jones as a computer technician had instructed Desmond Reardon to assess the injuries caused to me, Rachel Gordon. In other words, was I faking my memory loss?

Rhys had been on a course at Edinburgh University learning how to deal with setting up I.T. equipment for visiting dignitaries and celebrities who would be lecturing at events. Who knew? He was driving a university van.

I'm pretty sure Doctor Reardon went easy on me to begin with. Lulling me into a false sense of security. He started off by asking me to recall what had happened immediately before and after the accident. I did. (You've heard it all before).

Then the real investigation began. Many similar questions to the ones originally asked at Inglis Trust. Several times, James cautioned me as I gave my account much to Reardon's displeasure.

'You seem fairly certain that you would not cope in a classroom situation,' he said.

'Would you?' I asked. 'If I were to say to you that tomorrow you will be taking a primary five class for the week, would you be happy with that?'

'I am not a trained teacher,' the sod answered sarcastically.

'That's exactly how I feel. I have absolutely no recollection of standing in front of twenty-five baying nine-year-olds.'

'I'd hardly describe them as baying,' he laughed.

It was the first time I wobbled. 'Well, it would feel that way to me. Shitting my pants wouldn't suffice how I'd feel.'

Professor Warnock laughed at that.

'Yet you've refused to explore ways of perhaps restoring your memory?' Urging me to comment.

Professor Warnock warned me that this would come up

as Doctor Reardon had seen my hospital records but not the Professor's full report, only a summarized version.

I pointed out that 'refuse' was unnecessarily harsh. I was well aware that hypnosis might trigger some memories but they may not be real ones. I was frightened that the outcome would be worse than the one I face already. At least, I have learned to adjust to my new life. Plus, I've been assured that through time my memory should return. I'm prepared to wait for that process.

'Perhaps you feel that your new life, and with the possibility of reasonable compensation, would be more preferable than your old life.' Tosser. He was a doctor not a lawyer.

James Warnock shifted in his seat but I jumped in before him. I stood up.

'If you think this VERY lonely life is preferable to the one I had, then you have NO IDEA.'

I was thinking about you, Mum, and what you might say. Maybe not word perfect but this is what I thought I said.

'I CAN'T remember the wonderful bond I seemed to have had with my son and my daughter and my grandchildren. I can imagine it but that is totally different from knowing or feeling it. My poor grandson in Brentwood was so upset. There was no connection. I have no friends. My old ones, from my previous life, are hanging in there but I'm pretty sure I'll be dumped eventually. I visited my school. I didn't recognise any of the staff or children.

'My husband, Colin, has moved out. Couldn't cope anymore and his reaction to my memory loss was to terrorise me. He now faces criminal charges. As far as I'm aware, I led an uneventful, quiet life. Hopefully, happy. (Not true but kept that bit to myself.) Living with Colin since the accident has been incredibly frightening. I didn't know him, yet he expected me to be his wife, in every sense. (I eyeballed the two men to ensure they knew what in every sense meant. Both squirmed in their chairs.)

'I am terrified that tomorrow I might wake up and another new world awaits me. By that, I don't mean my previous life as Rachel Gordon, wife and teacher and mother to my children, I mean my son, (slight dramatic pause to emphasise my loss) but one with no recollection of any of my past memories.'

I was done. Exhausted. I fell back into my chair and the waterworks began. I bent forward, head and hands on my knees and let the pent-up emotions flow. I honestly was beyond caring how I was perceived by the devious Desmond.

After a few minutes, I dried my eyes and excused myself. I stood at reception looking out over gardens and to the white building of Gartnavel. Several minutes later, Professor James Warnock brushed my elbow.

'Coffee?' he suggested.

'A stiff gin,' I laughed.

# SIXTY-SEVEN

*Ruby's Journal*

**Sunday 3rd November**

Well, well, well. Big turn up for the books. Who did we spot (me and Annabelle) on Saturday in Perth? Only Jasper with another lady in tow. How he didn't spot us I don't know? We were busy gawping at the menu on the window of a cute wee cafe, Effie's, when I spied them through the window. All cosy, heads together, oblivious to everyone around them. We had only looked in Effie's because it's granny's name. It was Annabelle who noticed it. We had eaten already or we might have barged right in.

'What?' shouted my gobby pal. I jumped back and motioned her to have a neb. Two tables down on the right-hand side.

'No way,' she gasped. 'Is that Jasper? Holy moley.'

We both slunk to the side and giggled. Three lunch-time mojitos sanctioned our juvenile antics.

'Christ, you pick em.'

She raked in her bag for her phone. 'What the hell?' I whispered.

'Evidence.'

'For what?'

'Anything.'

Don't know what passersby made of us as we scurried away to review the incriminating shots, in another pub. We had taken the train for a wee day out. Could have been anywhere, but Perth was chosen as it was the first train leaving Edinburgh Waverley when we arrived at the station.

We took it in turns to watch from the doorway of the dive we had nipped in to. Annabelle saw them come out.

'Jeezo, I think they're heading here.'

We scrambled to the bar to hide. Ordered two V&Cs. If we had thought about it properly, we should have guessed that a smartly dressed, older woman would not have picked that dump to drink in.

'You did,' giggled Bella-Anne.

That was different.

The woman with Jasper must have been ages with you, Mum, probably older. Tall, slim (too thin), well turned out. Short grey hair. Neatly cut and styled. Beige dress, beneath a brown leather biker jacket and slouchy brown boots. Not unlike something I would have worn. Even Annabelle commented on her taste. Jasper had gone for the beige/tan look too.

Once they had passed, we downed our drinks and watched them from behind.

They strolled hand in hand, very comfortable, it appeared.

'Jealous?' asked Annabelle.

'Fuck no.' I wasn't. Positively relieved in fact, as I had felt rotten switching my allegiances to Charles.

'Two cheating men in a matter of weeks.' Annabelle shook her head.

'Three, if you count Ben.'

She gave me that don't-you-dare stare. 'Sorry,' I said. 'I retract that last comment. You can't cheat on your wife when you don't know she's alive and she is shagging other men.'

'Men?' She nearly choked.

Oops. I had forgotten to mention that. Was saving it for later.

On Friday night, after my show, Charles was waiting as always. This time he had a cheeky glint in his eye. I knew immediately that something would happen.

'Coffee?'

We had one Gaelic coffee each, prepared by Isobel, who announced a little too eagerly, that she was retiring to her bed as she put them on the glass table in his private lounge. Her face was unreadable but I guessed she was masking a smile.

Charles asked if I had finished decorating the spare room for Alfie and Nola. I nodded a yes and told him about the new bunk beds I had bought and the themes for each bed. Dinosaurs for Alfie and Unicorns for Nola. I had ordered new rugs for the living area and the master bedroom, apart from that, I had changed very little. I liked his taste.

'We are very similar,' he smiled and put his empty glass mug on the table.

Then it all happened seamlessly. We kissed for a while – all tongues – before he slipped his t shirt over his head. Within a few seconds we were both naked, him on top, as I lay on a pale grey rug in front of the log burner. Sparks exploded from the bloody fire as if heralding what was about to unfold. It made us both laugh. Similar minds.

Don't know about fireworks but it was beautiful. Slow, tender and intense. We climaxed together and clung on, pressing hard, until the last yummy tingle had melted away. I honestly didn't know whether to laugh or cry. It was so moving. Charles rolled on to his back with an enormous grin yet several tears trickled down the side of his face.

'You okay?' I asked.

'Never better,' he replied. Then he looked at me solemnly. 'It's been worth the wait.'

'What with me?'

He sighed. 'With anyone.'

I was frightened to spoil the moment but eventually had to excuse myself.

'Use mine,' he said and with his head pointed to the door in the corner.

The door opened into a small hallway. The bathroom was to the left and the other door (ajar) led to his bedroom. Both rooms were adorned with flickering candles. Pushing his optimistic luck.

When I returned, he was sitting in front of the fire with his back to a large armchair. He patted the floor in front of him and I sat down between his legs. Both completely starkers. He wrapped a throw around us. We talked for ages. He was desperate to reassure me that I could walk away at any time without any retribution from him or fear of losing my slots on Harbour Radio. Shit, I hope he hadn't had a wee poke at Maria. He found the suggestion hilarious.

His wasn't a lifestyle (stuck indoors) that was conducive to a long-term relationship and he didn't expect me to stick around forever. I appreciated his forthright candour but at this moment in time this arrangement suited me perfectly. I explained how much the future frightened me and that at any given time this time bomb in my head could explode rendering me incapable of remembering anything all over again. I knew that was a line I'd prepared for Desmond Reardon but deep down, I'm terrified, Mum, that you might reclaim what is rightfully yours. But not yet, eh?

So, on Friday night, I stayed over in Charles Rioch's bed and had a great night's sleep with a pleasant erect surprise in the morning.

**Friday 8th.**

We've decided that I'll stay over with Charles on a Tuesday night after my show and on a Saturday night so that we can have dinner together and neither of us are rushing to do or finish our programmes. The arrangement will be fluid rather than rigid. It's his birthday next Saturday and I've promised to cook for him and Isobel.

I asked Ben on Wednesday to talk me through the Iberian cheeks dish.

'It's for someone's birthday,' I said quietly. 'Next Saturday.'

'Jasper?' It was a rhetorical question.

He was not expecting another name.

'He's called Charles and at this point in time that's all I'm giving away. It's early days.'

I felt as if I was confessing to an affair. It was harrowing but his response lightened the mood.

'Fucking hell, Rachel. Sure, you're a dark horse. Now I know who Ruby took after.'

He nudged me with one side of his body (a nudge I had felt thousands of times). I blushed and he chuckled at my embarrassment.

He wrote down the recipe and added his own little twists here and there to the marinade then offered to make me mushroom pate for a starter. It was heartwarming listening to him explain to me how to prepare the dish. He's always so animated when he's in full flow.

That's when I took the opportunity.

'Ruby wouldn't want you to mope around forever. You're a young guy. You deserve to be happy again.'

He lifted his head. Those gorgeous dark blue eyes stared into mine. For a millisecond I hoped he would recognise me. I smiled and prayed that my eyes were not reflecting the pain that was buried inside.

'Thanks, Rachel, that means a lot but I don't think I'm ready.'

Oh, I knew differently. Didn't say, naturally. I had to break his gaze.

'Do me a favour though,' I could feel a bird-like rattle in my voice, 'I know that Ruby would want you to find someone that you liked or loved because they didn't remind you of her. Find someone completely different and don't make comparisons.'

I don't know how I found the strength to say that. Hope it wasn't to justify my infidelity.

'Has Annabelle said something to you?' he sounded miffed.

'Annabelle? No. How? Have you met someone?' My knees almost lost the power to stand. 'Wouldn't bother me if you have.' Tried to be more convincing than I felt.

'Nope. No-one I'd want to spend valuable time with, that's for sure.'

Suppress the grin I kept warning myself. Suppress the delight. Suppress the sheer jubilation. Hannah fucking Dunlop was gone. Off radar. Dust. Good effing riddance.

# SIXTY-EIGHT

*Rachel's Flat in Portobello. Thursday 9th January 2020.*

Rachel had done nothing for the past two hours other than read Ruby's diary.

She wandered around the apartment to ensure everything was ready for Rory's visit; she wanted to spend quality time with her son, something Colin had rarely granted her. In the past, Rory and his family would stop over at Ruby's or one of his university buddies rather than at his mother's house. Rachel realised now that all her excuses (the house is too small, it wouldn't be fair to wee Jack) would have been perceived as pitiful yet nothing was said, only endured.

The fridge was well stocked and there was plenty back up in the freezer. Her bed had been stripped and remade on her return from the butcher's earlier. The spare room –Alfie's and Nola's – needed little tidying other than having soft toys tossed onto the upper bunk. She would sleep there tonight. The damp bedding from the master bedroom was still airing on a white metal clothes horse near the radiator in the hall. If it hadn't dried by tomorrow, she would reluctantly put it in the dryer, something she hated doing. Those machines gobbled up money. Rachel hadn't yet become accustomed to controlling her income and not being chastised for wasting it.

Rory's flight was scheduled to arrive in Edinburgh at 6.30pm tomorrow. They would have dinner together and hopefully share a bottle of wine. There was a lot of catching up to do. Rachel hadn't seen her son (as herself) since he arranged respite care for her at Abbotsford Priory: fifteen months ago. No doubt they would be discussing and dissecting what she had been doing since the accident. Ruby's diary would be well hidden from inadvertent prying eyes. As with everyone else, she would make out that she had written a detailed account of the last nine months should she have needed it for future reference; to jog the memory so to speak or in case she had lost that too.

She was as nervous as she was excited at the prospect of not having to be looking over her shoulder to detect where Colin was hovering.

There would be no wine tonight. A clear head would be required for tomorrow.

As she stirred hot milk into her Horlicks, she thought about Charles and Jasper. Had Ruby no moral compass? Two men in the matter of weeks and as tempted as she was, Rachel decided not to flick through the remaining pages to confirm if she was still seeing Charles. What the hell would she do if that were the case? Surely, she would have to contact him and let him know. Annabelle hadn't mentioned it either. As soon as Rory leaves for Brentwood, Rachel would have to have serious dialogue with Ruby's best pal. Her mobile phone would surely contain the truth: it would all be there in text. All the intimate details. She flushed at the thought. Unless curiosity gets the better of her, she decided to persevere with the dairy. That way she won't miss any important developments.

And what about all those other things Ruby did? The radio show. The blog and the podcast (whatever that may be). If Rachel was being perfectly honest, she wouldn't mind trying them out but she loved teaching. Would it even be possible to return to her own school? She would have to consider it. She would have to fund this new lifestyle somehow and as far as she could gather, Tanya's family still occupied Carberry Crescent.

Her head began to ache as the what-ifs crammed her brain.

The end pages of the journal strummed through her fingers; not much to read now. Rachel looked at the clock on the kitchen wall: 8.42pm. She would read for another hour before turning in. In the morning, weather permitting, she might walk the length of the promenade and back. If possible, she would try to finish the diary before Rory arrives.

She hoped so.

# SIXTY-NINE

*Ruby's Journal*

**Sunday 17th November**

We had a fabulous time last night. Isobel was on good form. She is a lovely person. A real wee live wire with a dirty wee laugh to match. You can tell she is fond of Charles. No, more than that, you can tell she adores him and him her.

She is only 77. I don't know why I thought she was older as she has a beautiful complexion. Unblemished. Her dark grey hair is in a bun, permanently and I've only ever seen her in smart trousers and cashmere jumpers (in every colour). Short sleeves in the summer and longer in the winter, always worn with a string of fresh water pearls (a gift from Charles). She holidays twice a year, she told me. One week in spring and another in autumn to visit her only sister in Harrogate. Her sister reciprocates by visiting in the summer and winter, usually over Christmas. Hardly an exciting life yet she speaks as if she is the most fortunate woman on the planet. On Saturday she wore a short sleeved, white cashmere and slim fitting black trousers. Very Audrey Hepburn.

I had insisted we dress up for the occasion. Charles chose blue trousers and a light blue shirt with red tropical birds on it. Isobel joked that the shirt had to be twenty years old. (Quite possibly!) At least the birds matched my red dress (and my nails). I was chuffed with the way I looked. I felt younger than I have done in a long while. I've had your eyebrows microbladed and your eyelashes dyed. What a difference! You can actually see them now. I'm a size 12 or 10 depending on the retailer. Even Patricia passed a comment when I popped in to say a quick hello to her and Dad. I've said I'm seeing someone but not who. Patricia seemed genuinely pleased. No competition!!! Ha, ha.

The Iberian cheeks went down a treat and they praised the mushroom pate. Thanks Ben. Isobel had baked a birthday cake so I withheld the cheesecake I had made. Didn't want to steal her thunder. Charles blew out the candle. Number 56. A year younger than you, Mum. Not quite a toy boy!!

We locked up the studios while Isobel retired to bed with her latest John Grisham novel. Charles and I made love twice before retiring to ours. Can't believe I'm actually happy with a man who is old enough to be my dad. Changed days. No choice.

Claire texted me this afternoon. A foul-mouthed rant.

She had driven to Alderburn to challenge me about what I had said to Glynis. She had obviously blabbed to Claire. When Rina and Sofia told her to bog off, her only option was to text. I should have blocked her at the same time as I blocked Colin but wanted to keep communication open for Jade's sake. Won't be happening now.

I'm a nasty bitch and rotting in Hell isn't good enough for me after what I've put her dad through. It rolled on and on in much the same vein.

Succinct version – Glynis has dumped Colin and he has been forced to move back in with Claire and Jade. Not beneficial to his health. Or theirs, I imagine.

'Not my problem. Will be changing my number' was my short response.

Which I did. Only minutes ago, at the Gyle. Everyone who

needs to know has my new number. Despairingly few, as it turns out, but 'the only way is up' (Yazz sometime in the 80's).

Before I changed my number, I received a similar text from Colin. He also must have a new number or I wouldn't have read it. Kept the spew as evidence in case I need it. Jeezuz, hopefully never. Didn't expect a hateful mouthful from Jade. Have no way of knowing if she had been put up to it. I replied with a kind message. Told her I was sorry if I had upset her in anyway. Still loved her but for the time being we had to cease contact too. Perhaps in a few months, I would write to her. I actually cried when I typed it. More for her than me. I know she was extremely fond of you, Mum. So sad.

Annabelle just away. We had a fish n chips tea at a cafe on the High Street in Porty. I used to go there with Rory and Granny and Grandad at the beginning and end of the school holidays. Think I'll start taking Alfie and Nola. Got to start building new memories with them now.


### Friday 22nd November 2.00am.

Not easy slipping away from Charles. It must be the same with all men, regardless of their age. Once they get a wee sniff of sex, it's all they think about. Can't say I'm not enjoying it too. We did it in my studio tonight. Honestly, I feel as if I'm thirty all over again.

Can't believe I'm letting my journal slip. Thought I'd be writing in it every day but I keep putting it off plus get fed up repeating tedious stuff.

Yesterday was far from boring. The podcast is huge. I can't believe Elaine attracts so many followers. Our theme this week was stalking. (Last week it was hoarding, of all things.) The statistics are mind blowing and frightening.

Most stalkers don't see they have done anything wrong (sounds familiar) and the majority who are actually convicted (that process in itself is a long one) go on to re-offend. Not at all reassuring for anyone, (mostly women) who are on the receiving end.

Hundreds of responses and questions poured in. Both Elaine and I agreed that we would have to have a follow up programme in the near future. Too much to cover in an hour and a half.

Stalkers are insidious creatures. They develop an unhealthy interest in their victims. One woman in her 70's was quick to acknowledge she was no beauty. Yet an octogenarian at her church kept bombarding her with marriage proposals after she had handed in flowers when his wife had died. The more she rebuffed his unwanted notes, calls, visits to her home, the more bizarre and eventually violent his behaviour became.

The police did very little until he set fire to a letter of rejection and posted it through her letter box late at night. She was asleep in bed!!

So, to any one being stalked, the message seems to be that, it is up to you to keep a detailed diary of all contact.

The onus is on the victim to build a case. Where's the justice in that? And video evidence is crucial. Thank goodness I have stuff on Colin.

Talking of stalking, though perhaps unfair to categorise her like that, Hannah turned up at Deacon House last night in search of Ben who wasn't in. Turns out, he was not working at any of the restaurants. I thought he was over dressed for the kitchen. Smart shirt and his obligatory jeans (his better pair) but I assumed it was for going out after his shift. Obviously not.

Anyway, Hannah, slurring her words, demanded to talk to him. She wouldn't accept that he wasn't there so I invited her in. Her dress was far too short for those chunky thighs. I was in my jammies.

'Look for yourself,' I said, 'but don't you dare waken the kids.'

I could tell she was beyond reasoning with. Naturally, I followed her around the house. She knew the way. She'd been before with the rest of the girls although not as often as them.

I had to laugh. She asked to peek in the guest room at the other side of the house. When she was satisfied Ben was not at home, she marched indignantly to the front door.

'Do yourself a favour, Hannah, leave him alone. I won't say you've been. I can tell you've been drinking.'

Well, she swung round to face me, her face all smug.

'You've room to talk,' she sneered. Caught me by surprise.

'What do you mean?'

'You, Mrs Gordon, seem awfully keen to be with Ruby's best friend and her husband. Very creepy and I'm not the only one who thinks so.'

I struggled to find the right words. 'I think you will find that Ben and my grandchildren are very grateful for my help and I have known Annabelle since she was a wee girl. We find solace in each other's company.'

'What? Going out to pubs and clubs?' she snipped. (We have never gone clubbing.)

'I'm not going to argue or justify our friendship,' I said. 'And muscling in on Ruby's husband is a bit low, even for you.' I knew I shouldn't have but couldn't help myself.

'Hhhmmmff! You need to look closer to home. I think you will find I'm not the only friend who has strayed. At least I waited until Ruby went.'

I was aware I staggered. Her nasty tongue really did steal my breath. Don't know how long I stood in the porch, with the door wide open, ensuring that she had gone but I was freezing. Thinking all sorts of things. I listened to her boots clumping along the road until the noise faded. Everything outside was glistening with a beautiful night frost. Didn't soften the blow. Who the hell was she referring to? Please don't let it be Bella-Anne.

I was up early this morning. Couldn't sleep. Too many nightmares. I was waiting for the kettle to boil when Ben startled me. It wasn't yet six. He looked guilty as sin as he sidled past me.

'I'll have a quick shower and take the kids,' he announced before disappearing upstairs.

He'd come from the direction of the annexe.

I tiptoed to the corridor and listened. Couldn't hear anything but the door was closed and I couldn't risk opening it. So glad I didn't. Ben traipsed back into the kitchen within 15 minutes. Showered and dressed.

'I'll be half an hour at most, Rachel. Will you listen out for the kids?'

I could only nod. Next thing, the guest room door creaked and a young woman (younger than me) appeared beside my Aga. I recognised her but couldn't think where from.

A sheepish Ben introduced us. 'Helena this is Rachel. Rachel, Helena.'

Shit. She's the latest maître d' at Suthiez. She took over from Louisa's replacement and probably me. NOOOOOO!!! At least I'm going with someone twice my age. She can't be far off half of Ben's. What is he thinking? He's not. Trusting his cock too much. WANKER!!!

# SEVENTY

## *Ruby's Journal*

**Wednesday 27th November**

Ambushed Annabelle at her flat this morning. Sneaky and OTT but I had to see her face to face. I hadn't had a chance to speak to her properly after Hannah had dropped her bombshell. She was in London at a gin tasting until yesterday. Didn't want to bombard her with questions while she was away but did give her the heads up. We chatted briefly, yesterday, before my evening programme but there was too much unsaid.

I shouted out as I entered the hall.

'Christ, Roo, I haven't even showered. What's up?'

Before I could explain, she had nipped to the loo. Twenty minutes later, we were sitting at her coffee table sipping lattes and munching toast, her in her white towelling robe and a small pink one wrapped around her head. She reached for her glasses.

'Well?' I asked.

'Well, what?'

'Annabelle. Put me out of my misery. Who the fuck was shagging Ben before I died? I mean, my mum died. You know what I mean.'

She put her mug on the table and stared at the ceiling then at me. 'No-one was shagging Ben. He would never have done that to you,' she sighed. The pink towel fell from her hair.

'He did something according to Hannah fucking-slag Dunlop. Do you want me to phone her?'

She shook her head. Her chin dropped to her chest.

'I think she was referring to me. Something, totally insignificant, that happened years ago.'

'With you and Ben?' Of course, it was with Ben. Who else could it be?

My turn to pale. A hundred scenarios played in my mind. All lurid, involving my best friend and my husband. The room closed in on me. Annabelle was my only solid, sane link to my past and present and I was about to lose it and her. Was that wailing me?

Next thing I knew we were both sobbing and rocking in each other's' arms. She was all I had. With the palms of her hands, she held the sides of my face and forced me to look at her.

'Nothing happened. It was ages ago. We were both wasted. Nothing happened. Hannah is stirring.'

'Why would she say it though? Please, Annabelle. Tell me what happened.'

She rushed to the kitchen to splash her face with cold water.

When Nola was ten months old, JJ and I travelled to London together for a prestigious awards ceremony. We had been nominated for best presenters for local radio. It was such an honour for us and Fourth Waves. The buzz in the station that week was mind blowing.

Ben couldn't go. Rubiez had hired a new head chef (Karl) and he couldn't be left on his own. We were chasing a Michelin Star. Closing for two days was not an option. I was fully compliant but Ben asked me not to go. He felt it was too much. Unfair on the kids, especially Nola. I knew he was right BUT I was too stubborn. Accused him of being jealous and unsupportive. Which wasn't the case. Never had been.

Life had been far from easy since we had the kids. I was tired. Knackered. Not enough hours in a day. My fault. As everyone knows in radio, the morning presenters are obsessed with sleep (how much we were getting). While most folk wear fitbits to monitor their steps, we saddos discuss how many hours sleep we managed. I'm lucky, I've always survived on the minimum of sleep. Even as a teenager. Sacrificing my sleep meant I could help out more with the kids. But it was catching up.

The station was great after both pregnancies. JJ carried the programme until I could return full time. When Alfie was six weeks, I worked three days a week. Looking back, I was mad yet Ben rarely complained. I couldn't have done it without you, Mum. You stepped up too. (Pre-Colin). Seeing to Alfie before going to school on Mondays then staying over on Wednesday and Thursday nights to take care of Alfie the following days. After Nola, I opted for Thursdays and Fridays until she was four months. We employed a nanny when I went back to five days. She was great but she was homesick. The pull from New Zealand eventually won.

I truly regret not sharing those precious mornings with the kids. Totally selfish yet I couldn't see it. God, Mum, was I too busy chasing a dream instead of being a mum to my kids? Obviously. To everyone except me.

Sorry, I'm rambling. The Awards Ceremony. Nanny Jane had flu. You did the Thursday and I badgered Annabelle to stay on the Friday. Ben and I parted on very frosty terms.

Annabelle's version.

She took over from you (Mum) around midday. Took the kids to the big swing park in the Meadows. Tea, bath and bed.

She was exhausted. I smiled at that as it's her greatest wish to become a mum. She was asleep on the couch when Ben came in from Rubiez as high as a kite. On adrenalin not drink. They had had a really successful night. Some well-known celebrity influencers had been in. Taking selfies and sharing their posts on-line. One was a serious foodie. A millionaire by sixteen and a multi by twenty-five. He posted a picture of him on his knees pretending to be worshipping Ben. It went viral. (He was hammered, by the way!) Ben had phoned me and I hadn't answered.

'He opened a bottle of champagne and then another,' she apologised.

They got drunk too quickly. Ben was upset that I had ignored his calls and texts.

'Next thing, we were snogging,' she whimpered.

WHAM! POW! Direct kick to the heart.

'Nothing else happened. I swear to God. We crashed on the couch. It was stupid. Too much drink. Just two good pals comforting each other. Next morning, we were both mortified.'

Comforting. That's rich. What the hell did either of them need comforting for?

'Are you sure nothing else went on?' I asked.

'Positive. I'm so so sorry Ruby.'

I persevered. What if they hadn't been so drunk, would they have been tempted?

'NO! Definitely not. If we hadn't been so drunk that first kiss would never have been instigated.'

Then it struck me. Had they been lovers in Melbourne?

'I would have remembered that.' It was the way she sighed. Forlornly. Tinged with regret.

I had to ask. 'Did you have a wee thing for Ben?'

'No. We were great pals. That was all.'

It was not all. I can read her like a book. I remember how excited she was when she took me to Belfast. The first time I had ever met Ben and Pascal. Annabelle insisted that me and Pascal would hit it off. Two drop dead gorgeous human beings, she had been at pains to point out. You are going to love each other. But it was Ben and me who were instantly attracted. Gagging for each other. Poor Annabelle. Had she had high hopes for her and Ben? Had she stood quietly on the sidelines while her best pal sailed off into the sunset with the man she secretly hankered for?

She must have read my mind.

'I really liked Ben. We had a great laugh. He looked out for me in Oz. And maybe I did hope that when we met up in Belfast, he would realise how much he had missed me. But you know what? If he had liked me in that way, it would have blossomed over there. The minute I saw the way that you two looked at each other, I knew you were destined to be with each other.'

'Oh Annabelle. I'm so sorry.'

'Don't be,' she said so stoically. 'You and Ben are great together. My best mates and I would never change that. I would never deliberately hurt you, Ruby. Honestly? I would change souls with you now if I could. You could muscle in on Ben and let's face it, your mum is getting more action than me. You would have to teach me how to DJ.'

We laughed and cried for the rest of the morning. Annabelle skipped work for half a day.

After the London event, I scurried back to Edinburgh with my tail between my legs. We were runners up but it wasn't that. I shouldn't have gone without Ben. It wasn't the same and I'd missed him.

Ben suggested that we should get married asap. I pleaded with the station to allow me to do a four-day week. Fridays became a family day.

Oh, nearly forgot. Following year, JJ and I won. Best presenters. Ben and I stayed at the Ritz with JJ and Arjun. AND Rubiez got that coveted Michelin Star.

# SEVENTY-ONE

*Ruby's Journal*

**Sunday 1st December**

The kids were swinging from the chandeliers. Metaphorically. Advent calendars. I bought Alfie one with little cars behind each door. Nola's has bits and pieces for a unicorn kingdom. £75 each. Daylight robbery. Who cares?

I stayed for roast dinner. The kids had to judge who had made the best Yorkshire puds. Daddy or Granny? It was a draw. Nola voted for Ben and Alfie for me.

Their preliminary Christmas lists were written (and drawn). Every advert on telly is followed by 'I want that'. They are so funny. Ben has invited Annabelle and me for Christmas dinner. Mine was extended to include the opening of the presents in the morning. (Us two girls promised never to discuss our recent conversation about Ben with Ben.) Hannah was a very different matter. She got both barrels from Annabelle for stirring. Annabelle and I received a lovely box of flowers yesterday with an apology followed by a text. Another grovelling apology for her disgraceful behaviour. The demon drink!! Could we please say nothing to Ben?

Annabelle conceded that she would forgive her. I'm not ready yet but we agreed that it was something else that Ben didn't need to be lumbered with. I can't quite shake the notion that my wee pal was subjected to two loved up humping rabbits ruining her Belfast weekend and what else might have been. I have NEVER suspected.

Charles mentioned Christmas Day too. Isobel's sister will be staying and I have an open invitation to pop in anytime. I explained that I was desperate to see the kids' faces when they realise Santa has been. First time. I can't remember another (not entirely accurate). Promised to drive over to Cockenzie after breakfast as copious amounts of alcohol may be consumed later in the day. He hinted that a driver would be at my disposal in the evening should I need it. He is so thoughtful.

Charles always does the Christmas morning show live then we run with pre-recorded shows, from all the presenters, for the rest of the day. Same with Boxing Day. In fact, any of us can pre-record programmes for any of our slots over Christmas and New Year. He doesn't care. As he keeps reminding us, we don't get paid so he can hardly make demands. Any money that the station raises is used to upgrade our equipment and the rest (majority) is given to local charities. We are part of a lovely one that delivers presents to children on Christmas Eve. Schools and other services nominate children 'who would benefit' from such a gift. The words neglected or deprived is frowned upon. I wish Charles could venture out. He would make a fantastic Santa and he would love it. I've asked him to make a donation to the food bank I work in.

Rory, Alana and Jack are staying with me for three days. Arriving on Boxing Day. They don't usually stay with you, Mum, but I'm going to make a huge effort to make them welcome. They can have my room and I'll share with Jack. Apparently, he is so excited about that.

Before I left the house, Deacon House, Ben cornered me in the porch.

'Sorry about last Thursday. Won't spring anything like that on you again.'

'It's really none of my business.' I was proud of myself.

'Ruby would accuse me of having dick brain. Sorry.' And he pulled a forgive-me face.

That's exactly what I WAS thinking. Maybe I have flagrant fanny!!!

'Will you be seeing her again?' I queried.

'NO. Way too young.'

'Dick brain?'

'Yep. I've punted her to Rubiez.'

With that I left.

## Monday 2nd.

You will never believe this. Oh, my bloody days!!! Adrian phoned Charles on Sunday to ask about Robbo and ME!!!!! He had emailed earlier in the week and asked if he could discuss his proposals with us personally rather than going through him.

Although Robbo is a fabulous presenter, he is terrified to move on. He loves Harbour and his parents feel the pressure would tip his anxiety over the edge. I'll continue to coach him until he is ready to take up the challenge.

As for me, there is no way I am leaving Harbour. I love the anonymity of being Reya. I would feel foolish if the truth got out. Last week I had to tell Ben that I volunteered at Women's Refuge Centres. He had begun asking too many questions about what I did with my time. I explained that for the safety of the families, it was paramount that I never discussed where I helped out or what I did. It was totally plausible and he admired what I was doing.

Adrian was miffed. Too bad.

Then on Monday morning immediately after my show JJ phoned the station asking to speak with me. I've always been too curious for my own good. I called him back on his mobile from the station. That shocked him. He guards that number. Here's how it went.

'JJ, Reya here. What does Fourth Waves number one presenter possibly want with lil ole me?'

He found that amusing. Knew he would. 'I was wondering if we could meet for a chat.'

'Why? Are you looking for a new partner?'

I could hear him choke. 'Nothing like that,' he stumbled. My intuition told me differently. 'My husband listens regularly to your show and I had to tune in for myself. Find out more about the competition.'

I laughed. 'I hardly think so.'

Then he became very serious. 'People are talking about your shows and your podcast.'

'Really?' I had no idea.

'You are a natural presenter. Have you done it before?'

'I've dabbled,' I lied.

We had some light hearted banter (flirting) then he asked again if we could meet. To my astonishment, I said yes. At my wee cafe on Ferry Road. We set the date and time. If I chickened out, which was highly likely, I promised to text him. He, in return, promised not to tell anyone of our meeting. The blood was pounding in my skull. There was no way I would ever do a show with my pal but was vanity ruling my head?

I didn't say anything to Charles. Very deceitful.

**Saturday 7th.**

This week has been manic. Never ending. Trying to remember all the things you would do for Christmas. I posted cards to Canada. Rummaged in your loft for personal tree decorations (mainly the ones I had given you) as the kids are coming tomorrow to help me decorate my tree. Real one that Ben will drop off along with the kids. Rina was in her element with the huge box of decs. Your artificial tree is a sad specimen. I gave them an Amazon voucher to replace it.

I've made a list of all the presents I need to buy and the cards that you would want to send. Much shorter than normal but there's all these new friends and acquaintances to consider which is nice. Plus, I've had the time to think. A luxury not afforded to me in the past. I used to order everything (in haste) on line with very little thought given to what the recipient would really like. And I had a theme where all my pals received the same gift, with a little extra for Bella-Anne. Not now.

I met JJ this morning. So funny.

I decided to go for a run and meet him in the cafe. Right up to the second I spotted him loitering outside, I was sure I would bottle it. All week I had thought about what I would say and hoped he would accept my proposition. I knew I could trust him. So all sweaty, and in my running gear, I ground to a halt.

'JJ,' I shouted. 'Good to see you.'

'Rachel? Oh, my lordie, you've lost a heck of a lot of weight.'

I explained that I was out jogging and that Annabelle lived round the corner.

'This is my usual pit-stop. Fancy a quick coffee?'

He faltered. 'Er, I'm actually meeting someone. A business client.' A subtle hint that I should jog on.

'Reya? Oh, I know all about it.'

His face was a picture. Totally confused. I suggested we should wait for her together. We took our seats in the window.

'I take it you know Reya,' he coaxed.

'Kind of,' I admitted. 'JJ, Ruby always said that you were unequivocally trustworthy. Can Reya trust you never to reveal her true identity? Without that guarantee, she won't see you.'

'If she agrees to come into the station, everyone will see her,' he said. His voice less assured.

'It's complicated,' I said. 'None of her family knows she does radio, especially her ex-husband. He is a nasty piece of work. She won't risk unmasking herself. Will you please confirm that you will NEVER tell anyone who she is, not even Arjun?'

Poor Jacob Johnston. Hadn't a scooby yet he nodded his affirmation.

'Are you ready to meet her?'

He laughed as if the whole thing was incongruous. I launched into full Reya Enniskillen dialect.

'So, were you expecting that the mysterious Reya would actually be Ruby's mother?'

His face!! 'Jeepers, Jacob. For sure, it's not like you to be stuck for words.'

'I...I...you've fucking floored me.' Then the laughter started.

We were both hysterical. Young Steph, who approached us to take our order, had to wonder what the hell was going on.

'Had you any idea?' I asked.

'Not the foggiest.' He was still shaking his head. 'I should have though. You were too good in the studio. Ruby taught you well.'

We got down to business. I wanted a one-off slot on Fourth Waves, as Ruby's mum. A tribute to Ruby. Her life in songs. Preferably before Christmas.

Presenters are always begging for time off over seasonal holidays, in particular Christmas and New Year. I didn't want paid so anybody's space I took, wouldn't lose out financially. JJ agreed that most of our staff would bite my hand off at the offer. Being paid to sit at home or to catch up on sleep was a gift.

He asked about my husband. I spilled. It was so good to chat with my close pal (even if it had to be as you).

'I know someone who could sort him out. Just give me the nod.' JJ was serious.

He came from Drylaw. Born and bred. He was acquainted with some very dodgy characters. Salt of the earth but would stab you without hesitation if you crossed their granny.

'No thanks,' I informed him. 'Think he has been shafted already.'

If you met JJ for the first time, you would never guess he was gay. Seems so macho and looks too straight. The clothes are a give-a-way at times. Tight suit. Tee shirt. Loafers and no socks. Arjun less so. But both big hearted softies.

We shook on it then hugged for ages.

Before Christmas, Rachel Martin would dedicate two hours to Ruby. It helped that Adrian would be away that week. A secret tryst with Jemma.

She'd get on well with Hannah Dunlop.

# SEVENTY-TWO

*Ruby's Journal*

**Monday 9th December**

Told Charles this morning before my show that I would be hosting a tribute to Ruby on Fourth Waves as myself, Rachel her mother. He was relieved I wasn't going on as Reya. Confirmed that would never be the case.

Today's theme was food banks and how the community could help. The response was great. Not many folk understand how they function. Too many believe they are used by scroungers and lazy bastards. So not true. We discussed how to make cheap meals from tinned products and Christmas dinner on a budget. I was tempted to urge folk to volunteer but some smart arse might suggest that I should show up first. Couldn't risk it.

Had a fab time with the kids. Tree not huge but very cute. They brought me a lovely bauble with school/ nursery photos on either side. Only wobble I had was putting up the fairy (more like an angel). That was always Ben's job and we would toast her with a sherry and the kids with Irn Bru (the only time they were allowed it). With crystal sherry glasses, we continued with the Sutherland tradition. Alfie perched her precariously at the top.

I've bought and wrapped most of my gifts. I know, smug git. Mum, I'm sounding like you but it's a joy taking time finishing them off with ribbons and bows. Nola is right into Barbie so I've bought lots of bits and pieces. Alfie wants a Stretch Armstrong (his last one snapped) and football stuff. Bless him, he's not that good but we can only hope.

I've been busy mapping out my FW programme. Need to make sure I don't slip into my Reya voice. Wouldn't that be something?

Christmas songs are in full swing. Not nearly as bad as the bigger stations. By the middle of December, they feel like slitting their wrists every time a jingle or tune kicks in.

## 15th December, Sunday.

Had a lovely night last night with Charles. We put up his tree. The whole evening was cosy and romantic. Guess what he did? He opened a window and inhaled fresh air. I stood with him. It was only a few minutes but I was so proud of him. I cried. He smiled.

He has broken his seven-year phobia before. Several times in fact but something subconsciously re-triggers it. The longest break has been five weeks and two days. He doesn't venture far. Down to the harbour. A short drive along the coast. He enjoys country parks when they are not busy. At dawn or just before dusk. Sometimes just the length of his garden. Never into a supermarket. An Aberlady restaurant once screened off a large area for him and Isobel. They entered and left by the fire exit. I didn't ask but assumed he'd paid handsomely for the privilege.

The kids invited Auntie Annabelle to help them decorate their tree today. Not that I was envious – of course I was. My pal originally turned down the offer until I gave my consent. Had no option. She wasn't fishing for permission when she told me but not going just to please me wasn't fair either. Apart from meeting up with Hannah, Annabelle was slipping into

Billy-no-mates now that I stayed over with Charles on a Saturday. Fridays were taken up with my radio slot. I promised to switch nights next week and we would hit the city lights.

**9pm.**

Fucking Hell. Annabelle called me.

Colin turned up at Deacon House just as the kids were about to be bathed. He must have presumed that I was there as my cream Mini (new one) was parked in the drive. Annabelle's car had failed its M.O.T so she borrowed mine while I used the Audi.

He is off his fucking head. Annabelle said that when Ben opened the door, Colin was extremely tranquil and asked if he could speak to me. Ben tried really hard to convince him that I wasn't there. The kids ran to the front door, in the buff, when they heard his voice. They were excited to see him. He told the kids he was there to speak to Granny as he was lonely and missed her very much and could they tell her he was waiting for her? Annabelle said that his calmness freaked her out. They insisted I was at my own house. Thank goodness they didn't mention Portobello. At first, Alfie and Nola thought it was a joke because he kept cajoling them. He even asked what they would like for Christmas. Since they were starkers and freezing, Ben ushered them back inside. Even Annabelle tried to placate him and failed. Then, as if a switch flicked, Colin began screaming my name. RACHEL!!!!! The kids were terrified.

He barged past Ben and bounded into the house. He was ranting that he had no money while I was languishing in luxury. The thought of my two, naked, cowering on the sofa behind Annabelle turned my stomach.

At first Ben tried wrestling him out of the room but Colin

jumped into one of our chairs and clung on, refusing to budge. It was laughable. He looked as if he was glued to the fabric. At least the shouting had ceased (apart from weird moaning). Unbeknown to Colin and Ben, Annabelle had dialled 999 the moment he began screaming. Although, she didn't speak (dropped it when Colin flounced past her), the response centre heard the commotion unfold and located the call. By the time the police arrived, he was as cool as a cucumber and questioned why they were there. Annabelle was convinced he was on drugs. Funny that. I thought the same when he showed up at Alderburn once.

He was led out like a docile puppy dog wishing the kids a Happy Christmas and hoped that Santa would be generous. Nut job. What is it that makes him repeat this bizarre behaviour of turning up on doorsteps? He must surely realise that it never bodes well.

My initial reaction was to drive over but Ben was already in bed with the kids. They would sleep with him for the rest of the night. I just wanted to cuddle them. Reassure them. Annabelle said she would wait until the kids were asleep.

She sounded terrible.

'I might stay here tonight, Roo. I'm kinda spooked.' I couldn't respond. 'Don't worry, I promise to sleep in Nola's bed. On my own.'

My turn to feel awful. 'Thank you, honey. I know you will. Sleep well.'

I hung up.

# SEVENTY-THREE

*Ruby's Journal*

**Sunday 22nd December**

OMG. Two more sleeps and I'm on air. Christmas Eve. 2pm till 4. Can't wait. Slightly nervous but excited doesn't define it. Had to go in on Friday morning to 'try' out the decking with JJ. He will be my wingman during my presentation. I did point out that he could be catching up on much needed sleep on Christmas Eve but he was having none of it. Didn't take me long to find my rhythm. FW's equipment is more high-tech than Harbour's. News, weather and traffic are automatically updated. At Harbour, I have to remember to replace old information with new, manually and constantly. Can't have warnings of a traffic jam going out over the air when it was cleared hours ago. Jemma was less accommodating than last time. I stayed for half an hour tops or I would have swung for her. JJ was pleased with how well I had transferred my skills. Bless him, if he only knew.

Ray of Hope had a fantastic announcement. Laura the accountant is no longer with her husband. Eight months pregnant and rescued by her mum and dad. She was hospitalised after another beating. Nearly lost her baby. This time she summoned the courage to contact her parents and unload. They intervened. Nasty hubby has been charged with assault. Thank goodness. Her bully has had his final punch. Please don't go back.

At this time of year, domestic violent escalates. Money

pressures. Forced happiness and forced togetherness. Unbearably sad. Hopefully, Laura's courage will rub off on others.

Betty has high hopes for Christmas. Her man has promised to pay back SOME of the loans. Oh Betty!!!

I've told everyone who would be interested to tune in to the tribute on Christmas Eve. Ben was stunned. More so that JJ was instrumental in persuading Adrian to let me loose in the studio. JJ has been dropping it into his morning show for weeks.

Jasper asked to see me. He had heard of my presentation and was as intrigued as Ben. He wanted to know why I was avoiding him. We met for a coffee at the Fort Kinnaird on Friday.

'Hello stranger.' He smiled and kissed my cheek.

'Sorry been busy,' I fibbed.

'Too busy to text your good mate?' He admonished.

'I felt awkward.'

I told him that I had seen him with a very elegant woman in Perth and although I wasn't in the slightest bit jealous, I wanted to find the right moment to bring it up. Plus, I wasn't using his liaison as an excuse for no longer wanting sex with him

He chuckled. 'You don't mince your words.'

I laughed too but I didn't want to lose his friendship. I hoped that we could revert to being friends with no benefits.

He stared at me and smiled. For a very long time, before answering me. God, he is so good looking. Better than Charles but he doesn't come close in other departments.

'No hard feelings?' I asked.

He shook his head. How could I ask that when he was the one that should be apologising for not mentioning his other friend? We were hardly an item, I reminded him. We were two adults who enjoyed each other's company and I for one wanted that friendship to continue (defo no sex). He agreed. We drank our coffee and indulged in small talk.

'Spill. What's her name and how long have you been seeing her?'

Her name is Elizabeth. They met eight years ago. They have an unusual relationship. She has her house and he has his. It works. She doesn't quiz him or make unreasonable demands and vice versa. He is very attentive and in return she is very good to him.

'In what way,' I asked.

He shrugged. 'Holidays. Gifts.' He must have noticed that I pulled back. 'Nothing sinister. She has plenty money. She enjoys spending it on me. She has no-one else.'

'She seems a good bit older than you.'

'She is and it doesn't bother either of us,' he said. 'I've told you before. I'm attracted to older women. They're interesting. They've lived. I enjoy their company.'

He was at pains to explain that they were really good friends and he was very, very fond of her. He didn't mention love. Elizabeth liked living on her own but she also wanted companionship. Someone to share holidays with and to keep her 'happy'. He was willing to oblige. It was a mutual arrangement that suited them both.

As we chatted about my radio broadcast, I couldn't help but dissect everything he had casually divulged. How the other half lived. My previous life seemed very cosseted compared to everything I was now involved with. The unpredictable Colin and his sidekick, Bellatrix. The blog. The podcast. Food banks and now a gigolo who seemed unperturbed that a much older woman funded his lifestyle. Is that how he saw me? A future replacement.

Then it struck me. Betty. Elizabeth. Fuck! Was Jasper the younger man who was fleecing Betty from our blog?

'Do you ever ask her for money?' I blurted.

The utter disbelief and hurt on his face.

'Money? Why would I ask her for money?' I could tell I had kicked the breath from him. 'I have a really well-paid job. I live mortgage free. It's not a fancy house but it was bought and paid for by the money I earned in the China Seas before I met Elizabeth. I'm disappointed in you, Rachel.' He rose to leave.

I was so ashamed. My hand shot out and grabbed his arm. I pleaded with him to sit down and hear me out. He did, reluctantly.

I apologised for being so crass. Me and my big mouth and overactive imagination. I told him all about Betty who is on an on-line chat line that I take part in (didn't say what it was called or that I set it up) and that I had put two and two together and came up with five.

'I also volunteer at domestic abuse centres and I've become uncharacteristically suspicious of men in general.' I apologised over and over.

He kind of laughed but the hurt was still there.

'A,' he said, 'I could never intentionally hurt a friend, male or female.

B. Elizabeth would never under any circumstances refer to herself as Betty.

C. She is a strong independent, intelligent woman who wouldn't tolerate anyone asking her for money.

D. It's that kind of mindset that has probably held us back.' He jabbed his forefinger several times as he spat that last bit.

I couldn't understand what he meant. He scrunched his line-free, beautiful face. Other folk's perceptions of a younger man and a wealthy older woman. Elizabeth was fourteen years older. It was true. As a society, we rarely question an older bloke splashing his cash on a younger girlfriend but when roles are reversed, we use insulting jibes like cougar and money-grabbing or gigolo (so glad I didn't say that out loud). The age difference worried Elizabeth more than it did Jasper. She was certain he would abandon her for a younger woman eventually.

'Do you love her?' I asked.

He tilted his head back, eyes shut, boring into the ceiling.

Then his face lit up. Really beamed.

'You know what? I've just realised that I AM in love with her.' He was deadly serious.

'Have you told her that?'

'No.' He shook his head slowly as if he was digesting it all.

'What the hell are you doing here with me? Away and tell her,' I urged.

I apologised again. He couldn't care less. He was about to give Elizabeth her best Christmas ever. We don't tell the people we love often enough.

I swear, Jasper glided out of that cafe like a wee boy who had just been given the key to Santa's Grotto. I was unbelievably chuffed for him.

Annabelle was gobsmacked when I told her but was as happy for him as I was. She laughed, 'has your mother the face that attracts oddballs?' With the exception of my dad, of course. But it was true. Maybe it's the combination of your appearance and my personality. A potent cocktail.

Talking of which. We guzzled too many concoctions and neither of us surfaced until late afternoon.

Charles was touchingly sympathetic when I wasn't able to face my dinner and had to skulk off to bed at 8.00pm.

**Monday.**

Was a blubbering mess. Santa was visiting Nola's nursery. Ben couldn't go so I went after my show. They sang Rudolf the Red-nose Reindeer and Little Donkey. Oh, my days. Hardly a dry eye amongst us. Nola beamed as Santa handed her a beautifully wrapped gift. No more than £5, we were warned. I chose a princess activity book. She loves dressing up little figures with the sticky clothing labels. She skipped up the Royal Mile with all the joy and happiness Christmas brings.

**7.30pm.** I'm busy preparing my FW show.

I have always written the framework of my gig in an A4 hard back book (but only after umpteen drafts on scrap paper) then I take my book to the studio. The first half of the programme is on one side, the other half on the other. JJ was the total opposite. Winging every show. I'd be a quivering wreck if that was me. Meticulous planning. That's me. Once in the studio, I transfer everything into the computer. The exact time of each piece of music is worked out to the nano-second and the countdown begins from the very first output. You always know what time you have left. Sometimes you have to fade a song out quickly or cut it out altogether, at others, you have to find another song. I'm really lucky. I've been given free rein to use whatever songs fit the presentation BUT I had to submit them ALL to Adrian last week for vetting.

Must go. Lots to do.

# SEVENTY-FOUR

## *Ruby's Journal*

**Tuesday, Christmas Eve**

I have palpitations. In six hours' time, I'll be back in my old studio. I've already pre-recorded my Harbour night slot. Two broadcasts in one day might be too much. If this one goes badly wrong there was no way I could be bubbly at night. Not fair on my listeners. This way they get a cheery (non interactive unfortunately) Christmas broadcast.

I'm well organised for Christmas and my visitors. All my presents have been handed out. I popped in to see Auntie Lisa, Auntie Vera and Tanya and Sean on Saturday morning. I'll see Charles tomorrow after I've watched the kids opening their presents. I'm truly grateful, Mum, that I have been given this second chance. I promise I will make every second count.

I've written out my agenda for my show so many times. One more won't do any harm. Here goes. P.S When I write JJ contribution, it's because he has organised our listeners to send in a short memory message about me. I guess there will be a lot of tears. I contacted everybody I can think of about the song choices. Don't want to be accused of making it up.

Christmas Eve: **RUBY**
A Life in Songs
**14.00** News/Weather/Traffic/Fourth Waves jingle

**14.03** Introduction

**14.05** Rocking Around the Christmas Tree/Brenda Lee (*Home Alone with Rory then Alfie*)

**14.08** Streets of Philadelphia by Bruce Springsteen (*with Rory London Olympic Park*)

**14.12** Our jingle/ Big Prize Quiz/ JJ contribution

**14.15** My Life would Suck Without You by Kelly Clarkson (*Ruby karaoke*)

**14.19** Adverts

**14.22** Do They Know it's Christmas? By Band Aid. (*Year Ruby born. 1984.*)

**14.26** Don't Cha by Pussy Cat Dolls (*for best pals*)

**14.30** Fourth Waves jingle and Traffic

**14.32** Short quiz and JJ contr.

**14.35** Pencil Full of Lead by Paulo Nutini (*for the jivers Rach and Lisa/godmother*)

**14.39** Let it Go from Frozen. Idina Menzel (*for Alfie and Nola*)

**14.43** All I Want for Christmas by Mariah Carey (*Love Actually fav film*)

**14.47** Adverts/ Our jingle

**14.49** Mysterious Girl by Peter Andre (*first day at High School R&A*)

**14.52** A Million Love Songs by Take That (*concert Ruby &Ben at Wembley*)

**14.56** Heroes by David Bowie (*for Ruby's dad*)

**15.00** News, Weather, Traffic

**15.03** Fourth Waves jingle

**15.04** Last Christmas by Wham (*all the girls loved film The Holiday*)

**15.08** Same Jeans by The View (*for Ben*)

**15.12** Recap quizzes JJ contribution

**15.15** You're Still the One by Shania Twain *(JJ& Arjun first dance)*

**15.19** West End Girls by Pet Shop Boys *(supported Take That concert)*

**15.23** Adverts/our jingle

**15.26** Dancing Queen by Abba *(Stars in Your Eyes/School/ Ruby & A-Belle )*

**15.30** Traffic/Fourth Waves jingle

**15.32** Mistletoe and Wine by Cliff Richard *(a favourite of my granny)*

**15.36** Good Riddance by Green Day *(Fav song)*

**15.40** Quiz winners and JJ contribution

**15.44** You Needed Me by Anne Murray *(tent on West Highland Way R&B)*

**15.49** Mr Tambourine man by Bob Dylan *(Ben loves it)*

**15.53** Thank yous and acknowledgements/Our jingle

**15.55** Fairytale of New York by The Pogues *(THE family favourite)*

**Extras:** Lewis Capaldi/Florence and the Machine (if needed)

# SEVENTY-FIVE

*Ruby's Journal*

**Boxing Day 10.00 am**

Never in a million years did I think my broadcast would lead me to this moment. Don't know whether to say it imploded or exploded but WOW!!! My head's mince. Totally mixed up. And quite honestly, I don't know where I go from here.

I need to start with the show itself. **Christmas Eve.**

I arrived at the studio an hour and a half early to programme my show as I had done thousands of times before. JJ was in the sleep hub (not used that often). It's a tiny room no bigger than a cupboard but there's a bed. And it's quiet. He was grabbing a much needed kip.

The hour whizzed past as did the actual show. I had to fade out several songs. More than I've ever done. Too much hilarity. With the content we had and all the ideas that were popping up, we could have done a four-hour slot no bother.

I kick started with *Rocking Around the Christmas Tree* by Brenda Lee. Rory and I loved Home Alone and Alfie got into it last Christmas.

There were so many poignant moments that tears had to be swiped quickly and composure regained. JJ was touched that I had included his first dance with Arjun. It was as if I had never been away. Our bonhomie rippled through the building. Even David on the front desk knocked on the window to give a thumbs up. The mood was most definitely festive and buoyant.

Dozens of our devoted listeners sent in moving tributes and memories including my mates from *Haud Yer Wheesht*. Amber Rose donated a haircut as a prize for my quizzes (as did Rubiez). Questions were all about me. How long have (oops had) I been working at Fourth Waves? (6 years & 2 months) and what was my most memorable interview? Sorry Lewis but nothing could top David Bowie. We aced that one. Happened to be in the right place at the right time. There were many other silly questions that JJ had thrown in. Like what was my shoe size? Six and a half.

My favourite entrant, the lovely Ashlyn, phoned in. She was bubbling as she thanked me for her baby's present. She didn't win anything this time so I threw in lunch at Suthiez for her. She was cock-a-hoop. Honestly, the phone lines were red hot with callers as was our Instagram page.

All my girls had tuned in. I kept getting distracted reacting to them. After *Don't Cha,* each of them texted in 'WET BREEKS'. So funny. Annabelle sent a tearful emoji during *Mysterious Girl.* Likewise, nearly all my mobile contacts followed suit when Frozen's *Let it Go* was played for Alfie and Nola who had sent in a little voice recording for Mummy and Granny. Plucked the heart strings big time!!!

Dad loves David Bowie. Got me and Rory into him so had to include *Heroes*. Mum, you loved Elton John and anything rock n roll. Even though technically not your era, Auntie Lisa's sister taught you both how to jive. You owned the floor, ladies.

The last time that Rory and I were at something on our own, no spouses, was in London at the Olympic Park Stadium to see Bruce Springsteen. Fantastic night. Wee brother and sister got wasted after it. Happy days.

Then there was my soul mate. Couldn't not play The View's

*Same Jeans*. Ben lives in his jeans. Our favourite concert ever was Take That at Wembley in 2011. They were supported by Pet Shop Boys. Struggled to choose a favourite but plumped for *A Million Love Songs Later*. At least West End Girls was more upbeat as were most of my other chosen songs. Not my next one. When we first dated, Ben and I walked the West Highland Way. Stayed in a tent as money was tight. We were saving like mad for our first restaurant. One cold night, under canvas, Anne Murray's *You Needed Me* was playing and we both agreed that the words were exactly how we felt about each other. I cried at that one and poor JJ had to take over for a couple of minutes.

JJ showed me a text he had received from Ben.

Great show mate. Thanks for helping Rachel put it together and all your support.
    Appreciated.

JJ replied.

No help required from me, man. All down to her. She's a natural like her daughter. In fact feel as if it is Ruby sitting next to me. We've had a blast. Merry Xmas, man. And the kids.

Aww, bless my JJ.

Had to finish the show with *Fairytale of New York* by the Pogues. It is THE family favourite of all time.

That was it. Finished. I was overcome. Hugs and kisses all round. Arjun gave me a huge bouquet of flowers and JJ popped the champagne as he shouted at the top of his voice that Fourth needed to sign me up NOW. That wouldn't be happening but I have to admit I was buzzing.

After the swirl of emotions (a roller coaster full), it was time for me to leave. I stepped out on to a cold Windsor Street slightly giddy from the champagne and the excitement. It was quiet and dark. Several Christmas trees lit up the bay windows opposite and the trees ahead lining London Road twinkled with bright blue lights. I remember feeling slightly dejected but I immediately perked up when I thought of Alfie and Nola and how fortunate I was that I would be spending Christmas morning with them. I picked up my pace.

That's when I heard him. Directly behind me.

'Mrs S. where are you hurrying to?' At first, I thought I'd misheard it but the soft familiar voice said it again. Oh man!

I nearly fainted. Only one person called me Mrs. S. I immediately froze. Daring to breathe or move a limb. I was terrified to turn round. But I did, ever so cautiously.

I stared at him for ages. Tears running down my cheeks. I was afraid to speak or respond.

There he was. My Ben. In a brown suede donkey jacket. Brown boots. Obligatory jeans and the Sutherland weathered tartan scarf I bought him years ago.

'Nice scarf,' I said.

'My wife bought it for me,' he replied.

'She wasn't your wife then. Not even a fiancé.'

'From a shop in Fort William I believe.'

'I think you will find it was bought in Oban.' I pointed out. 'You put it on and dribbled brown sauce down the front.'

'The worst fish n chips I've ever had,' he laughed.

My heart was pounding so much, I was sure it would burst through my coat. It was red. The coat. Red leather. I bought it from Zara's last week.

'I take it you were listening to the show?'

Ben nodded. We hadn't moved towards each other. We must have been five metres apart.

'Why are you here?' I was terrified that the reply would not be what I wanted to hear.

'To see you.'

My turn to nod. Honestly, Mum, I have played out this encounter so many times since it happened. Even as I write this, I'm frightened that I've misinterpreted the last forty hours.

'When did it register,' I asked.

'From the opening song. How did Rachel know about Alfie and Home Alone? She has no memory before the accident.'

'That's it?'

'The whole show was riddled with inconsistencies. You couldn't possibly have known what me and Ruby spoke about in that tent.' He eyed me suspiciously.

'More holes than a calendar?'

We both chuckled at that. Annabelle said it once and Ben and I have used it ever since.

'Deep down, I've always suspected but if I voiced them then I might have been put away along with you,' he laughed. It was a quiet laugh as if he couldn't quite believe the words that were leaving his mouth. (Neither could I.) 'You knew the house too well. Where everything was kept. It was like you brought Ruby in with you each time you came. I liked it.'

'I tried hard to fool you all.' I couldn't control the fear any longer. Tears erupted down my cheeks.

Ben walked towards me and wrapped me in his arms. I hid my face in his chest and sobbed.

'Don't cry Scooby Doo.' And he kissed the top of my head.

# SEVENTY-SIX

*Ruby's Journal*

**Christmas Eve**

Arm in arm, we walked to his car. I clung on. He was going nowhere without me. The kids were at Libby's and we drove to pick them up. I could feel Ben's eyes penetrating my soul.

'What do you see when you look at me?' I had to ask as we reached his car.

He hesitated. 'I can't lie. I see your mother.'

Thought he would. What else would he see?

'What do you think happened?'

What indeed? 'I don't know.' I answered truthfully. 'I woke up in hospital to manure breath. Nobody believed my version. I was fecking terrified. What could I do? I had to leave with the devious wee shite.'

'I'm sorry, Ruby. How was I to know? How did you cope?'

'Couldn't have without Annabelle,' I confessed. 'Think I would have thrown myself under a train,' I winced because it would have been a complete waste of a second chance.

'I sussed that. You two were thick as thieves, so you were.'

'We can't tell anyone,' I barked.

He nodded. Sadness and pain etched on his face. He was as frightened of the future as I was.

'Let's just enjoy the moment,' he urged and kissed my nose.

God, how I longed for his lips but realised that someone

might recognise us. It had to have crossed his mind too. We kept our opinions and hands to ourselves for the time being.

All the way to Libby's he probed me about things only the two of us would know. Some surprisingly intimate. Like what did I actually say after the first time we fucked? The exact words. He could hardly have said 'made love' as we were like two horny gorillas on speed. That would be, 'That's how I want it from now on.' Corny but true. He needed to be certain. I get it.

The kids were so excited to see their granny and even more so when Ben announced that I would be sleeping over. Couldn't concentrate on anything properly after that as the sleeping arrangements dominated my thoughts.

After supper, we watched the last part of Polar Express. Kids were still high on sugary sweets from Auntie Libby's. Treats were left out for Santa and the reindeer then PJ's then bed. We snuggled into Alfie's bed, all four of us, for *The Night Before Christmas*. I was on one of the outsides. Kids in the middle. Not once did either of them question why Granny was in the bed too. Honestly, Mum, I didn't want the evening to end. I must have been breathing (sighing) loudly at times as Ben would reach his arm up and over to pat my head.

Nola wanted to say a prayer for Mummy. No arm this time. He was too busy brushing his tears. I kept dabbing my eyes with the duvet. The kids chose to remain in Alfie's bed together.

'Will Santa know I'm here, Granny?' she whispered as I was leaving.

'Absolutely, Sweet Pea. Cuddle in. See you in the morning.'

'Love you to Australia and back,' she said.

'Love you to the moon and back,' I replied.

'Granny,' she admonished. 'Australia is further away than the moon.'

'Aww, thank you, honey.'

Ben and I bustled about setting out all the presents, especially Santa's. Ben had bought Alfie a John Deere electric car and Nola a new bike. We've always put the bigger tree in the conservatory as we can see it from the kitchen. It looked particularly beautiful this year. Fairy lights lit up the patio outside. It felt magical. Special.

We couldn't put it off any longer. The serious discussion. (One of many!!)

'Nightcap?' he suggested.

I opted for Amaretto. Ben for a Macallan. We sat at opposite ends of the long sofa. Perched like two stuffed Christmas turkeys, hands between our legs. I had on my black dress (with the cherries) minus my black, slouchy boots. Ben was in his bare feet, jeans and a black Christmas T-shirt that the kids chose last Christmas. Homer Simpson in a cooking apron.

We both spoke at once.

'Sorry you go.'

'No, you.'

Ben took control.

'What do we do now?' he asked.

I wasn't sure if he meant in the next five minutes or the next five years. Would he even want to have sex with his mother-in-law? I sure as hell was gagging for it BUT realistically concluded it wouldn't happen. Would it?

'Truthfully? It's opened a shitty can of worms,' I sighed, miserably. 'I'm so sorry, Ben. It's a mess.' Characteristically, I began to cry. It's the new me!!!!

'Hey,' he said and slid across the sofa next to me.

'How can we possibly be together? It would be too weird. For you. For the kids. For our families. Fuck, Ben. How would that work?'

He found the funny side. 'Rachel the cougar,' he said.

I immediately thought of Jasper and Elizabeth. Then I blushed. FUCK!!! I've been extremely intimate with two men recently. But so has Ben with two women. Awkward.

'You blushing Mrs. S?'

Ben liked to remind me that I was his missus.

'Can we kiss? Please? You can close your eyes.' I didn't beg but there was a note of urgency in my tone.

He kept his eyes firmly closed. OMG. His mouth on mine. It was joyous, heavenly, sexy. Everything I could remember. It lasted for ages. Then I felt it. The familiar bulge. Hard and erect on my pubic bone. We had manoeuvred our bodies into that position. Too late. He opened his eyes. In that split second, I understood that we could go no further.

'I can't,' he gulped. 'All I can see is your mother's face.'

'Don't worry,' I assured him. Over and over again. I held him close until our passions eased and our breathing returned to normal.

We finished our drinks. Most unexpectedly, he persuaded me to join him in bed. No sex. We talked for ages. About his work and mine. He'd never heard of Harbour Radio. Didn't mention Charles. I told him that if I had my time again (my earlier life), I would not have been as obsessed with the station and especially T.V. I was truly sorry. He gave me a ticking off. We both enjoyed our lifestyles. In our own ways, we both sought fame or recognition for what we did. We were a dynamic couple. He got a real kick showing me off. I was pleasantly surprised. I had always thought that Ben had shrugged the limelight but on reflection he was just blasé about it all. Like yeh, I like being famous but it's not what I set out to be.

Eventually and reluctantly, we drifted off to sleep.

The alarm woke me with a start. It took a few seconds for me to establish where I was. Ben was zonked. I wondered how he heard the kids. Yet, he must do. He always said that he blanked out my early morning buzzer. All those mornings I missed sharing with the kids and Ben.

Rather than sleep downstairs on my own, I crept in beside them. My two wee cosy munchkins.

Christmas morning, 6.30 am, was mayhem. Wonderful and exciting. Parcels were ripped open as I wrote down what was from whom. Ben prepared pancakes and bacon, with slivers of smoked salmon for the adults.

I had to nip home to shower and change. Didn't waste any time. Rushed back to the bosom of my beautiful family. Several times Ben referred to me as Mummy, much to the kids' amusement but a poignant reminder that being together wasn't going to be without its problems.

Unperturbed, we pledged to enjoy our day. And we did. Oddly enough, we didn't invite Annabelle to be part of our charade. Don't know why.

It was still great to see her. She complained that Ben and I had been too generous with our gifts. Think we were both grateful for everything she does for us.

I had to excuse myself. I had someone to see. I had discussed it with Ben already. I would only be gone for a couple of hours. Ben wanted me to stay over again on Christmas night so driving over to see Charles was something that had to be done. I had no idea how we were going to get rid of Annabelle later although she had seemed keen to call in on Ros in the evening as she was having friends round for drinks. Ben had politely declined the invite.

Standing in the porch, Ben kissed me tenderly on the lips. We both smiled then immediately sprang apart when the doorbell rang. Someone's finger was glued to the buzzer.

My first reaction was shit. Please don't let it be Colin.

'SURPRISE!!!' It was the whole fecking Sutherland squad.

Ben looked as stunned as I felt. Stunned and slightly resentful. Our evening had been scuppered.

Obviously, we squealed with delight and hugged as they pushed past, one by one, including Carrie's brood. Laden with extra gifts and hampers bulging with food.

'Rachel, pet. Please don't say you're going?' howled Margaret.

I promised I would be back.

The Sutherlands had stayed at the Balmoral overnight (where else?) and wanted to surprise Ben and the kids. It worked. We were gobsmacked. I'm being bitchy. It was very gracious of them.

Guess what? They're staying until the 2nd. At least, Margaret and Kenneth are. Carrie and Dale plan to spend New Year with friends in Belfast. What with me hosting Rory and his lot, the Sutherlands bedded in at Deacon House, when were Ben and I going to have any time together? Shit. Shit. Shit.

I dropped in on Cockenzie.

It was actually really nice to be there. A guilty pleasure. And a safe haven. I had no idea what lay in store for me and Ben or Charles. I was drowning in doubts. Charles was overjoyed to see me. Even if it was for only half an hour. Isobel's sister was lovely. A little taller and wider but she had the same gentle manner as her younger sibling.

We exchanged gifts. I had a coffee and shortbread. Home-made. We kissed in the hallway. I'm a first-degree hussy. Jeezo, he only opened the outside door for me. Worth another kiss.

Confused. Befuddled and dejected. What a mess sure enough.

# SEVENTY-SEVEN

*Ruby's Journal*

**Boxing Day 10.30 am**

I've just this second called Annabelle. Rory et al are arriving around 4.30 pm. They decided to travel by train, first class, so I have plenty of time to get to Pitt Street. Another ping from Ben. He must have texted me a hundred times since yesterday.

It's one o'clock in the afternoon. Brought Annabelle up to speed about what actually happened after my tribute. Shocked doesn't cover it.

I confessed that I wished Ben had never found out. That fucking broadcast. My ego got the better of me. What an idiot.

'He would have found out sooner or later,' she acknowledged. 'Let's be honest. I think you wanted it brought to a head, Ruby. Why else did you do the presentation?'

True. I practically badgered Ben into tuning in. But now? How many times does one person wish the clocks could be turned back? Too many!

*

When I got back from Charles's on Christmas Day, Deacon House was in full swing. Ben was singing and dancing at the stove, beer in hand. Normally, I would have loved it but I was frightened he would spill. Not the wine but our secret. He practically sprinted towards me.

'Rachel, you look fantastic. Doesn't she?' He shouted seeking approval from the room.

'Grand. You're a sight for sore eyes that's for sure,' responded Kenneth kindly.

Annabelle caught my eye and pulled 'a what-the-fuck' face. I chuckled nervously. A glass of red was plonked in one hand and a plate of home-made blinis topped with a variety of Ben's pates in the other. Starters have always been casually served and eaten in our house. Finger foods. Allows us to mingle, chat and drink pre-dinner.

Ben was desperate to catch me on my own but it was impossible so we texted instead like we were involved in some clandestine affair. Can't deny it was intoxicating.

I sat between Carrie and Dale. Annabelle between Margaret and Kenneth. The kids huddled in a wee gang at the bottom of the table. Ben commanded the top end. Top dog. He loves cooking for family and friends, from his own kitchen. He was brighter than I had ever seen him. God, how I love him. The table was beautiful. I had excelled myself.

Carrie complimented my dress. Chocolate box purple. Velvet wrap around. Then as a gesture acknowledged Annabelle's who looked drop dead gorgeous in her red dress. She could easily pass for being Spanish or Italian. It's her shiny dark hair. Carrie had a tight fitting (funny that) black sparkly cocktail dress. It would have cost an arm and a leg. Same with Margaret's cream and sparkly ensemble. Without doubt, Annabelle was the most glamorous woman in the room. She peeked over those black specs and mouthed 'Primark' for us all to hear. Hard not to snigger.

It would have been a great day had I not 'come out'. I adored being with the kids. I videoed the whole present opening morning and reviewed it again and again last night.

Without looking in his direction, I could feel the pull. Ben and I would have preferred if it had been the four of us, no-one else. After all this time, we still couldn't be together. It was actually harder than before. We were now in this bizarre situation where we were desperate to be together but explaining it to others would have been unintelligible.

By 7.00pm Annabelle was itching to be elsewhere. She understood that I would want to be with Ben and the kids for as long as I could.

Everyone was stuffed. Kenneth was snoring in the lounge away from the hustle and bustle. I helped Carrie and Margaret organise the kids' bedrooms. Lara was sleeping with Nola and the boys would share with Alfie. I kissed my two and left them with their grandma and auntie. Had to give them their place. I have to say, for all their money, Margaret and Carrie are truly kind and generous (with their time) to family. Especially my two.

Downstairs, I signalled to Ben that I was leaving. He shuffled me into the utility room.

'Don't go. Please. Stay the night.'

The idea was totally impractical. Carrie and Dale were in the downstairs room. Margaret and Kenneth in the annexe. Where would I sleep? Certainly not with Ben. Wasn't going to happen. Jeezuz, Ben was rat-arsed. He actually fumbled with my boobs and tried to finger me down below. Mortified doesn't give it credence. At any given moment, Kenneth or Margaret would amble past on their way to their room. I felt dreadful shrugging him off.

'Come tomorrow,' he begged.

I agreed knowing full well that it wouldn't happen. On a clear head, he would be less impulsive.

I ordered a taxi to take me home.

Ping. Ping. Ping. Ping. The texting continued all night. Poor Ben. Welcome to my world.

And you know what? I can't fathom why I telephoned Charles. But I did. Usual guy picked me up. One hour later I was shagging the brains out of Charles wishing he was Ben. What a sham.

Happy fucking Christmas!!

\*

So here I am. Boxing Day. Waiting for Rory, Alana and wee Jack desperately wishing I was ensconced in Deacon House without the rest of the clan.

### Sunday 29th December.

Rory, A and J, have gone to his pal's out at Barnton until the 31st. Like Carrie, they will be heading back for New Year. Not sure if I managed to execute my hosting duties as well as I had hoped. I tried but mind elsewhere. Rory thanked me profusely when he left so maybe I did. We all went to Ben's for lunch yesterday. Good craic. Good camaraderie. Ben looked dreadful though. The strain is telling on him.

He came to Portobello to see me after the Brentwoods had gone. We hugged and cried. So draining.

He had this wonderful, hapless plan that the four of us should pack up and move away. Australia or New Zealand. Anywhere but here. Start again.

I pointed out that my body was seventeen years older than

him. In ten years time I would be 67!!! He didn't care. I was his Ruby and that was all that mattered. What about the kids? How would we explain that Granny was the new mummy? Still didn't care. Don't get me wrong, I had prayed for this. That Ben and I and the kids would find everlasting happiness elsewhere and listening to Ben, I believed it was possible. In fact, I got caught up in the euphoria. Selling up. Moving on. Embracing an exciting new life. BUT? There's always a but.

What if, one day I woke up and my memory was gone and I didn't recognise anyone. Ben or the kids. What would he do then? Especially if we were abroad somewhere. Or worse? A stroke or heart attack. I do occupy an older body. Any illness could take me.

It's a small world these days. No matter where we hid, someone would recognise us. How would we convince family and friends to accept us?

'Fuck them all, Ruby. It's you, me, Alfie and Nola. That's all that matters.'

I believed him. For a few precious minutes I was sucked in.

We stood on the balcony and looked out to the Forth and imagined us sailing off over the horizon. We snuggled and cuddled. Giddy at the prospect of new beginnings.

Ben took my hand and led me indoors. He pushed me on to the sofa and we kissed working ourselves into a frenzy. He yanked off his shirt. I pulled my sweatshirt over my head. He danced out of his jeans. I slipped out of my joggers. He shook his pants from his feet. His hard on was enormous. It sprang from his body, waiting and wanting. Then he stopped rooted to the spot. It was as if an electric shock had surged through his spine and registered in his face. His palms shot to his cock, covering it up.

'I'm sorry. All I can see is your mother. I'm sorry.'

He flopped on to the sofa. I grappled to put on my clothes. We sat forever.

'Give me time, Roo. It'll get easier. I just need to get my mind round it.'

'It won't though. Every time you try, it will get harder.' I wanted to say more but it would have been too truthful, too hurtful for both of us. Ben was in bits. He was physically shaking. His stomach muscles were convulsing.

I held him as if I was soothing Alfie. I coaxed him to get dressed as I made us a coffee.

'The coffee was a giveaway too,' he said, blowing the piping hot mug.

'You always preferred my coffee,' I teased, holding back the tears. I knew I had to be strong. I watched him take tiny sips. 'It's been a lot to take in. For both of us. I think we need to digest it.'

He agreed.

He would have to get back. He lied. I've a lot to do too. I fibbed. We kind of fumbled awkwardly when we hugged goodbye.

I wailed uncontrollably when I heard the outside door close behind him. I wandered aimlessly around the apartment, stripping beds and generally tidying up. Every ten minutes or so I allowed myself the luxury of breaking down again. This went on for over an hour.

I phoned Annabelle.

'Minute,' she said as she answered. I could hear the telly fade as she moved to another room. 'Ben's here,' she whispered.

Didn't surprise me. Like me, who else would he turn to?

'How is he?' I asked.

'A mess,' she replied.

'Phone me back when he's left,' I begged.

That hour seemed like ten.

**4.27pm (exactly).** Annabelle persuaded me that there was no more to be said. I wanted the conversation to continue.

'Listen, bbz, you have to hang up now,' pleaded my best pal. 'You're going to give yourself a headache. We've been over it (their conversation) a hundred times. I'm sure he just needs to get his head round it. He loves you, Ruby.'

Ben had gone straight to Annabelle's from mine. She's on holiday until next Monday.

Anyway, Annabelle said he was inconsolable. Worse than he was after my accident. Not sure I liked that. She clarified. As much as my death had been devastating, my unfathomable reappearance (resurrection sounds too biblical) has been harder to take.

He should try being in my shoes. Correction – your body.

Ben desperately wants to be with me BUT the reality of shagging his mother-in-law is daunting. He feels he is letting me down.

'He won't abandon you, Ruby. He's determined to make it work.' Annabelle assured me but her enthusiasm didn't quite ring true.

We discussed all the scenarios that Ben had put forward. Annabelle agreed with me. What would people think? Especially the kids.

I'm away to console myself with Charles which makes me a right fraud. Poor Ben is at his wits end yet I can swan off and fuck another man. Maybe, I'm hardening. I hope not.

I wish, wish, wish that I hadn't been so foolhardy. Right now, I wish that I hadn't even told Annabelle that way I would be hurting nobody but me.

# SEVENTY-EIGHT

*Ruby's Journal*

**Monday 30th December Nola's Birthday**

Big decision made today. I'm in tears as I write this.

Stayed overnight with Charles. Couldn't hide my sadness. Didn't tell him the truth only that being with the family over Christmas had stripped off the sticking plaster that had been tentatively holding us together. I'm on the outside looking in. Not far off the mark. I know, I'm a lying cow but I can hardly tell him that Ben is struggling with my real identity. There had been no bombardment of texts from Ben only one sincere apology and a promise that we would catch up soon.

It is so comforting being with Charles. He accepted the new me. Mind and body. Something Ben will never be able to reconcile.

'What are you going to do?' he asked hesitantly.

I honestly didn't know then but I have come to terms now with what I'm going to do next. It may be rash but I see no alternative.

If someone (think I mean God) had asked me if I would give up everything to make love to my husband one last time. I would have said 'show me the bed.' BUT that would have meant never seeing my Alfie and Nola ever again. That is a sacrifice too far. My children mean more to me than any physical contact with Ben. So why am I contemplating this?

Nola had chosen the soft play centre near my Belvedere apartment to celebrate her birthday. Four nursery friends, Libby's two plus Alfie and Jack had been invited. Alana brought Jack while Rory played snooker with uni pals. Carrie and Dale were already onboard sailing to Larne.

I pretended to be bubbly. Hey, I had more energy than all the other adults put together.

'I'll have whatever you're on, Rachel,' hollered Libby over the jubilant screaming.

Several times Ben put his hand on my bum as I crawled in front of him. I found it insulting. He couldn't do it when it counted so don't do it now. I was being unfair. Last week, I would have found it exhilarating. Actually, last week, he would have been mortified if he'd touched me there.

Nola loved every minute of her party. Alfie loved playing with his big cousin.

When Nola blew out her candles and we all belted out *Happy Birthday* there wasn't a dry eye amongst us. Ben walked over. Hugged me and kissed my cheek and whispered in my ear,

'Thank you, Ruby, for giving me two amazing children. I do love you, you know.'

To sympathetic onlookers, it would have looked like a grieving son-in-law propping up his dead wife's mother.

Ben had organised with Kenneth to take the kids home on the pretence that he had something to fix for me at the flat. He would follow on shortly. I had phoned him first thing this morning asking for a meet. I promised not to ravish him. Wasn't able to disguise the sarcasm. Could feel him squirm at the other end. I felt like we were strangers.

We walked to the apartment in silence. No small talk even though we could have chatted about the birthday girl.

Several times our knuckles brushed causing us to gaze at each other.

'Only me,' I shouted as we entered my lobby.

Ben seemed to panic. I took his hand and kissed the back of it softly.

'It'll be fine,' I promised.

Annabelle jumped to her feet as Ben followed me in. I caught her mouthing sorry to my beleaguered hubby.

'Sorry for the subterfuge, guys, but I want you both to hear what I've to say.'

I poured a large wine for me and Bella-Anne. Ben was driving.

There was no point procrastinating so I launched right in.

'I'm going on a sabbatical as soon as I've sorted my affairs here. It's only fair, especially to you, Ben.'

Inevitably, the tears fell but not for long. Big breaths.

Ben protested vigorously and promised to try harder. Annabelle sobbed but I was determined to be heard.

I confessed that it would have been easier for all of us if I had hidden the real me from them but I acknowledged that I would never have coped with Colin if Annabelle hadn't had my back. Every day, I'm faced with the monumental task of being you, Mum. It's wearing being on high alert all the time. Watching what I say. Not giving the show away. But most of all the reality that Ben and I cannot be together is too much to bear. Or to witness him moving on to someone new.

'I'll try harder,' pleaded Ben. 'Please stay, Ruby. I've just got you back.'

Annabelle and I were rendered helpless. Waterfalls fell. I had to be strong and say what needed to be said.

I told Ben that he was NOT to blame. He fell in love with me, Ruby Martin, the whole package. I couldn't imagine that

I could ever jump into bed with Kenneth. (Perish the thought. Yet it didn't stop me humping Jasper or Charles!!!!)

Leaving Alfie and Nola would be the most difficult part but the three of us together could prepare them for my departure. It wouldn't be forever. I was planning to return in twelve months at most. And I would FaceTime them regularly. Not the adults. Only the kids. I wanted to give Ben and Annabelle time to readjust without me around. If and when I did return, I would probably start all over again elsewhere.

'Where will you go?' asked my tearstained pal.

'Travel. Explore. Australia, Canada, North and South America. Not sure'

Ben and Annabelle had taken time out when they were younger to work in Oz while I, the boring predictable fart, had stayed at home. I wanted to catch up on what I'd missed while I was fit enough (in your body) to do so.

Ben would have to employ a nanny. Preferably a lesbian, I joked but actually anyone (male or female) who truly liked the kids would be good. It's not as if we couldn't afford it. Both of our life policies paid off the mortgage on our deaths. A substantial monthly saving on our outgoings. Plus, everything else we had in the bank. Not sure what the Welsh University will eventually cough up. Ben used to joke that I would be a very wealthy widow should he cop it. He was now the very wealthy widower. Talking of which. I asked Ben if he would fund my adventure.

'If I said no, would you still go?' He knew my answer. 'We could tell everyone the truth,' he blurted. Bless his wee cotton socks.

We would be a laughing stock. Ridiculed by everyone we knew. It would have a detrimental impact on the businesses we had made sacrifices to build. God, how he tried to convince me.

'Ben. Would you believe Dale and your mum if it were her and Carrie in this mess? Be honest.'

Of course, he wouldn't. It would be preposterous.

'Take whatever you need. What's mine is yours,' he conceded.

'And what's mine is my ane!' Another wee joke we shared.

We chatted about all the practicalities of my trip. Keeping safe. Travelling with organised groups. Reporting back regularly.

I had thought about nothing else since the dangly dick fracas. Staying here was no longer viable. Ruby Martin would have to exit their lives for another time.

# SEVENTY-NINE

## *Ruby's Journal*

**Tuesday 31st Hogmanay**

I've had an unremarkable day so far. Very calm. Hope it's not before a storm!!

Forewarned Ben and Annabelle that I wouldn't be bringing in the New Year with them at Dick Place. Too emotional and I mean to go on as I've started. Distancing myself from them. Don't get me wrong, it's bloody hard but can't risk being with them fuelled with alcohol. Something would give in front of witnesses.

I'll keep going to the house, look after the kids as normal as I want to cram as much time in with them as I possibly can. We'll tell them about my new adventure once Kenneth and Margaret have left. Ben and I have agreed that there will be NO sexual advances made by either of us from now on. I know there will be cuddles. It would be hard not to but no trying to change my mind either. This is definitely the sensible route.

I did the podcast with Elaine today. Decided not to divulge my plans just yet. Will do once I've finalised my travel destinations. Wish I could be excited. Big empty hole in my heart and soul. Our programme was all about isolation. In all its forms. Very apt given my present predicament and we touched on hoarding. It was fascinating. The majority of hoarders rarely have visitors. Too embarrassing. I admire Elaine so much for opening up all these topics for discussion and with humour too yet never patronising or lacking empathy.

Blog updated. As predicted, too many women and their kids subjected to terrifying abuse over the festive season. One contributor said her partner smashed up the TV on Christmas Day because of the racket the kids were making. Laughing at 'Despicable Me'. Then gathered up all their laptops and game consoles and locked them in the boot of his car before he buggered off with a mate to God knows where for two days. Gave her several serious slaps for reminding him it was Christmas.

At least Laura (accountant) and her new baby boy had a safe and wonderful Christmas at her parents' house. Betty still with the fleecer. Do hope he's not Jasper.

I might ask Elaine to run my blog while I'm away. Maybe I could contribute while I'm travelling.

Bringing in the bells later with Charles and Isobel. My new safe haven. Funny how life can turn on a sixpence. One of your many quotes, mum.

**Thursday 2nd January.**

HAPPY NEW YEAR!!!!

Wish I meant it. Saw the New Year in with my two dear pals in Cockenzie.

Charles had prepared supper. His usual repertoire. A selection of tapas. I wore a grey sparkly dress. Isobel and Charles wore the same outfits they had on at Charles's birthday. They certainly can't be accused of flashing the cash. Around 11pm we switched on the telly. BBC. Charles's choice, however, I do like Susan Calman. Loved her on Strictly. A programme about Scottish adverts followed which was odd considering the BBC doesn't do adverts. Remember the one about 'Pea and ham from a chicken'? Rory says it even now. In fact, he definitely said it when we had lunch with Ben and the Sutherlands on Saturday.

Seems like weeks ago.

After midnight, we toasted the New Year and Isobel retired with a book. Charles and I snuggled up on the sofa in front of the log burner with our large nightcaps, courtesy of Isobel.

'Come on,' he prompted, 'what have you decided? You've been noticeably quiet all evening.'

Hadn't meant to be. Thought I was chirpy. Shit. You think my tear ducts would be exhausted. I'm totally fed up with crying. There must be rivulets hollowed into my cheeks.

I explained that I had made a decision to leave but only for a while. His body immediately stiffened. I was fifty-seven years old, I said, and can't remember what it was like to be young although Charles had given me an insight. He chuckled at that. My family and friends were strangers to me and I found that to be not only sad but very lonely too. Not wholly true but was seeing it from your perspective, Mum. I wanted to explore. See the world before it was too late but most of all I wanted to find peace within myself.

He clearly contemplated his response but it was no more than I would have expected. He understood fully.

'Wish I could come with you,' he sighed.

'Me too.' I honestly did. 'Will you wait for me?'

He held me close. 'Where else will I be?'

We made love and savoured every second of it like lifelong partners who knew how to please each other without the need to rush. This time, I thought only about Charles and how reassuring it was to be with him. Afterwards, my thoughts returned to Ben.

My lovely husband who lost me, and me him, nine months ago. Thankfully, Charles had no reason to question my tears.

I'm off to see Ben and the kids today. Please let it be easy and harmonious.

I've had a nagging headache all morning. Don't let it be pneumonia again. Doc thinks it might have been a different virus last time as I recuperated quicker than anticipated.

**Friday 3rd.**

I had a lovely time with Ben, Alfie and Nola on Thursday. Told them that Granny was thinking about going on a long holiday. They were neither up nor down. Actually requested to come along as well. There were lots of cuddles, with Ben too, and lots of reminiscing. I left them with a real sense of inner calm. That everything had been resolved. It wouldn't be easy between Ben and me but he finally agreed that he would need that distance and space to come to terms with our new relationship. Like Charles, he volunteered to assist me with the planning.

Popped in to see my bestie. She, unfortunately, is finding it hard to cope.'

'I could come with you. I'll take unpaid leave or pack it in altogether. I'll easily get another job,' she begged.

Where would she get the money? Didn't want to remind her that she was in debt up to her eyeballs. Not exactly but she was hopeless at saving and struggled to clear her credit cards each month. Plus, I wanted to be on my own. To accept that I was now an older woman despite being young inside. Lots of women feel like that anyway. How many times have you heard someone say that they feel the same way as they did twenty/thirty years ago? You used to, Mum, until you shacked up with the weasel. He turned you into an old woman before your time.

Wish you had had the chance to sort him out for yourself. Wish I had seen what was going on. Love you so much, Mum. Missed you at Christmas. Miss you every day.

'Ben and the kids are going to need you and you them,' I reminded Annabelle. 'Coast is clear. You know, for you and Ben.'

'Don't, Roo. I could never consider that. Please don't say it again.'

'Well, if you ever did, you have my blessing. I want you both to be happy.' That was hard to say but I meant every word.

We hugged for ages. It wasn't as if I was leaving the next day, for goodness sake.

Did the morning show, this morning (Friday) and have recorded my show for later. Tried to be upbeat but didn't feel great. Have stayed with Charles since Hogmanay. Looking forward to a lazy day in Porty and vegging on the sofa in my jammies.

**Saturday 4th 6.30 am.**

Been up since early doors. Nothing shifting this headache. Think it's with everything that is going on. Don't know why but I've written a letter to Ben and Annabelle. What else is there to do at that time in the morning? Hidden them in my underwear drawer at the back. I'll probably rip them up later and write them another before I actually set off. It's laughable really (would if my head wasn't so bloody sore) that me, Ruby Martin is going anywhere on her own never mind the other side of the world. For all my bravado and seemingly worldly-wise allure (all put on), I'm a home-bird at heart. Even you used to say that, Mum. Couldn't get the plane to Belfast without working myself up. Ruby, you would say, you won't end up in Timbuktu. Think my poor sense of direction has something to do with it. Not now. I HAVE TO DO THIS.

Shit. Head not any better. It's 8.00am and the darkness is lifting. I'll take a brisk walk along the prom (not raining) then it'll be another day binge watching *Line of Duty* and whatever else I need to catch up with.

# EIGHTY

*Rachel's Flat in Portobello. Friday 10th January 2020.*

Rachel read the last three pages of Ruby's journal again and again; touching the writing with her fingers desperate to hold on to her precious Ruby. For five days, her life had been consumed with the book she held in her hand with its deck chair and palm tree. She was frightened to close it, instead, she left it open at the last page and placed it at the bottom of Nola's bed. She had to hunt for those letters in the master bedroom.

She found them exactly where Ruby said they would be – tucked under her knickers right at the back. Two white envelopes sealed; one for Ben the other for Annabelle. It was only as she stared at their names did it register that Ruby's handwriting had been evolving since she first began the diary. Although, the handwriting was still hers (Rachel's) there was more and more of Ruby's right slant creeping in.

Rachel immediately texted both Annabelle and Ben. It was most unlike her to be so impulsive or intrusive but needs must.

Hello, it's Rachel.
Ruby left letters for each of you. They're here if you want them. Rory arrives today at 4.30pm. Either come beforehand or wait until he returns to Brentwood on Sunday.
Rachel xx

Rachel texted a separate ending to Annabelle.

Does Charles know about my accident? I've finished the diary and I understand Ruby was still in a relationship with him. I can't text the man myself. I'm so embarrassed.

The familiar ping of a text fired back. Then another. Rachel couldn't get over how quickly youngsters read their messages and responded almost immediately. She didn't expect a response until morning. Ben said he would call in after dropping the kids off. Annabelle replied,

Thanks bbz.
Can't wait so I'll pop in before work. I'll bring the coffees. And yes Charles does know. He was in bits when I went to see him on Sunday evening. Thought it was only fair to tell him in person. He will wait until you are well enough to contact him.
P.S Says he loves you loads. Xx

Annabelle always finishes her texts with several emojis. This time with beating hearts, sad faces, teary faces and kisses.

Rachel awoke with a start. Her intercom was dinging. She lifted her head from her soaking wet pillow: tearstained, and checked her alarm clock. 8.35am. It was most probably Ben as Annabelle had a set of keys.

She rushed to buzz him in and then to the bathroom to splash her face with freezing cold water. It was a shock to the system but one she needed to waken her up properly and to help her focus. Within seconds, several taps drummed on her door.

'Minute,' Rachel requested and she grabbed the first thing from her ironing pile; black jogging top and bottoms.

Ben stood on her doormat. It was at that precise moment she realised that they had never seen each other (at least she hadn't) since the accident.

'Ben, I'm so sorry,' she wept. 'Ruby has gone.'

Gone being the operative word. Not only had Ruby died in the crash but was no longer here either. Mother-in-law and son-in-law were locked in an emotional embrace until Annabelle's voice broke the bond. She held aloft a large brown paper bag.

'Coffees and croissants from your favourite cafe,' she whooped, trying too hard to bring a sense of merriment to the doorstep. 'Oh, sorry. Meant Ruby's favourite.'

Rachel forgave her faux pas and invited them in. She apologised for looking a sight but it had been a long night and she had overslept into the bargain.

As Ruby's husband and best friend settled onto the sofa, Rachel opened the blinds. Light poured in. It was surprisingly bright for January. Her two guests were sitting in Ruby's lounge (didn't feel like hers yet) for one thing only. It was up to Rachel to put them out of their misery.

When she returned from the spare bedroom, she handed them the letters. Both laid them on the coffee table simultaneously and continued to sip their coffees. Ben was mesmerised by the white rectangles in front of him. His eyes rarely deviated from the spot.

'How's your head, Rachel?' asked Annabelle, rising to inspect the scar.

'A little tender but fine I think.' Her hand automatically reached for the wound as if confirming her diagnosis.

'Looks good to me.' Annabelle peered over her new dark purple specs. 'No inflammation.'

Rachel smiled as 'nurse' Annabelle squeezed in beside Ben.

'Can you remember anything about the last nine months?' Ben probed his mother-in-law.

Rachel flushed as she tried not to look at his crotch. The dangly cock episode would be a hard one to forget. 'Only what I've read in the diary,' she swallowed. Like Ruby, tears were waiting to pounce whenever the opportunity arose. 'One small consolation. Ruby had no inclination that her time was close. She'd been having bad headaches and was worried that another bout of pneumonia was looming. I truly hope that she did drop like a stone like those who saw her witnessed. She didn't suffer the first time...' Rachel sucked in a deep breath.

The two friends exchanged looks. Annabelle bit her lip. Ben gripped her hand tightly. Too tightly as Annabelle clearly winced. Annabelle pulled a sad face but nodded her head to encourage Rachel to reveal more if she could.

'The last time she was with you all, she loved it,' she spoke directly to Ruby's husband. 'The cuddles and the reminiscing. She felt a sense of calm when she left. As if some kind of acceptable resolution had been achieved. The thought of deserting you all over again was heartbreaking for her.'

Ben was about to say something but changed his mind. He had been sorely tempted to persuade Ruby to stay that day. Her visit had lifted their spirits, especially his. There were several times when their banter was in full flow that he wanted say to Ruby that it could be like this all the time. Yet hiding their true feelings behind closed doors wasn't fair to either of them. Letting her walk away that day would haunt him forever.

As if reading her son-in-law's thoughts, Rachel reminded him that the right decision had been made. 'Don't beat yourself up. Deep down, I'm convinced Ruby knew she was on borrowed time and I'm proof of that. She kept saying to me *not yet, Mum.*

She stayed here to help you and the kids and say her goodbyes.'

It was Ben's turn to weep quietly. He wasn't one for showing his emotions. The women allowed their tears to fall freely too. There were no theatricals. Both were as reserved as Ben.

'Did she say anything about me?' pried Annabelle.

Rachel smiled. 'She appreciated your offer to travel with her but Ruby could only have come to terms with existing in my body by living as me; or at least accepting that she could survive a future in an older body. She could only leave because she trusted you to look out for her family.' Rachel left out the part where Ruby encouraged Annabelle to make a move on Ben.

There were a few moments of reflection before Rachel lifted the letters and handed one to each of them.

Ben intended to read his in the privacy of his car. Annabelle waited behind with Rachel. Ben embraced both women and left.

He is a lovely lad, thought Rachel. She wished him the happiness he truly deserved.

Annabelle fiddled with the envelope: turning it over and over with her fingers until she dropped it.

'For heaven's sake, Bella-Anne. Read the bloody thing.'

They both laughed at the reference and Ruby's pal said she wouldn't object if Rachel used it now and again.

Subconsciously, Rachel had slipped on the jogging outfit Ruby had worn on her last day.

'You look great, you know. Ruby done a good job.' Annabelle nodded approvingly.

'Have you any idea how much she admired you?' Rachel insisted. 'Ruby thought that on Christmas day, you outshone every woman in the house. You need to have more self-belief, Miss Jeffries. Go on read it.'

Annabelle decided to read it out loud. After all, Rachel knew everything about her so there would be no surprises. She slipped her fingers in and pulled out the letter. It was handwritten. Annabelle breathed deeply.

*Saturday 4th January*

*To my best pal in the whole wide world, Annabelle Jeffries.*

*It's four in the morning and I'm pissed off because I can't sleep. I took two paracetamol and two ibuprofen earlier but it hasn't shifted. So, what else was there to do but write a letter to you and Ben?*

*By the way, this is not a goodbye for ever letter. I will be back. (Said that in my best Terminator voice!! Ha, ha.)*

*Thank you so much for believing me all those months ago. I couldn't have done it without you. You kept me sane. You kept me alive. Honestly, if it wasn't for you, I don't think I would be sitting here right now. Thank you, my bestie, for everything and for the friendship we've shared since nursery. Jeezuz, it's been a journey but a fabulous one. Ours is a friendship that others can only dream of. I hope I have been as good a friend to you as you have to me.*

*Love you my honey to the moon and back (although Nola thinks Australia is further away. Wee soul). You are funny, lovable, unique and drop dead gorgeous. You must be the only person who doesn't see it. You deserve to find a decent guy who loves you, everything about you. Don't settle for less.*

*Talking of which, you could do a lot worse than taking on Ben. You two adore each other. You have a great friendship. Great foundations for a long-term relationship. The kids love you so no hurdle there and who knows? Alfie and Nola would love a wee brother or sister. I honestly mean that. I couldn't think of anyone better for Ben than you.*

*I'm so sorry to be gallivanting to the other side of the world and leaving you again but I truly believe it's the right thing to do for all of us. Anyway, an old woman like me cramps your style.*

*I will keep contact but only indirectly through the kids. Charles will have my full itinerary and I'll check in with him every day. I am so lucky to have him in my life. Please don't say that to Ben. It's hard to explain even to myself.*

*I intend to keep a travel journal. Just in case. If anything ever happens to me, please make sure that the relevant authorities know that Rory is my next of kin. I informed my lawyer of that ages ago. My lawyers are Ben's too. Colin and Claire must never be granted access to me. AND I'll hand my diary in to you for safe keeping before I go. Please don't read it. It's too personal and full of drivel anyway.*

*Take care my Bella-Anne. Love you always.*

*Ruby-Roo.*


Rachel stared at Annabelle but Ruby's young pal said nothing; she was too absorbed in the notepaper in her hand. Ruby was right. Annabelle is a strikingly beautiful young woman with her curvy figure and a mane of wavy dark hair. Not forgetting those glasses. Who else carries off large frames with such aplomb?

Eventually, Annabelle lifted her head and smiled. No tears. Not yet,

'That was a tenderly written letter, honey. Ruby loved you so much.'

Annabelle continued to smile as she zipped up her red jacket. Her black polo neck peeked out over the collar.

'I'm going to go before I have a meltdown. I'm too busy at work for swollen eyes and a blotchy face. I'll catch you on

Sunday.' Her attempt to sound cheery failed miserably. At least she conjured a weak smile.

She gathered up her hat and bag and wiggled the envelope into an outside pocket. As she opened the door into the staircase, she called out, 'love you' to her best pal.

Rachel sat at the glass dining table. What a day. What a week. Rory wouldn't be arriving for a while yet. She set the alarm hoping to grab a couple of hours sleep before he arrived. She placed the diary carefully on to the floor and slipped into the unicorn bed. After Rory's visit, she would go and meet Charles.

She wondered if Ruby might visit again.

Meanwhile, in the car park at the back of the Belvedere apartments a young man turned up the heater in his Eiger Grey Range Rover. He was bloody freezing. He'd stood too long staring out over the Forth, saying his farewell to Ruby, without a jacket. He blew into his hands to warm them up. On the passenger seat beside him a white envelope with his name on it beckoned.

His hand trembled as he unfolded the letter. He smoothed it out on the steering wheel.

*Saturday 4th January*

*My darling Ben (My Mr Bean)*

*It's very early in the morning. I've just scribbled a letter to Annabelle and now I'm writing one to you. Don't know where to start. Didn't say all the right things to Annabelle and no doubt this note will be destined for the bin and a rewrite too.*

*I am so so sorry to dump all this baggage on you. You have had enough to deal with.*

*Thank you for taking such good care of our two wee munchkins. You are a great dad. It breaks my heart that I can't be at your* side to raise them but whatever happens I know you will do great things with them. Hopefully, when I return, I can be the granny that my mum never got the chance to be. I will give it my best shot.

I love you so much Ben Sutherland. Always have, always will, but you understand as well as I do that our life as husband and wife is over. I wish it were not the case but know this, it has been a joy and privilege to be your Mrs S, your Scooby Doo. I have loved every precious second of it. The minute I saw your face in that Belfast bar, I was hooked. Kerpow!! Love at first sight and I have continued to love you ever since.

All those months when I couldn't confide in you were so difficult but I wish you hadn't found out then I could have continued to support you and the kids in my own way. I wish I could turn the clock back but I can't. So now I'm giving you time to contemplate a life without me again. It's shite, isn't it? It's bad enough for me but somehow, I feel it's worse for you. Please, please rebuild your life.

I know this is rich coming from me but slow down. Take time out to be with Alfie and Nola. Trust me. You only get one shot at it. The restaurants are established. Manage them from the sidelines. You won't regret it. I was given a second chance and still scuppered the fecking thing. Honestly Ben, I wasted my chances. I should have spent more time with the kids first time around. I shouldn't have let my ego get the better of me the second time. That fucking broadcast. AAAAARG!!!!

Talking about second chances. You do realise that our Annabelle has carried a torch for you all these years. I spoiled that opportunity for her. She is convinced she is over it but I think otherwise. You two would be good together and that's not easy for me to say. If you find that a step too far then be a good friend to her. She'll need you when I'm gone. AND stay away from Hannah Dunlop. Anyone but her.

Please don't try to track me down when I go. I hope that I can *find some sort of peace living in this body and accept that I won't be young again. But for my mum's sake, I have to be thankful that I'm here. Alive and breathing when she is not. I miss her so much and I'm so angry that I'm the only one grieving for her.*

*Sorry, I'm ranting. Tired now so I'm signing off. Away to see if a Horlicks will work its magic. Paracetamol and ibuprofen didn't.*

*Love you, Suthie, to the moon and back.*

*Forever yours*

*Ruby (your Mrs S.) xxxx*

# ACKNOWLEDGEMENTS

As an author of a debut novel, I am so grateful to my band of readers who gave up their time to read *Take Me Instead* and for your constructive feedback; particularly Sandra and Val who were bombarded on a weekly basis! Your warm words of encouragement enabled me to get this far. I don't have the luxury to employ others to proofread or do research for me, so thank you Maureen, for your diligence (my friend since our first day at High School). This is not my only novel but it is the one I have chosen to publish first.

Many thanks to my wonderful family for your ongoing support; especially to my husband, Ronnie, for his patience and for taking on all the household chores.

So many professionals gave up their valuable time to answer my many, many questions. Thanks to P. McGlashan (police procedures), Fee Mackay (banking), Kate McFadden (worked for a recipient of a Michelin star and is now the proud owner of Kate's Edinburgh). Shauney Millar (events). I am indebted to Cat Harvey at Forth FM and to Mags Foster at Radio Saltire. Their input and insight were invaluable. Likewise, thank you to staff at Radio Tay.

A hearty thank you to my nephew, Mark Stevenson, for the outstanding photograph on the front cover and to his model Mia Foster. I was extremely fortunate to have had Duncan at

Lumphanan Press recommended to me. He has guided me through the process of self-publishing on a tight budget. He went above and beyond.

To all those affected by domestic abuse, remember you are not alone. Stay safe and seek advice.

If you enjoyed this first novel of mine, please look out for future books that will follow shortly: *Sleeping Partners* and *Three's a Crowd*.

Faye Stevenson grew up in an East Lothian mining community. She graduated with a teaching diploma at Moray House College, Edinburgh. As well as teaching, she helped her husband run the family businesses in hospitality for over thirty years. Now in semi-retirement, she has returned to her love of writing.

Her next book, *Sleeping Partners*, is forthcoming.

Printed in Great Britain
by Amazon

34488395R00290